THIRD MATCH
OZONEZMA THE CAPRICIOUS
"YOU HAVE A SWORDSMAN'S BODY, I SEE. NO OTHER WEAPON WORKS FOR YOU."
"Just look at you… That's quite the form you've got there…"
SOUJIROU THE WILLOW-SWORD
FOURTH MATCH
KIA THE WORLD WORD
"…So you're Rosclay? …Aren't you cool."
"Thank you. Please don't be too hard on me."
ROSCLAY THE ABSOLUTE

"Apologize to her...to that bride whom I wasn't able to protect! The Sun's Conifer!"

TU THE MAGIC

RIQUE THE MISFORTUNE

NASTIQUE THE QUIET SINGER

...I can aim at Tu from here.

KUZE THE PASSING DISASTER

ISHURA

IV

Judgment of Light and Shadow

Keiso

ILLUSTRATION BY
Kureta

YEN
ON
New York

IV

Keiso

ILLUSTRATION BY

Kureta

Translation by David Musto

This book is a work of fiction. Names, characters, places, and incidents are the product of the author's imagination or are used fictitiously. Any resemblance to actual events, locales, or persons, living or dead, is coincidental.

ISHURA Vol. 4 KOINEIYUKEI
©Keiso 2021
First published in Japan in 2021 by KADOKAWA CORPORATION, Tokyo. English translation rights arranged with KADOKAWA CORPORATION, Tokyo, through TUTTLE-MORI AGENCY, INC., Tokyo.

English translation © 2023 by Yen Press, LLC

Yen On
150 West 30th Street, 19th Floor
New York, NY 10001

Visit us at yenpress.com
facebook.com/yenpress
twitter.com/yenpress
yenpress.tumblr.com
instagram.com/yenpress

First Yen On Edition: July 2023
Edited by Yen On Editorial: Payton Campbell
Designed by Yen Press Design: Andy Swist

Yen On is an imprint of Yen Press, LLC.
The Yen On name and logo are trademarks of Yen Press, LLC.

The publisher is not responsible for websites (or their content) that are not owned by the publisher.

Library of Congress Cataloging-in-Publication Data
Names: Keiso (Manga author), author. | Kureta, illustrator. | Musto, David, translator.
Title: Ishura / Keiso ; illustration by Kureta ; translation by David Musto.
Other titles: Ishura. English
Description: First Yen On edition. | New York : Yen On, 2022.
Identifiers: LCCN 2021062849 | ISBN 9781975337865
    (v. 1 ; trade paperback) | ISBN 9781975337889
    (v. 2 ; trade paperback) | ISBN 9781975337902
    (v. 3 ; trade paperback) | ISBN 9781975337926
    (v. 4 ; trade paperback)
Subjects: LCGFT: Fantasy fiction. | Light novels.
Classification: LCC PL872.5.E57 I7413 2022 | DDC 895.63/6—dc23/
    eng/20220121
LC record available at https://lccn.loc.gov/2021062849

ISBNs: 978-1-9753-3792-6 (trade paperback)
       978-1-9753-3793-3 (ebook)

10 9 8 7 6 5 4 3 2 1

LSC-C

Printed in the United States of America

The identity of the one who defeated the True Demon King—the ultimate threat who gripped the world in terror—is shrouded in mystery.
Little is known about this hero.
The terror of the True Demon King abruptly came to an end.

Nevertheless, the champions born from the era of the Demon King still remain in this world.

Now, with the enemy of all life brought low,
these champions, wielding enough power to transform the world,
have begun to do as they please,
their untamed wills threatening a new era of war and strife.

To Aureatia, now the sole kingdom unifying the minian races,
the existence of these champions has become a threat.
No longer champions, they are now demons bringing ruin to all—
the shura.

To ensure peace in the new era,
it is necessary to eliminate any threat to the world's future,
and designate the True Hero to guide and protect the hopes of the people.

Thus, the Twenty-Nine Officials, the governing administrators of Aureatia, have gathered these shura and their miraculous abilities from across the land, regardless of race, and organized an imperial competition to crown the True Hero once and for all.

POWER RELATIONSHIPS

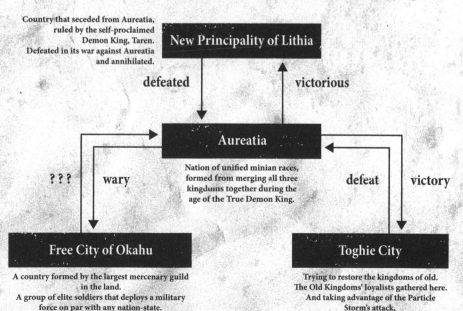

Country that seceded from Aureatia, ruled by the self-proclaimed Demon King, Taren. Defeated in its war against Aureatia and annihilated.

New Principality of Lithia

defeated

victorious

Aureatia

Nation of unified minian races, formed from merging all three kingdoms together during the age of the True Demon King.

??? wary

defeat victory

Free City of Okahu

A country formed by the largest mercenary guild in the land.
A group of elite soldiers that deploys a military force on par with any nation-state.
Completely independent of any outside authority.

Toghie City

Trying to restore the kingdoms of old.
The Old Kingdoms' loyalists gathered here.
And taking advantage of the Particle Storm's attack,
declared war on Aureatia and were defeated.

ROSCLAY THE ABSOLUTE

Knight Minia

Sponsor
ELEA THE RED TAG

JIVLART THE ASH BORDER

Vagabond Minia

Sponsor
HARDY THE BULLET FLASHPOINT

SOUJIROU THE WILLOW-SWORD

Blade Minia

Sponsor
YUCA THE HALATION GAOL

OZONEZMA THE CAPRICIOUS

Medic Chimera

UHAK THE SILENT

Oracle Ogre

Sponsor
NOFELT THE SOMBER WIND

ZIGITA ZOGI THE THOUSANDTH

Tactician Goblin

Sponsor
DANT THE HEATH FURROW

SHALK THE SOUND SLICER

Spearhead Skeleton

Sponsor
HYAKKA THE HEAT HAZE

MELE THE HORIZON'S ROAR

Archer Gigante

Sponsor
CAYON THE SKYTHUNDER

Sponsor
HARGHENT THE STILL

LUCNOCA THE WINTER

Silencer Dragon

Sponsor
HIDOW THE CLAMP

ALUS THE STAR RUNNER

Rogue Wyvern

Sponsor
MIZIAL THE IRON-PIERCING PLUMESHADE

TOROA THE AWFUL

Grim Reaper Dwarf

Sponsor
QWELL THE WAX FLOWER

PSIANOP THE INEXHAUSTIBLE STAGNATION

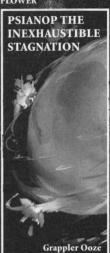

Grappler Ooze

SIXWAYS EXHIBITION

ZELJIRGA THE ABYSS WEB

Clown Zmeu

Sponsor
ENU THE DISTANT MIRROR

MESTELEXIL THE BOX OF DESPERATE KNOWLEDGE

Creator/Architect
Golem/Homunculus

Sponsor
KAETE THE ROUND TABLE

TU THE MAGIC

Juggernaut

Sponsor
FLINSUDA THE PORTENT

KUZE THE PASSING DISASTER

Paladin Minia

Sponsor
NOPHTOK THE CREPUSCULE BELL

GLOSSARY

◈ Word Arts

① Laws of the world that permit and establish phenomenon and living creatures that physically shouldn't be able to exist, such as the construction of a gigant's body.
② Phenomenon that conveys the intentions of a speaker's words to the listener, regardless of the speaker's race or language.
③ Or the generic term for arts that utilize this phenomenon to distort natural phenomena via "requests" to a certain target.

Something much like what would be called magic. Force, Thermal, Craft, and Life Arts compose the four core groups, but there are some who can use arts outside of these four groups. While necessary to be familiarized with the target in order to utilize these arts, powerful Word Arts users are able to offset this requirement.

◈ Force Arts

Arts that inflict directed power and speed, what is known as momentum, on a target.

◈ Craft Arts

Arts that change a target's shape.

◈ Thermal Arts

Arts that inflict undirected energy, such as heat, electrical current, and light, on a target.

◈ Life Arts

Arts that change a target's nature.

◈ Visitors

Those who possess abilities that deviate greatly from all common knowledge, and thus were transported to this world from another one known as the Beyond. Visitors are unable to use Word Arts.

◈ Enchanted Sword • Magic Items

Swords and tools that possess potent abilities. Similar to visitors, due to their mighty power, there are some objects that were transported here from another world.

◈ Aureatia Twenty-Nine Officials

The highest functionaries who govern Aureatia. Ministers are civil servants, while Generals are military officers.
There is no hierarchy-based seniority or rank among the Twenty-Nine Officials.

◈ Self-Proclaimed Demon King

A generic term for "demonic monarch" not related to the One True King among the three kingdoms. There are some cases where even those who do not proclaim themselves as a monarch, but who wield great power to threaten Aureatia, are acknowledged as self-proclaimed demon kings by Aureatia and targeted for subjugation.

◈ Sixways Exhibition

A tournament to determine the True Hero. The person who wins each one-on-one match and advances all the way through to the end will be named the True Hero. Backing from a member of the Twenty-Nine Officials is required to enter the competition.

CONTENTS

✥ *SIXTH VERSE:* SIXWAYS EXHIBITION II ✥

AUREATIA TWENTY-NINE OFFICIALS

First Minister
GRASSE THE FOUNDATION MAP
A man nearing old age.
Tasked with being the chairperson who presides over Twenty-Nine Officials' meetings.
Not belonging to any of the factions in the Sixways Exhibition and maintaining neutrality.

Second General
ROSCLAY THE ABSOLUTE
A man who garners absolute trust as a champion.
Participates in the Sixways Exhibition, supporting himself. The leader of the largest faction within the Twenty-Nine Officials.

Third Minister
JELKY THE SWIFT INK
A bespeckled man with the air of a shrewd bureaucrat.
Planned the Sixways Exhibition. Belongs to Rosclay's faction.

Fourth Minister
KAETE THE ROUND TABLE
A man with an extremely fierce temperament.
Sponsoring Mestelexil the Box of Desperate Knowledge.
Possesses preeminent military power and authority and is resisting Rosclay's faction.

Fifth Official
VACANT SEAT

Sixth General
HARGHENT THE STILL
A man who yearns for authority despite being ridiculed for being incompetent.
Sponsoring Lucnoca the Winter. Has a deep connection with Alus the Star Runner.
Not part of any faction.

Seventh Minister
FLINSUDA THE PORTENT
Corpulent woman adorned in gold-and-silver accessories.
A pragmatist who only believes in the power of money.
Sponsoring Tu the Magic.

Eighth Minister
SHEANEK THE WORD INTERMEDIARY
A man who can decipher and give accounts in a variety of different scripts.
Acts in practice as First Minister Grasse the Foundation Map's Secretary.
Maintains neutrality just like Grasse.

Ninth General
YANIEGIZ THE CHISEL
A sinewy man with a snaggletooth.
Belongs to Rosclay's Faction.

Tenth General
QWELL THE WAX FLOWER
A woman with long bangs that hide her eyes. Sponsor for Psianop the Inexhaustible Stagnation. Timid and always trembling in fright. For some unknown reason, even compared to the rest of the Twenty-Nine Officials, she possesses superlative physical strength.

Eleventh Minister
NOPHTOK THE CREPUSCULE BELL
An elderly man who gives a gentle, kindly impression.
Sponsor for Kuze the Passing Disaster.
Holds jurisdiction over the Order.

Twelfth General
SABFOM THE WHITE WEAVE
A man who covers his face with an iron mask.
Previously crossed swords with self-proclaimed demon king Morio and is currently recuperating.

Thirteenth Minister
ENU THE DISTANT MIRROR
An aristocratic man with slicked-back hair.
Sponsor for Zeljirga the Abyss Web.
Infected by Linaris the Obsidian and now under her control.

Fourteenth General
YUCA THE HALATION GAOL
A simple and honest man, round and plump. Doesn't have a shred of ambition. Head of Aureatia's Public Safety branch.
Sponsoring Ozonezma the Capricious.

Fifteenth General

HAIZESTA THE GATHERING SPOT

A man in the prime of his life with a cynical smile. Prominent for his misbehavior.

Twentieth Minister

HIDOW THE CLAMP

A haughty son of a noble family and at the same time a popular, quick-witted man. Sponsor for Alus the Star Runner. Sponsoring Alus to ensure he doesn't win.

Twenty-Fifth General

CAYON THE SKYTHUNDER

A one-armed man with a feminine speaking manner. Sponsor for Mele the Horizon's Roar.

Sixteenth General

NOFELT THE SOMBER WIND

An abnormally tall man. Sponsor for Uhak the Silent. Originated from the same Order almshouse as Kuze.

Twenty-First General

TUTURI THE BLUE VIOLET FOAM

A woman with grizzled hair tied up behind her head.

Twenty-Sixth Minister

MEEKA THE WHISPERED

A stern woman who gives a rigid and rectangular impression. Acting as the adjudicator of the Sixways Exhibition.

Seventeenth Minister

ELEA THE RED TAG

A young, beautiful woman who rose up from her prostitute ancestry. Supervises Aureatia's intelligence apparatus. Sponsoring Jivlart the Ash Border. Keeping Kia the World Word a secret to use as her trump card.

Twenty-Second General

MIZIAL THE IRON-PIERCING PLUMESHADE

A boy who became a member of the Twenty-Nine Officials at just sixteen years old. Possesses a self-assured temperament. Sponsoring Toroa the Awful.

Twenty-Seventh General

HARDY THE BULLET FLASHPOINT

A man who sincerely loves war. Sponsor for Soujirou the Willow-Sword. Prominent figure accompanied by the largest military faction. Regarded as the largest rival to Rosclay's faction.

Eighteenth Minister

QUEWAI THE MOON FRAGMENT

A young, gloomy man.

Twenty-Third Official

VACANT SEAT

Previously the seat of Taren the Punished. However, it is currently vacant following her secession and defection.

Twenty-Eighth Minister

ANTEL THE ALIGNMENT

A tan-skinned man wearing dark-tinted glasses.

Nineteenth Minister

HYAKKA THE HEAT HAZE

A small-statured man who supervises the agricultural division. Straining himself to become worthy of his position in the Twenty-Nine Officials. Sponsoring Shalk the Sound Slicer.

Twenty-Fourth General

DANT THE HEATH FURROW

An exceedingly serious man. Commands the northern front army, containing Old Kingdoms' loyalists' forces. Part of the Queen's faction—and harbors ill feelings toward Rosclay's faction. Sponsoring Zigita Zogi the Thousandth.

Twenty-Ninth Official

VACANT SEAT

ISHURA

Keiso

ILLUSTRATION BY **Kureta**

Sixth Verse:

SIXWAYS EXHIBITION II

It was around the time the True Demon Lord's reign of terror had begun to spread across the world.

Kuze the Passing Disaster was not yet a cleaner, nor had he earned his name of the Passing Disaster, but instead he was a normal young man aiming to become a priest, wandering from one almshouse to another to learn the Order's teachings.

In some frontier city, all communication to the outside world had been cut off overnight, and every person who left to investigate never returned. However, even with such little information, everyone at the time seemed to have a hunch that it wasn't because of some sudden uprising or an outbreak of a new plague.

In the early days, people tried to ignore the very existence of the city. There was someone who said there had surely been some terrible disaster, and the rescue attempts were met with trouble. That Izick the Chromatic, who had already managed to lay waste to several cities, or the vampires that were still hidden among the minian races were far bigger problems—and that *they must not let some unrelated city on the frontier concern them.*

The younger Kuze believed this explanation. Nevertheless, he soon understood this wasn't the case.

The more necessary it was to go around saying that one mustn't let something concern them, *the more it weighed on everyone's minds.*

As far as Kuze understood, both adult's and children's minds were seized by anxiety, and yet the fates of the city's residents remained a mystery, with any investigative activity being placed on hold for over a year.

It was abnormal.

Before long, there came a rumor that a hamlet adjoining the city had *apparently* disappeared. Any investigation related to the True Demon King never yielded much. The one who barely managed to make it back didn't say anything about the extent of the damages, or the safety of the residents. They only left a single statement behind—*"There's something terrifying there."* Then he died.

His death wasn't from any physical abnormality. The extreme terror and exhaustion had killed him.

It wasn't *"There* was *something terrifying,"* but that *"There* is." The word was short, but that was what truly expressed the staggering terror of the True Demon King. In all likelihood, he had never even encountered the True Demon King at all. He encountered the Demon King Army in that ruined place—and learned from himself that something terrifying *was still there...* And because of this unfortunate realization, he perished.

The people feared this unseen terror.

Someone began referring to the overwhelming threat as the True Demon King.

They were more than a tyrannical monarch standing in opposition to the One True King. They were a malevolent entity unlike anything the world had seen before.

The head priest of the Order gave a proclamation to the people. Either the royal family or the head priest had to or else unabated disorder would continue to spread.

"Every life on this planet, joined in understanding with Word Arts...has persisted from time immemorial into the present day because they have overcome the threat of annihilation again and again."

The Order faithfully undertook their duty, trying to expel the curse of fear that tormented the hearts of the people.

"There will be many sacrifices, just as there were during the plagues and the Viledragon Disaster. Be that as it may, just as with those calamities of the past—this terror will inevitably come to an end."

Kuze believed this, too. He could entertain the hope that if they endured it for just a little bit longer, an unknown Hero would slay the True Demon King.

However, this proclamation itself may have been the worst possible crossroads for the Order to put forth.

The First Party, the hopes of many on their shoulder, was wiped out, and the Order's charity work was unable to hold back the wave of ruin, with everyone around the world dying, dying, and continuing to die.

All the kingdoms were on a war footing, and the support for the Order, tasked with maintaining social welfare, continued to dwindle as the years went on.

The Order, their doctrines leaving them unable to supply any military aid, began to be coldly regarded by the people, and as all kinds of despair spread across the world, faith was the very first thing to disappear.

If the Wordmaker supposedly created this world, then why did this Wordmaker allow something like the True Demon King to exist?

The head priest who made the first proclamation died just a year later.

He was stabbed by a vagabond who had lost their family to the Demon King Army.

"If you're intent on the priesthood, Kuze…"

The priest Kuze was learning from at the time, Rozelha the Ruminator, let these words slip.

"Don't give it up until the very end, long after everyone else. No matter how much the True Demon King torments the people… You need to protect the correct teachings up until the very end. That's the hardest job a priest is tasked with."

"…*Ha-ha.* Is it now? I mean, you're always giving up on temperance yourself, Father Rozelha."

"No… *Hee-hee*, that's different. It's a completely different topic altogether, you understand, Kuze?"

"...Everyone comes seeking salvation from the Wordmaker. They feel that if even the First Party proved unable, they want someone who can do it, to go and kill the True Demon King. There were some trying to grant these wishes. I don't really think those guys are wrong. But believers have begun abandoning their faith and trying to join the subjugation forces... What am I supposed to do for people like them?"

The True Demon King couldn't be allowed to exist. Kuze himself wished he could become a savior to the people. Not just to protect the refugees who escaped from the Demon King and give the people peace of mind, but to eliminate the problem at the source.

If it was possible to comprehend the True Demon King through the use of Word Arts, the actions necessary to slay them would, for the Order's believers, also mean discarding their faith.

"...'Thou shall not hate.' 'Thou shall not harm.' 'Thou shall not kill'—these conditions make the task rather tricky."

"Do you think that everyone who went off has...given up?"

"I'd say so. They weren't able to stick to their priestly ways of saving others. That might be a cruel way to put it, though."

Kuze knew that Rozelha's faith in the Wordmaker was deeper than anyone else's. Even if his behavior was unbecoming of a clergyman, Kuze had never seen him break any of their religious precepts.

"You see, Kuze, when I say keep going until the very end, longer than anyone else, I mean that I want you to outlast *even me*. If all the people of the world fight, and seek to kill each other; if there's no one there to protect our teachings until the last man standing, who will pass them on to the world to follow? That's what makes it the most difficult responsibility of all."

Rozelha took a single gulp of the small remaining amount of booze in his bottle.

"There will be times when you'll want to fight for justice. When it seems like there's a better way to improve the world than through the Wordmaker's teachings. When your faith beings to waver, the words of the Wordmaker will be your anchor. We need to be there for those in need, even the ones who've had their faith waver. Even if it doesn't seem like the right thing to do."

"...I wonder if I can become the sort of priest you're talking about, Father Rozelha."

Kuze didn't think he had lived a life of misfortune. Though he had been an orphan abandoned at an almshouse, having never known his birthplace, he was surrounded by friends in the Order.

Then there was the angel—whom no one else could see—that always watched over him.

If there were going to be more and more children with circumstances like Kuze's in the age of the True Demon King, then he wanted to practice what he'd learned from his teachings and save as many of those children as he could.

"I'm scared of the True Demon King, too."

Kuze feebly smiled.

"Lately, I've been afraid that before long...I'll go against our teachings, just like everyone else has."

"*Heh.* That's 'cause you're kind, Kuze."

"Father Rozelha. I don't have the courage to kill—or the courage to die. Everyone who went to join the subjugation force were all much more impressive than I am. Do you think someday…everyone will come back to the Order, and we'll be able to do things like we used to?"

"…'Course we can. We continue protecting the Wordmaker's teachings for just such a day. Whatever happens to the world out there, the good things, the things that save the soul, won't change at all."

Priests act as embodiments of this everlasting truth—this must have been what Rozelha wanted to say. In the Order, those who voluntarily broke the precepts of their teachers would be unable to become priests.

"Kuze. I know plenty well enough that the ones who have separated from the Order are experiencing the worst hardships of all. Because they have to believe for themselves in the justness they were willing to abandon the Wordmaker's teachings for—the decision to harm and kill someone. They might have to live right up to the end holding firm to this sense of justice. That is a truly agonizing thing. That's why we will wait."

"……"

Even then, if they were all to return to their faith, the Wordmaker's teachings made it clear.

If they returned to the Order, their sins would be forgiven.

"Lately, I've been dreaming that I'm…I'm in Cunodey's almshouse like I was way back when…truly just like I was, doing stupid stuff with Nofelt, teasing Ina… Imos was still alive, too."

To Kuze, faith in the Wordmaker was no different from the memories of such happy days.

A majority of the friends Kuze had lived with had also broken off from the Order. There were some who would never come back.

"I... I want to be waiting here for everyone."

"...I know. That's what faith feels like. I'm sure it will be okay. Kuze..."

Putting down his glasses, Rozelha smiled.

"You'll be able to find happiness."

Kuze, just an orphan on the path to priesthood, had never met someone's true intent to kill until the spiraling slaughter born from the True Demon King spread out over the world.

Therefore, at the time, he had no way of knowing about Nastique's unusual ability to automatically bring instant death to all who confronted him.

◆

A long time passed.

Kuze was looking at a church pelted in a downpour of rain.

Close to twenty years had passed since he had his conversation with Rozelha, and the terror of the True Demon King still continued to exist in the world.

"...How did things end up like this?"

Drenched by the rain, Kuze gave an exhausted smile. A self-deprecating smirk.

There were six dead bodies lying around him. All of them were armed.

"I've become a murderer myself, Father Rozelha."

Kuze the Passing Disaster wore a robe that closely resembled a priest's, but it was black. He wasn't a real priest. He was no longer young, and he had lost the ambitious glimmer in his eye. There was also a stubbly beard on his chin.

For a long time, the rank of paladin within the Order had been discontinued.

In the era of the True Demon King, where no one could rely on any other power and needed to protect themselves with violence, there was a class of warrior assigned once again to a single individual. The cleaner for the Order.

The armed group that attacked the church that day even included an ogre over twice as tall as Kuze in their ranks. This ogre, too, had collapsed and was leaning up against the wall. It had attacked this church and eaten many of the children here, and yet the look on his dead face was peaceful, as if he were asleep.

There were some who attacked the Order to pillage them, but Kuze knew that a majority weren't like that.

They were filled with hatred toward the Order, and their teachings, that did nothing to help them.

Kuze looked up to the top of the roof.

There was a being that had been watching over Kuze ever since he was a child.

"Hey there, Nastique. That's where you're sitting today, huh?"

On top of the roof, doused in cold rain, her palely glowing form was the one thing that would never get wet.

Pure-white hair. Pure-white clothes. Pure-white wings.

Her soft, short hair and delicate frame made her look like a young boy, but her appearance was elegant and graceful.

When Kuze noticed Nastique's presence, she replied with a faint smile.

The corners of her mouth relaxing meant a smile. The angel's expressions were so indistinct that it took Kuze a long time until he understood even this much. She seemed like a whole different being from anything else.

"Are you okay?" Kuze was convinced this was her salutation to him.

"I'm fine, I'm fine. We were just saying hi to each other, really," Kuze said, trying to show that he was tough.

He knocked on the church door. If Nastique wasn't watching, he might've still wavered.

"Pardon me, the rain's really coming down out here..."

The priest and children inside were safe, and they'd holler back their reply. That was the fantasy he played in his mind.

"Could you lend me your roof for a little while?"

Silence at first. Then there came a reply. The sound of a crossbow pulling back.

Kuze readied his large shield. Twisting the handle as he gripped it tight, he braced for impact.

The storm of arrows that pierced through the doorway rushed

toward the steel shield. Kuze lowered his body. He withstood. If he grew scared, he'd be repelled, and his fears would become reality. The shield he raised became riddled with arrows.

"Sheesh... Not very kind of you."

The class of paladin was meant for combat, but they could not equip themselves with swords or bows. The only thing they carried with them was a large shield to defend against their enemy's violence.

Stepping inside the church, Kuze tried to continue his thought.

"If you're in there, then you gotta say so; come on, now..."

Kuze saw a lump of flesh dangling from the ceiling and closed his eyes. He hadn't wanted to see it.

The person who he had wished was waiting for him inside was no longer there.

"...Ah, Father Rozelha... *Bweh-heh-heh*, so that's how it is... You didn't make it, either, huh...?"

The gang that had taken hold of the church aimed their arrows at Kuze.

In the rear of the church, someone was sitting on a bench with their back to Kuze. Turning their sights to the entrance, their face and eyes met Kuze's. The face, hideously burned, was covered in worn bandages.

"...A glimpse of my face—"

The voice sounded much, much younger than Kuze had imagined. It was practically the voice of a young prepubescent boy.

"—doesn't frighten you, does it?"

"...*Bweh-heh-heh*. So I take it you're the one in charge here?"

Kuze didn't even plead for his life, simply offering a weak laugh. His attitude was abnormal for someone currently surrounded by death on all sides. He felt the same way himself.

Be sure to talk things out. People were bestowed Word Arts by the Wordmaker in order to communicate with one another.

"Well, I heard that the church here's been making a bit of noise lately. See, I got the message from the Order, and, well... I thought I'd try to settle things peacefully. I'm Kuze the Passing Disaster, and—"

Crunch.

There was the sound of metal splintering. The tip of the chain, brandished by the man on the bench, chipped Kuze's shield.

"......"

The attack was instantaneous. His foe still had his back turned to Kuze, and he was still seated.

Even when sitting, his attack reached far back behind him near the entrance of the church. If Kuze had been even a second slower with his shield, he would've been severed clean in half, bones and all.

"Go ahead; continue. My name is Hyne the Swaying Indigolite. A long, long time ago......I was the first formation rearguard of Obsidian Eyes."

Suddenly, a slash attack was launched at his blind spot on the right. Kuze narrowly deflected it with his gauntlet.

The long and limber chain was being sped up with just his fingertips. Hyne the Swaying Indigolite's weapon took an unexpected trajectory, as if it were a writhing live snake, and transformed into high-speed slashing attack.

His subordinates also nocked their arrows in quick succession and began peppering the intruder with arrows.

A brutal onslaught from every direction, which the defense of his large shield alone was utterly unable to handle.

"Okay, okay, I lost, I give up..."

He deflected an arrow with the round of his shield. Right before the chain tried to snap up into the air, he stamped down on it.

"Just calm down! Uh-oh, whoa!" Jumping under a bench, he dodged the hail of arrows. This was a familiar church. He had played tag with the children here, before then being scolded by the aging priest.

He had found a slim means of escape. He kept finding them.

If he didn't desperately cling to that scant opportunity, he'd lose sight of it forever.

Kuze had long since gotten used to fights like this.

Raising his large shield up like a roof over his head, he blocked the deluge of arrows. Ultimately, he was unable to defeat anybody.

On that day, he hadn't been able to go off and defeat the True Demon King, either.

Thanks to a wonderful miracle, we no longer live in solitude. All creatures with a heart and soul are our family.

"...Back. Keep your distance." Hyne mumbled quietly. Was he really being cautious of Kuze's nonresistance?

"You might try to punch with that shield of yours. Or maybe you're preparing to use some Word Arts?"

...See, I can't do anything like that.

The tempestuous assault continued. Hyne continued to precisely assail Kuze from all sides with his chain, as though it was filling in any gaps between the arrows besieging him.

Please, no more killing.

Hyne the Swaying Indigolite. Just how dedicated he must have been to train and develop his skills to this level.

Even that dedicated training hadn't been enough to erase his hatred for the Order.

Blood. Severed arms, legs, eyeballs, innards—no matter what he did, the left-behind traces of the tragedy that occurred in this church reflected in Kuze's eyes as he continued to live on and survive.

I'm begging you. Don't try to kill me.

In the thick of a world where anyone and everyone kept meeting their ends, Kuze raged against the inevitable.

The bench concealing Kuze was severed in two, iron frame and all. Hyne's chain was picking up speed. Kuze readied his shield again, fortifying against the arc of the chain's slash.

......Shoot.

One of the gang members who had drawn in near his blind spot was readying an arrow.

The destruction of his cover had thrown off his calculations. He couldn't block it with the armor on his arms or legs, either. That was the moment facing him.

Kuze prepared for death—

The attacker's legs twisted, and they collapsed.

......

Their boss, Hyne, picked up on the obviously strange event, too. "…What did you do just now?"

Kuze didn't answer. He had prepared for death—and nothing more.

—The death of his enemy.

Kuze was the only one capable of perceiving it.

Nastique's figure as she teleported behind the back of the one directing their killing intentions Kuze's way—and stabbed them with her short sword.

They were beings who had been scattered at the time of creation, when the Wordmaker gathered a great number of visitors together and this world began. They were tasked with establishing the laws that govern the world.

When the time of creation ended, so too did their responsibilities. As time marched on, the angels disappeared….and perhaps the people stopped trying to see them, turning them into mere figures of legend, even within the Order.

Death was her domain.

Kuze referred to the sinister red blade, ill-matched with her elegant, white body, as Death's Fang.

Thou shall not hate. Thou shall not harm. Thou shall not kill. Treat others as thou would treat thy own family.

Taking advantage of the gang's attention being drawn to the inscrutable and sudden death, Kuze fled to the wall.

A fresh member of the mob readied their short spear and charged toward Kuze. The impact sank through the shield. Matching the movements of the spearhead's thrust, he pulled back his shield. Pulling his assailant down to the ground after his stance faltered, he pinned him down.

"...Phew..."

Still pinning the attacker down against the wall, he covered the other side of him with his shield, forcibly making a safe zone. At long last, he could take a deep breath.

Nastique floated right next to Kuze and fixed her eyes up at the lump of flesh dangling from the ceiling. *"Who is this person?"*

"...See, Father Nozelha has taken really good care of me for a long, long time."

Nastique was not a heartless angel.

Kuze believed that she must have a heart that mourned for people, lamented, and tried to do good.

This was why he continued to talk to her. Even if he never got a reply.

"He was super good at making potato soup, let me tell you. All the kids in the almshouse, and I mean all of them, loved it... Though, for a priest he was pretty loose, and he'd have his mistresses and stuff, but he was a kind man. Always caring deeply for all of us..."

"Curse you, lemme go......! Like I give a damn about whoever the hell you're talking about!"

The rogue Kuze kept pinned down yelled out. He must have believed Kuze was talking to him.

"You know, I tell you...... Oh, really? You don't know him? You didn't hate him or anything, and you killed him anyway?"

He always prayed that no one would get killed. And yet things never went that way.

Each time a person killed another, Kuze's faith faltered, and he'd drift further away from some potential happiness.

"He's the guy you have hanging up there. He...he was my teacher."

The short spear–wielding rogue must have tried to attack Kuze without waiting for the answer. Either with some concealed weapon he could use while held down against the ground or maybe some type of Word Arts.

However, he never put his plan into motion. The angel silently cut up the rogue's side with her short sword.

Without exception, a single attack from Death's Fang would prove lethal. No matter how tiny of a scratch it may have left.

The gusting carnage of chain and arrow also meant nothing to Nastique, as she didn't possess a corporeal form in their world. Without anyone being aware of her, Nastique and Nastique alone, protecting Kuze, was always claiming the lives of others without any of them being able to fight back at all.

"Are you okay?" She must have been concerned for him.

Turning to Nastique, Kuze laughed. A fatigued laugh.

"...Bweh-heh-heh. Well, now he's dead."

He understood. It was almost certain that none of them would put down their weapons.

They must have had a reason driving them to go to such

lengths. And yet Kuze could only flounder in meaninglessness, desperately trying not to kill anyone and trying not to be killed himself. He didn't even want to keep making his angel add to her sins.

He shouted. "Oh yeah, so I forgot to mention something! I came out here to kill all of you guys!"

After he acknowledged it once, the only thing left was to carry it out to the end.

"Sorry, but...I'm gonna need you to die. All of you."

"You think after the Order couldn't save anybody...they have the right to kill us now, huh?!"

"I guess I don't. Maybe, if we had just talked things over a bit more, we could've worked things out... Truly. But the thing is..."

He planted his humongous shield at a spot on the floor with a large image of an angel spreading her wings.

Behind Kuze the Passing Disaster's back, the angel of death, invisible to everyone else, was unfurling her pure-white wings.

"Apparently the angel...isn't going to forgive you for what you've done."

Kuze began walking toward Hyne, sitting on a bench in the back of the church.

A rogue with a long sword slashed at him from his flank. Nastique's short sword brushed against the man's neck. With just this, the attacker lost his strength and collapsed.

"What's with this guy...?!"

Hyne twisted his bandage-wrapped face and shouted. One

who had tried circling around him. One who had charged with a short spear. And just now, one wielding a long sword. All of them died.

From their perspective, none of them was hit by any attack at all, and Kuze was just defending himself...and yet they were the only ones losing their lives. That was how it all looked.

"Everyone, stand back. I'll get him! *Haine io quqiciku! Hamn nagre, meg 9fran, orped borg, 5,1,8,6! Zaido lebehe!*" (From Haine to Kuqeciku's cord! Running ecliptic, right elbow axis, touch skylight, five, one, eight, six! Shred him!)

The thick chain glowed red-hot and rent the church from the floor to the ceiling with a six-meter-long arc.

A combination of Thermal Arts, Power Arts, and iron chain techniques using both fingers. It was a crystallization of all the combat prowess that Hyne the Swaying Indigolite had trained in, as a warrior for Obsidian Eyes, nevertheless—

"......!"

Hyne's technique cleaved the bench, the altar, and his remaining subordinates, while also incidentally twisting and breaking the fingers serving as the basis of his technique.

"It can't be."

These fingers of his were now lying at his feet. While only a red cross section on his wrist remained behind.

The instant he unleashed his ultimate technique, his hands were cut off at the wrists, and he lost control.

"Impossible. There's no way."

"There sure is. These things happen."

Hyne vacantly gazed at the nub where his hand had been severed by some unseen force.

"Wh-why…is it always like this? Irrational absurdity, over and over."

He groaned.

Death would come. Taking a hit from Nastique guaranteed such a fate.

He was supposed to be a violent ruffian who massacred Kuze's former teacher and all the orphan children in the man's care, and yet he wore the expression of a sobbing child. The terrible burns beneath the bandages told Kuze the kind of life the man had led up until now.

"It's always like this."

"……You're going to die, Hyne the Swaying Indigolite. Your time has come. Just as it comes for everyone else."

"B-but…who gets to decide that? Why do these things happen…? Tell me. Did the Wordmaker decide it was my time to die…?"

Kuze slowly walked until he came to a halt in front of Hyne.

"…It's the same way for everyone, right? The Wordmaker isn't responsible for anything and everything."

"No. No, you're wrong…!"

Underneath the bandages, Hyne twisted in hatred.

"It's, the Wordmaker, and you Order people's fault. All of it… You praise the Wordmaker for the creation, for being omnipotent, and despite all that, the Wordmaker doesn't bear any responsibility for their own world?!"

The terror of the True Demon King would inevitably come to an end. Kuze believed those words, too.

Everything went just as the murdered head priest once said. Nevertheless, it all came too late.

The True Demon King continued to terrorize the world, and before long, a whole twenty-five years had passed. What had the Order actually saved from that reign of tyranny?

"...Yeah. Everyone suffered, more than was ever necessary. How about we chat about the salvation of this world...the Wordmaker's salvation."

Kuze sat down on the half-demolished bench.

The church had transformed into a crucible of atrocity, drowned in a sea of blood.

However, when Kuze first saw him, Hyne was sitting on this very bench, looking toward the altar.

Kuze knew—the ones who hungrily sought the Wordmaker's salvation...were the ones who fell the deepest into despair.

"I'm still a clergyman when all is said and done. I'll listen here until you die. Confession time. Gathering confessions is all that'll save people."

"Then, why—why didn't the Wordmaker save us? Was I...were we all...abandoned?"

"...Well, you're wrong there. Think about all the things or people who've saved your life up until now. Might've been some random chance, heck, maybe been a stroke of good luck. But see... The salvation that the Wordmaker bestows on people? Me, I don't think that it really manifests in some amorphous good fortune or anything like that."

Lifeblood poured incessantly from the severed remains of Hyne's arms.

There wasn't anything Kuze could do as he gazed down at the sight.

"...No one's been abandoned. If your cruel treatment came at another person's hands, then you must have been equally saved by another person's goodwill. A conscience to save others. The Wordmaker was there in each and every moment. See, if they're the god that created this world? Then they can't favor only one race, right? That's why they created a world where people would save other people. That's the salvation...that the almighty Wordmaker bestowed on us."

"I-in that case... In that case, why...did the people who saved me, why did all of them die?"

"Because they're people. If it's not the sort of tragedy a person's strength can help save...then people can't save at all."

"No... No, that's wrong... They should have the power, more power that could save everyone...! Curse them all... The Wordmaker...the Demon King..."

Kuze knew what drove them into despair.

It was because they wanted to believe there was some hope amid a hopelessness beyond the reach of any person's helping hand.

The hope that someone, an unknown righteous somebody would save everything and correct the world to how it should be.

"...Da...mmit all...not scared...this face........."

The scars left behind by the True Demon King continued to torment all who lived in these times.

"...Yeah. It's over."

Watching Hyne's death, Kuze addressed the empty air. Floating there was an invisible angel.

The young, white girl smiled faintly.

"Thank goodness."

Without a doubt, she was genuinely concerned for Kuze's life. Kuze understood that.

"Thank goodness you were able to survive, huh?"

Now, in the present day. Kuze the Passing Disaster was a hero candidate in the Sixways Exhibition.

His sponsor was Aureatia's Eleventh Minister. Nophtok the Crepuscule Bell was a veteran within Aureatia's Twenty-Nine Officials, but the older man was the least like the rest of the Twenty-Nine Officials.

Without any exceptional great ambitions, or displays of wit, he obediently handled the work assigned to him and nothing more, going back and forth between the assembly hall and his own home slowly, with the gait of a pigeon.

But on that day, with the Sixways Exhibition drawing near, Nophtok stopped.

"…Excuse me, you there."

In a narrow alleyway, hidden away from the sights of the people going down the main road, a small girl crouched down.

The clothes she was wrapped in were brand-new, but they were likely stolen. Her arms and legs were emaciated, and she was clearly in a poor state of health.

"Are you all right?"

"...Yeah."

The girl nodded blankly. They were the eyes of someone who never expected any goodwill or help from the start.

"It's not much, but have some."

He presented her with a hard piece of bread. He had been carrying it with him for lunch.

If she was a beggar and learned in the techniques for receiving charity, then she wouldn't have been hiding away from the eyes of others. He thought she might have been a child who only recently drifted into Aureatia after losing her hometown in some strife, such as the Lithia War or the Particle Storm.

"......"

"You must be thirsty. I do have a water flask with me."

The girl accepted the bread, and seeing her begin to eat, Nophtok let out a sigh of relief.

"...Th-thank you...... Mr. Stranger Man."

"I see. You don't know me, do you? I see, then."

Nophtok smiled with his eyes, hidden behind his thick white eyebrows. Nophtok's presence among the Twenty-Nine Officials was weak. He was nominally the leader in charge of the Order's division of the government, but within the younger generation of the Order, there were many who didn't even know the man's name.

"There's a big avenue over there. Do you know which one I'm talking about?"

"...Yeah."

"If you cross it and head toward the general store with the

yellow roof, you'll see a church. If you don't have anywhere to go, then let the Order shelter you. It'll be far better than sleeping out here on the street like this."

"The Order..."

The large eyeballs fitted into her emaciated face looked at Nophtok.

"...are liars."

"......Are they, now?"

"I was told that the Wordmaker doesn't even exist, but they lie... and collect donations. And they just do bad stuff with it instead."

"Well, that's no good, now, is it?"

Nophtok couldn't bring himself to ask who had taught the girl such things.

Even the large-scale massacre that destroyed 90 percent of the minia races' living sphere was nothing but one facet of the true hopelessness brought forth by the True Demon King. The most irrevocable destruction that the True Demon King bestowed on this world was completely killing the faith in the Wordmaker that had existed from the beginning of time.

"...If I could help you myself, I would... Forgive me."

"It's okay. Thank you for giving me food, mister."

"If things get rough for you, get someone to share their food with you again. You need to have the courage to ask for help. You shouldn't steal. Got it?"

"......Okay."

Nophtok left the girl behind and began walking along his usual route.

At this point, the Order can no longer bear their function as a social welfare organization. Should we keep allowing an organization to exist when they can't save anyone?

The Order's destitution wasn't solely because Aureatia's financial support had stagnated. The contributions from the faithful continued to decline, and the nightmare the True Demon King unleashed on the world was still breeding individuals beyond all salvation. Due to lack of capital necessary to help said people, they now had difficulties picking up those who had been abandoned by society, teaching them, and returning them back into the world.

Nophtok still remembered the incident that a man called Hyne the Swaying Indigolite brought about. Though he was an orphan raised by the Order, he was ultimately drawn into the societal underworld, Obsidian Eyes.

"Master Nophtok."

When he started down a different street, a man in a hat approached him without making a sound and called his name.

He was wearing an outfit that would allow him to disappear into a crowd of townspeople, but there was a perilous gleam in his eyes.

"...Oh. It's you. Good day."

"The attack on Kuze the Passing Disaster has failed."

Nophtok had ordered the assault. Before the Sixways Exhibition opened, and the bracket was set in stone, he needed to get a precise calculation of Kuze the Passing Disaster's fighting capabilities.

"This is the second time we've attacked him in his sleep, but again, he killed all his attackers. This would then mean that he is able to enact his mysterious and deadly counterattacks whether the man himself is conscious or not."

"...In that case, no matter how many assassins we send in, we're probably not going to glean any more information."

Nophtok himself was simply an older man without either wits or ambitions. The purpose of the Eleventh Minister's very existence was questionable, without any achievements to his name, yet without causing any scandals as well and lacking the power to sway the Aureatia Assembly.

—Naturally, that was how he made things seem.

One other cause behind the Order's decline in recent years was that Nophtok, the man with jurisdiction over them, would intentionally delay procedures and communications. He also didn't counteract any of the false reports of criticism circulating among the citizens.

The overseer of the Order, Nophtok the Crepuscule Bell, was absolutely not the Order's ally. He was a negligent saboteur, tolling the twilight bell unbeknownst to the organization he was tasked to manage.

The answer was already clear. An organization unable to save anyone should not be allowed to survive.

The problem didn't lie in the Order's benevolence or lack thereof. As long as they didn't establish an alternative social welfare apparatus, there would only be more and more citizens who continued to slip through society's cracks. Just like the young girl from before.

"If there's anything I can assist with, please tell me. Being able to act independently of Aureatia is really the only advantage a blackguard like me has at his disposal."

"Ah yes. Thank you very much. Is there any other reward besides coin that I could give you?"

"I was raised by the Order, too. They can't keep going the way they have. They've distorted the teachings of old...and nowadays, they're even using hit men for their own goals."

"......"

"I'll do anything I can, if it'll help correct the Order's current path."

Finished with his short conversation, the man left, going in the opposite direction at the fork in the road.

Possessing a close relationship with the Order, Nophtok the Crepuscule Bell could use his connections to freely mobilize members of the criminal underworld without any direct link back to Aureatia itself. However, such individuals were, precisely speaking, none other than the outcasts who had slipped out of the Order's helping hands.

It was the world's irredeemable irony, the weak consuming each other.

If the True Hero was established through the Sixways Exhibition, Aureatia would be democratized. Then a social welfare system, managed by a new institution, instead of an Order that has fallen into dysfunction, would be able to support the nation.

Nophtok the Crepuscle Bell was Kuze the Passing Disaster's sponsor. His goal was simply to drag the Order's strongest weapon out onto the Sixways Exhibition stage and dispose of him in the public eye. The assassin who caused the New Principality of Lithia to surrender was worth an entire nation's military might. By erasing him, for the first time, he could commence with the massive enterprise of dismantling the Order that had existed for several millennia.

Nophtok had lived a long time. Nor did he have any attachment to his own life. His mind was always at peace, even if his role was without honor or he had to stain his hands with dirty business.

But the same was not true of the world around him. It needed a champion to serve as the cornerstone of their hearts and minds.

"We really will need you to win it for us, Second General."

◆

"Sorry to disturb your rest, Rosclay. Mind if we talk?"

In the courtyard of the Aureatia Central Assembly Hall, Third Minister Jel sat down next to Second General Rosclay.

Rosclay had just returned from visiting different regions, beginning first with the areas damaged by the Particle Storm, to offer his sympathies, and was taking a brief moment of respite.

"…Not at all. Today's a busy day, isn't it?"

"This is something that can't be brought up from a council chair. I don't really want anyone else to hear us."

Jel put a finger up to his thin glasses. He wore the same rigid, high-strung expression as always.

"...What do you yourself think, regarding the treatment of the Queen?"

"You're talking about...after I become the hero in the Sixways Exhibition, yes?"

"The smooth opening of the Sixways Exhibition was largely due to your efforts. I'm also grateful that you gave your name as a hero candidate for this purpose. However, after you, as hero, have finished changing this country, what exactly do you plan on doing with Queen Sephite...? I haven't heard your answer directly."

"I suppose not. Queen Sephite is still young. We need to consider the possibility that those scheming to overthrow the new regime raise the abdicated Queen back into a position of power."

"...Rosclay."

Jel observed Rosclay's expression.

The beautiful, composed face, bringing peace of mind to the people, was unchanged.

"Of course, I don't want to outright execute her. The Queen is perfectly innocent and doesn't deserve such an end... The best strategy would be to continue keeping her close at hand as a symbol, someone who doesn't get involved with politics, but make it clear she herself acknowledges the new regime. If we're the ones to sever the long history of the royal family, I think it's best to assume there would be an even greater uprising than if we continue to let her live."

"If that's how you see things, then I can relax...for the time being."

The Sixways Exhibition. The proposer of this historically

massive undertaking, Jel the Swift Ink's designs were a parliamentary democracy, and the complete abolition of the monarchy, as well as the Twenty-Nine Officials.

However, the Sixways Exhibition's hero candidates are the only ones who should shed blood. Not ever making the Queen or the people spill blood themselves. It may be too naive, too idealistic, but...

He believed that was the best path.

He needed to back the new symbol that everyone of the age was longing for to prevent a civil war fighting over making the sole remaining member of the royal family, Sephite, a puppet and to avoid a future where the citizens and Sephite herself were drawn into wars and strife. A true hero.

"...I do feel it's a bit hasty to be worrying about what will happen once I claim victory, though. The bracket hasn't even been settled yet."

"Still, you're bound to be victorious. Am I wrong?"

"If you were, I'd be far too terrified to fight."

They would give *the appearance* of a fair match—and avoid the true danger. Rosclay's camp had already won over others in the Twenty-Nine Officials and, as the largest faction, continued to expand their operations.

"...At the very least, with regard to the first round."

Hidow the Clamp, Alus the Star Runner's sponsor.

Nophtok the Crepuscule Bell, Kuze the Passing Disaster's sponsor.

The administrator of the Sixways Exhibition—Rosclay the Absolute—had joined forces with more than just these two men.

"There's a high chance I'll be matched up against a hero candidate who we already *have an agreement with*."

The threats propagating the land would crush each other, and the last one who should be left standing was the minian champion.

The largest undertaking in the history of the minian races, intrigue and violence mysteriously entwined together. That was the true face of the Sixways Exhibition.

A young girl was walking along the roofs of the homes lining the hilly road. Though she was high enough up to guarantee injury if she ever fell, the girl's long legs were completely exposed, without even a pair of shoes on her feet.

Her chestnut-colored braid swayed behind her like a tail as she walked. Her name was Tu the Magic.

"Hey, Rique, mind if I ask you something?" she asked her companion down below.

"It's dangerous up there," Rique the Misfortune replied, exasperated. The dwarf was a famous mercenary, but in the streets of Aureatia, he was dressed lightly and not carrying his bow.

"Tu, you may be totally fine if you fall, but anyone who sees you is going to be in for a shock."

"So tell me. Why do you think some houses have nice, tidy roofs, but others are falling apart?"

Tu liked high places because they gave her a clearer view of the far-off landscape. Having lived her whole life in the desolate wastes of the Land of the End, for Tu, everything about the Aureatia townscape was novel and strange.

"That's gotta do with if someone's got the money to repair their roof or not. Everyone's circumstances are different, but there aren't any run-down roofs in the nobles' section of town, that's for sure."

"Nobles are people like Flinsuda, right?"

Tu the Magic was also a hero candidate appearing in the Sixways Exhibition. Known as the Demon King's Bastard, not only was she without any relations to speak of, but her very race was suspect; it was thanks to the support of her sponsor in the tournament, Flinsuda, that she was able to live a comfortable life in luxury.

"The Seventh Minister... Flinsuda's a really special case even among the other nobility. That woman's the head of the Aureatia Assembly's health care division. She's probably the richest person in the country, second only to the Queen herself. You think if I became that rich I could see Sephite whenever I wanted?"

Tu had decided to participate in the Sixways Exhibition as a hero candidate for a chance to be reunited with Queen Sephite, who she met in the past. It was quite possible that 70 percent of the responsibility for this string of events was the result of Krafnir's maneuvering the hero candidate Flinsuda originally planned on sponsoring.

Tu was a candid and honest young girl. At the very least, the motives she gave for herself were truthful.

...But why?

Neither Rique nor Krafnir knew the reason why. Though she seemed not to keep any secrets, the naive and unsophisticated Tu wouldn't talk about this single point.

This girl, origins unknown and possessing tremendous individual fighting strength, sought an audience with the Queen for reasons she couldn't speak of to anyone else.

Nevertheless, for Rique, Tu didn't appear to be plotting the Queen's assassination.

"There is technically another way to meet with the Queen, Tu. Do you know where we're headed today?"

"Nope! Not a clue."

"You came along without knowing?"

Tu the Magic was a powerful being, beyond any of the monsters Rique had seen in his life as a mercenary, yet on the inside she was like a young child. That may have been why she had taken like a baby bird to people like Rique and Krafnir—the furthest from honesty and integrity one could get.

"An Order almshouse. They take in orphans…and children from houses unable to raise their offspring—and educate them. History, writing, Word Arts, arithmetic, and the like."

"Sounds hard."

"Nowadays there are some places that teach even harder stuff than that. Aureatia's government-operated schools, well, they're even more complex… That's where kids are studying stuff like natural sciences or economic theory. Queen Sephite attends school herself. She's still eleven, after all."

"Then if I join this 'school' place, I'd could meet Sephite, too."

"Now there's still a super-tough exam you have to pass to get in. An academic exam, at that."

"…I—I think I'll stick with the Sixways Exhibition then…"

"You might be right about that. At the very least, the Queen will be spectating the matches starting from the second round. If you and the Queen know each other, then she might recognize you."

For the school the Queen attended, the issue of one's social standing also was a major factor. Even supposing one received a recommendation from Aureatia's Twenty-Nine Officials, to actually attend, one would need to be, at least, a commoner's child.

At the present moment, with Nagan Labyrinth City's college in ruins, it was impossible for people like Rique, who lived in the world of violence, and Tu, her very status as a member of the minian race dubious, to receive an advanced education.

The Sixways Exhibition to decide the strongest being across the land—the fact that proving victorious in such a battle was more realistic spoke to how far apart the world's light and shadow stood from each other.

"Tu. That's the wrong way."

"Oops."

Tu was heading toward a different forked road that ran along the residential roofs she was traversing. However, she immediately kicked the third-story roof and, spinning twice in the air, landed on one leg down on the pavement.

A feat even an acrobat would've found impossible, yet Tu was totally unharmed.

Invincible. It was Sixways Exhibition hero candidate Tu the Magic's greatest quality. She could get hit directly with a castle's cannon fire, let alone the landing impact from a three-story fall, and come out of it without a scratch on her.

"*Ah-ha-ha*. I was about to lose sight of you."

"Not that there's any reason for you to come with me in the first place. It's personal business anyway."

"So there's someone you want to see, too, huh, Rique?"

"I'm just dropping by to say hello to a friend who's helped me out before. I was contracted way back to do some bodyguard work for the Order, see."

"Now that you mention it, this work of yours, it's almost always escorting people or guarding someone, huh."

"Most of the time, I guess. I've always been good at sniffing out danger, ever since I was born."

Rique came from a mercenary family. Both his grandfather and mother had been mercenaries. It was because he bore such a pedigree that he would always pick and choose jobs based on his own set of standards, to help people.

Naturally, in the current age, there were more mercenaries like those in the Free City of Okafu, who carried out their commissions regardless of their morality, with money the only criteria they went by.

As long as they lived in an era where friend and foe, and the side of justice itself, was in constant flux, as a profession, Rique felt that their stance was also worthy of respect. Still, he needed to believe proudly in his vocation, or he'd be unable to pass on his wisdom and skills as a mercenary to his children or grandchildren.

Rique was indebted to the person he was going to see today, and it bolstered confidence in his beliefs.

"We're here. This is the building."

Tu joined Rique to look where his finger pointed.

"The roof's shabby, huh."

"…Yeah. I didn't notice."

Rique tried his best to answer like it didn't bother him.

When he rang the bell at the entrance, two young men, appearing to be priests in training, came to greet the pair.

"Um, good morning. The chapel's that way, but do you have some business here?"

"Pardon the sudden visit. I'm Rique the Misfortune. I wanted to stop by and give Aiten the Wood Oar my regards while I was here in Aureatia."

"Oh, and I'm Tu the Magic!"

Tu hopped behind him to make herself known, but she was already tall enough for that to be totally unnecessary.

"Aiten the Wood Oar, is it? He left Aureatia quite a long time ago."

"Did he now? Was he dispatched to another city?"

"No. He quit the Order. Said he had to get a proper job to support himself… Though, I remember hearing he was headed for Lithia, so… After the great fire there, I haven't heard what became of him."

"…I see. Got bad enough for someone like him to abandon his faith, huh……"

Rique himself didn't necessarily believe in the teachings of the Wordmaker. Still, he was acutely aware of the depth of faith of those raised by the order.

"Now, all the people best suited for the clergy have up and

gone, so I was put in charge of this almshouse. My name's Naijy the Rhombus Knot."

"...At your age?"

"Yes. I only have a vague memory of the scripture at best, so I'm not at all confident I can manage, though..."

The young lad scratched the back of his head, looking troubled. He was a good-natured young man. However—

Can the Order maintain their education and welfare in a state like this?

Rique looked back to Tu behind him. Tu blinked her eyes.

"There isn't anyone else here who's helped you out before?"

"No, not here. I first met Aiten on a job outside of Aureatia, too. The stuff about him being a priest for the church in Aureatia's Western Outer Ward was just something he told me back then, too."

"Huh, that so...?"

"I am sorry. After you came all this way to visit, too."

"It's fine. We're probably the ones putting you out here. It may not be much more than a small gesture, but could you let me inside and donate to the church?"

"Huh?! Y-yes, of course, absolutely!"

As they were shown inside the building by the suddenly chipper young man, Tu, following behind Rique, consulted him by quietly whispering in his ear.

"Should I give something to them, too?"

"Don't."

"Like empty bug shells or something?"

"Don't."

They passed by classrooms where children were learning. Rique felt the number of children was very small for an Order institution in the minian races' greatest city. If it meant there were less orphans and impoverished children in the world, then it might've been something to celebrate, but he knew this wasn't so.

Then there was a man walking toward them from the far end of the corridor.

Rique gasped.

"......You!"

"Well now, if it ain't Rique the Misfortune. And look at this fine woman you got with you!"

Rique immediately focused his attention on the position of the short sword concealed inside his clothes.

"Whoa, whoa, no need to square up now."

The other man shrugged. He had a large mouth, and his hair was combed back.

"*Ha-ha!* Either way, you're a just a chump without that bow of yours."

"...You may be right. Though even if I am a *chump*, I'm pretty sure that's enough to take you on."

Taking stock of the sudden change in atmosphere, the youthful guide posed a question to Rique.

"U-um... Rique? Are you an acquaintance of Master Jivlart the Ash Border?"

"'Master'?"

Rique frowned at young man's word choice.

Jivlart the Ash Border. The boss of Sun's Conifer. Rique knew this man.

"These guys…are a band of punk thugs from a country town. Ever since a job of mine two years ago, I made up my mind to never trust these Sun's Conifer dregs. What's all this 'Master' nonsense about, then? Jivlart?"

"A country town… *Ha-ha!* A real nasty way to refer to a man's beloved hometown, wouldn't you say?"

Jivlart jogged forward and looked down right in Rique's face. Though his dress itself was rather high-class, the distinctive violent and boorish air to him hadn't changed at all since Rique last saw him.

"Though, you're not wrong."

Sun's Conifer, rising up from a frontier village and rapidly making a name for themselves in recent years, proclaimed to be a guild. They behaved like a band of skilled and capable mercenaries, and a majority of the city's citizens believed their act.

However, in reality, this brute force only ever pointed their blades at those weaker than themselves who they could exploit.

"Um, Rique…"

"If you're in charge here, then you listen, too. A while back, I took up a job guarding the daughter of a wealthy farmer. I had to escort her to the family she was marrying into. The ones the client hired to act as the on-site guarantor were Sun's Conifer. When I successfully escorted the girl, I handed her over to these guys. But."

Though he had only a relatively short relationship with her, the girl was cheerful and loved to make small talk. Rique had thought she'd be able to live a happy life in her new home.

"For *some reason*, that girl's finger was sent to the wealthy farmer's house. The girl who I had definitely escorted safely to her destination had apparently been abducted by bandits. The young girl who returned in exchange for a ransom was no longer in any state to present to her fiancé…and ultimately, she died."

"*Ha-ha!* Well, that sure is a straaange story, eh? Though, I wonder which is stranger, that or a bungling mercenary trying to push a past failure onto someone else."

"There are children living in this home—"

Rique pulled his hood back over his eyes.

"—and I'm not going to dirty it with blood. Step out front. You're the boss, so you're gonna take responsibility for the job you did."

"Ya know, I wonder why they all start sounding the same to me. The jabbering drivel of pretentious guys like you."

Jivlart's smile disappeared, and he put his hand on the sheath of his long sword.

"At least have the guts to say you'll kill me *right here on the spot*."

"Hold up."

Someone butted into the powder keg mood in the air—Tu the Magic.

"Inside, outside, it's not happening either way. And Rique—"

Tu unexpectedly pointed to Rique.

"Don't try to kill someone before asking about the situation in front of you!"

"Hold up, Tu... You think *you* get to tell me that?!"

Back when Tu and Rique had battled each other in the Land of the End, if the Demon King's Bastard, Tu the Magic, had actually asked about why Rique and Krafnir were there, they never would have needed to fight in the first place.

"I learned my lesson! So you gotta learn yours, too!"

"Flipping the script is really unfair, you know that?!"

"...Um?"

The young priest in training, scared by the current state of affairs, timidly spoke up from behind the pair.

"Master Jivlart is donating to our facilities here. It's largely thanks to him that I am even able to run the almshouse all by myself..."

"...What?"

"So if there is indeed some misunderstanding between the two of you...... Please, I ask you to put away your swords. A-at the very least, I would ask you to respect the Wordmaker's teachings in these halls..."

Rique looked again at Jivlart.

He absolutely couldn't trust the man. There was a possibility that like his past escort mission, the man had some nefarious schemes up his sleeve. However, at present, Rique couldn't see any benefit to Jivlart currying favor with the Order in its weakened state.

"What's your angle?"

"Angle? Is there any angle to charity?"

Jivlart stuck out his tongue to needle Rique.

"I'm real kind to kids, and the kids here are really well-behaved. Who wouldn't want to give them a bit of spending money?"

"……"

"Those are the eyes. People like you are always like that, eh? Arbitrarily judging and labeling whatever a person does as they see fit. Raised up nice and proper into a righteous prick. What the hell do you know about me? Dragging on some moldy grudge of yours and getting a buncha random other people wrapped up in it, too."

"And you, too, Jivlart!"

Tu butted in. She wasn't intimidated by the violence in the air.

"That's going too far. You may not like Rique, but none of that's got anything to do with the Order, either! If you got your own case to make, then make it!"

"…Who're you?"

"Tu the Magic."

Her green eyes, faintly glowing, stared hard at Jivlart.

Jivlart the Ash Border once again slowly placed his hand on the hilt of his long sword.

An imposing move. When it came solely to making a show of brute force, Jivlart's skills might have excelled more than those of a true mercenary like Rique.

"……I'm Jivlart the Ash Border. Hero candidate. I was invited to the Sixways Exhibition and came out here to Aureatia."

Tu didn't look intimidated in the slightest. It almost seemed like she didn't notice his aura at all.

"That so, huh?! We're in the same boat, then! I'm a hero candidate, too."

As Tu stretched her hand to Jivlart, a smile blossomed on her face.

"...You gotta be kidding me."

Jivlart couldn't bring himself to return Tu's handshake. His fingers stayed on his sword hilt.

"A woman like you, a hero candidate?"

"She's telling the truth."

Rique grumbled.

"You'll see once they announce the matchups. Tu's an official hero candidate, backed by the Seventh Minister, Flinsuda."

"*Ha-ha!* So this woman's stronger than you, huh? You're so spineless I can't help but laugh, Rique."

"*Pfft, heh-heh-heh...* Stronger than *me*? No, that can't be right."

Rique laughed. He hadn't thought there'd be anything to make him laugh when confronting Jivlart.

"She's stronger *than Krafnir the Hatch of Truth and me combined.*"

"......"

"Uh, um..."

The silence continued. Jivlart remained stock-still before the inscrutable young girl, while conversely, Tu also wasn't sure what to do with the hand outstretched before Jivlart.

"Makes me sick."

"Screw this."

Jivlart backed off. He shoved the hand affixed to his sword into his pocket and cracked his neck.

"I'll be by again."

"Oh, um, u-understood...... Thank you, as always."

He departed without returning any of the numerous bows from the priest in training.

Tu was frozen in her current pose, her hand still outstretched.

"H-hey, Rique..."

"Tu. Thanks for stopping me."

Rique grabbed her hand instead. Tu happily shook it up and down.

"...I wasn't thinking things through clearly... Whether he's a bad guy or not, it wasn't right to rush to conclusions without trying to learn anything about him."

"Right? Maybe Jivlart's actually a good guy, after all?"

"Maybe."

Tu probably wanted to believe he was.

The success Tu had achieved that day likely made her happier than ever.

The experience of talking things out with Rique and Krafnir, on a mission to subdue the Demon King's Bastard, and coming to a mutual understanding.

That was why she was still so attached to Rique and sought the very same thing from all the people she met here in Aureatia.

Having been a mercenary for a long time, Rique knew that the world wasn't like that. Folks who it was meaningless to try talking it out with—just like the those Tu had long expelled from the Land of the End—accounted for a large majority of people out there.

That day, Rique had been unable to meet the person he was indebted to, but he donated more money than he had first planned on.

He stayed there until the sun sank low, without forcing his travel companion to go back ahead of him.

Rique watched Tu from behind as she joined in the children's playtime and pondered.

...*"Maybe," huh...*

Jivlart's group, Sun's Conifer, was an organization from a frontier village that had rapidly and suddenly distinguished themselves and had risen up in the world.

A guild founded by a group of poor youths with neither lineage nor learning to their names. In order to grab success for themselves, without anyone at their backs supporting them, they might not have had any other methods besides dirtying their hands with the sort of vile, underhanded jobs that Obsidian Eyes, for example, had formerly taken on for themselves.

The worlds of light and shadow stood so far apart that those born in squalor were forced to further stain their hands with such dirty methods.

There were the Order's destitute, who the inhabitants of Aureatia paid no mind. There were children that even the Order had failed to reach. Poor people on the frontier who only had brute force and violence at their disposal. Alternatively, there were the victims, left behind in the Land of the End, that Tu had kept under her protection.

I don't think I can forgive Jivlart. But...

Rique was a mercenary. He had always chosen jobs he could take pride in.

Had he ever been able to save even a single person faced with such circumstances?

Tu, I want to believe that there's salvation out there for everyone.

Leisha sincerely loved Kuze the Passing Disaster.

Though he was always busy making rounds across different regions and could only drop in on the almshouse where she lived about three times a year, and though she had yet to pass her tenth birthday, she felt sincere love for Kuze.

And yet even when she expressed her feelings openly to her teachers and friends—even to Kuze himself—for some reason she couldn't understand, they were always treated like a joke.

"I truly, truly love you, Father Kuze."

Resting against his large back, she whispered words of affection. At that moment, Kuze had a small child resting on his lap, and he was teaching them the Order's script. Wearing the same black clothes, with the same disheveled hair, and the same scruffy beard.

"I love all of you. Everything, even down to your beard."

"Stop with the 'Father,' stuff! How many times must I insist?!"

Kuze gave a troubled smile.

She hadn't been trying to embarrass him, and the most important part of what she had said definitely wasn't how she was addressing him.

"Besides, this old man's only here in Aureatia for the time being. You should find yourself a much more upstanding suitor than an aging man who wanders around aimlessly."

"I think I'm a really pretty woman, though."

"Yup, yup. I've been around to many different towns before, among all the ten-year-old girls I've seen, I haven't met anyone who's as beautiful as you, Leisha."

"I'm not talking about ten-year-olds."

Leisha stood up from her affectionate snuggling against his back and put her hands on her hips.

"I meant I'm beautiful, even compared to adults."

"*Bweh-heh-heh*, I wonder…"

Her hair was always neatly brushed, and she even put a lot of care into maintaining her skin, too. She used a skin lotion from the stems of yellow willowseed, which the previous priest had taught her about. The other kids were quick to destroy their clothes by roughhousing, but Leisha didn't. She chose the old clothes made from good fabric that were very rarely donated by the nobility and would wear them whenever Kuze visited.

She was beautiful, and that was why her adoption was decided before anyone else her age.

"My boobs are coming in, and I can handle cooking duty totally by myself, so I'm definitely ready to become a wife. It won't be too long until I perfect my etiquette, too."

"Yeah right, Leisha, you're a total munchkin!"

A boy playing with a shuttlecock top hollered.

"The big lady who came today was way prettier than her!"

"If you're so set on being a grown-up, you gotta get boobs like hers!"

"Stupid boys! What's wrong with you?! Pipe down, pervs!"

The boys always acted like children and never really thought anything through.

Leisha was so serious about her feelings, too. She couldn't stand them.

"That so? This young lady visitor played with all of you, did she? What sort of girl was she?"

"I don't care. I can't believe that Tu the Magic, or whatever her name was. Baring her legs so much—and her chest... It was obscene! She's the worst! I don't want to think about her!"

"...Tu the Magic."

Kuze quietly murmured.

"So she's the hero candidate Flinsuda's sponsoring, huh?"

"Father Kuze, do you know her?"

"I suppose you could say that. I've heard about her from a friend. Was she nice?"

All the children besides Leisha chimed in one after another.

"She was super nice!"

"She dashed up the trunk of a tree to get our ball! It was amazing!"

"My writing was better than hers, though."

"Those boobs of hers were something else."

"Ugh!"

Leisha kicked one of the boys. She had to remain ladylike.

"She can write in the Order script, huh? I wonder who she learned it from."

"Uhhh."

"…She did mention it."

Leisha had a good memory and remembered what Tu had said to them.

"She said she had learned it *from her dad*."

"Really…?"

"Aren't I great? I gave you the best answer just now," she said, clinging again to Kuze.

Unlike other adults, for some reason Kuze smelled like ashes from a fireplace. For Leisha, it was a soothing smell.

"You did, didn't you? You're a very observant girl, Leisha. I'll need you to be a big sister to everyone and continue to look after them."

Kuze complimented her, proudly stroking her hair. She was convinced that the warmth she felt welling up inside her from his words was because Kuze did love her.

"Um, Father Kuze. There's a whole lot of good reason for you take me as your wife, you know."

Soon Leisha would be taken very far away. To an affluent frontier family without an heir. They chose her because Leisha was beautiful, something she took great pride in.

But would it mean she wouldn't be able to see Kuze, making rounds for the Order, anymore?

"I'll make you egg dishes that smell like flowers every day."

"*Bweh-heh-heh.* Eggs every day, huh…"

"I'll wear expensive makeup…and become a really pretty wife you can brag about to everyone."

"I'm sure you will."

This time, Leisha sat in Kuze's lap. Just like when she was younger, sitting in his lap every day, never once growing tired of it—before Kuze was as busy as he was now.

"I'll even maintain that beard of yours for you."

"Aw, and you used to love playing with it so much."

"You can't be untidy forever if you're going to have a wonderful wife like me."

The truth was, even now, she liked Kuze's unkept beard.

"I'll build a small house, too... Our house. As the woman of the house, I'll run a tight ship and make sure the wallpaper doesn't peel or crack. On cold days, I can light up the fireplace early in the afternoon."

"Well, doesn't that sound nice."

"And—and then, Father Kuze. Aaah..."

She loved him so much that no matter how much she fantasized about their wonderful married life together, it didn't feel like enough.

Even if that future was indeed impossible for Leisha to achieve.

"You'll be really, really happy, Father Kuze."

She stroked his face, right at the same height as her own, and smiled.

Just like a wife, far more beautiful and far happier than anyone else would.

"Really happy. More than anyone else in the whole world."

"*Bweh-heh-heh*. Oh Leisha...... I'm sorry..."

Kuze averted his gaze and pressed down on the inner corners of his eyes.

"I'm sorry."

"Hey! You made Father Kuze cry, Leisha!"

"It's 'cause you're always making things hard for him!"

"You're always giving him trouble, Leisha!"

"Ugh! Be quiet! I... I'm being really serious here! Idiots!"

Leisha was slightly grateful for the boys' immaturity as they jeered at her again.

Grateful because she could convince herself that even if she got teary-eyed herself, it was out of anger at their taunting.

◆

Nighttime in Aureatia.

Though the light from the gas lamps illuminated the streets aboveground, the canal that stretched under the bridge was very dark.

Therefore, if someone happened to be collapsed on the ground and seriously wounded, their voices would very rarely be heard.

"Listen."

Kuze the Passing Disaster squatted down next to the bound man lying on the edge of the canal.

He looked like a powerless, good-natured, middle-aged man.

"Leisha felt proud that she was getting taken in by you, you know that?"

The head of a wealthy frontier farming family without an heir.

It had all been a lie.

Feigning their social status, these people would take in children with exceptional features and looks—and sell them off for abhorrent purposes.

Currently, with the Order's authority fading away, and lacking the strength for proper investigations, it was difficult to pick up on criminals with these objectives in mind. Kuze couldn't blame the young man left in charge of the almshouse.

Starting a few years ago, many people had begun hearing tragic stories about children in the Order's care being swept up into the criminal underworld. This exacerbated the persecution of the Order and the expulsion of the poor that had spread across society, and as a result, the Order began to see the power to save others taken from them. A vicious cycle.

"See, she said she was getting taken in because she was the prettiest..."

Kuze was looking at the white angel sitting on the gas lamp on top of the bridge.

The man had lost consciousness and couldn't hear what Kuze was saying to him.

"But why hasn't she been saved yet?"

Leisha had the right to be happy, and that happiness had nearly been taken from her forever.

A person's heart holds the will to save others.

That was the blessing bestowed by the Wordmaker. That alone was something Kuze truly believed existed.

"After all, Leisha's a really good kid..."

This man was a small-time scoundrel. Crimes like this had

existed for a long time, and Kuze was only able to glimpse a handful of instances of this commonplace and worldwide activity.

Those with power took from the weak.

Violent gangs attacked almshouses, and slavers targeted orphans.

Aureatia aimed the citizen's criticism toward the Order, and all the sinless, pious faithful were being forced into becoming martyrs to maintain order for the ones living in comfort.

Kuze gave a weak laugh.

"...Bweh-heh-heh."

"Should I kill him?" He felt like he heard such a voice.

He turned to look at the gas lamp over the bridge. Nastique the Quiet Singer was staring at him.

"It's okay."

His reply came out as a sigh. He didn't want to kill. He never did.

Kuze the Passing Disaster was invincible. In this world, Kuze alone was protected by an absolute authority that could deliver death to any being. A power that only ever killed his enemies and never truly intended to rescue who he wanted to save.

"I made it in time. Without anyone needing to die..."

He was trying to calm himself. Leisha was safe now. That was enough.

When Cunodey died, and when Rozelha died, Kuze was able to give up. He could accept that there was nothing he could do about a tragedy that had already come and gone.

All the deceased had been just as important and cherished as Leisha. In which case, he should have been overjoyed right now that this time he had been able to save her.

"*Bweh-heh-heh.* I have to keep my smile, you know, but I wonder... What is it feeling...?"

"What you're feeling is fear, Kuze."

Just below the bridge that crossed the canal. There was another voice from the darkness.

The voice belonged to a young boy with gray hair. He looked just as old as the almshouse orphans.

His name was Hiroto the Paradox.

"It looks like you're scared, to me, Kuze. Sometimes the future, which we have the ability to change, can feel more terrifying than a cemented past. 'What if I had been just a little bit later?'...for example."

Hiroto's troops had captured and bound the man underneath the bridge.

Kuze had merely arrived afterward.

"It's a good thing you made it in time, while you could still make an impact."

"...Yeah. I feel the same way."

"And that's not the only reason for your fear, Kuze, I'm sure. 'Is this sort of thing happening *right now* all across the Order and just out of my sight?' 'Am I standing by the wayside and letting down kids that I should be able to save...that I should be able to reach?'"

"*Bweh-heh-heh.* You're a nasty man yourself, Mr. Hiroto."

Given his involvement with the criminal underworld as a cleaner, Kuze knew the Gray-Haired Child's voice. That he had made contact with him like this, before his opponent in the

Sixways Exhibition was to be decided, made his objective that night perfectly clear to Kuze, too.

"So that's why you gave me the information on this guy for free, eh?"

"With our forces, it would be possible to track the whereabouts of all the children in the Order across the whole land. I have some information on organizations we already have a grip on, as well."

Kuze stayed standing stock-still and looked down at the blood-soaked man.

If he had been too late today, what would have happened to Leisha? In this day and age, it wouldn't have been unthinkable if tomorrow another one of the children Kuze held so dear fell victim.

"...Not good enough. That's not enough."

With the white angel watching over him, Kuze stepped into the bridge's shadow, where Hiroto lingered.

"I have another condition. If you have that much power, then I want you to save everyone in the Order for me. After the Sixways Exhibition is over. If you guys manage to win. I want you to make it so all the children can go out into the world on their own and continue our...continue the Wordmaker's teachings that've brought us salvation."

"Education and welfare for the people are absolutely necessary to maintain a civilized society," Hiroto earnestly replied to Kuze.

A politician's superpower was being able to see through to what someone truly desired—and make them believe in a future where it can be made real.

"Aureatia may be planning on using a new governmental body

to take over those functions, but even from the perspective of a non-believer like me, I think it's far more efficient to construct such an institution by using the already existing Order as the foundation. That is our reason for wishing for the future existence of the Order."

"...*Bweh-heh-heh*. Think you can do it?"

"I moved the very Free City of Okafu itself into action with the power of my oration alone. I promise that I will closely protect the Order and free them from their current persecution."

"If...if that does happen, that'd be fantastic. Truly..."

"We have already secured two spots among the sixteen participants. You would be the third."

Regardless of whether he believed him, Kuze had no choice but to collude with Hiroto. In order to realistically save the entire Order, it would require an unrealistic degree of power, on the scale of a nation-state, at the very least.

But then, more than anything:

...*Listen. Powerful players like you all aren't the only ones hatching schemes, you know. Hiroto the Paradox.*

For *the real reason* behind Kuze's participation in the Sixways Exhibition, too, would require their strength.

All Kuze wanted was to keep the faith and bring salvation to the followers of the Order.

For this, he would sacrifice anything.

"Let's join forces, Kuze the Passing Disaster."

"I accept."

He took the hand spread out before him. Hiroto's hand was small. A petite hand, like the orphans Kuze knew.

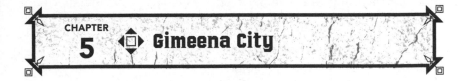

Twelve days before the start of the third match. Unlike the first two fights that featured appearances by legends like Toroa the Awful, Alus the Star Runner, and Lucnoca the Winter, there weren't many who recognized the names of the hero candidates fighting in the third match.

A visitor swordsman, Soujirou the Willow-Sword. A chimera of origins unknown, Ozonezma the Capricious.

Mysterious, obscure—but powerful fighters.

In Ozonezma's case, the citizens of Aureatia hadn't even had the chance to see what he looked like. As if to keep all information about him a secret, he was staying in nearby Gimeena City.

Gimeena City—a metropolis of a far different nature than Aureatia.

Rice fields stretched out in between the brick buildings, with trees lining the streets in equal distances along the roadways criss-crossed by carriages. The atmosphere, carefully managed nature quietly melding into the surrounding civilization, was almost the exact opposite of Aureatia's noisy and flamboyant city streets.

Gimeena City was also affiliated with the Aureatia Council, and there was one member of the Twenty-Nine Officials who owned an enormous mansion there. A giant of a man, rotund, yet one who left a cordial and amicable impression. The Fourteenth General, Yuca the Halation Gaol.

A strange beast had been residing in his large estate for the past several days.

"YOU ALWAYS LOOK BUSY, YUCA."

"Well, suppressing a rebellion isn't just about cutting someone down in a fair fight or anything. Besides, right now, I gotta keep these Old Kingdoms' loyalists in check somehow."

An eight-legged beast with blue-and-silver fur, who appeared almost like a streamlined version of a wolf. Ozonezma the Capricious.

Completely ignorant when it came to political bargaining, Yuca was oblivious to the fact himself. But as a result of being caught up in Hiroto's behind-the-scenes maneuvering, he had been enticed into sponsoring Ozonezma the Capricious.

"The other military officers can work when war breaks out, and that's enough for them, but my work always ends up being a lot to deal with."

"I PERCEIVE YOU ARE HAVING ISSUES."

"Nah, you're a big help by not being difficult to handle, Ozonezma. Hidow and Haade seem like they're having a real hard time."

Even when stripping away the details surrounding the sponsorship or the chimera's own temperament, Ozonezma and Yuca got along better than they imagined.

Ozonezma found Yuca's mild-mannered and generous personality pleasing, while Yuca was also grateful that even with the chimera's strange form, Ozonezma didn't make any excessive demands of him and stayed put here in Gimeena City.

Yuca also showed interest in Ozonezma's vast knowledge, and although he couldn't comprehend everything the chimera spoke of, he was still an excellent listener who could express his honest admiration and astonishment about the details of the topic at hand.

"When all is said and done, I'm preventing a big uprising from happening. I'd say they can probably start the Sixways Exhibition now."

Within the Twenty-Nine Officials, Yuca's responsibility was leading the nation's public safety branch.

Fortifying against enemies not from abroad but from within, he stood on the front lines to suppress rebellion and uprising, in some cases purging his own compatriots when necessary. While this role was an essential presence in keeping the nation safe, it was definitely not a job that would turn him into a champion, living in the light.

However, Yuca the Halation Gaol handled this assigned job, completely contrary to his own benign temperament, without complaint.

"YOU COULD LUMP SUPPORTING A CHIMERA LIKE ME INTO THIS AS WELL, BUT...ARE YOU NOT BEING PUSHED INTO TAKING ON DISADVANTAGEOUS ROLES?"

While Ozonezma placed his trust in Yuca's character, he did this with a twinge of anxiety.

Was his kindness that made him unable to refuse any requests going to be his ruin and make discontent grow within him? There was a possibility that, when the time came, it would become an unexpected rift for Ozonezma.

"Nah, it's not like that, I'm telling you. I volunteered for it myself. Surprisingly, folks like me are suited for this work, you know. 'Cause I'm good at not thinking about anything. Even if someone carefully considers how to do this job, no matter how good things go at the start, I think it'll quickly get harder and harder for them."

Sinking his corpulent body into the big chair, Yuca talked to himself.

"The types who have to resort to rebellion and violence are usually real weak and powerless."

"...THAT IS FAIR. NO MATTER WHAT SORT OF CONSPIRACY MAY BE BEHIND THEIR ACTIONS...THE ONES WHO STAND ON THE FRONT LINES FOR SUCH ACTIVITIES ARE USUALLY THE WEAK WITH THEIR BACKS UP AGAINST THE WALL."

Even knowing full well this exploitative structure, Yuca could clearly separate himself from this understanding to fulfill his role and brandish his blade. He could use his own strength to ensure that no one else would be burdened with this feeling of guilt.

That was the understanding Ozonezma had of Yuca's character.

"IN THAT CASE, WHAT DO YOU THINK ABOUT THE ORDER?"

"Not the Old Kingdoms' loyalists? The Order, huh... Hmmm.

Well, I'm pretty sure there are a whole bunch out there who want to reverse the way things are currently going for them. But unlike the Old Kingdoms' loyalists or the Lithia remnants, I guess they don't present a very big threat to be wary of."

"I BELIEVE THEY POSSESS A CONSIDERABLE AMOUNT OF ORGANIZATIONAL POWER, THOUGH."

"Organizational power, sure. But in their current situation, the Order has almost no warriors who could let them resort to violence. I mean, historically, yeah, they had plenty of their paladin-class soldiers or what have you, and there were some periods when they had military on par with the kingdoms of the day, but none of that's there now. Tenets of the Wordmaker dictate things to be that way, after all."

"SO YOU ARE SAYING BY MAKING THEM OBEY DOCTRINE...THEY'VE HAD THEIR FANGS DULLED OVER MANY YEARS."

"I mean, I seriously doubt that this current state of affairs was something they were planning for. I think the fact that the kingdom had always protected the Order with military force meant that part of it was them telling the Order that they'd bear responsibility for the nation—and to focus on their teachings instead. Though, I guess the country's true wish was to have a grip on their leash should anything happen, right?"

Yet during the era of the True Demon King, the Order lost the power meant to be spared for their protection. Spears had been pointed at the Order, filled with the anger and sadness toward a calamity beyond any means of salvation, and their existence was slowly fading away.

As of now, with the destruction of the kingdoms meant to have a tight control over them, the Order were livestock dying of starvation while shackled in their pens. They no longer had the power within them to rebel against the nation.

"THANK YOU. I WAS ABLE TO UNDERSTAND THE CURRENT STATE OF AFFAIRS MORE DEEPLY."

"We weren't even talking about anything that important, and there you go again with the formalities. You're a hero candidate, Ozonezma, so you could stand to act high and mighty, you know," Yuca said jokingly.

"YOU AND I ARE EQUALS IN A COOPERATIVE RELATIONSHIP."

"*Ah-ha-ha.* Suppose you're right."

Equals. Ozonezma wasn't the one asking for instructions, even when dealing with Hiroto the Paradox. Ozonezma didn't take a single step out of Gimeena City, while he continued to receive radzio communications regarding the Aureatia hero candidates he had a chance of fighting—or if not that, information on the ones sponsoring them.

The current circumstances of the Order was something he needed to know about, too.

THE ORDER'S HERO CANDIDATE IS KUZE THE PASSING DISASTER. AN AUTOMATIC COUNTERATTACKING ABILITY THAT INSTANTLY KILLS ANY LIVING CREATURE THAT TRIES TO ATTACK HIM.

If he did indeed possess such a power, then that would make him one of the strongest hero candidates in the field.

As long as Hiroto the Paradox was manipulating the situation, the yet-finalized bracket wasn't likely to have Ozonezma and Kuze facing each other—however, if he didn't ascertain the properties of this ability beforehand, Kuze was strong enough *to potentially put up a tough fight,* even with the trump card that Ozonezma was concealing for himself.

INDEED, IT IS NOT THE SORT OF STRENGTH THAT CAN REVERSE THE ORDER'S CURRENT PREDICAMENT. HIROTO POSSESSES TRULY OUTSTANDING WIT. TO DETERMINE THAT KUZE'S POWER WOULD BE NECESSARY AND MAKE CONTACT WITH HIM DIRECTLY AS HE HAS.

Or perhaps, it could have been a subconscious and supernatural power to sense omens of future events—and hold sway over such fateful encounters themselves. For someone like Ozonezma, a mere chimera with no one to support him, to break into this tournament, it had been necessary to meet with Hiroto and form their cooperative relationship.

Hiroto and Ozonezma were equals. Ozonezma wouldn't fight for the sake of his camp's ambitions. Nor would he fight for Yuca's sake, either. Ozonezma's goal behind throwing himself into the Sixways Exhibition ring was singular.

"Still, Ozonezma. Aren't you bored, spending all your time cooped up in this mansion? I imagine the feeling's the same for chimeras as it is with anyone else."

Ozonezma was holing himself up in Gimeena City, without showing his body in Aureatia at all, while also being a hero candidate. He had information that there were other organizations outside of Hiroto's camp and Aureatia's own that were investigating the fighting strength of the hero candidates. Supposing there came a time when he engaged with these sorts of attempts on his life, even in the worst-case scenario, he couldn't expose *his trump card*.

"...TRUE. I DO NOT MEAN TO PRESENT MYSELF AS SUPERIOR, BUT...THERE IS ONE FAVOR I WOULD LIKE TO ASK WHEN THE TIME COMES TO DEPART GIMEENA CITY FOR AUREATIA."

Therefore, this was a request that was entirely out of Ozonezma's own interest, unrelated to his goals or tournament strategy.

"TU THE MAGIC. I WOULD LIKE YOU TO SET UP A MEETING WITH THE HERO CANDIDATE BY THIS NAME."

◆

...Then there were five days left until the start of the third match. The noontime Gimeena City main road was quiet.

Yet at the same time, there were enough people there to fill the street to capacity. The quiet throng was eerily intimidating, sinking the entire city into silence.

The scene outside was visible from the windows of the estate built up along the mountain.

"Hrmm, well, looks like things have really turned sour."

They were in a large dining hall on the estate's first floor. Ozonezma replied to Yuca's grumbling as he sized up the situation outside the window.

"THEY DO NOT SHOW ANY SIGNS OF STOPPING."

Ozonezma was able to surmise the identity of the throng.

"THEY'RE OLD KINGDOMS' LOYALISTS, ARE THEY NOT?"

"Probably."

The Old Kingdoms' loyalists crowding into Gimeena City were targeting Yuca the Halation Gaol.

The main road, ordinarily lively with voices from the shops and merchants, had gone silent, and the armed throng continued to gather as time went on. The wave had continued to grow stronger from morning that day.

"See, usually, there's some signs with this sort of stuff, but welp. Times like this are when you get the relatively serious types. You can't hear any angry cries or speeches or anything, right...? Actually, you probably don't get any of this, huh."

"...NO. I UNDERSTAND. THOSE WHO HAVE ALREADY RESOLVED THEMSELVES TO ACT DO NOT NEED TO ENERGIZE THEMSELVES. CONTROLLED ACTION, NOT PROPELLED BY FEAR OR ANGER."

Having always taken the lead in quelling uprisings, Yuca had profoundly earned the hatred of rebellious forces, such as ones outside the window. He was a valuable fighting asset who was the one in charge of leading an insurrection would want to eliminate before all else.

However, together with the execution of Gilnes the Ruined Castle, the Old Kingdoms' loyalists had lost their main constituents—and were supposed to have been already cleaned up entirely—

SAFETY IS NOT GUARANTEED OUTSIDE OF AUREATIA. THEIR TRUE TARGET MAY ACTUALLY BE ME.

Naturally, a disorderly group of however many thousands surging toward him couldn't possibly be enough to defeat Ozonezma the Capricious. However, the same wasn't true of his sponsor, Yuca.

"THE SITUATION IS BY DESIGN. A MANIPULATED UPRISING."

"Hmmm. Well, thinking through it all logically like that isn't really going to do anything, to be honest. *Something's* gotta be done about the situation first. After this is all over, there'll be someone else to think about all that stuff."

"I CAN FACE THEM."

"No, no, no. Quelling uprisings falls under my jurisdiction, after all, and I can't owe you a favor, Ozonezma."

Yuca was already donning a red suit of light armor. Very sparse armor, preventing arrows from piercing through to his vitals— and nothing more.

"BUT ESCAPE SHOULD BE THE FIRST PRIORITY. YOU AND I ARE EQUALS. I WANT YOU TO BUY TIME."

"*Ha-ha-ha.* Well, you got me there. And here I thought I'd just fight through them all on my own."

"...THERE IS A MOUNTAIN BEHIND THIS MANSION, YES? SURELY YOU HAVE AN ESCAPE ROUTE PREPARED."

"I'm surprised you knew that."

"MERELY CONJECTURE."

Yuca's manor had a steep mountain behind it. It was for times like now, suddenly under attack, to restrict the defensive area to its facade. It was an approach very appropriate of a military official.

Even if the attackers had sensed the presence of an escape

route through the mountain, Ozonezma concluded that the troop strength capable of deploying in the tangled mountain wilds would be more restricted than it would be in front of the mansion.

"LET US MOVE TOGETHER UNTIL WE PASS INTO THE MOUNTAIN PATH. I WILL KEEP OUR REAR SAFE. ONCE YOU ESCAPE, GATHER SOLDIERS AND POUND THIS FORCE BACK AGAIN. WE SHALL DIVIDE OUR ROLES BETWEEN US. THAT SHOULD BE ACCEPTABLE."

"I didn't want to trouble you like this, you know? Didn't you want to keep your skills hidden until the day of your match?"

"I AM THE ONE WHO SHOULD BE THINKING ABOUT THAT. LEAVE IT TO ME."

"Of course. Well then, let's go with that."

With the matter settled, the two moved quickly. They were both warriors who had fought through a great number of battles.

When they passed through the wooden corridor that stretched out from the hidden back exit in the mansion's basement, they immediately exited out into the middle of the mountain. After cutting apart the entryway, concealed by bushes, they both dashed down the wet crags, without wasting any breath between them.

Ozonezma ran in front of Yuca, ensuring the mountain road was safe. The mansion at their backs would likely be up in flames before long. Though, the best plan would be to bring the situation under control before it met such an end.

"By our hands, the kingdom will rise again!"

"Expel the Twenty-Nine from the assembly!"

"Take the Fourteenth General's head!"

The people's shouts could be faintly heard far off in the distance.

This throng of theirs wasn't the true threat. There were likely those mixed in their ranks who hadn't been Old Kingdoms' loyalists in the first place. People agitated into a frenzy, their misfortune, oppression, and discontent used against them.

THE ONES FORCED TO STAND IN THE LINE OF FIRE... ARE THE WEAK, DRIVEN UP AGAINST THE WALL.

If this was a purposefully planned raid, then the force in front were, in part, a feint—

There was a *whoosh* of something slicing through the air. Simultaneously from three directions. Continuing to run at a high speed, Ozonezma *caught* the arrows flying from the gaps in the trees.

Tossing the arrows aside, he declared, "RANK AND FILE."

The fingertips that caught the arrow shafts with abnormally precise movements did not belong to any of Ozonezma's eight legs. They were part of the crowd of humanoid arms that grew out of the fissure in the center of his back.

Within Ozonezma's enormous body, not reminiscent of a chimera at first glance, housed an innumerable number of people's arms, like a nightmarish cnidarian creature.

"IS THIS THE EXTENT OF THE ENEMY'S STRENGTH?"

"I mean, they really can't do anything but hide and shoot from afar, right? They can't use fire attacks in the middle of the mountain, either."

Yuca was facing archer fire himself, and yet his tone stayed carefree and easygoing through it all.

On top of this, as he spoke, he dashed out from behind Ozonezma. In a straight line toward the mountain fighter, perfectly aware of their position after judging the trajectory of their shots moments prior.

They aimed at Yuca as he ran—and fired off the second volley. Too slow. Ozonezma's movements were faster than the arrows' flight. The countless arms blocked the arrows' arrival like a wall. Yuca had gotten in close to the archer.

"Yuca the Hal—!" the archer shouted, the distance between them neutralized.

Of the three of them, the archer likely hadn't ever imagined they would be the one to die and see their end come so abruptly. The gleam of a curved short sword flashed through the air.

"Hrrrm."

The flash of Yuca's sword severed their abdominal artery. The blade cut off the small intestine, dragging it out into the air.

"Sorry about this."

Yuca told the soldier plainly, yet with a look of regret, before continuing deeper into the mountain. Jumping, accelerating, fatally injuring, then escaping—it was a rapid performance, like flowing water.

The entire chain of movements showcased ability inconceivable of his outwardly obese body.

"...FITTING OF THE TWENTY-NINE OFFICIALS."

Naturally, at that point, Ozonezma's attack was over, too.

Instantly exterminating the other two archers, he was collecting the exceptional latissimus dorsi muscle from the first—and the well-conditioned pulmonary artery from the second. With their windpipes ruptured, they weren't even able to let out death rattles.

He stopped there and watched Yuca's back recede into the distance.

"NOW THEN, I SUPPOSE I WILL BE...KEEPING ALERT FOR PURSUERS FROM BEHIND."

The instrument stored inside Ozonezma's body was exposed. A large radzio transmitter.

It was one of the reasons he had let Yuca continue on ahead. While Ozonezma was a chimera, he could control radzio with a level of precision beyond any minia.

"DO YOU HAVE A GRASP OF THE SITUATION, ZIGITA ZOGI? THE MEMBERS OF THE ASSAULT FORCE ARE OLD KINGDOMS' LOYALISTS."

<...You're finally able to get in touch, I see, Master Ozonezma. I estimated that if you kept yourself hidden without entering Aureatia, eventually someone would do something drastic, but... This is quite something, indeed.>

"IN ANY CASE, THIS IS NOT A SIMPLE UPRISING. EVEN I AM ABLE TO REACH THAT CONCLUSION."

<First, allow me to give you my read of things. The one behind those loyalists is, in all likelihood, Aureatia's Twenty-Seventh General. Haade the Flashpoint, I'd say. The military officer supporting Soujirou the Willow-Sword, the opponent for your first match, Master Ozonezma.>

The third match was determined to be between Ozonezma and Soujirou.

In which case, the obvious approach was to eliminate the opponent beforehand. However.

"IS AN AUREATIAN BUREAUCRAT CAPABLE OF MANIPULATING THE ANTI-AUREATIA OLD KINGDOMS' LOYALISTS?"

<After losing Gilnes the Ruined Castle and Romzo the Star Map, the Old Kingdoms' loyalists around the land are nothing more than raucous hens with their heads cut off. They don't have any clue where their orders are coming from. Replace the "heads," egg them on a bit, give them a target, and manipulating them like this is quite possible. Not a particularly uncommon fate for the remnants of a defeated army.>

"...HOWEVER, THE OLD KINGDOMS' LOYALISTS ORIGINALLY HAD A RELATIONSHIP WITH YOU, DID THEY NOT? ZIGITA ZOGI, EVEN WITH YOUR POWER, YOU WERE NOT ABLE TO KEEP THE OLD KINGDOMS' LOYALISTS UNDER YOUR CONTROL?"

<That would be the difference between influencing an organization temporarily and using them long-term. In fact, with this latest development, I grasped that there are spies from Aureatia infiltrating the Old Kingdoms' loyalists. If one was truly going to take command of an organization, then it would be more efficient to do so after waiting for them to make a move like today's, where our enemy has revealed the pieces they have in play. Though, it has caused some trouble for you unfortunately, Master Ozonezma.>

"...INTRIGUING. IN THAT CASE, WHAT WILL HAPPEN TO THE SCENARIO AFTER ALL THIS?"

Zigita Zogi the Thousandth. His might was fundamentally different from that of individual strength.

It was the strength of his tactical foresight and intellect, and the more cooperators he had, the more he was able to share this power. Introduced through Hiroto the Paradox and now collaborating with the goblin, Ozonezma could make use of his own personal fighting strength as a champion through strategies and tactics based off the goblin's optimal situational judgments.

<The enemy's true target is Master Yuca. Without any preliminary information, they decided to neutralize Master Yuca instead of you, Master Ozonezma, given they knew nothing of your origin or fighting strength—would be what I would surmise. Since you haven't openly shown yourself in Aureatia, if you were to lose your sponsor, then you would no longer have any means to enter the city... To go one step further, Master Yuca positions himself in the line of fire—and has suppressed the uprisings of reactionary forces. The Old Kingdoms' loyalists have plenty of reason themselves to attack him directly.>

"YOU MEAN TO SAY THAT IT IS AN EASILY INCITED OBJECTIVE FOR THEM."

<...And with that, first they seek to eliminate Master Yuca. It's likely that they will try to capture him alive. Thereafter, using the "head" that was previously concealed within the Old Kingdoms' Loyalist ranks, guiding them... Master Haade will suppress the Old

Kingdoms' loyalists under the pretext of rescuing Master Yuca. With that, he will be able to largely dispose of the loyalists in a position to know the particulars behind this series of events. Master Yuca would then be in his debt, there'd be no leftover friction, and then once the third match is over, well... I imagine this is the likely the scenario he's operating under. If so, then our enemy has thought up a rather interesting plan, I would say.>

"IF THIS 'HEAD' IS HERE NOW, I MIGHT BE ABLE TO CUT IT OFF MYSELF... ARE YOU FINE WITH ME MAKING A MOVE?"

<Thrilled. If our enemy is putting this scheme into motion, at the very least, the one in charge of agitating this uprising must be mixed in with the group out in front. Do not worry about what's behind you. My commando unit has already taken care of the ones placed along Master Yuca's path of retreat.>

The radzio communication was cut off.

Zigita Zogi... As expected of a strategist recognized by Hiroto the Paradox. He was always reading two or three steps ahead of his enemy, weaving webs of initiative and taking every precaution. If he was guaranteeing Yuca's safety, then Ozonezma believed he must have indeed been truly safe.

As if to prove this fact, a single soldier came running up to Ozonezma.

"Heeey, Ozonezma!"

It was one of the Fourteenth General's bodyguards, who he had seen several times before.

"IS YUCA SAFE?"

"Yeah. Our unit's already begun moving to put down the uprising. The Old Kingdoms' louts are moving much slower than expected. You should retreat now while you have the chance."

"BECAUSE THEIR FORWARD-FACING ACTIONS...WERE ALL A FEINT TO LURE US INTO THESE MOUNTAINS. THUS THE SLOW PACE."

Then their best troops were hunted down by Zigita Zogi's soldiers. No matter how meticulously prepared and planned their forces may have been, they couldn't possibly put up a fight against a goblin colony moving in accord with the truest tactical strategy.

Ozonezma lifted his enormous head and captured the citizen mob in his gaze from atop the mountain.

Their individual heads looked like poppy seeds from afar, but for Ozonezma, that was more than good enough.

"OF COURSE, I WILL OBEY THE ORDER TO RETREAT. HOWEVER, BEFORE THAT, I HAVE SOMETHING TO TEST."

"What's that...?"

"*Yaogoyurrg yogog. Yogm agenyeryu. Yesgef goyuyarg. Yayoymc yuuya. Yarhatyu.*" (From Ozonezma to Gimeena soil. Shadow of queued divergence. Swimming horn. Reflected in a white line. Assemble.)

With this, he scratched the dirt with his colossal forelimbs.

Countless silver lights appeared from beneath the thin layer of soil. The weapons Ozonezma created with his Craft Arts were surgical knives used for medical treatment.

"THERE WAS A MAN... A RENOWNED MERCENARY NAMED ALBERT THE SUMMER RAIN."

Far...far away. Ozonezma observed the throng, tinier than ants at this distance.

Ozonezma could distinguish all the bodies in the rabble from each other. Along with each of their movements. Even down to their breathing, too.

Though they consciously tried to hide it, he was able to grasp the movements of an Aureatian soldier.

It wasn't relevant who the Old Kingdoms' loyalists were outwardly propping up as their leader. Haade the Flashpoint was a trueborn soldier, which meant that the subordinates he sent for the task would be, too. Ozonezma identified three targets. Haade's undercover agents, sent into the Old Kingdoms' loyalist ranks. The "head" guiding the organization from within.

The minian arms that sprouted up in droves from his back picked up the blades formed from soil.

Then—

"WHILE THEY MAY NOT BE AS ACCURATE AS 'SUMMER RAIN' WAS..."

A shrill sound of slicing through the air, like a flute.

With it, his throw was finished. The three Ozonezma had in his sights were eviscerated by surgical knives launched at bullet speed.

"...IN TERMS OF RAW POWER, I WOULD SAY MY CAPABILITIES ARE QUITE IMPRESSIVE."

"Y-you killed them? From this distance...? Impossible..."

Leaving the still-stunned guard behind, Ozonezma quickly departed the area. He reported back to his own camp on the other side of the radzio.

"I DISPOSED OF THE 'HEAD.'"

<...I heard about your exchange. This is Dant. If Haade really is behind this, then this 'head' or what have you doesn't end with the ones standing out in the open. There had to be others who saw your attack.>

The Twenty-Fourth General, Dant the Heath Furrow. Zigita Zogi's sponsor.

"THAT IS NOT A CONCERN. AS LONG AS THE ONES OUT IN THE OPEN HAVE BEEN DEALT WITH, THEY WILL HAVE LOST THEIR CONTROL. IT SHOULD ALSO HELP WITH PUTTING THE UPRISING DOWN TO SOME EXTENT."

<...So you're saying the attacks you showed off weren't everything, huh? In that case, what's your trump card, then? I haven't been told yet about how you fight.>

"DANT."

Ozonezma glumly smiled without answering Dant's question. A bestial smile that couldn't be expressed through the radzio.

"I AM GRATEFUL. YOU MADE THE CORRECT CHOICE. THE SPONSOR YOU PREPARED FOR ME, YUCA THE HALATION GAOL... THE MAN DOES NOT TROUBLE HIMSELF WITH SCHEMES AND IS NOT LOOKED AT WITH CAUTION BY THE BUREAUCRATS. BUT...HE HAS OTHER STRENGTHS AS WELL."

Ozonezma had a goal. An objective that had remained unchanged from the moment the True Demon King's era came to an end.

"IT IS HIS AUTHORITY OVER THE PUBLIC SAFETY DIVISION. HE HAS A SPECIAL PRIVILEGE THAT NO OTHER GENERAL POSSESSES. THE RIGHT TO SLAUGHTER HIS COMPATRIOTS. AS LONG AS ANY SUPPRESSION HAS RECEIVED HIS APPROVAL... EVEN IF I KILL AUREATIAN CITIZENS, I WILL NOT BE DISQUALIFIED FROM THE TOURNAMENT."

Haade had used Yuca's position, which incurred hatred among reactionary forces, and dispatched troops in their ranks.

Right now, Ozonezma had simply used that for himself.

The archers from earlier, and the "head" mixed in with the throng. All of them were nothing but unfortunate victims, created in the process of suppressing revolt. That was how it would be seen.

"YOU WILL UNDERSTAND MY OWN SPECIAL PRIVILEGE BEFORE LONG, AS WELL."

◆

In the barracks situated in central Aureatia, Haade the Flashpoint learned the results of his surprise attack.

Dry white hair, with a long scar running down his right cheek. This elderly general, having lived through fiercer wartimes than any of the other living Twenty-Nine Officials, commanded Aureatia's military, as well as a faction in the government to rival Rosclay's own.

"The Gimeena City plot was put down. We failed to capture General Yuca. Is it at all possible that General Yuca saw through our surprise attack?"

Haade blew cigar smoke at the staff officer's report.

"No. I know Yuca very well. Putting ambush troops on the mountainside, anticipating our movement there, none of it's, well...it ain't his cup of tea. That man prefers his nightly beauty sleep over constantly being on alert for surprise attacks. If he had actually foreseen the siege on his mansion, he would've been able to make his escape right then and there, too."

"Then, does that mean his hero candidate, Ozonezma, prepared for the attack ahead of time and worked out a scheme of his own?"

"...Most likely. He's either really sharp for a beastfolk, or he was getting help from someone sharp. It doesn't matter either way."

Was it shrewd subterfuge or a magnetism capable of allying himself with such wits?

The more collaborators on one's side, the more it was possible to share that kind of talent with others.

"But, Lord Haade, I have one piece of good news. The 'nerves' that were sent into the Old Kingdoms' loyalist ranks were apparently murdered by short daggers flown from far in the distance. Sniping the 'nerves' of the operation with deadly precision, while they hide among that peculiar frame. It would mean our enemy possesses the ability for such an incredible long-range attack."

"It's a trap."

"...Huh?"

Haade placed his cigar on the ashtray. He was thinking about what these results meant.

If Ozonezma had indeed readied for this ambush, then he purposefully went out to fight for himself. That's where the problem lay.

"He killed them to announce to us what his fighting style is like. He wants us to get it in our heads that he utilizes long-range attacks. With that...he's trying to coerce us into setting match conditions that would take advantage of Soujirou's close-quarters sword range. Ozonezma wants to use Soujirou's sword to work in his favor. Only natural that's the direction my mind'd go."

"Is there anything to base these suspicious on, sir?"

"Hmm, various things, sure. But for starters, on the battlefield, you don't see such convenient things happening often."

At the very least, Ozonezma wasn't going to fold just by getting in close. He had some trick to use when in sword range.

Throwing knives were far too conspicuous to be used for assassination. He was trying to make Haade inform Soujirou about this technique and instill an incorrect preconception into Soujirou before the match. Poison mixed in with information.

"...In any event, nothing to worry about. The dead here are nothing more than Old Kingdoms' loyalists who got nothing to do with me; Yuca even earned himself another notch in his belt. Good for him, eh?"

"We'll make our next move."

"Got it. At the bare minimum, for the second round... We gotta make sure we're going at it against Rosclay."

"Understood. We will see to it that Soujirou will advance through the first round."

The staff officer departed.

Haade grinned wide to himself. A smile that anticipated bloodshed.

"I can't wait. You'd better entertain me, Rosclay."

A day after the Old Kingdoms' loyalist uprising. A major thoroughfare in Aureatia.

What am I doing?

Yuno the Distant Talon had this on her mind inside the carriage.

There were two people riding with her. One was a slightly elderly man, Twenty-Seventh General Haade's envoy. The other was a short young man, wrapped in a unique dark-red outfit. His name was Soujirou the Willow-Sword.

The carriage was headed to the postwar negotiations. The war between Aureatia and Okafu had ended with Zigita Zogi the Thousandth—and the entire Free City of Okafu itself with him—submitting to Aureatia as a hero candidate, but in order to wrap up the war diplomatically, there were still other huge affairs that needed to be hammered out.

The scenery going by outside the window was the very same everyday landscape that Yuno was familiar with. And she couldn't believe that she was on her way to sit in on such important negotiations.

"You don't need get yourself so worked up there, lass."

The envoy spoke up, showing consideration for Yuno, her body stiff with nerves.

"I'll generally be doing all the talking. You can simply sit there and watch. This meeting will be for ironing out the finer conditions, one of many more negotiations to come... Ummm, you lass, the new secretary. What was your name again?"

"Y-Yuno. Yuno the Distant Talon."

"Right, right, Yuno. Slipped my mind for a second there. I'm counting on you to ensure Soujirou here fulfills his duty as bodyguard."

"Y-yes...sir..."

"What the hell's that about...? I ain't Yuno's damn pet or anything..."

Lying down in his seat, Soujirou's objection was mixed in with a yawn.

The details behind Yuno the Distant Talon, naught but an average young girl who once lived on the frontier, being employed as Haade the Flashpoint's secretary was the result of a number of coincidental events.

Having lost the person he was originally going to sponsor, Kazuki the Black Tone, Haade the Flashpoint now needed to decide on a different hero candidate to participate in the Sixways Exhibition. The powerful fighter he picked out was a visitor who had already earned a certain amount of military achievements in the conquering of the New Principality of Lithia, Soujirou the Willow-Sword.

Yuno, as one of the few people involved with the visitor from a world separate from their own, as Soujirou's *accessory* so to speak, mediated the dealings between him and the top echelons of Aureatia. Her status as a scholar of ruined Nagan, now an unfortunately rare breed, also aroused the interest of the Twenty-Nine Officials to some extent.

As a result, Yuno remained in her role as Soujirou's manager of sorts, and together with Soujirou's sponsorship, she had been made into a secretary in Haade's care.

I'm sure that what the old me was striving for...

A path open for anyone to claim glory, no matter what sort of past they had—or their racial or social status.

She had even dreamed of such a future.

...was this sort of good fortune, wasn't it?

For the current Yuno the Distant Talon, even this dream turned reality was hollow.

She only had one goal in involving herself with the Sixways Exhibition.

Revenge against the powerful fighter who destroyed her hometown of Nagan.

Whenever her thoughts turned to her revenge, she'd ask herself: *Just what am I doing...?*

"Do you have any questions about your job this time, Yuno?"

"Um... For the time being, Soujirou's being treated as a hero candidate, right? I feel like his fighting power's a bit excessive to serve as a bodyguard for these negotiations."

"I see. That is a very good question."

The gentlemanly envoy answered with a composed look.

"But, my dear Yuno. They say that on Okafu's side, there is a visitor called the Gray-Haired Child. In order to prepare ourselves in the unlikely event of an Okafu attack...we need a bodyguard who can handle the *methods* of the Beyond, yes? It is not about having more or less fighting strength, but that it is only another visitor who can match up with the standard tactics and ways of thinking used on the other side. Understand?"

"...I do. However, the need for such preparations means that Okafu and Aureatia's relationship is in a strained enough position to warrant them, doesn't it...?"

"Are you scared of battle, Yuno?"

The envoy flashed a toothy smile. A ferocious and brutal smile incongruent with his facial features.

"Come now. Soujirou here is just our precaution against a worst-case scenario—and nothing more. Besides, if you're going to be working under Lord Haade, you'll need to grow accustomed to some degree of barbarity."

"......"

Yuno lowered her head to avoid meeting the envoy's eyes.

Not many days had passed since she was placed under Haade the Flashpoint's command, but there was one thing she had come to learn.

The air that surrounded Haade and his subordinates was completely different from the followers of the other Twenty-Nine

Officials. They seemed to intrinsically crave combat. Just like Soujirou the Willow-Sword.

"Sniper attack," Soujirou suddenly murmured, still lying on his back.

Yuno couldn't surmise the meaning of his comment. It happened in a brief second.

"Huh?"

There was a loud bang. Something had pierced the carriage wall. Still lying down, Soujirou had drawn his sword, and the diverted bullet had grazed Yuno's hair before flying off somewhere.

"What?!"

Outside the window, the citizens were coming and going the same as always. A scene of everyday life.

"How—?"

"We're taking sniper fire! Turn into the nearest alley!" the envoy shouted, and the carriage accelerated suddenly. Soujirou broke the window and jumped out of the carriage's passenger car, blocking the bullet aimed at the driver at the last moment. He groaned, annoyed.

"Ugh, give me a break…! I gotta defend three people like this?!"

"No… There's no way. Right?! We're in the middle of town!"

"Yuno! Get your head down!"

"Yo, it's coming from the fire tower! There's two more shots on the damn way!"

Soujirou performed an acrobatic leap through the air, and flying backward against the carriage's path, he cut off the roof on a diagonal. The arc of his katana blocked the shot aimed at the envoy, while a scattered fragment of the carriage roof blocked the shot aimed at the driver.

The carriage catapulted into the alleyway with enough force to roll the vehicle over.

Horse hooves crushed piled-up wooden boxes filled with fruit. The loud roar and tremors assailed Yuno inside the carriage.

"...*Koff...* Ah!"

Her brain was rattled. Her insides were thrown into chaos in the span of a second, to the point of nausea.

Her life was being targeted, too. In the middle of this everyday scenery, without any warning.

No one had noticed. Even the overturning of their carriage, in the eyes of the citizens, likely appeared to be a simple runaway carriage accident.

"Yo. Get out, Yuno. They're gonna pick you off."

The carriage door, warped from the impact, was instantly cleaved through. Soujirou was peering inside the carriage car.

"What about the envoy?"

"He jumped outta there a while ago. You're the only one still dillydallying."

"Seriously... Why is it always like this...?!"

Led by the hand, she guardedly looked over the narrow alleyway stretching out in front and behind her. But then, her senses couldn't determine the snipers' location, or if they still had their sights set on Yuno's position.

It was sniper fire, but there weren't any arrows piercing the carriage. Our enemy's definitely using guns.

They were using the bustling city noise to cover their gunshots—and attacking them without revealing themselves.

If Soujirou's intuition hadn't sensed the sniper fire, then they all would've been assassinated right in the public eye. Yuno tried to get her breathing under control.

"*Hah... Hah, koff.* Soujirou. You knew about the attack... before they fired?"

"How many thousands of times do you think I was under sniper fire back in my other world? Just going off experience here."

Whether she knew the tricks from the Beyond or not, Yuno understood one thing. Soujirou the Willow-Sword's level was far beyond this attack. At the very least, for him, this didn't even register as being in danger.

"Do you think we can hold out if we hide in this alleyway?"

"Nah. That big main road back there was one-way despite how many people were on it, yeah? If we suddenly come under fire, we don't got a lot of options for side streets to escape, too, neither."

"Th-then...they've dispatched enough fighting power to chase us down no matter which side street we escape down..."

Prompting Yuno's group to then flee into the present alleyway. It meant the enemy had finished encircling them again—if the enemy truly intended on assassinating them.

"Geez, protecting weaklings is such a pain in the ass..."

Soujirou scratched his head while he followed through with

his sword, gripping it upside down. There was the metallic sound of a bullet being repelled.

With the sound behind her, Yuno desperately dashed over to the shadows behind stacked wooden crates of fruit.

The envoy and driver were already hiding there. The envoy stroked his beard as he spoke.

"I'm glad you're all right, Yuno."

"Y-yes, barely."

She turned around. Soujirou vaulted in a zigzag between both walls of the narrow alley and rushed up to the top of the buildings with tremendous momentum. These were abnormal physical abilities.

No gunshots came. Not yet.

"D-does Okafu...intend to oppose Aureatia? Sniper attacks. Well-trained gunmen. They knew we would be passing by here today, too. Mercenaries from Okafu are the only logical explanation."

"Judging by the current situation, I see no other interpretation! Reluctant as we may be, there's even the chance war will break out inside Aureatia's borders! At the very least, subduing the hero candidate Zigita Zogi and the Free City of Okafu is all but unavoidable at this point, isn't it?!"

"...Subduing?!"

In situations where it was evident a hero candidate participating in the Sixways Exhibition attacked another participant, the other hero candidates were obligated to put the attacker down.

Would the Free City of Okafu set up an attack like this knowing full well about this rule?

"But then what does Okafu's side have to benefit from—? *Eek!*"

Yuno screamed. A mysterious burning mass had fallen from the rooftop. It was a mangled minian corpse.

Soujirou landed on the ground after it. He had been fighting the fallen man moments prior.

"The guy went and blew himself up," Soujirou said with displeasure.

"I cut down four of 'em, but they'd all had some kinda explosive in their bodies. Weird."

Yuno covered her mouth with both hands. The urge to vomit from the carriage's rollover welled up inside her again. She still couldn't come to grips with the terrible battlefield opening up before her eyes.

"Do you think it's to cover up their association...their association with the Free City?"

"That really all there is to it...? Get the feeling that torching everything, body and all, is a little much."

Soujirou kicked the corpse with the tip of his foot. The burned torso blocked the latest rifle bullet flying their way. Soujirou looked toward the main road.

"Those guys are a bit far away."

Hearing Soujirou's words, the envoy made a window with his fingers and measured the distance to the spot they believed the sniper attacks were coming from.

"...About three hundred meters, I would say. Can you capture them alive, Soujirou, my boy?"

"I mean, I tried. I ain't some bloodthirsty killer or anything, okay? They all blew themselves up when I got close; it's a real pain."

"Just try to do what you can. I'd like to recover one of them."

"No guarantees."

Smacking his shoulder twice with his sword, Soujirou dashed off again. He was as fast as the wind.

No matter how imposing the target, Soujirou didn't hesitate to cut them down. In the blink of an eye, he had traveled an impossible distance.

"The enemy—"

Yuno wiped cold sweat from her cheeks.

"—must have known that Soujirou was here escorting us, right?"

"What do you mean?"

"I can't see their self-destruction prep work as anything but these snipers anticipating *a counterattack*. They're the ones encircling *us*, yet…blowing themselves up the moment Soujirou gets close makes it seem like they knew they'd lose from the start, doesn't it?"

"…Still, if the Okafu's side knew about Soujirou the Willow-Sword's presence, they would never have thought their ambush would succeed in the first place. Personally, I feel like that doesn't mesh with meticulously setting up a sniper attack and cutting off our route to escape on the way to the meeting."

"Yes, and that's why it's strange. Pardon me, envoy, but do you have a *replacement*?"

It was a truly rude question. Yuno herself felt as much even saying it.

"…Replacement?"

"If you were truly an irreplaceable member of Mr. Haade's, someone worth assassinating, even when taking into account the sacrifices it would require...then maybe in that case, it might be possible that they'd risk the small chance of success to ambush us. But if that isn't the case... Um, I don't think there's much benefit for Okafu's side."

"You, my girl..."

The envoy raised his eyebrows slightly and looked Yuno in the eye.

"...have very good combat intuition, don't you? Indeed, military provocation is the only result one could anticipate from this attack. There aren't many young girls who could calmly come to such a conclusion in this situation."

"...I've had something far more terrifying than any armed force standing beside me for a long time."

Regardless of the motive, that only means any hope Yuno and the others had of making it out of this situation lay in Soujirou the Willow-Sword.

Until he returned and told them he had secured their safety, they couldn't go anywhere.

"However, the fact remains that there are a limited number of individuals who knew about the postwar negotiations being held today—and who could obtain our route to the meeting. Taking that into consideration, I don't think our attackers could be anyone but the Free City of Okafu, but—"

"Ah!"

Yuno let a small cry slip out. Another carriage tried to enter the alleyway they were hiding in and was showered with sniper fire before rolling over. It was likely a civilian carriage, wholly unrelated to the situation.

For a brief second, she was able to see the small child inside the carriage.

"......*Mn!*"

Right as she instinctively went to dash over, the envoy grabbed her shoulder.

"You'll die if you go out there, Yuno, my girl. Wait for Soujirou."

"B-but... Soujirou won't save them!"

Soujirou the Willow-Sword wasn't a fiend, only capable of killing others. Yuno knew that. He carried what resembled his own form of duty and obligation, which was why he was trying to carry out his job as bodyguard for Yuno and Haade's envoy.

However, he didn't show any compassion for those who lost their lives.

Uninvolved bystanders, people who jumped into the jaws of death on their own, along with the worthy strong who battled against him.

For all these people, he thought if they ended up dying, there was nothing he could about it.

I'm different!

Yuno flew out from the shadow of the wooden crates. She hadn't summoned her courage. It was the reckless willpower that had continued since the fall of Nagan, and she had simply found herself wanting to resist.

Depending on the model, reloading a musket can take longer than a bow! If their target's the envoy for the negotiations, then they won't prioritize shooting a simple tagalong like me! Soujirou's closing in on the snipers, too; they might not have a moment to ready their next shot!

A number of rationalizations passed through Yuno's mind. All of them completely unfounded.

Clinging to the rolled-over carriage, she kicked in the glass on the door with the heel of her shoe. A desperate move, indifferent to how it may have made her look.

"Hurry and get out of there!"

A small hand took her own outstretched hand.

"Yuno the Distant Talon, yes?"

"......!"

The child inside the carriage was dressed in high-quality black clothing. His hair, an almost gray-white.

Looking up at Yuno from inside the overturned carriage, the young boy spoke to her unfazed.

"Thank you. My name is Hiroto the Paradox."

"The Gray-Haired...Child...!"

"Since you didn't appear on time for our scheduled meeting, we came to you. Please forgive me for not noticing your crisis sooner."

Hiroto the Paradox was here, right now. The mastermind leading the Free City of Okafu.

Without a moment to think about what its development meant, the sound of a bullet impacting rang out behind her.

Sending her hair fluttering into the air as she whipped around, she saw the goblin driver holding up a shield made of what appeared to be resin. A twisted fiber-like structure peeked out from the cross section opened up by the enemy's gunfire.

"First, I shall get straight to the point. We would like to protect you from this attack."

"Wh-why…? Isn't this attack something the mercenaries in the Free City planned out?"

"It's extremely difficult to explain the details properly."

Hiroto held up his hand. At this signal, a goblin force began gathering in the alleyway.

With their shields up in a close formation, they began assembling a wall that would protect everyone there from the sniper fire. The movements were efficient and extremely well disciplined.

"You are correct to assume that the ones fighting us right now are mercenaries from the Free City of Okafu. However, their actions are neither under orders from myself nor the arbitrary whims of Okafu's leader, Morio the Sentinel."

"Are you trying to say someone else *made these mercenaries betray you*?"

"Indeed. There are a countless number of spies infiltrating any of the forces involved with the Sixways Exhibition, not just Okafu. We have taken to calling this group the invisible army and are trying to tackle the issue."

"……"

Spies that Aureatia wasn't aware of, who had infiltrated Okafu and were capable of highly disciplined strategic maneuvers.

It was a terribly outlandish story. It would be more realistic to explain it away as a select group of Okafu mercenaries going out of control. Yet his words coincided with Yuno's analysis.

...They used Okafu mercenaries to attack us because they're trying to cause a rift in Aureatia and Okafu's relations and ensure their mutual destruction... If true, it would be consistent with this inexplicable ambush. But...

"It appears we will need to prepare our negotiations with His Excellency Haade anew. This is likely an extremely big problem for Aureatia."

"......"

There were no new gunshots. Either they saw the goblins' shield wall and determined they were meaningless or Soujirou had reached them and put the snipers to the sword.

Sitting on the edge of the overturned carriage, Hiroto turned back to Yuno.

"It seems we can relax for the time being. Yuno the Distant Talon, to shift the conversation to the future for a moment... Can I ask you for your testimony regarding this ambush?"

"...All right. If that will possibly prevent war. But there's one thing I want to know."

Hiroto the Paradox. He called Yuno by name from the very start. Her second name and all.

"How did you know my name?"

"I investigate anyone I have the possibility of forming a collaborative relationship with."

As far as Yuno could see, he was just a child. She didn't sense that he was a powerful individual.

However, he, too, was a visitor, deviant to the point of abnormality, in a way that differed from Soujirou.

"Yuno the Distant Talon. You're a survivor from the ruined Nagan Labyrinth City, yes?"

A supernatural power of fate, bringing him to opportunity and forming cooperative relationships.

"......That's right."

"Do you know anything about the hero candidate Mestelexil the Box of Desperate Knowledge?"

◆

Wind was blowing through the fine gaps in the steel frame.

A fire tower was far removed from where Yuno's group sat, on the other side of the main road. Soujirou was able to scale its heights with just the strength of his own legs and look down at the five-story buildings.

"...I don't wanna let ya escape."

The shot pierced the ground. Atop the steel frame, with no room to escape, Soujirou parried the gunshot, grazing it with the tip of his hilt. From this range, he didn't even need to swing his sword.

One story above where Soujirou stood, a bright fire was burning. It was a sniper. They set themselves alight as they pulled the trigger.

"But if you escape to the world beyond, how the hell am I 'posed to chase after ya?"

Soujirou scratched his head. Killing was his forte, but he

always had trouble letting people live. Whether it was his enemies or his allies.

"Hold up, are they even safe over there?"

The alleyway that Yuno and the others were hiding in was being protected by a group of goblins with shields. He had seen troops in the Beyond use a closed formation like it before. Their behavior suggested they were hostile, but Soujirou's gut intuition didn't tell him any more about the situation.

Turning back to the sniper's dead body, he tried searching it to see if anything was left behind after he burned up.

Something to identify them or who sent them, for example.

"......Whoa."

His intuition alerted him to the danger. The shape. The smell. The atmosphere.

Then he immediately jumped down from where he was.

"What the hell, c'mon!"

In the span of a single breath, an explosive fireball burst above Soujirou. These flames weren't just to cover up any evidence left behind. It was a *delayed explosion*, using gunpowder with a different rate of reaction.

A trap that saw through, and planned, for Soujirou's attempt to collect evidence.

"...*Hyaaah!*" Soujirou shouted. The flash of a blade ran through the air.

On the tip of his sword, he snatched a high-speed projectile.

The weapon had a blade that encircled a metal ring and was known as a chakram.

This thing...

Soujirou's gut had told him.

...was the real trump card. They've been gunning for me this whole damn time.

Midair, with nowhere to escape. A totally different trajectory and stopping power from the previous gunshots. There was a sniper hiding somewhere on these streets that was on a completely different level from the mercenaries who had first ambushed them—even concealing their murderous intentions within the encirclement around Soujirou's group.

In the middle of his descent, he put his heels on the tower's steel frame, controlling his posture and center of gravity like a cat while he descended.

"...Some bastard's comin' out with the exciting stuff now."

Soujirou's intuition was not omnipotent by any means. It didn't show him the correct tactics to use, nor did it make all the facts detailed and clear to him.

In spite of this, there was one thing he was able to understand.

The objective of this unseen enemy...was not the envoy's assassination, nor did they wish to spark a war with Aureatia. Their goal was none other than Soujirou the Willow-Sword himself.

◆

It took a day to gather information and testimony regarding the ambush.

Yuno was scared there'd be more ambushes, but there currently didn't seem to be any signs they would continue.

At the very least, their present location was safe—the office of Aureatia's Twenty-Seventh General, Haade the Flashpoint.

"Yuno. You've finished making the reports on the ambush, right? Can you make a clean copy of some other data for me? I want to make a list of everyone involved at all with the Sixways Exhibition."

"Y-yessir! Right away!"

In the midst of cleaning the carpet, Yuno immediately ran over at Haade's call.

Although his appearance looked aged, Haade seemed to brim with nigh limitless stamina and vitality. In the simple motion of handing over documents, he was far more forceful and spry than the still young Yuno.

"It's not totally impossible to read, but so much of the handwriting's messy, it's not easy on the eyes. Nagan people are great to have around. Can write clean and legibly."

"Th-th-thank you, sir..."

Even amid the Twenty-Nine Officials, the bearers of supreme power in Aureatia, there were some who saw Twenty-Seventh General Haade, and his control of the nation's greatest military faction, as the dominant figure.

People involved...in the Sixways Exhibition.

As she browsed the documents, Yuno thought back to the events of the previous day.

...Mestelexil the Box of Desperate Knowledge. At the time, she had been on guard against the Gray-Haired Child's rhetoric skills. Although she hadn't been able to ask him what he was trying to get across to her...

"...K—"

...when she saw the list of participants, she learned what Hiroto had been trying to say to her.

Someone involved with Mestelexil the Box of Desperate Knowledge.

"Kiyazuna...the Axle!"

"Whoa there, what happened?" Haade asked, his suspicions raised by the concern in Yuno's voice.

"O-oh, no... It's nothing... Lord Haade."

"Definitely didn't sound like nothing."

Haade roared with laughter.

Nothing?

Yuno was shaking with rage.

It was rage at herself. If she wasn't right before Haade's eyes, she would punch herself bloody.

O-of course... Of course it's not nothing! How could it be?

Kiyazuna the Axle. Kiyazuna the Axle. A name she'd never forget.

A fearsome self-proclaimed demon king who made labyrinths and dungeons with her own hands. The creator of the Dungeon Golem who destroyed her homeland.

As Yuno's hands transcribed data, she dug the nails of her

left hand into her upper right arm. Enough to draw blood. She broke the nib of her pen twice before fully transcribing the name Kiyazuna the Axle.

...I'll kill her. Kill her dead. I'll murder her, no matter what it takes. Kiyazuna the Axle—until I make you pay for everything you've done and kill you, I'll never find peace.

Up until that moment, how could she let herself be so languid and listless?

Had she simply *decided* it would be impossible to search out Kiyazuna the Axle and kill her, and thought instead she'd go from being a survivor of Nagan City to a secretary for one of the Twenty-Nine Officials, to grab peace and happiness for herself?

Disregarding the dead, disregarding Lucelles in the process.

"You're looking pale, Yuno. Everything okay over there?"

Haade asked in a slightly more serious tone than moments prior.

Did being one of the Twenty-Nine mean they possessed excellent skills of observation as well? No—it must have been that Yuno's demeanor in that moment was simply that perturbed and unusual.

"...Lord Haade."

Lifting her head, Yuno looked at Haade. The red tint to her vision was likely because of the tremendous amount of blood shooting through her eyes.

"I-is this... Is this really, right?"

"...What?"

She was about make an irrevocably improper remark.

However, it was too late for regrets. Yuno had already begun to speak.

"Am I? Is this how—how *things should be* for me? With my homeland destroyed. Th-the demon king who caused it... Kiyazuna the Axle, still alive. Why—why was I able to pretend everything was fine? It's ridiculous. Not Soujirou, nor Dakai, but *her*. She was the one I should've killed first. Otherwise, everything about getting revenge would've all been a lie. I mean, Lucelles. Didn't I love her? Yet it was all useless. The entire time... Even if it cost me my life, even if it meant being slaughtered without a fight, I should've gone after Kiyazuna the Axle to kill her. I needed to prove myself, whether it took five years or a hundred. Dammit... Just what are my feelings supposed to be, then? Why—why wasn't it until I saw her name...until I had the possibility of making it happen thrust in front of me?! Why aren't my feelings making me feel that *this is how I want it to be*?! I want... I want vengeance! If I'm going to forget, then I'd rather be dead. *I* needed to fight! Me!"

"............"

"I—I, um...forgive me. I'm sorry...Master Haade."

Haade observed the girl without interrupting her, until she had spewed out all her emotions. With a raptorial glare, quiet yet keen.

"I get it now, Yuno."

Then he twisted his lips, enough to show his gums, into a smile.

"*So you like war, too?*"

"............Wh-what?"

For Yuno, in her stupor, it was a totally incomprehensible comment.

War... There shouldn't have been anyone in the world who could derive pleasure from such a terrible thing.

Perhaps, just maybe, that was the meaning contained in her spewed rambling.

Why was Haade smiling? Was it okay to even consider his expression as "smiling" in the first place?

Was it affirmation? Or denial?

"What do you mean...?"

"Sheesh, and here I figured you were just a little girl along for the ride with Soujirou, but it seems I've made quite the find with you, Yuno the Distant Talon."

Haade put his large palm on Yuno's right shoulder.

"Want to try killing Kiyazuna the Axle?"

It was unreasonable.

An inconsequential young girl, who had only fallen into her secretary job by coincidence, ranted and raved, spitting out incoherent nonsense to none other than the most influential player in Aureatia.

It would've made perfect sense for her to be seen as deranged and fired immediately—if anything, that was the correct course of action.

"I—I... I don't understand..."

"*Bwa-ha-ha-ha.* You won't, in the beginning. You don't have to understand it at all."

"Will I understand eventually?"

"Oh yes. There'll be plenty of opportunities from here on out. First up, three days from now, I plan to kill Ozonezma the Capricious. Let's hope that'll be enough to stoke the fires of war."

Haade put on his overcoat, looking in high spirits, and opened the study door.

"During the Sixways Exhibition, act however you want. You have my permission."

"……"

For a moment after the door closed, Yuno stared at both of her hands, dumbfounded.

There was still a small amount of blood left over on the nails of her left hand she had dug into her arm while working. However, they were just as much the fists of a plain young girl from the frontier.

Right now she was composed. She was fully aware she had lost her head and blurted out awful things to *the* General Haade. Yuno had returned to her senses.

Still, should she really think like that?

Perhaps instead, what she should have been *returning* to was the true Yuno—the Yuno that had definitely been there moments ago, pelting her feelings at the leader of the military without fear, present that time when she challenged Dakai the Magpie to combat amid the fall of Lithia, present at the beginning of it all when she had sworn her revenge against Soujirou in Nagan after losing everything.

She needed to get her hands on something—big enough to take on the apathy of the strong, that allowed Yuno to oppose them.

"You get to decide where you go, and what you're gonna do."

I'll be able to become them both. Fully embrace them... From now on.

She needed to decide...because now Yuno was free.

Fallen leaves covering the brick road crunched underneath young Linaris's leather shoes.

She was seeing a dream of a day gone by. How many years had it been since she had raced through town at midday like this?

"Father!"

The image of her father in his formal garb was exactly like her vivid memories of that day.

Rehart the Obsidian. Her outstanding father, who she revered more than anyone else.

"Get your breathing under control."

His golden eyes were fixed on her. A low voice, calm and mild.

"In that state, both your appearance and your language will grow sloppy."

"…I-I'm sorry… I had something I wanted to ask you, no matter what…"

"An important topic, is it, Linaris?"

Linaris nodded, tears welling up in both eyes.

"Father… Is it true…that your job involves uncovering people's secrets a-and…murdering them? The lord of the last town…and the nobles in the town before that, were they all the work of Obsidian Eyes?"

"...Ah, I see. Who did you hear that from, Linaris?"

"Yufick...said all of that... I love you, Father, and you're always so kind, so... I—I didn't want to believe any of it, but—but!"

A large palm was placed on Linaris's head. Just like always. Rehart solemnly whispered.

"It's necessary."

"...Father."

"You know this, Linaris. The weak make up many of the Obsidian Eyes members. I don't mean physically weak, but the weak who are unable to live in society. What do you think it is, Linaris, that differentiates them from the strong?"

Linaris answered in a thin, strained voice.

"I don't... I don't know."

"It's whether they can keep secrets."

Her father stooped down and rubbed Linaris's back as if to make her understand.

"Those who have to steal nobles' money to survive. Those who betrayed their lord for the sake of their lover. Those who have killed many of their own friends. The people who join Obsidian Eyes are those who have had secrets they wished to keep hidden exposed to the light of day. Everyone knows their sins—and that they're unforgivable. Despite surely wishing for nothing of the sort."

"But everyone is...so nice... They're even nice to frail children like me... Children unable take care of themselves..."

"You're right. They're no different from any of us. Who can

possibly save them? The nobles, the military...even the royal family has secrets they wish to keep to themselves. They kill their siblings, exploit the people, and hide their wealth, yet the weak are persecuted. They are different from our friends in one way only. Their secrets have yet to be exposed."

Her father whispered, bringing his face in close. He would always do this, teaching her what was right.

...However.

"The weak need to eat secrets to live. They've lost their own, so they need others' secrets. All of it's necessary to help everyone...to help our friends."

"For everyone's sake..."

"You're a sharp girl. You understand, right, Linaris?"

"Yes... Thank goodness... I was right, Father... You're a nice person."

Linaris wiped her tears. Looking at the golden eyes they both shared, she did her best to smile.

Lies.

Even at a young age, before she had reached puberty and before she had awakened to her vampiric powers, Linaris had another inherent ability. The power to read the minds of others and deeply study their thoughts. The power to expose secrets.

This was why she could understand.

The justice her father talked about was a lie.

Obsidian Eyes was not an organization for saving the weak.

With the power gained from devouring numerous secrets, Rehart the Obsidian wished for the arrival of bleak and chaotic war.

She hugged her father. Though she understood everything, she couldn't stop herself from feeling the way she did.

Father, I love you. I love you. Even though you're doing such awful things, I'm sorry. I still love you, Father. I love you. I love you. I love you...

The next day, Yufick was gone.

She learned that those who had lost their secrets would go on to die.

◆

Midnight had come and gone. Even within Aureatia's borders, the mansion was located near a tranquil waterfront.

"...My lady."

The voice outside the door woke Linaris from her indulgent nap.

She pulled the sheets up to her chest.

"Mhhn..."

In the dark room, absent the light of a single candle, her porcelain skin and the gold eyes peeking out from her long eyelashes were the only things giving off any light. The night air filtered in and chilled Linaris's bare skin.

"My lady. There's been movement among Okafu's troops."

"...Thank you. I will hear the details in my father's stead. May I have some time beforehand?"

Linaris answered the voice on the other side of the door. It was always Frey's duty to summon Linaris from her bedroom.

"It is not critical news. You must be tired, my lady. Please, relax."

The sound of footsteps faded into the distance.

"......"

Linaris once again went to lie down on her bed.

"Father."

The beautiful vampire tenderly stroked the cheek of her father, continuing to sleep right beside her.

The body, still preserved even now with Life Arts, was exactly the same as it been before. Even if it no longer sent any words her way or guided her.

"I, Linaris...promise...to devote myself to your glory."

Though she possessed the supernatural ability to make anyone obey her, she wanted to obey someone, to be controlled, more than anything else.

Even in death, her father controlled her just as she wished.

After she fully dressed herself, Linaris descended to the large room downstairs.

Her mansion was always enveloped in quiet. Many of the agents of Obsidian Eyes were entrusted with espionage duties in various places around Aureatia, with a limited number of personnel guarding the manor. Currently, there were merely two within its walls.

A housekeeper and staff wielder, the leprechaun woman was the organization's oldest serving member—Frey the Waking.

A lycan warrior from the Zehf Tribe, Hartl the Light Pinch.

"Good evening. Miss Frey, Miss Hartl, welcome back."

"Indeed, my lady. It is a lovely night."

"Thank you, my lady. My apologies for summoning you from your slumber with my report."

"*Tee-hee-hee.* Please, not at all. I should be apologizing for making you wait here so long."

"It involves one of our pawns in the Free City of Okafu. Frey here can provide the details."

The "pawns" Obsidian Eyes spoke of were members of another organization who had been turned into corpses.

In general, unless a corpse remained in close proximity to their vampire parent, they would preserve their original self, and making them execute advanced orders was considered impossible.

However, Obsidian Eyes was different. Just as it had been with Atrazek the Particle Storm, through the destruction of the host's mental barriers by the vampire's domineering infection, they were able to create sleeper agents capable of reliably executing orders without being close to their parent. The technique to destroy the mind, instead of the body, was a special characteristic of Obsidian Eyes, passed down from the previous generation.

Through their power to control these pawns, distinctively different from simple corpses, Obsidian Eyes had developed into what was known as the greatest spy guild in the land.

"Yes, yes. Now then, let's go through the report. Before nightfall, at least seventy Okafu soldiers departed Aureatia. I believe they plan on withdrawing all the personnel they had infiltrate the city."

"...How honest of them. It would have been so much nicer if they wavered on their next move for us."

The ambush attack on Soujirou the Willow-Sword was one part of the large-scale operation of Obsidian Eyes.

Haade the Flashpoint, head of the military faction and known for his highly belligerent nature. His long embattled opponent, the Free City of Okafu. By manipulating Okafu soldiers to stage the attack on Haade's envoy, the objective of their operation was to fan discord between both parties.

That wasn't the entirety of it. The other objective was to give Soujirou the Willow-Sword a *grazing wound*.

The chakram he had blocked at the end of the fight belonged to an Obsidian Eyes marksman named Veeze the Fluctuation. Linaris's corpses didn't inherit her unique airborne transmission of the vampire pathogen. However, by using a trace amount of her blood coated onto a weapon, they could force a transmission through blood.

...However, both objectives ended in failure.

The trap set for Soujirou had admittedly been, in some senses, an ancillary plot.

However, despite handing Haade the ideal excuse to go to war with Okafu, not only was there no declaration of war, but there also weren't any hints of sanctions against the city, either.

If Master Haade fully accepted the Gray-Haired Child's claims and wasn't questioning Okafu's responsibility at all... Then it's almost as if Haade himself was purposefully trying to avoid war.

Putting her index finger up to her pale, tinted lips, Linaris followed her enemy's line of thought. Her talent was the power to discern the minds of others and thoroughly pursue them.

The Gray-Haired Child, as part of the negotiations around this latest incident, might have used the withdrawal of Okafu troops from Aureatia as a bargaining chip. The withdrawal of Okafu forces was a move that promptly discarded his advantage, the ability to openly bring troops in and out of Aureatia, while also fundamentally being the best way to deal with the situation.

As long as they weren't here in Aureatia, Linaris would be unable to manipulate the Okafu soldiers. She could, of course, control them to ignore the withdrawal order, but in that case, Okafu's side would be able peg the soldiers disobeying the orders as suspects behind the ambush. If they pursued things even further, there was a chance they'd discover Linaris's camp was controlling the situation behind the scenes.

Presently, the one she considered to be behind their strategic plans was a Sixways Exhibition hero candidate named Zigita Zogi the Thousandth. As well as Hiroto the Paradox, known as the Gray-Haired Child. Once they had identified a breakaway group within the Okafu soldiers, it had taken them just under two days to bring Aureatia to agree to this large-scale withdrawal.

With this, they couldn't expect any further progress in their plan to lay suspicions on the Free City of Okafu or make the other hero candidates off each other, either.

"Let's kill them."

The lycan Hartl spoke up with his arms crossed.

"If the Okafu soldiers investigate their pawns, there's a big risk they'll look into our identity. Dead bodies reveal our existence more than anything else. If they autopsy the body of the infected, and happen to examine their blood, we'll end up handing over proof to them all on a silver platter that a vampire is maneuvering behind the scenes."

Infection and control through airborne transmission. At first glance, it seemed like an unrivaled power. However, it was ultimately still a power based on the racial nature of vampires.

There existed an antiserum for the vampire virus that protected against infection.

The manufacturing process was extremely unique. With fears of possible side effects, adoption was limited to a select group of people, those involved in medical treatment and the like. But the instant it was suspected a vampire was spreading their virus, there'd be measures taken against them.

Furthermore, the vampire virus that Linaris possessed could only infect through the air if it was coming from Linaris herself. The moment she infected another, and the virus took hold, it would turn into an ordinary virus transmitted through blood.

"My lady. I can kill and incinerate the ones we'd turned into pawns immediately. The biggest strength of corpses is that they can be prepared quickly—and easily replaced. There's no need to hold on to them for dear life. In any case, Okafu's likely already discerned that there is another organization besides Aureatia executing their own espionage operation."

The members of Obsidian Eyes, while Linaris's corpses, were

not under mental control. Making it possible take their opinions into account—determined by their own observed experiences as individuals, swearing loyalty of their own volition—made Linaris's Obsidian Eyes distinct from a normal vampire colony.

"Quite so."

Accepting the dangerous proposal, the young lady smiled with grace.

"Miss Frey. If they're suspicious of a collaborator, then Okafu is performing an internal investigation, yes?"

"Yes. They appear to have already begun. They're also investigating if there have been any secret acts of sabotage from other organizations as well. It goes without saying that our pawns will not be identified that easily."

"From among those targeted by Okafu's investigation, would it be possible to take two or three of them who aren't our pawns... and kill them without infection? Not only Okafu, but let's kill the ones in Aureatia, in Sun's Conifer, and in the Order as well. We'll make them out to be our spies."

"...I see. People from several different powers disappearing all at once. For those who know the truth to some extent, that there's been sabotage behind the scenes, they'll simply correlate these organizations to the deaths all by themselves."

"That's right. Given that our opponent is looking into us... making them believe the scale of their enemy is much bigger must be more convenient, wouldn't you say? For Zigita Zogi, as well as Aureatia."

It was also in part a diversionary tactic against the Free City of

Okafu to delay their cooperation with other powers. It'd be impossible with the information they had to determine which powers in Aureatia she had sunk her hands into.

Additionally, a slew of suspicious deaths occurring simultaneously with the Okafu army's large-scale withdrawal would be reason enough for the suspicious eyes of the other powers in play to turn their focus on Okafu. Obsidian Eyes would set a quiet attack on all the players at once in order to sow these seeds of doubt.

Petite Frey's smile remained as she repeated Linaris's orders.

"Yes, yes. Then, let's kill a few of them at a time. The job can be done in three days if we rely on Veeze's sharpshooting."

"Please do, then. As I'm sure Father is hoping for just such a thing."

Linaris the Obsidian spelled disaster.

Just as Atrazek the Particle Storm or Kia the World Word could do the same themselves, it was perhaps possible for her to control the nerve center of the world, including the Aureatia Assembly, and annihilate the current minian society.

However, the existence of Obsidian Eyes couldn't be exposed. The pestilent vampire would lose a large amount of her superior positioning the moment her existence was uncovered, and measures were put in to combat her.

Linaris was the only person who could infect through the air, when her corpses were unable to do it, too. It was a shortcoming at first glance, but when looking at it as a survival strategy, she considered it an advantage, if anything.

If all of Aureatia was inflicted with disease by way of

indiscriminate airborne transmission, the minian races would band together, pursue the origin of the infection, and put an end to her. The same conclusion as any normal epidemic.

However, as long as Linaris didn't make any moves, she could keep the path of infection completely within the palm of her hand. Additionally, with warriors of the caliber of Obsidian Eyes under her command, meeting the conditions for blood transmission was simple.

Therefore, it was necessary for Linaris to choose her targets carefully.

In order to achieve her goal, simple destruction wouldn't be enough.

She needed to usher in discord among the minian races' fellow members and bring forth *a voluntary demand for chaotic war*. Ensuring Obsidian Eyes didn't become a mutually hated enemy, she would create a world where only those capable of living in darkness would be allowed to exist.

That was what the Sixways Exhibition was for. If, by using this special event, she could sow decisive seeds of doubt between a power with plenty of reason to oppose Aureatia—the Free City of Okafu—and Aureatia itself, then the maelstrom of conflict she wished for would descend on the world.

Yet Haade avoided starting a war.

She had thought that Haade the Flashpoint was the first person she should set her sights on. Linaris might have been mistaken in her choice of targets.

…The first round. In the third match, Haade's champion,

Soujirou, will battle against Ozonezma, who has Zigita Zogi at his back... But after that, there was the second round...then the third round. If Haade is setting up what I fear he is, then the meaning behind his attempt to avoid war...

A plague that could think. She would only ever take action herself when she had her sights on a truly vital target.

"...I entrust dealing with the Okafu side of things to you. I myself will probe into Haade's movements."

"My lady. Are you sure?"

"Yes. I'm able to investigate much deeper secrets than anyone else in Obsidian Eyes."

Behind her composed smile, Linaris was afraid.

She feared her comrades dying. She feared coming to an end without being able to honor her father's dying wishes. These fears could very well become reality.

If she let the moment pass her by, the decisive secret that lay behind this Sixways Exhibition would slip out of her reach.

"...And with everything staying a perfect secret."

Once again, she brought her index finger up against her lips.

Until the match began—and even after it had, she couldn't let anyone catch wind of her true identity. She would take hold of all the secrets and achieve her goals under the cover of shadow. Such was the way of the Obsidian Eyes.

"Because if we don't, we won't be able to survive."

The office in the soldier barracks was where Haade the Flashpoint usually spent his time. He would always stay on base, keeping an eye on the soldiers' morale and discipline, and he almost never visited the Central Assembly Hall in the course of his daily duties.

There was also a visitor who was freely allowed to go in and out of this office as well.

"...Soujirou. Have you been using that sword this whole time?"

Soujirou the Willow-Sword was sitting down, leaning up against the wall.

While his eyes were closed, he wasn't asleep. He simply didn't like any superfluous or bothersome activity. He had never even practiced any of the techniques he knew.

"Yup."

"That's a Nagan training sword, you know. Not only that, but Nagan's no military school, so the build quality isn't anything special, either. Basically...it's a light sword, just enough to get you used to the bare minimum basics. Sure, it isn't incapable of killing people, but cutting down a single minia should be enough to ruin it for good. Start talking about a zmeu or anything like 'em, and it couldn't cut down a single one."

"Oh yeah? Okay, so how come I can kill people with it, then?"

It was a rare state of affairs for Soujirou to show interest in the principle of something.

"Because you aren't slashing with raw strength. You slash the eye or an opening in something—which is admittedly something the masters here in our world do, too, more or less. Your technique just goes far, far beyond that."

Just as Aureatia had done with all the visitors they secured for themselves, they repeatedly analyzed and experimented with Soujirou's skills as well.

The tip of Soujirou's drawn blade never failed to penetrate steel armor like water seeping in. The story was that his sword attack had even sliced through Nihilo the Vortical Stampede's deep celestial charsteel armor.

With a slash of that speed, it was possible to slice through material of any quality with the very first cut. Not only that, but while accompanied with an abnormal amount of technical skill, the trajectory of his blade never wavered until he was finished with his follow-through.

…However, if that explanation was enough to detail his entire abilities, that would truly place him in the category of "abnormal technical skill."

Soujirou could slice a clean line through an ooze corpse that would collapse at the slightest touch, pull off curved slashes that seemed impossible to explain, judging by his sword's trajectory, and even manage to slice through a gun while it was pushed against his blade.

A being existing in a realm that even Haade the Flash Point, having witnessed the skills of soldiers more than anyone else, was unable to comprehend. That was what it meant to be a visitor.

Just as it was with a dragon's forelimbs, a gigante's long life span, or an enchanted sword or magic tools—those first initial abnormalities were impossible to replicate no matter what Word Arts or types of science one used.

That was why they were all banished from the Beyond and brought to this world.

"Soujirou. Are you particular about that sword or something?"

"I can figure out whether a sword's good or not, too, ya know. If I picked myself up another sword, then I woulda used that."

"...I see, then. Since you're appearing in the Sixways Exhibition, are you gonna need a higher-quality sword?"

"If ya don't got one, then I don't need any."

"I'll give you an enchanted sword."

Haade opened the package on his desk and took out a sheathed sword.

The long sword had a blade that gently curved with a single edge, as if it knew of Soujirou's origins back in the Beyond and had chosen him specifically.

"Here in this world...there are swords that'll explode just by touching the tip, swords that'll spit fire, swords that'll move on their own. Enigmas beyond analysis, one being worth as much as a whole army."

"Don't need 'em."

"*Pfft!* Knew you'd give me that. Relax. This one's got nothing to it."

The exploding sword jumbled the recoil from hitting something. The flame-spitting sword was already not really a sword, considering the range of destruction and its behavior. Swords that moved on their own and their ilk were out of the question while in the middle of subtle and intriguing sword techniques.

It was indeed true there were genuine monsters like Toroa the Awful, who were capable of manipulating even these characteristics of various enchanted swords to be part of his own technique.

However, it was the fantasy of those who didn't know the way of the sword to think an enchanted sword would unconditionally lead to unrivaled power. Gilnes the Ruined Castle, for example, wielder of the enchanted blasting sword, was a fearsome swordsman because he wielded it while fully aware of this fact.

Haade casually tossed the enchanted sword, after speaking of its scarcity and value, to Soujirou. With his eyes closed, Soujirou remained seated as he grabbed the sheath in midair.

"Alcuzari the Hollow Blade."

"What sorta sword is it?"

"It doesn't break or chip. That's it. Its metal's flexible, sure, but no warping or bending's left behind. Not only is that an inexhaustible sword, but it's an impregnable shield. That should be good for you, eh?"

"...*Heh-heh.*"

Soujirou stifled his laughter.

Several traces of light flashed through the air. With the follow-up clack of the hilt, Haade then realized he had tried out the sword by slicing through the air.

"Ain't nothing special. No different from the average sword. The shield stuff doesn't matter, neither. I've never blocked with my sword before."

"Looked like a pretty good match just now."

"Yeah, I guess."

Haade had witnessed Soujirou's swordsmanship with his training sword.

Now that he had swapped out to the weight of a common sword, it seemed as if the difference in heft had been converted to speed.

To say nothing of the power should such a slash connect—it was impossible for Haade to imagine.

The swordsman was sneering, like a beast impatiently waiting for his premonition of bloodshed to come true.

"*Heh-heh......* Hey, Haade. You're thinkin' up something awful, aren't ya?"

"*Bwa-ha-ha...* Yeah, I guess."

The same smile spread across the Twenty-Seventh General's face.

The third match was about to begin.

◆

In front of the long bridge in Aureatia...

A steam automobile stopped right before it had finished crossing the bridge. The driver shouted.

"This is it! I can't go any farther!"

"UNDERSTOOD."

The door of the car's bed promptly opened, and a monstrous beast jumped out of it.

He stamped down the city road. Colors streamed through their sights as they raced.

Even with the portly Fourteenth General, Yuca, on his back, his running speed still surpassed any and all of the automobiles around him.

"Hoo boy, we sure are late, huh? But at least it looks like we made it in time for the match."

Despite the tremendous headwind he was facing on Ozonezma's back, Yuca the Halation Gaol wasn't shaken up at all. For Ozonezma, he was grateful for the man's calm composure.

"...DO YOU THINK SO? WHEN WE DEPARTED GIMEENA CITY, WE INITIALLY HAD A THREE-DAY LEAD TIME."

"Rotten luck, wasn't it? We didn't have a vehicle, and there was that detour midway, too."

"DOES AN AUTOMOBILE COAL DEFICIENCY COUNT AS 'UNLUCKY'? EVEN THAT SMALL AMOUNT OF FUEL WAS ALL SCRAPED TOGETHER ON THE BLACK MARKET, WASN'T IT? RIGHT BEFORE WE LEFT, THERE WAS A LARGE-SCALE SEIZURE OF FUEL. CONCENTRATED ENTIRELY AROUND GIMEENA CITY."

"Well, I mean, that stuff just happens sometimes, I guess?"

After the long time he had spent together with Yuca, Ozonezma had come to understand something.

He certainly wasn't as stupid as he made it seem to those around him. He must have long since realized that the course of events surrounding them was probably a form of sabotage from Twenty-Seventh General Haade. It was likely partly out of Yuca's pride that he understood this—and still remained calm and collected.

However, if it wasn't for Zigita Zogi's warning—if their departure had been delayed even a half a day later, there was a chance that Ozonezma wouldn't have been able to even step on the battlefield and would have lost his match without putting up a fight.

"...IS IT TOO LATE TO MAKE TIME TO MEET WITH SOMEONE?"

"*Ha-ha-ha.* It's no skin off my back if you lose, Ozonezma, so we can do that first if you want. But noon's almost here. If you don't head straight for your match, you might not make it."

"UNDERSTOOD."

It was Ozonezma himself who chose to tactically delay his arrival to Aureatia until the very last moment.

Of course, he was resigned to the considerations he'd have to make as a result, but he still had some regrets.

TU, WHERE ARE YOU RIGHT NOW?

He had memories of Aureatia's layout from the map he had obtained from Zigita Zogi's men beforehand.

Turning at a sharp angle in the alleyway, he kicked the wall to dodge a carriage, continuing at such extreme speeds that the eyes of the passersby didn't register his passing. Such full-power speed, when compared to the battle he was about fight, didn't tire him out in the slightest.

"You're talking about Tu the Magic, right? Sorry 'bout that. Flinsuda and I actually get along pretty well, and she might've brought her out to Gimeena City if I asked her to."

"A FAR TOO OPTIMISTIC VIEW. ANOTHER SPONSOR LEADING THEIR CANDIDATE OUT OF AUREATIA BEFORE THEIR MATCH... EVEN PROPOSING IT WOULD INVITE SUSPICION FROM THE OTHERS. IT'S IMPOSSIBLE."

"Still, though, are you sure you shouldn't meet up with her first? You could just as easily get heavily injured in this upcoming match, too."

"...YOU WON'T GO AS FAR TO SAY I MIGHT DIE, THEN?"

He came to a sudden stop. His monstrously huge frame used a small building's window frame as a foothold and climbed up as if his body weighed nothing at all. It was mobility that far eclipsed the speed of automobiles or horses.

"Geez, it might've been better to run on your back from the start."

"FOR THREE WHOLE DAYS?"

"Sure, you could do that, right?"

"YOU WOULDN'T GET THROUGH IT UNSCATHED."

In fact, Ozonezma's acceleration should induce a horrifying amount of physical strain to a minian body.

Despite this, Yuca was composed enough to chitchat with

Ozonezma just like he always did. He was a tenacious man. Supposing Ozonezma's sponsor had been a regular civil bureaucrat instead, he wouldn't have been able to act so recklessly.

"IT IS FINE IF I AM UNABLE TO MEET TU THE MAGIC. NO MATTER WHAT PATH THAT ONE CHOOSES TO GO DOWN... IT DOESN'T DIRECTLY INVOLVE ME EITHER WAY."

"You almost sound like you're friends."

"...I WOULD WAGER SHE DOESN'T KNOW ME AT ALL."

"Then, what is she?"

"............A DIFFICULT QUESTION. IF I HAD TO ANSWER..."

Jumping over rooftops, he crossed two roads before coming back down.

The match would start soon. Just as Yuca said, there was no time for him to converse with Tu the Magic.

Straight at the end of this alley was the garden theater where the match was being held.

Ozonezma answered.

"A YOUNGER SISTER."

Kicking the ground again, the grotesque chimera rushed on.

While this was Ozonezma's first time stepping foot into Aureatia, he couldn't afford to take in the glittering and gorgeous scenery around him.

However, he could win. Up until the moment the match started, both Haade and Soujirou remained totally ignorant of the true methods he would use.

I will win this first battle.

It was the first round and would be the fight that would prove the most difficult.

His enemy was Haade the Flashpoint, leading a faction that rivaled Rosclay's own, and the tangible and intangible sabotage from his organizational strength was driving the chimera up against the wall before the match even began.

Nevertheless, if Ozonezma defeated Soujirou in the first round, he could destroy the opposing faction in Aureatia that was rivaling Rosclay's. Haade's faction, governing Aureatia's military, would become an isolated player within the Sixways Exhibition.

This held a completely different meaning than defeating Rosclay himself, the majority faction's leader. Precisely because Haade's faction was not the largest player, even after it collapsed, their common enemy in Rosclay would still exist.

Haade's faction would be placed in a situation exactly like the Old Kingdoms' loyalists in Gimeena City—if there happened to be someone who could bring together their scattered forces again, that person would then become a new "head" for their group.

As long as Ozonezma had Hiroto the Paradox as a collaborator, such an operation was all too easy. By directly connecting with the envoy for Haade's camp, Hiroto had already laid the foundations to do so. This fight would be the most difficult, but it was also an arrangement that Hiroto the Paradox had negotiated for when devising the tournament bracket.

...I MUST WIN.

Therefore, for this first-round match, it had been necessary to assemble an absolutely flawless surprise attack.

Having remained outside of Aureatia, Ozonezma wasn't directly acquainted with the appearances or personalities of the other participants. He knew the fighting strength of his bracket from Zigita Zogi's investigations and came up with his counter-measures based solely off that.

He was unconcerned with the goals of the other hero candidates fighting in the Sixways Exhibition. It wasn't necessary.

Whatever objectives Soujirou the Willow-Sword had, their match moments away, were irrelevant.

Even if it had been Tu the Magic instead, he had resolved himself that, if it was necessary, he would have no other choice.

Ozonezma had one goal.

TO ERADICATE THE FALSE HERO.

◆

The castle theater garden was a facility that had been used to hold royal games before the beginning of the Sixways Exhibition.

There were passageways set up below the stone audience seats for the players in royal games to use, and the Twenty-Nine Officials sponsoring hero candidates could now remain here on standby and watch over their candidates' matches.

Currently, only Haade the Flashpoint was there. Yuca the Halation Gaol had yet to arrive.

An elderly secretary sped to his side and passed on a message to the general.

"General Haade. I have something to report."

"Couldn't stymie their transportation?"

"...Yessir."

Obstructing Ozonezma from entering Aureatia itself—it was one of the plans that Haade's camp had devised, much like the Old Kingdoms' loyalist insurrection in Gimeena City to try to clear the first round.

The maximum amount of sabotage that was possible without things getting out to the public...or to be more specific, without Yuca *making it public.* As far as Haade's plans were concerned, he couldn't scheme anything more extreme than what he had.

"Getting put on the back foot with the steam automobile hurt. The central registry for steam vehicles is still too lax. They had a car they purposefully kept hidden from us. Someone like Jel would've been able to take care of it, I bet."

"Ozonezma will arrive at the arena. There's no choice but to fight against him."

"I know. Soujirou's there for when we get forced to fight. Get in touch with Dant."

"Master Dant... Contact Zigita Zogi's sponsor."

Contact with the Twenty-Fourth General Dant—it meant contact with the Okafu, and the Gray-Haired Child, first and foremost. While it was a backup plan, itself bringing danger, Haade wasn't a man who hesitated in situations like these.

"Is Master Dant involved in this incident...?"

"Ninety percent of it. Ninety percent, for sure. First, there's the loophole in the steam automobile system, and then the instant he got wind of our movements, the bastard went and got control of the fuel on the black market. 'Cept it's not a stunt he could've pulled off with just smarts. He'd need hands that could reach far and wide. A military force. That's Zigita Zogi—and his command of the Free City of Okafu, right?"

"...and what of the possibility it was Master Rosclay's army?"

"Nah. The scale of our enemy's movements wouldn't be possible with the soldiers Rosclay can call to action outside of Aureatia. During the negotiations after that sniper incident, Zigita Zogi and the Gray-Haired Child...they didn't flinch about expelling the Okafu soldiers who were given Aureatia citizenship out of the city. Might've been part of what they were aiming for. To make them be there to support Ozonezma outside the city."

There was no one but Zigita Zogi who could mobilize a military force that rivaled Aureatia's own army.

Kaete and Rosclay could similarly command their own military forces, but those were still, in some ways, Aureatia soldiers. Even if they mobilized a selection of troops from the bigger whole, their movements would get leaked to the other members in the Twenty-Nine Officials as well.

Mobilizing troops outside the city, like Haade was now, had been a high-risk gamble that left a large hole within Aureatia's borders. This was likely how the other players saw it.

"Zigita Zogi and the Free City of Okafu. No doubt that Gray-Haired Child's mediating between Ozonezma and the Okafu mercs."

"...Is their aim to defeat us in the Sixways Exhibition and incorporate us into the Okafu camp?"

"If so, there's a way to take advantage of that, but... At any rate, they aren't any normal mercenaries. No doubt there."

With this, the war specialist Haade was outsmarted. As far as he was concerned, what he truly needed to be cautious of was not Hiroto the Paradox, stepping into an organization and winning them over to his cause. Nor was it the self-proclaimed demon king, Morio the Sentinel, who led the Free City of Okafu.

The tactical prowess to efficiently mobilize a large-scale force, read the opponents' next moves, and dispatch said force accordingly—

Zigita Zogi the Thousandth was a far mightier and more dangerous presence than Haade had imagined.

"I'll arrange things with him directly right now. If their aim's to bring us into their forces, then I'm all for it. When Soujirou loses, my only option'll be to join up with them myself."

"...Will Soujirou the Willow-Sword lose? A visitor like him?"

"Now, I didn't necessarily say that."

Soujirou was strong. Haade had chosen to use him because he was the real deal.

However, he wasn't confident in a surefire victory, either. He needed to advance through this first round, but there had been a limit to the schemes he put into play against Ozonezma, who hadn't been present in Aureatia until that day. There wasn't anything Haade could do for Soujirou while he faced off against Ozonezma in the public eye.

He had already tried every means of winning before the fight started. The warmonger was simply thinking over his means of victory *after the battle was fought.*

"It's the same for Soujirou or anyone else—once a battle's started, there's never a hundred percent chance of victory. Not even the person fighting can predict what'll happen on the battlefield. That's why it's about always making the first move. Time to leave the arena."

"I will coordinate a meeting immediately. I believe it would be best for you to accompany me directly, sir."

"Always planned to. Things're getting interesting. Let's go... Well, now."

Haade stopped. His adviser halted shortly afterward.

A colossal beast, almost taking up their full field of vision, appeared ahead in the brick corridor.

An unnatural wolfish beast, with bluish-silver fur. The largest of the Twenty-Nine Officials, Yuca the Halation Gaol, even looked small when lined up with Ozonezma.

"YOU MUST BE HAADE, THEN."

"Hello there, Ozonezma the Capricious."

The Twenty-Seventh General wasn't perturbed by the monstrosity and instead had stopped and waited for his arrival.

He took a cigar from his breast pocket and stuck it in his mouth. His adviser, walking out from beside him, lit it.

Haade closed his eyes and took a puff of the cigar.

"...Took you long enough, eh? The audience's growing impatient out there. Run into some sort of problem?"

"WE ARE NOT LATE. THERE IS PLENTY OF TIME TO FINISH UP OUR BUSINESS. RIGHT HERE…RIGHT NOW."

Ozonezma was directly in front of the corridor.

He'd have to pass by him, or he wouldn't be able to depart the garden theater.

In order to head for his destination, Haade the Flashpoint would have to pass right beside the brute force capable of massacring minia with a single touch.

"*Pwa-ha!*"

Haade laughed, blowing smoke.

"Sorry, but I got important business coming up soon, see. Fine if I sneak by you, right?"

"*Ha-ha-ha.* Don't go getting up to anything too nasty, Haade." Yuca said, upbeat and without any concern for the tension in the air.

Though they currently were working with different powers, they had confidence in each other as fellow military officers. Haade, feared as a merciless tactician, might have been showing diffidence, in some ways, to the man in front of him.

"Well, if there were any injuries to the citizens, I couldn't overlook that, now could I? Looks like we both lucked out, eh?"

"…Right."

Shaking his head slightly, Haade passed his finished cigar to his adviser.

"Ozonezma. I'm coming through."

"……"

Even as he passed by Ozonezma's side, Haade didn't quicken

his pace a single step. To Haade, war meant that death was always close at hand.

"Oh right, Yuca. Your birthday's in about ten days, isn't it?"

"I guess so, now that you mention it."

"Looks like my mind hasn't gone yet. Lemme do something for you to celebrate."

The elderly general went on his way without watching the match that was about to begin.

The warriors for match three had gathered.

Ozonezma the Capricious versus Soujirou the Willow-Sword.

◆

Twenty-Sixth Minister Meeka the Whispered, tasked with adjudicating the Sixways Exhibition, would be categorized as having a large build for a woman. Even with the beast dwarfing the two of them, her large stature still made him look noticeably small.

"Combatants, are there any objections to the true duel arrangements?"

"NO."

"Nope."

After reaching the same agreement that was laid out in the first match, Meeka left the area.

The spacious garden theater. If the opposing participants had both wished for it, they could have started from midrange instead.

However, Ozonezma chose to start in sword range on purpose. Soujirou went along with the decision.

"Well, look at you… That's quite the form you've got there…," Soujirou mumbled in a low voice.

"IT SEEMS THIS IS YOUR FIRST TIME WITNESSING A CHIMERA, VISITOR."

An explosive sound echoed in the air. The cannon shot from the brass band to announce the start of the match.

Nevertheless, both parties remained still.

Regardless of Ozonezma being in range of his sword, the blade master hadn't tried to cut him down.

"…*Heh-heh-heh.* How many lives you got there, huh…?"

Soujirou's eyes narrowed. There weren't any vulnerable areas.

Even without his opponent moving a muscle, Soujirou had a deviant fighting instinct that could recognize the quality of his enemy's fighting skills with a single glance. Far beyond a mere sixth sense, it was an infallible intuition, on par with true precognition.

Ozonezma's abnormally colossal body was constructed entirely out of champion-level muscles and bones. Every fiber was intricately woven around each bone to achieve peak performance. Far beyond just Soujirou, the chimera's physical abilities likely outstripped those of the arachnid tank he had fought against in Lithia.

This wasn't all. Fatal weak points, present in all living creatures, were missing from this chimera.

"YOU HAVE A SWORDSMAN'S BODY, I SEE. NO OTHER WEAPON WILL WORK FOR YOU."

Ozonezma, too, had finished his observations of Soujirou upon first glance.

However, in his case, this was not a natural gift but insight into a body's construction that he had accumulated through experience. Though he was a chimera, he was also a doctor. Whether it was above or beneath the skin, he was the creature who had observed the most champions out of anyone else across the land.

"AND YOU HAVE YOUR GUARD UP."

In fact, Soujirou was actually putting distance between himself and Ozonezma. Two sword lengths away. He surely had techniques to slash at Ozonezma even from this distance. However...

"……"

"ARE YOU THINKING I HAVE SOME METHOD OF COUNTERING YOUR ATTACK? DO NOT WORRY. IT IS NOT THE TYPE OF METHOD YOU ARE IMAGINING."

He held a secret trick he could employ within sword range.

For Ozonezma, keeping it hidden until the location of their match was decided on had been an insurance for him. He could match Soujirou's slash, and precisely match the method of attack, to defeat him in a single blow of his own.

Still, the hand he kept as his final trump card, once the match had started and they faced each other at this distance, would chip away at the opponent, completely irrelevant of whether they figured out its lethality, qualities, or even its true nature.

"THAT REMINDS ME: I HAVE ONLY HEARD THIS AS A RUMOR, BUT...IT SEEMS THERE IS A GIRL NAMED YUNO THE DISTANT TALON."

"...Huh?"

"DO YOU KNOW HER? SHE IS—"

The air trembled with a hum, and silver streaks of light swooped in on Soujirou. The ground exploded.

The streaks of light were actually six scalpels thrown simultaneously.

Perfectly simultaneous precision bombing, utilizing six of the numerous arms that appeared out of the gaping hole in Ozonezma's back.

"...Geez!"

The cloud of dust blew away. Soujirou survived the nightmarishly destructive rush. Ozonezma's arms weren't the only things that had caused tremors in the air.

How was Soujirou the Willow-Sword able to dodge the six perfectly synchronized projectiles?

As he pulled back his right leg, targeted by one of the scalpels, he repelled the one heading for his shoulder with the heel of his left palm. Following through with a slash from the enchanted sword in his right hand, the flash of steel brought down the two scalpels that were aimed at his torso simultaneously. An efficient slash, rubbing the side of the scalpel blade to kill its momentum. His body, twisted down diagonally over the course of his movements, dodged the remaining two.

Within the normal principles and laws of the universe, it would have been interpreted as miraculous good fortune.

That Soujirou, coincidently, was in a position that made it possible to dodge them all.

This wasn't the case.

VISITORS. THEIR EXISTENCE IS THE MOST TERRIFYING OF ALL.

Ozonezma's eyes had clearly observed Soujirou's muscles' entire kinetic mechanisms.

No matter how superb someone's physical abilities were...even if they were indeed a powerful champion, they possessed bones and muscles, moving in accordance with this logic.

Visitors were different. The dodge just now occurred as if it was inevitable.

Even his skills of visual observation, capable of perceiving everything down to a singular muscle fiber, couldn't perceive the mechanisms of this movement.

He felt an unknown uneasiness, and by the time he realized it, Soujirou was moving with physical strength and speed impossible of a minia. A category of terror that was difficult to resist, shaking the foundation of all the laws of nature.

IT IS IRRATIONAL—THE VISITOR'S VERY EXISTENCE...AS WELL AS ALL THE PHENOMENA THEY CAUSE.

Ozonezma's myriad arms readied new scalpels in succession. His body was formed entirely of the muscle fibers of champions, of nerves that had achieved illustrious status.

As a medic, he was a chimera capable of remodeling himself, thus forming only the greatest, carefully selected, materials. This was Ozonezma.

The arms sprouting from Ozonezma's body were visibly prepared to throw their scalpels. Soujirou responded with signs he would evade them.

As the beast threw his projectiles, his eight legs switched directions. He charged. To Ozonezma, it was ultra-close range. He reached it in a bound.

"...!"

Soujirou sent out a flash of his sword.

"TOO SLOW."

Ozonezma's acceleration, that seemed ready to knock down and trample over Soujirou, stopped still right as his snout was lightly cut. Inconceivable muscular strength and body control capable of halting the momentum of his colossal body.

"A BLUNDER UNBECOMING OF A SWORDSMAN. MENTAL DISCORD, PERHAPS?"

"Yo... What did you do?"

"VERY WELL, SOUJIROU THE WILLOW-SWORD. I WILL REVEAL MY SECRET—"

Together with a crack, he fired off silver lines of light. Direct fire from super-close range.

Sent flying by Soujirou's slash upward were forceps thrown in a spiral toward him.

"Ya know something... You—"

An initial movement, unlike all the throws Ozonezma had made up to that point, laughing with just a back-and-forth motion. A surprise attack that anyone who was on their guard against the previous simultaneous throws would be incapable of evading— was deflected by Soujirou. Even from this close range.

"Definitely gotta have a nasty personality."

"IF YOU FEEL VIRTUE IS NECESSARY IN A BATTLE TO

THE DEATH, THEN YOU CAN BE RESPONSIBLE FOR THAT YOURSELF."

Ozonezma was already shifting his movements for his next throws.

Soujirou lowered his sword slightly and ran to cut off the line of fire. He anticipated the trajectory of the destructive meteor. Right arm and liver. Left eye and chest. Throat. His right shin at super-high speed. Right palm, right elbow, right upper arm, and left flank.

"Yo...! Can't you! Do anything else! But throw stuff?!"

Each individual projectile had the force to kill instantly. On top of it, Ozonezma showed no signs of fatigue, opening up space where he had the advantage and pelting Soujirou nonstop with his weapons.

"WHAT'S WRONG, SOUJIROU?"

The tempest continued to rush at him. While it resembled the bombardment from a military siege, the power was on a completely different level from mere bullets or arrows. Soujirou held his own, constantly moving the tip of his sword with impossible speed, leaving behind not just a single line but a whole surface of slashes in the air.

"DON'T YOU WANT TO FIGHT IN SWORD RANGE?"

"Give it a rest!"

"*YOU COULD SLASH AT ME.* WITH YOUR PHYSICAL ABILITIES, YOU SHOULD BE ABLE TO BREAK THROUGH AN ONSLAUGHT LIKE THIS."

A majority of the audience watching the match couldn't know

just how abnormal it was. However, an extremely mysterious situation had developed.

Soujirou the Willow-Sword was backed against the wall of the garden theater and rotating into a defense stance.

The difference in range between his sword and the projectiles. The difference in build and physical ability. It was as if the visitor was giving in to ordinary logic.

"Gaaah… Dammit. Why's it always gotta be like this…?"

He took a deep breath and let it out.

The silver streaks of light passed by him. He was dodging them.

Kicking the wall behind him, Soujirou jumped up at an angle.

The arms, like gunfire, fixed their aim on Soujirou in midair. Scalpels. Second slash. Third slash. Soujirou raised his blade and deflected them. Though he was pressing the attack, Ozonezma's eight beast legs were free. While Soujirou was still in midair, he was able to open up space between them again. But…

"……!"

A blade was buried deep inside one of the eight. It wasn't Soujirou's.

"THE SCALPELS."

One after another, in the knee, at the base of the thigh, scalpels dug into flesh.

Soujirou flew into the air and enticed the continuing projectile attack. He had aimed to send the *repelled* scalpels back down over Ozonezma's head.

Even if he didn't hold it in his hand, the technical logic of swords themselves remained under his control. A blade master too aberrant for this world.

"Your life's…"

The instant the repelled scalpels had halted Ozonezma's movements Soujirou was right up inside the chimera's reach.

Within the projectile range. Stance ready to launch his sword from his sheath, bearing down on his neck.

"…mine no—"

A charge from short range grazed him. He was sent flying.

He should have been able to unleash his finishing slash.

During what was an unbelievably golden opportunity, Soujirou *didn't do anything.*

Soujirou ricocheted off the garden theater's ground and clumsily fell flat.

"*Koff, hngh…!*"

He got hit by a colossally terrifying attack. A charge he should have been able to dodge.

Yet more than that, he felt a threat that convinced him getting hit by the attack had been the best option.

Soujirou had dodged *something* he didn't really understand himself.

…A threat.

That ain't it. Something's not right. Even since I first missed my swing, something's been off.

As he tried to stand up, Soujirou looked at his own arm.

There was a scalpel stabbed in it. In an area that hadn't been hit by any of Ozonezma's attack.

What the—?

Soujirou was injured.

Who stabbed me?

Someone's hand was trying to sever Soujirou's artery. Whose?

It's me.

That someone's hand was Soujirou's own off hand.

"...What the—? What's going...? Hey. What's happening...?"

Something terrifying was there.

Out in front. Soujirou looked at what he had tried to dodge.

Without him realizing it, there was now only one arm stretching out from Ozonezma's back.

That singular arm slid back into the darkness of his body.

The numerous arms that grew inside Ozonezma's back were corpse white, modified, and reinforced with tendon and gold wire, the several varieties of muscle brilliantly joined together.

That one arm was the only exception.

Soujirou had only glimpsed it for a brief moment, but he thought it was an incredibly beautiful arm.

Soujirou the Willow-Sword felt it.

The terror.

Why was the master swordsman, capable of instant death, unable to cut off the head of his opponent with his very first slash?

Why did he wait for a chance to counterattack and switch to a defense stance so he could keep defending against his opponent's attacks?

How was it even possible that Soujirou the Willow-Sword could harm himself and be unable to make his move?

"...What the hell is that thing?"

Ozonezma the Capricious was a chimera whose entire body was constructed out of the best organic material.

It could be said that one arm was the strongest, and the most terrible, organic material. A trump card that rendered even the likes of Soujirou the Willow-Sword unable to fight, without even touching him.

He had a special privilege. One that none of the other hero candidates had.

"THE DEMON KING'S ARM."

The special privilege of the True Demon King.

◆

He no longer remembered how many years ago it had happened.

He did, however, remember the shadow of the collapsing transmission tower.

The scenes of the Beyond had remained in Soujirou's memory.

A tower burning up in flames and melting, on the other side of the piled building rubble. Thinking it was a very strange way for a tower to fall, Soujirou watched it crumble.

"Hey! God dammit; I told you: Quit going on ahead, Soujirou!"

A man in his forties was calling Soujirou's name. It was Tsu-kayoshi. Soujirou had finished cutting down all the infantry sol-diers a long time ago, yet Tsukayoshi, just walking along, came three minutes behind him.

This man was dressed in a casual kimono with no *hakama*, which looked like a joke smack-dab in the middle of the urban battle.

Tsukayoshi Yagyuu. He claimed to be the last true successor to the Yagyuu Shinkage-ryu school of swordsmanship, but was he really?

"It's 'cause your outfit's hard to walk around in, dumbass."

"Y-you little... Listen, you keep making fun of your master like that, and I'll cut you down before you can blink. A quick moon-shadow, and it's off with your bratty head."

"Master, my ass."

Bodies were strewn about the area, cut up in round slices, level IV body armor and all.

Soujirou was rolling a severed infantry soldier's arm with the tip of his foot. The soldier's assault rifle still gripped tight in their hand.

In the world of the Beyond, Soujirou's sword was undoubtedly peculiar.

"Who's ever heard of a master who's weaker than their appren-tice? When the hell are you even going to draw that sword, huh?"

"Don't you forget who I am... See, me, I'm beyond the stage where swinging my sword around like a little kid's enough for me.

Oneness, yeah, that's what this all is, didn't I say that? Becoming one with the universe and yourself, matching your breathing with your opponents, and they'll back off by themselves without firing a single shot. Basically, see, the peaceful path, free of fear's the real—"

"Didn't that guerilla attack earlier have you pissing yourself?"

"No, that was, uh, just another form of strategy, yeah..."

"Weren't you swinging your sword around like an idiot when you ran away, too?"

"......"

Fed up with the man, Soujirou returned his sword to its sheath.

Not a single drop of blood from the veins he severed could catch up to the speed of his lightning-fast strikes. And with this single sword alone, he had cut down far more lives than he could hope to remember.

He wondered how much time had gone by since he first met Tsukayoshi. Soujirou was accompanying him under a sense of duty, simply for being given his very first sword.

He tried to remember any memories of being beholden for some other reason, but there wasn't much of anything.

"Ain't another M1 gonna show up or what?"

"...Listen, tanks are only gonna show up when things really go south. This ain't like when the seventh atomic bomb dropped, okay? Next time they come, we're seriously all going to die."

"Nothin' but infantry and armored cars; it's boring."

"...Dammit, why the hell can you slash through tanks anyway...? You're not even human. There's no way."

As far as Soujirou was concerned, a tank frame was just begging to be slashed through, so what else was he supposed to do?

It was indeed true that Soujirou wasn't all-powerful, and somewhere out there in the world there was definitely *something* he couldn't slice through. That and tanks were much harder to cut through than other things. He wasn't going to deny that.

Nevertheless, there was still a large discrepancy between his senses of perception and those of other humans.

"Be weirder if I couldn't, right? They didn't spring outta the ground as fully formed tanks or anything."

No matter how encased in armor, as long as something was built by someone's hands, there had to be somewhere along the process they bent or melted down the armor. They couldn't shape it how they wanted if they didn't. On top of that, given that it was assembled together, there was no possible way to make it flawlessly without any gaps or warps. There wasn't any logical reason why someone wouldn't be able to destroy it. Soujirou was simply doing all this with his katana.

He was always making this case in response to Tsukayoshi's comments.

"Listen... Do you even get how they process metals...? No, guess you wouldn't, huh? Your generation has no idea at this point, do they? Hell, there aren't any schools to teach it anymore, either."

"Yup. School. Was it fun for you, Tsukayoshi? More fun than cutting down tanks?"

"...How the hell can I even compare the two? Let's talk about Yagyuu instead."

Tsukayoshi scratched his head. Whenever Soujirou would bring up these topics, Tsukayoshi would never fail to try to change the subject.

Claiming to be the Yagyuu Shinkage-ryu successor, now impossible to verify, he spouted dubious swordsmanship knowledge, dressing in a casual kimono, and wore a sword at his waist.

If anything, he seemed to loathe his life back when there was peace.

But instead of the talks of useless principles, Soujirou preferred the conversations about back then.

Just what sort of life did they live, without any war or soldiers coming in to bring them goods and resources?

What had the world been like before Shiki Aihara appeared? From the time he was born, it had been a mystery.

"...So really, you ain't a Yagyuu or anything like it, right?"

"Excuse me?! I-I'm the real deal, you know! You little... This is exactly what I'm talking about! You're just a corpse-eating *kasha* at this point. Don't be sorry when someone comes and chops you down."

"Oh, hey, that's a bomber, ain't it?"

"Eek?!"

He was an appallingly weak master.

He couldn't do anything, not only being unable to deflect bullets with his sword or thrust his blade into a moving armored car, but even simply enjoying battle itself was impossible for him. Grand only in his words and demeanor, he hadn't once done anything useful.

It was mysterious that regardless of just how weak he was, he still believed he could fight with his katana.

Surviving for less than two years from that day, Tsukayoshi Yagyuu met his inevitable death.

That might have been why Soujirou had arrived in this alternate world.

◆

"IT IS A CORPSE," Ozonezma declared. The unique voice of a chimera, like several different voices combined into one.

"NOTHING MORE THAN A MASS OF PROTEINS. IT HOLDS NO MEANING."

Soujirou was unable to properly swing his blade as he had moments prior. However, things were already different.

"Stop."

Soujirou mumbled. He was trying to stop his other hand from cutting open his own artery. Of his own volition. With his own body.

It was decidedly different. It wasn't the same as moments before, when he had been able to fight fearlessly.

Ozonezma knew. There wasn't the slightest bit of the True Demon King's past influence left over in the Demon King's arm.

It was just a simple dead body—and even when connecting it to his own body, Ozonezma had been able to grow accustomed to it after *nothing more* than several big months of nightmarish insanity where he killed himself over and over again.

It was now just a dead girl's arm, without any abnormalities at all.

All of it had just been the terror of when she had been alive. The current Ozonezma understood that, too.

...However. For those who laid eyes on this trump card of his for the first time?

"...*Haaah! Haaah...!*"

Viscous sweat endlessly trickled off Soujirou's entire body.

He had sliced through everything that could be cut down across the entire Beyond. That was why he understood all too well.

Right now he couldn't even be certain of the fingers gripping his sword.

Can I... Can I not...

He saw a young girl's arm.

That was the extent of it. His enemy remained the same; both of their skills and powers hadn't changed at all, either.

...cut this thing down anymore?

While it had only been a glancing blow, he had been hit with Ozonezma's body slam. Were there cracks in some of his bones?

He stared at the blood gushing out from his own left arm. The scalpel he extracted was on the ground. He had to use it to slit his throat—no, doing it with the sword in his hands would be faster.

He was compelled to do so. It was terrifying. Too terrifying, driving all of his thoughts into insanity.

It was something everyone in the land had avoided facing, incomprehensible and impossible to defeat.

"I-I'll, cut you, dead."

He felt the sensation of cutting through flesh. He was trying to slice through his own abdomen.

"Haah! Haaah!"

"EMOTIONAL PERSPIRATION. YOUR HANDS ARE SWEATING."

Ozonezma didn't attack. If anything, he was speaking slowly, as if to tease his opponent.

"I SUGGEST YOU FOCUS ON WHETHER YOU CAN GRIP YOUR SWORD PROPERLY. CONTROL YOUR BREATHING AND CONCENTRATE ON YOUR HANDS. THIS IS A LIFE-OR-DEATH AFFAIR. YOU CAN'T LET IT DROP... NO MATTER WHAT."

The earth burst open like an explosion from a powder keg. Ozonezma charged forward again.

"Aaaaaaaaaaah!"

Soujirou shouted, readied his sword, and clearly saw Ozonezma charging for him from the front.

He could hold up his sword. The enchanted hollow sword, absolutely indestructible. He'd cut him down before he got to him.

He could kill him. Within Soujirou's dulled senses of perception, he knew it was possible.

He could cut him. Three more paces left. Terror. Cut him down. Two steps left.

Terror. He couldn't kill him.

He was scared.

"......!"

A cloud of dust kicked up. Soujirou slid forward, passing Ozonezma by in a low, froglike stance.

A meager space around his feet that was only made a mere millisecond right before he reached him. He had crept under his belly, where the Demon King Army couldn't physically reach him.

From this position...

"Hii...yah!"

A streaking flash of steel. Ozonezma's torso, above Soujirou's head, was severed.

As it separated, a mumble came out from the front end of Ozonezma's torso.

"SLOW."

Soujirou had understood it himself. His technique was too slow. Far too slow. The terror was ruining his swordsmanship. He hadn't been able to cut him at all. This was Ozonezma's self-amputation.

"YOU'RE SLOW, SOUJIROU."

Ozonezma's front half alone moved independently.

Soujirou turned around and kept Ozonezma's front half in his sights. Ozonezma had opened out his arms in a wheel, before there was the flash of countless scalpels. Simultaneous projectiles.

Defend—no. He had a gut feeling. What he needed to be wary of was the chimera's back half behind him.

"Hwoooooooh?!"

Soujirou shouted. He kicked the arm that closed in from a blind spot at his feet and jumped.

There was another one.

The chimera's headless *back half* was writhing eerily, with many arms and back legs growing out of it. It was executing the simple order from its nerve ganglion to grab and capture its enemy.

"I TOLD YOU."

The intelligent front half was already lying in wait at the end point of Soujirou's dodge.

Another charge. Accelerating while simultaneously using his innumerable arms. Soujirou raised his katana.

"NO MATTER WHAT, YOU CAN'T LET YOURSELF DROP IT."

The blade of his sword was caught in Ozonezma's teeth. Before the fierce impact could break off his wrists, Soujirou let go of his hands. The charge grazed him, digging into the flesh on his side.

The master swordsman had his sword stolen from his hands.

The attack wasn't over. As he passed by Soujirou, the enormous mass of arms assailed him. They weren't throwing their scalpels, but slashing at him with them.

Within the extremely condensed moment in time, Soujirou looked at the blades rushing toward him.

Each individual arm. Their range of movement. Their speed.

The silver blades stabbed, one after another. He would be dissected. Together in the flurry, three arms flew into the air. Three arms.

They were the arms of the dead.

"Muto...dori!"

Soujirou finished his slash with the scalpel he stole from one of the arms.

He had managed to do so without brushing up against the Demon King's arm, sent out simultaneously.

"...St...op...it!"

With the momentum of the scalpel follow-through, Soujirou tried to pierce his own windpipe.

He was scared.

It was definitely just a young girl's arm.

However, he was convinced that if it truly did touch him, there would be no going back.

The horrible second had come and gone. The second of terror that would have taken the life of a normal person many, many, many times over.

Ozonezma's front half passed by his recently severed back half and, with a single leap, finished reattaching his body together. Without leaving even a seam behind.

They both readjusted their stances—

But far faster than that, the air shuddered with another roar. Soujirou wasn't even given a single second to breathe.

The chimera's grotesque body was capable of immediately switching to the offensive from any situation.

"Gwah!"

The Otherworld master swordsman turned away and repelled seven scalpels that flew his way. That much was clear.

Even at the limits of tremendous exhaustion, it had been possible for Soujirou the Willow-Sword.

However, as for his mental, not physical, exhaustion?

"…JUST NOW. DID YOU THINK MY ATTACK WAS OVER?"

Soujirou let out a muffled voice.

"*Gngh… G-gwaugh!*"

They were agonizing groans.

The True Demon King's terror. Driven far past its limits under such pressure, his mental state…

"RIGHT AFTER THE TERROR'S GONE—"

Soujirou lost his right leg. It hadn't been due to a direct hit from one of the scalpels.

Simultaneous with the slash that had defended against Ozonezma's whirlwind of projectiles.

"THAT INSTANT IS WHAT CREATES THE BIGGEST HOLE IN ONE'S MENTAL STATE."

Soujirou had sliced off his own right thigh.

He did something he shouldn't have.

No matter how powerful one may have been, they would lose control over their own body, their own will, absolutely everything.

That was terror.

The loss of his right leg.

"*Geh-heh… Heh.*"

Everything was over.

In Soujirou's hand was a single scalpel blade.

Blood gushed from his severed leg. It would likely be impossible for him to perfectly unleash his techniques as a swordsman forever.

Nevertheless, Soujirou sneered.

…Right then, he saw it all.

He could see how things would unfold from now. *There was nothing more he could do.* He understood that.

From here, Ozonezma would charge and extend the Demon King's arm.

An absolutely perfect opportunity—his enemy stepping within his range of their own accord—would come.

Soujirou couldn't slash at him.

The arm would arrive, and from then on... Even Soujirou's intuition couldn't tell him. That was the end.

Soujirou had no possibilities available to him.

But he figured it out.

"I saw it. I saw your life."

◆

A night in the Beyond. He wasn't sure if the memory was before the steel tower or after.

Tsukayoshi had his katana drawn and looked to be training in some old-school swordsmanship style. It was the same katana he had emphasized that he didn't draw lightly, but Soujirou didn't intend on pointing out that fact now.

Tsukayoshi's practices weren't a consistent habit to begin with, little more than self-gratifying training that he only ever did on a whim when he was bored.

To Soujirou, it didn't seem like anything but a magnificently useless waste of effort, but it was too much of a bother to get up and go point this out to him, so he kept his mouth shut.

"Soujirouuu. How do you do that thing where you block gunshots? The thing from yesterday."

Tsukayoshi shouted from outside the tent. Soujirou wanted to pretend he was asleep. Why did this man insist on asking about things totally beyond him?

"I ain't blocking them at all. If I blocked them, the blade'd break, stupid."

"Hey, don't call your master stupid."

Soujirou truly thought it was a giant nuisance, but if he didn't answer, then Tsukayoshi would probably come talk to him about something. He was old enough to be Soujirou's father, yet he acted like a child.

Even as he rubbed his sleepy eyes, he continued with his half-hearted explanation.

"...All right, so. With that, I ain't hitting the bullet tip, see? I sorta smack the side of the bullet with the flat of my katana, thrusting it into its flight trajectory, see... That way, see, with the sideways force, the blade acts as a springboard. Match the bullet's rotation, give a hard pull, and it'll deviate on its own away from ya."

"Hold up... Yeah, no way, nu-uh. Run that back again. We're talking about rifle shots here, right? What you're talking about's a whole lot stranger than just blocking them, you know that?"

"And that's why I'm saying it's impossible for you. You're way too weak."

Soujirou could manage about ten rifle shots coming at him at once. He had never attempted any more than that before, but considering their shot grouping at midrange, it was possible for him to maneuver effectively against their firearms.

However, that level of technique wasn't enough to survive in this world. When flamethrowers or grenades showed up, he would need a completely different method of dealing with them.

Tsukayoshi Yagyuu was too weak to fully deal with everything using his katana.

"If it's swords or knives flying at ya, though, there's probably a better way of deflecting them. Vertical rotation's part of it, so ya can't smack their central point from the side."

"Vertical? So if a bullet's rotates sideways, a knife's vertical?"

"...I mean, a knife's sideways, too, I guess. Which one's vertical then?"

Soujirou wouldn't be defeated by a blade.

Even in another world, this should have been an unchanging fact.

◆

Soujirou the Willow-Sword had cut himself.

As Ozonezma had told him, the taste of relief brought about the nightmare. An unhinged madness ordinarily unthinkable to see from Soujirou.

It had all been under the control of the singular arm, Ozonezma's trump card.

The Demon King's arm, its mere existence terrifying, was the wickedest deterrent in the land, operated with intelligence and strategy by the butchering beast, Ozonezma.

The situation was beyond the realm of merely *keeping his guard up against* the trump card's counterattacks when he was in sword range. From the moment Soujirou had established this distance, from the opening moment of the fight, he was checkmated.

As long as he fought Ozonezma from close range, he would be unable to resist the ultimate terror.

Don't got time to stop the bleeding...... Hell—

Soujirou thought with a foggy mind. He was experiencing hemorrhagic shock.

His blood pressure dropped, his motor functions were deteriorating, and he was wearier than he had been at any point during this third match.

Minia were awfully fragile, descending into this state just from losing their left leg.

...I can't even move at this point, huh.

Still, he had to move.

Brandishing the scalpel in his hands straight out in front of him, he showed he had no intentions of surrender.

Even if doing so was entirely meaningless, it was necessary.

"BRILLIANT COURAGE."

Ozonezma didn't speak long before galloping again.

As he ran, the chimera's head split. A delicate white arm lithely stretched out of it. The Demon King's arm.

Soujirou could see Ozonezma's life as he pressed in.

It wasn't the life of the myriad organisms that composed the chimera's entire body.

If there was indeed a life within him that, with one clean cut, could end all of them at once.

Don't lower your sword.

He was frightened. Terrified.

Just maybe, this was how his master has been feeling.

While Soujirou had enjoyed himself in that inferno of battle, had Yuno felt the same?

Why the hell are you thinkin' about all this stupid stuff now?

All he had to do was stab his blade and slice through the beast's life.

That would easily give Soujirou the victory.

With certain death awaiting him, there wouldn't have been any reason for him not to do so.

Five more paces left. Four.

Ozonezma's trajectory and speed should be exactly as Soujirou's intuition had forewarned.

He just needed to cut him. That would end it all. It was terrifying.

...Don't ya dare lower it, dammit!

His arm tried to relax, counter to his will. What was it trying to slice?

It was horrifying.

The Demon King's arm. It hadn't even touched Soujirou.

Like a tidal wave swallowing a metropolis, levees and all, the terror unilaterally destroyed all in its progress.

Soujirou wasn't able to move.

With an unreliable single short blade, he was facing off against this terror.

It hadn't arrived yet. Even as Ozonezma charged with such terrific speed, rushing through such a short distance.

Not yet. Not yet. He had space to think.

He just had to cut him down. It was too late.

Even if he started his slash now, at this range, it wouldn't make it in time.

The terror. The horror. It was frightening. Dreadful.

Time was slowing down, just like one's consciousness moments before death.

In such a state of awareness, he simply *understood that there was nothing he could do.*

The terror, bordering on madness, was prolonged several times over, gnawing at his mind...

One more step. Then.

Don't lower...

He, at last, realized he didn't feel the scalpel in his hand.

Beads of sweat bubbled to his forehead. He absolutely couldn't let it slip.

White.

A white hand was right in front of his eyes.

Ozonezma was extending the Demon King's arm.

The master swordsman from another world lost to the terror.

"UNGH!"

Ozonezma was the one to let out a groan.

The Demon King's white finger bent seconds before it could touch Soujirou and missed its mark.

"......! WHAT...DID YOU...?!"

Ozonezma looked at the abnormality in the Demon King's arm.

A scalpel had pierced through its elbow.

Ozonezma should have been able to crush the stopped Soujirou in his jaw, but he was in an abnormal state of confusion. Right in front of Soujirou, he halted then groaned.

"MY ARM."

He couldn't afford to stop, either.

Next, a different scalpel, with a spin, twisted off the flesh of the Demon King's arm.

The beautiful arm was shredded mercilessly, separating from Ozonezma's body and flying into the air.

Though he shouldn't have had any ability to feel pain, Ozonezma shouted.

"HNGAH, GAAAAAAUGH!"

It was the second scalpel—no.

The crunching and mashing sounds continued. In a position shifted slightly from the two scalpels, there were five sticking up from the ground. More than seven scalpels had rained down from the sky... In other words—

"AH, AAAAUGH... MY ARMS... IMPOSSIBLE... Y-YOU... REPELLED THEM...?! IN THAT MOMENT!"

The transcendent swordsman was capable of precisely repelling the blades thrown his way.

Which was precisely why Ozonezma was confident he had outdone Soujirou's ability to counter him with a surprise projectile attack, immediately after he had instilled him with terror. Then he chose to charge him as a method of finishing him off. Instead of projectiles that risked deflection, he had tried to eradicate Soujirou through direct contact with the Demon King's arm.

"YOU LAUNCHED...THE BLADES UP INTO THE AIR...?!"

Soujirou had no possibilities available to him. Soujirou understood that.

In which case, what if Soujirou's own will didn't intervene at all then?

A direct attack from the Demon King's arm, the best guarantee of bringing instant death to the frozen Soujirou.

Confident, with his superpowered combat intuition, that the chimera would choose this method of attack...

What if there was an unearthly technique that made it possible to sync up the free fall of Ozonezma's scalpels previously deflected high up into the area, to that certain future?

1181, the fourth year of Jisho.

There was an anecdote of a warrior-monk who fought bravely under Minamoto no Yorimasa, named Gochi-in no Tajima.

Facing off against three hundred Heike horsemen, the imperial forces battled them on a bridge with fifty horsemen of their own. Gochi-in no Tajima, with just his *naginata*, cut down all the Heike's hailstorm of arrows and was given the nickname of Tajima the arrow-cutter.

* * *

It was not simply slicing something that could not be cut, nor was it slashing at speeds faster than his opponent could.

Even within a nightmare horrible enough to sever his own right leg, Soujirou the Willow-Sword was able to do it.

He looked at Ozonezma. Even with the Demon King's arm lobbed off, he had physical abilities that far outstripped Soujirou. An extremely crafty intelligence. A myriad of lives, more than he could kill.

Nevertheless, right now, he could cut him down.

Soujirou grabbed the scalpel that had severed the Demon King's arm in midair. The scalpel was a new weapon.

It was plenty.

"*An accidental death's* all I got," Soujirou bellowed. "An accidental death, to kill that thing for good!"

"GWA-GWAAAAAAAH!"

Ozonezma spread out his numerous arms.

Within distance to touch each other, the two beasts clashed swords.

Nevertheless, even should he lose a leg, even should death be right before his eyes.

For the master swordsman from another world, in the realm of bladed combat…

The small blade pierced Ozonezma's heart as it passed by, severed a ganglion, before splitting open another heart. Lethal. Lethal. Lethal. All of them were fatal spots in Ozonezma's body.

...That was as far as he got. The thin scalpel blade shattered in Soujirou's hands.

"Huh?"

Any other living creature would have died by his hand.

Ozonezma's fur blocked him, armor itself. His muscle, as dense as steel, blocked him. More than anything, however, the terror and fatigue he had accumulated throughout the fight had hindered Soujirou's technique.

Just as Soujirou possessed unrealistic swordcraft, Ozonezma had an unrealistically strong body. That was all.

The deviant swordsman from another world had, for the first time, broken a blade.

Ozonezma's forelegs were closing in.

"......"

There was wet slapping sound.

"HNG, AUUUGH... GLLRG... NGH, AUUUNG."

Ozonezma moaned vaguely.

Once again, his claws came down. Next, bones shattered, and it lost its original form.

Still unable to stand, Soujirou watched the chimera's movements.

Ozonezma didn't even glance at the minia gazing at him, and he continued to focus solely on destruction. On destroying the severed arm of the Demon King.

"HAAH, HAAH... HN-GAUUGH... NGH... HRN..."

His groaning voice trembled. He was scared.

The unrivaled beast was haggard, as if the recoil from the entire fight had hit him at once.

Once again, his claws tore at the carcass.

It was nothing more than a corpse. Transformed into a meaningless lump of flesh.

"Looks like I was right. That was the one, eh. That one was your life, huh."

The strongest chimera of all, an amalgam of physical abilities capable of surpassing the inscrutable visitor, tactics based on his many fights against other champions, and a trump card that brought instant death to all the living creatures of the world.

Ozonezma the Capricious was truly a fearsome monster.

But there was something even more terrifying.

"*Ain't no way you ain't scared* of something like that. No way you got used to it. You probably get it by now, but... Me, you, we've both been freaked out by that thing."

"*NGH, GAAAAH... I... I...*"

"...... You... You were going to die by suicide, weren't ya? You were fighting to try to get yourself killed."

The terror of the True Demon King... Dying by suicide and killing those you're close to.

Unable to remove it, even escape was impossible.

It drove you mad all without you even realizing it.

"N-NO... I WILL KILL THE FAKE HEROES! IT IS MY ONLY WAY TO ATONE! THAT IS MY OWN WILL... IT SHOULD

HAVE BEEN...! I—I...! THE DEMON KING'S ARM! SUCH BLAPSHEMY...! *HNG... AUGH...* THE TRUE HERO... IT'S NOT TRUE; THAT'S NOT IT...! I'M SORRY...OLUKT...!"

"I don't give a crap about whatever you got goin' on... Ya hear?"

Soujirou thrust out the broken scalpel in front of him.

This time, it wasn't a bluff from sensing he would give in to terror.

Even if this battle continued, Soujirou likely had no chance of winning. Understanding that it would end as he simply waited to bleed to death, he remained with his weapon raised, because despite everything, he would fight.

To fight, and fight even more.

Especially after learning what terror felt like.

"I just wanna have fun, see?"

"I... I..."

Ozonezma, trembling at the fear he had finally become conscious of, barely managed to squeeze out his words.

"...SURRENDER."

"......"

"HAAAH, HAAAH... VICTORY IS...YOURS...SOUJIROU!"

No matter who it may have been, it was impossible to resist that one singular fear.

Having lived through the age of the Demon King, he should have known it better than anyone else.

Soujirou looked at the pool of blood that had formed on the ground.

"......"

While Ozonezma had thrown away victory in the match—perhaps, in fact, all while throwing away his own life, long, long before any match at all—the young girl's arm, destroyed at last, radiated terror no longer.

◆

After the match, Ozonezma was taken into a huge carriage, specifically for beastfolk.

Riding along in the freight car, Yuca spoke to him with concern.

"Are you really all right? You're wounds look terrible, but do you think you'll last until the doc gets here?"

"...I AM A DOCTOR. PHYSICAL WOUNDS...DO NOT PRESENT ANY CONCERN..."

"Really, now. I just thought I'd listen to any final words you had if it looked like it was too late for you."

While there certainly was no small number of those in the audience who had been exposed to the terror of the Demon King's arm in the match earlier, it was interpreted as fear from seeing the grotesque chimera itself.

Now that the arm was gone from this world, Yuca would also never know the truth Ozonezma held.

"...YUCA."

"Hmm?"

"...WAS I...TRYING TO DIE?"

He definitely hadn't ever been aware of it himself.

Ozonezma had been convinced he was acting in accord with his own sense of justice.

He couldn't abide a false hero. He had believed that now he was the only one in the land who knew of that battle he had witnessed. Believed that the ones left behind had an obligation to do so.

However. What had he expected to happen when, after using the True Demon King's power to kill all the self-proclaimed heroes and advance through the tournament, he revealed the truth before the people?

Ozonezma's thoughts never once extended to the tragedy that would occur afterward.

He had been rushing headlong into destruction. He himself had chosen death—and no one else.

Suicide.

Had he not understood any of it until that moment?

"Hrmm. I don't really get it, but you fought hard, Ozonezma. Hell, I've never seen such an incredible fight before. Look, if you had had any chance of winning, however slim, then it definitely wasn't suicide, right?"

"...IN WHICH CASE...WAS CHALLENGING THE TRUE DEMON KING SUICIDE?"

"Conversation's heading in a real strange direction." Yuca smiled awkwardly.

The general who was chosen by happenstance, simply as an easily manipulated pawn. To Ozonezma, as long as he had a sponsor in name only, that was enough. Nevertheless, it was good fortune that this man had been the one to do so.

Ozonezma spoke as his profound exhaustion brought him to the verge of sleep.

"SOUJIROU...SAID IT WAS AN ACCIDENTAL DEATH. THAT IT WAS THE ONLY WAY TO DEFEAT THAT TERROR..."

"I mean, that's about the only way I can see that Demon King kicking the bucket. Sure, whoever makes it through the Sixways Exhibition'll be declared hero in name, but...for the citizens who've never stepped on a battlefield themselves, they'll never truly understand that terror."

"...THAT IS NOT IT."

Ozonezma knew the full circumstances behind the Demon King's demise.

It may have been true that, among those involved in the Sixways Exhibition, only he knew.

"THE TRUE HERO DOES EXIST."

The True Demon King had definitely been defeated right before his eyes.

"...IT IS TRUE... THERE IS SOMEONE IN THIS LAND... WHO DEFEATED THE DEMON KING... I WANTED...TO TELL..."

Right before his eyes closed, he got the feeling he had seen them among the crowds passing by.

It was assuredly an illusion of the past, seen through the gaps of his fading consciousness.

The Final Party.

Olukt the Drifting Compass Needle was there. Ozonezma the Capricious was there... As well as—

"...SETERA..."

This was one of the outcomes of those who once challenged the True Demon King.

The True Demon King died, and at the end of a long journey, their physical carcass had now been fully destroyed.

However, a little longer of a wait would be necessary before learning what happened over the course of such events.

And this was, after all, a story about determining a single hero.

Match Three. Winner, Soujirou the Willow-Sword.

Shortly before the beginning of the third match, in the complex corridors underneath the castle garden theater's spectator seats.

With Soujirou the Willow-Sword's match imminent, Yuno had been ordered to remain there on standby. Her assignment was trivial, simply recording the climate conditions before the match—and the state of the audience.

...I don't have the time to be doing this.

Ever since the moment she laid eyes on the name Kiyazuna the Axle, vengeance was the only thing on her mind.

I couldn't let things stand the way they were back then. I decided to get my revenge on Soujirou...

It was why Yuno had brought Soujirou this far. The only place under the horizon where death awaited, where someone more powerful than Soujirou the Willow-Sword could appear—the Six-ways Exhibition. If Soujirou was defeated in this match, she'd be able to carry out revenge on yet another. She could believe that there were still things she was capable of...

...because she needed to kill Kiyazuna the Axle no matter what.

Has the match already started?

With her papers sitting on her lap, long finished with her recording work, she had nothing do as she waited for Haade's return.

Yuno looked at the clock.

That's strange. He should have been back by now...

Unable to continue waiting, she stopped one of the patrol soldiers and asked them.

"Excuse me. I'm the Twenty-Seventh General's secretarial assistant, Yuno. Do you know where General Haade is?"

"Oh, Lord Haade?"

At Yuno's question, the soldier answered with a similarly pondering look.

"He appeared to have departed the garden theater before the start of the match. Maybe he had some urgent business to handle."

"What...?"

Did something happen? Where had he gone? Neither of those were the issue.

She had believed that, for Haade, Soujirou's match today had his entire political career riding on it. That he was risking everything on this battle, just like Soujirou was. Had she been mistaken?

In spite of all that, he was so ready and able to leave the match for some urgent business or another.

Much more than that, a young girl like Yuno was, compared to this urgent business of his, someone he didn't give any second thought to leaving behind.

"Th-then, am I...?"

She clenched down on her recordings, nearly crushing them. Meaningless and destructive actions flashed through her mind.

She had known. Even if she thought she had acted together with the deviant visitor Soujirou and gotten Haade to acknowledge her existence, ultimately Yuno was still an *inconsequential* presence.

"Am I still on standby?"

"Like I have any idea—Lord Haade's the only one who could tell you that. Did you want to go up and watch the match?"

"That's not...that's not what I mean...!"

She understood that talking back to this soldier wasn't going to accomplish anything.

When it was all said and done, Yuno was still totally ignorant, whether it came to General Haade or this Sixways Exhibition.

"...Pardon me!"

With a violent bow, Yuno left her position.

It's not enough. Not enough. Not at all.

She had left her recordings behind. She was sure to be reprimanded by Haade for her actions, but to Yuno, that was the least of her concerns. Everything was—

Not enough. For my vengeance, everything, it's still—it's not enough!

With her thoughts in chaos, she continued walking.

Before she knew it, she had reached the deepest recesses of the complex corridor network.

The one area she was in was dark, with the lights on the walls extinguished.

"...Oh."

She stopped. A young girl, close to Yuno's age, appeared from out of the door in front of her.

She wasn't one of the garden theater staff.

"……"

The girl silently stood there, her golden eyes looking at Yuno.

...*Unbelievable.*

The young girl was so beautiful that she felt her chest tighten before her thoughts could go anywhere else.

"Um, are you—?"

Yuno shut her mouth as soon as she opened it. From a crack in the open door, she saw a soldier sitting up against the wall. They were unconscious...or perhaps dead.

Right. There should have been one of Haade's guards...in the corridor I just turned down.

Yet Yuno had been able to trespass this far just by wandering around aimlessly. Where were the guards? Haade had left the scene, and in that time, a foreign presence was infiltrating the area.

In which case, she was an enemy. Haade and Soujirou's enemy.

The gears in Yuno's head weren't slow. She was able to reach the conclusion within moments of their encounter.

"You're..."

"……"

If she was indeed an intruder, what was Yuno supposed to do to this girl?

The girl didn't appear to wield any weapons. Her hair black as night, her skin terribly white.

"Hey. Someone's over there. Who're you? Give me your name!"

Suddenly, a voice from behind Yuno interrupted her thoughts.

A different patrolling soldier had approached them.

I can do...whatever I want.

Yuno the Distant Talon was still not enough in every way—but now...

"I'm Yuno the Distant Talon! My apologies... She's my, um...a friend. She's my friend. The spectator seats were all full, so we were coming to inquire if it was possible to watch the match from the players' passageway. Do you know where General Haade is?"

"Distant Talon. General Haade's secretary? Outsiders aren't allowed to be inside the premises. General Haade is gone, as well! Where is the guard who was positioned here? Does that friend of yours have some identification?

...It's no use.

Yuno closed her eyes. Why did she want to try saving this girl?

Simply by covering for this girl just now, she could be tried under suspicion of being a spy.

"Please wait, sir."

The young girl spoke. She took the soldier's hand and showed him a small seal.

"I have my authorization right here."

It was meaningless. A seal that could be stolen after she infiltrated the area wouldn't serve as a pass through the security. The seal was handed over when one passed into the area—and returned only when one left. That was exactly why guards like them were patrolling the area.

This girl's trespassing, after all. Why am I doing something so stupid...?

"...I've confirmed your authorization's valid."

"Forgive me for the trouble. Let us be off."

Her delicate hand pulled Yuno's own.

Even after they had started walking off, Yuno hadn't the slightest idea about what had just happened.

Why? There's no way that excuse should have worked. It didn't seem like this girl did anything, either. Why...why is she holding my hand?

Even while they went up the stairs to the surface, they continued to hold each other's hands.

If she was being honest, Yuno was in such a state of confusion that she didn't have the presence of mind to let go.

"J-just...," Yuno asked, her voice cracking, "...who...are you?"

With but a few words, she made the soldier submit to her. Was she some sort of preposterously important person, like the Queen herself, and Yuno simple didn't know it? When the girl stared back at her, Yuno's heart pounded for reasons she didn't understand.

"Um."

The young girl averted her eyes apologetically and spoke with a thin voice.

"Thank you kindly. You tried your best to help me out."

"...It's fine. You're...an enemy of General Haade and Soujirou, aren't you?"

"......"

"If it's difficult to answer that, then forget it. I'm Yuno the Distant Talon. You are?"

"...My apologies. I owe you a debt a gratitude, yet I failed to first introduce myself. I am Shadow Laden. Linore the Shadow Laden."

A young girl whose blouse and skin were almost transparently white, yet with an evanescence, like she would melt into the darkness.

Her face was once again close to Yuno's. Her beauty was enough to make even another woman like Yuno sigh at the sight.

Perhaps, she could even more than Lucelles.

What—?

She turned her head aside and expelled the thought from her mind.

What am I thinking...?! There isn't anyone out there prettier than Lucelles. To me, it was she, and she alone... That should be a given, so why...?!

She couldn't let it be otherwise. That was why this was different.

"Why did you offer me your help?"

"If...if you really are their enemy...I want to defeat Soujirou, too."

"...Miss Yuno, you're Mr. Haade's secretary, correct?"

"Do you think that's weird? But really... This isn't what the Sixways Exhibition was supposed to be like for me. I need to get revenge. Before I start anything else. Faster... Before I settle into my current position and find peace. I need something...any sort of lead, any sort of first step. A starting point for my vengeance."

"Revenge..."

Yuno as she was couldn't even land a single blow in a battle between the powerful. It was possible she held some sort of expectation in her heart for Linore, who was taking action despite being a girl close to her in age.

On the other hand, it also seemed like that was less than half the reason why. Perhaps, ever since seeing Kiyazuna the Axle's name, she had been in a constant state of desperation.

Until the two of them exited the garden theater, it appeared they wouldn't be questioned by any of the soldiers.

However, the third match was starting. Yuno wouldn't be able to see the results.

A bit of hesitation and guilt came to her—until.

"Oh."

Next to her, Linore unexpectedly fell to her knees.

Yuno instinctively supported her with her shoulder. There was a pleasant smell, like a pale flower.

"Whoa there."

"…P-please…do not…worry yourself."

"Are you okay? Was that little bit of running enough to tire you out?"

"…I do not…handle sunlight well. I am quite ashamed to say…"

Linore weakly smiled. Her loveliness was enough to send a shudder down one's spine.

"We're outside at this point, so no need to rush anywhere. Let's rest in that street stall over there."

"…We've only just met, Miss Yuno. I cannot ask you to continue showing me such kindness…"

"I'm not really doing this out of goodwill or anything anyway."

She needed to ask about her circumstances. That much was for certain, at the very least.

The two ordered the same drink and sat down opposite each other out in front of the street stall.

"…Well then, are you ready to tell me? Why exactly were you back there?"

"Um."

Linore began, looking timid and nervous.

"Miss Yuno, why are you going out of your way to be so kind to me? Well, um… I… I could be planning on doing you harm. Much more, there's no guarantee that I will be useful to you at all."

"…Good question! Maybe because you're pretty?" Yuno hotly replied. She had to be upset, she thought.

She was absolutely biased. Without a doubt, this girl was a dangerous and suspicious individual. Supposing if the person she had encountered was a much shadier older person, or a terrifying ogre, would she had have come to their aid and been as interested in them as she was now?

"Um."

Linore cast her eyelashes down.

It was devious. It was her fault for being pretty. Despite being someone other than Lucelles.

"…Pretty…?"

"What, is that weird? Answer me, what were you doing back there?"

"…Y-yes, um, well. If it's not any trouble to you, Miss Yuno, I'd like to repay you for your kindness."

The young girl placed a document on the table.

She had likely knocked out the soldier in order to steal this document.

However, the document used a system of writing with a low adoption rate. Nothing a mere soldier would write.

"This is a document written in welkin language. With written communication, subordinates won't be able to decipher it, and even if the person who wrote it isn't there to exchange the message directly, it's possible to confirm the original writer by their handwriting. This is likely the way Mr. Haade, or someone in a similar high position, uses soldiers to relay vital information."

"From the 'cerebrum' to the 'brain stem.' Depending on results, it may be necessary to adjust 'terminus excision' period. Negotiations underway with 'insect.'"

"...! You can decipher what it says?"

"I mean…yeah. I *was* a Nagan scholar at some point, after all. Luckily, I just happen to know welkin language. The words actually written on the page, though… It's all military code top to bottom, so I still don't really understand it anyway."

"In that case…"

Linore brought her face in close and peered down at the document with Yuno.

Long eyelashes. Golden eyes. Why was such a beautiful girl sitting beside her?

"…can you read it for me?! I will decode what it means!"

"S-sure… Got it. Um, can you give me a bit more space…?"

"Oh, m-my apologies."

"It's just a bit harder to um, read… That's all, okay? Sorry…"

At the end of what must have been the hundredth of these awkward exchanges, Yuno read out the contents of the document, while opposite her, Linore interpreted what everything actually meant.

As they conversed, Yuno was hypnotized by Linore's attractive features.

Insight far more precise than any of the Nagan scholars Yuno knew. Just who was she?

"In other words, this is…"

"Indeed. Miss Yuno… If by any chance you intend on exposing Mr. Haade's secrets. This plan is far too dangerous for you to get involved in. The meticulous planning of whoever thought this up…… It's unbelievable."

Linore grabbed both of Yuno's hands. Yuno searched for the words, but she couldn't find any.

"……"

Striking back, getting a blow in—this posed a far bigger problem.

"…You have my thanks, Miss Yuno. I promise, no matter what, I will repay this favor in kind."

Vengeance against the powerful who laid waste to her homeland.

The Sixways Exhibition, set to decide the absolute strongest existence in the land.

A mere inconsequential young girl like Yuno wouldn't have possessed a single means of facing off against such magnitudes.

However, an accidental encounter had gifted Yuno the possibilities to do so.

The first was a plan unknown to Twenty-Seventh General Haade.

The other was a single shura, making schemes behind the scenes of the Sixways Exhibition. Her true name was Linaris the Obsidian.

Nearly three big months had passed since Kia had begun studying at Iznock Royal High School.

She still experienced strange looks from people, as a girl born and hailing from the untrodden and secluded land of mystery, Eta Sylvan Province.

Iznock Royal High School had originally been constructed for the children of the royal family and nobility. Even in Aureatia, gradually opening the doors of education to the masses, a majority of the students who studied there were from respectable minia families.

The elf Kia attended the elementary section of the school, for children a full ten years younger than herself, and even then her grades were abysmal.

Adding to things, her crabby, arrogant disposition hadn't changed in the slightest.

However.

"Kia! Let's eat lunch together."

"It was amazing how you solved that problem all by yourself, Kia."

It was the hour of their noontime break. Yet again today, a number of the female students gathered around Kia's desk.

The rude elf girl from the frontier had been so warmly welcomed into this new world that it was mysterious. At the very least, on the surface, the girls were all friendly.

Kia's eyes stopped on one of the girls within the group.

"......"

Velvet hair glistening silver white. Large eyes filled with enigmatic depth.

Kia was indifferent to minia standards of beauty, but even then, she could tell her presence was completely and radically different from the other girls.

Her name was Sephite.

The Queen ruling over the minian races. The very person who lived in the beautiful palace she witnessed on her first day in Aureatia.

"Hey," Kia said with irritation. For the past several days, she had constantly been in a sour mood.

"Aren't you making things hard for the Queen? I mean, she certainly doesn't seem like she wants to talk with me."

Sephite was not the type of Queen she had envisioned.

Sephite was far wiser than Kia, despite being three years younger, and excelled the most out of everyone in her class, but to Kia, her gloominess betrayed all of Kia's ideals of a Queen, her facial expressions were lacking, and she was little more than a brooding young girl.

There was always a shadow of despair inside Sephite's large eyes.

Kia couldn't help thinking that a country that had a girl like her sitting at the top was destined for ruin.

Kia had the expectation that if she was the master of the dreamlike scenery she saw on her first day in Aureatia, then surely she must have been so brilliant and blessed the people with so much happiness.

"That's not true, right, Queen Sephite?"

"Queen Sephite wouldn't discriminate against her elven schoolmate."

"Kia. Her Majesty is quiet, but she truly wished to be your friend."

The way Sephite's cronies insisted on pulling Kia into their circle of friends also felt a bit eerie and weird to Kia.

She might have felt better if she was isolated from the girls or bullied, instead. Since no matter how many enemies she may have faced, Kia was confident that, if it came to blows, she was invincible.

Sephite spoke in a dull monotone.

"...Sorry, Kia. If it pleases you, would you like to join us for lunch?"

"...Sure. But Her Majesty shouldn't be using words like *sorry*."

Kia also sometimes thought that maybe her home tutor, Elea, was giving unneeded attention to the situation behind the scenes.

She had only recently learned for the first time that Elea stood in a high-ranking position as one of Aureatia's Twenty-Nine Officials.

Kia didn't know any specific details about what sort of work she did. If it was true, though, she wondered why Elea was content with the sort of life she was living.

If she's such an important figure, she needs to have more fun in her life. Isn't that what being a bigwig's all about?

Trying to keep some distance from the crowd surrounding Sephite, Kia headed toward the same lunchroom as they did. She tried not to think about the house she would go home to. It would only sour her mood even further.

There were still all sorts of fun things waiting within the streets of Aureatia. New friends who weren't one of the Queen's cronies, too. On the way home that day, she was going to visit the traveling carnival. She heard that in there was a zmeu's street show in the western district, too. Moreover, even the food provided at the school, though not very big, was much, much higher quality than what they had in the Eta Sylvan Province.

As she ate the well-simmered bean dish, she sized up Sephite sitting opposite her.

"Is it always like this for the Queen?"

"…What ever do you mean?"

Sephite stopped picking at her food. Her white neck titled slightly, and she looked at Kia.

Kia had her elbows up on the table and was gripping her fork in a tight balled fist.

"Don't you ever get tired of allllways having your back up straight? With the way you eat, you won't get dirty at all, even without draping that napkin over your lap, right?"

"I suppose so."

Sephite fluttered her long eyelashes, her expression remaining largely unchanged.

"I do get tired. Very much so."

"...I mean, if Your Majesty's fine with it, then whatever, I guess."

Kia wanted to be free. Nothing had changed from when she was living in the Eta Sylvan Province.

She didn't have any desire to join in the conversations of the girls around her. Kia's plate soon emptied.

Doesn't she ever get sick of it? She can't even ask for seconds in front of the other kids.

"Oh my. Kia, you're done eating already?"

"You're so fast."

"Not really. You sure you're not all just slow?"

Kia pulled out one of the small berries she had in her pocket and plopped it into her mouth.

The Queen's cronies all looked at her dubiously.

"Um... Kia, what is that? Food?"

"What? It's the yellow willowseed from the courtyard. They aren't growing it there so we can eat it?"

"Yellow willowseed... Wait, is it all right for us to eat that?"

"Beats me...?"

In Eta, it had been totally normal. For all these girls, it wasn't.

Ignoring the other girls exchanging glances with one another, she purposefully placed one of the berries in front of Sephite.

"...I'm sure Her Majesty's never eaten one before, right?"

"......"

Sephite stared hard at Kia without saying a word.

Dark pupils. As if scenes of ruin were forever burned into the deepest recesses of her eyes.

The Queen took the pale-pink berry and tilted her head slightly with a smile.

"Thank you. I'll try it."

Kia sighed. She briskly departed the lunchroom.

...Hmph, please, you're not really smiling at all.

◆

In a district far removed from the school in the hills was the mansion where Kia lived. It was the house of her home tutor, Elea, a pretty structure that was ten times bigger than her house back in her homeland.

Just as Kia returned home, a man was opening the door to exit. A wide-mouthed man with his hair combed back behind him.

"Well now, if it ain't little Kia."

"...Ugh."

Kia glared at the man with all the contempt she could muster. Jivlart the Ash Border, leader of a guild called Sun's Conifer. However, for Kia, he was nothing more than a tyrant staying at Elea's house and acting like he owned the place.

Kia knew that Jivlart was violent with Elea almost every day. He would drink booze in Elea's house and enjoyed extorting money daily, foisting unreasonable demands on her and abusing her.

"Hurry up and leave."

"Ha-ha, what do you think I'm doing?"

While Kia was in class, this man was always here in Elea's house. No matter what sort of fun she was having, or what food they provided for her in the lunchroom, Kia's mood would always sour whenever she remembered.

"I know that you hate me. I gotta be gentle with the kiddies, though, right?"

...*Coward.*

If Kia was there to witness it all, she would absolutely knock him senseless.

But whenever Kia would return home from school, she'd always arrive after it was all over.

"Don't ever come here again."

"Well now, that all depends on that woman's attitude, doesn't it? You better warn her, too, Kia. If she wants me to win the tourney, she's gotta come up with *terms better than Rosclay's! Ha-ha-ha.*"

"Get lost! I'll make you disappear for good; I mean it!"

"Yeah, yeah, I got it, I got it."

Jivlart took his leave, a nasty smirk still on his face.

He liked children—there was no way.

Even now, Kia wished she had truly let the command "*disappear*" cross her lips.

"...I'm home, Elea."

Inside the house, Elea was cleaning up the messy living room, illuminated only by candles.

"You're home late today, Kia."

"……"

Kia frowned, seeing the brand-new bruise at the base of Elea's throat.

They were Jivlart's doing. Both the disordered room and Elea's wounds.

Ever since he was selected to be a hero candidate, Jivlart's tyranny only continued to get more dreadful.

"Was school fun?"

"…Sort of, I guess."

"If there's anything you're worried about, you can always talk to me about it, okay?"

"Not really… There's nothing to be worried about at all. I can do anything."

Kia averted her eyes. She wasn't worried about anything—concerning herself.

But Elea's lifestyle, compared to the version of her tutor she had long been familiar with, was an unimaginably desolate one.

Elea had no family or friends. Besides Kia, the only people she involved herself with were the hero candidate Jivlart or his scoundrel underlings.

There was broken glass and ceramic fragments scattered all over the floor.

It was possible that it wasn't just Jivlart who had come to the house that day.

Not just him, but those Sun's Conifer losers, too.

…*Gives me the creeps.*

Just what was so fun for them?

"Elea. I don't want to cook today. Let's go eat out. I'll finish cleaning this up later."

"*Tee-hee-hee.* Will you now? You can't use Word Arts to clean up, you know."

"That much is fine, isn't it? I mean, I did it all the time back in Eta."

For the time being, she wanted to go outside. She didn't want to have to look at the aftermath of Jivlart's violence.

Why was he able to get violent with people weaker than himself?

Did people like Jivlart, when faced with the same awful treatment from someone stronger than themselves—someone like Kia—really think they'd accept the injustice without any complaints?

Who cares about "evidence" or whatever. Next time I see him, I'm bringing him to tears.

As of now, Kia had followed Elea's orders forbidding her from using Word Arts. On a previous day when something similar happened, she had healed the cut on Elea's arm, but Elea herself got unbelievably angry at her for it.

Nevertheless, when the time came when her patience truly wore out, she wasn't going to sit there silently and do nothing.

"Elea, did you know? At a place nearby the school, they serve Lithia-style seafood."

Kia continued as she pretended not to pay any heed to Elea's wound.

"It might be a bit expensive, but… Not even the Queen can eat fresh fish every night!"

"Honestly... You're talking like it's all but decided that we're going out tonight."

"Let's go, Elea."

Kia changed her shoes. The shoes were small and adorable, totally different from what she wore when living in Eta.

Elea had bought them for her.

"We're not making any detours to the theater now."

"I know, I know!"

The two exited into the street.

The Aureatia streets were often noisy and filled with people. Kia always felt strange, wondering if, with so many people, they could actually all fit inside the buildings when it came time to sleep.

"...Hey, Elea. Can I bring some friends over to the house? I'm sure that would make things a lot more fun."

"Fun?"

"I mean, you're lonely, right?"

Elea looked surprised for some reason. She turned her eyes away from Kia and talked about something else.

"...Are you bringing friends from school, then? You're pretty friendly with the Queen, right?"

"Nope. They're kids I met at the plaza by the reservoir. The six of us had a tree-climbing competition, and I was the fastest. I didn't even use any Word Arts."

"They're probably military children. There's a family dormitory for Aureatia's army near there."

"...Military."

When she thought about it, the friend she played with that day had bragged about their father, too.

That child's father was supposedly a magnificent soldier and favorably viewed by the Twenty-Seventh General, Haade, who gallantly fought against the Old Kingdoms' loyalists and freed the conquered Toghie City.

"You learned in class, right? Aureatia was originally a final bastion built to protect the minian races from the True Demon King, so...there are a lot of citizens who have some involvement with the military. The owner of that bakery you're always going to has two children in the military themselves, and even at school there are some who serve as civilian employees for the army."

"Really...? I didn't know. So that's how it was."

The Aureatia army. Up until just recently, she might've brushed off the topic as something unrelated to her.

"Do you have friends in the military, too, Elea?"

"...Does it look like I would?"

The sun was beginning to sink into the horizon, and night was covering the zenith above her.

Elea was at a gap in the gas lamps lining the street, and it seemed like even her smile had a shadow cast over it.

"I just thought, well, since you're one of the Twenty-Nine Officials, that maybe...you'd have an acquaintance or two in the military."

"Is there something bothering you?"

"Hmm..."

Really, it wasn't that important. Since it was nothing more than a rumor.

"The Aureatia army... They're not going to attack Eta or anything, are they?"

"......"

It was simply a rumor she had heard at school. If it turned out to be true, then it likely never would have reached the ears of a child like Kia in the first place.

"It was just something the teachers were talking about together, and it's just... They said that Aureatia needed to gather the resources to maintain the country from somewhere else. That since the Demon King didn't ravage Eta, it sort of checked all the boxes."

If Kia had questioned the instructors talking about it then and there, she could've figured out for sure how true the story was. But if that was indeed the case, what then was Kia supposed to do?

"...Truthfully, that topic has come up before in the assembly."

"......!"

"But I lived in Eta and actually saw everyone living out there... So I absolutely don't want to let that happen. Though, my position definitely doesn't give me any say in the way the army does things. But that's how I feel, regardless of Aureatia's policy."

"But...if it does happen, is there even anything that can be done about it?"

"Yes. If I win in the Sixways Exhibition, I'll be able to save everything."

"The winner'll get any wish of theirs granted!"

They were words Kia heard on her first day in Aureatia.

Right. Jivlart's her hero candidate.

That was why Elea put up with all the violence that came her way and propped up a hero candidate in the Sixways Exhibition. To save Kia's homeland.

"But...even then, I don't want someone like *him* coming to the rescue. Besides, whatever happens to my homeland... It doesn't really concern you anyway, right?"

"Of course it does."

Elea patted Kia's head.

When she had been Kia's home tutor in Eta, they were always at each other's throats, quarreling like sisters even, yet ever since they had arrived in Aureatia, Elea had grown totally gentle and kind. Thanks to the loneliness of her current life, she had become feeble and dispirited.

"After all, Kia, you're my student."

"...U-um, s-supposing!"

A carriage was passing through the main road.

It was an army carriage. In Aureatia, the soldiers had become part of daily life and could be found wherever Kia looked.

"Just supposing Eta really does get attacked, I... I'll stand up to the whole Aureatia army myself and beat them. I'll protect Eta."

"Yes. You might be able to do that."

"Right? After all, I just have to say, 'Blow them away,' and no matter however many thousands come at once, I'll send them flying in a gust of wind. I could even make them blow up with fire— or make the earth swallow them up."

This wasn't merely a child's braggadocio.

Kia was capable of turning even these grand boasts into reality.

Whether it was changing the weather with just a word or making an endless military force disappear in the blink of an eye. Such omnipotent power had been gifted to her from birth.

"......"

"*Hee-hee.* I know that. You wouldn't do anything like that, Kia."

"...Don't say that like you know for sure."

Each individual soldier in the Aureatia army might have had a family of their own. Like Kia's friend or the bakery owner. There may have been more interconnected relationships within the army than she could possibly imagine.

Fighting the Aureatia army is absurd.

Kia had *spent too much time* in Aureatia to declare that whatever happened to them didn't concern her.

Moreover, after she exterminated a military force to defend Eta, would all the people in her homeland still show her the same love that they had before? To a murderer of so many people?

"You're a kind child, Kia. That's so much more valuable than being invincible. That is what I believe."

"......"

She looked at the sky. The two moons should've been out in the sky, but a thick cloud was blocking them from her view.

Kia was close to whispering "*Clear up.*" Just like she had casually whispered on a whim one day back in her homeland.

I am invincible.

With just a word, she could turn any and every intention of hers into reality.

Even when it came to the very shoes on her feet, she could make as many of them as she wanted.

There wasn't an enemy in the land who could threaten Kia. No matter what threat confronted her, Kia's Word Arts could eliminate it.

...Still. Is there any "enemy" out there who would truly make it necessary to go that far?

Time continued on toward the Sixways Exhibition.

To what would be a fight between Rosclay the Absolute and Jivlart the Ash Border.

◆

Later that night.

Elea had an apartment separate from the estate where she lived with Kia, under a different name. An apartment for receiving radzio reports from her liaison.

"It seems Kia's caught wind of the Eta offensive perfectly. I was able to confirm things on my end, as well."

<That is good news. I thought about filling her in myself directly, but thankfully she's a much more perceptive kid than I thought.>

On the other end of the radzio was an instructor at Iznock Royal High School. His public persona, at the very least.

"That concludes your assignment. There'll be no more communication until the end of the Sixways Exhibition, and you're to stay undercover. Understood?"

<Understood. Well then, Minister Elea. Until we meet again.>

Elea cut the line.

There were several of Elea's undercover agents who had infiltrated Iznock Royal High School, as it was one of the few places where it was possible to make direct contact with Queen Sephite. They would carry out orders through exchanges of conversation and every day commodities, and she would pay them when they achieved results—that was the extent of the relationship. Her agents would never inquire about their given orders. One group of them acted as Sephite's cronies and attempted to make Kia come into contact with the Queen.

A few days ago, the matchups for the tournament had been decided. Everything was proceeding exactly according to her schemes.

Elea had deliberately ensured information on the Eta invasion was leaked to Kia. Even if it was a slight seed of doubt at first, once planted, it would be difficult for a young child like Kia to uproot the danger from her mind.

"...Useful resources aren't only things visible to the naked eye."

Leader of Aureatia's intelligence division—Seventeenth Minister, Elea the Red Tag.

Even if an assault on Eta did indeed become a reality, she herself would be the one responsible for it. Depending on how Kia acted going forward, she could either send her squads into action or stop them.

Furthermore, the information itself that Eta would be attacked could be used as a resource of its own.

With it, she would narrow the available courses for Kia to protect her homeland until only one remained.

She rubbed the bruise on the back of her neck. A mark from where Jivlart had hit her.

However, Elea had known full well that she would be subjected to this sort of violence.

It's okay. I'm not the same as my mother.

Jivlart the Ash Border, like Kia, was a necessary piece in her plot. Those who lacked character were easier to manipulate, and when it came time to discard him, she could do so without any regrets.

"Terms' better than Rosclay's" had been his words.

Jivlart should already be wrapped up in Rosclay's camp's schemes. Rosclay's moves during the Sixways Exhibition are far more discreet and thorough than I had expected.

Jivlart was set to receive a far greater reward than victory by safely losing the first-round match. He likely intended on adding weight to his own accomplishments by claiming he crossed swords with the world's strongest knight.

It would then tie to Sun's Conifer's reputation as well, and with his relationship with Rosclay's camp, he could gain a stabler foundation for his activities in Aureatia going forward.

Clever. I didn't want him thinking things through that far.

To Elea, Jivlart's role was to be the bait ensuring a first-round fight against Rosclay. There may have been someone even stupider than Jivlart—someone actually convinced that they stood a chance at victory over Rosclay the Absolute—but within the limited amount of time, Elea's individual efforts hadn't been able to find someone more suitable than Jivlart, possessing both fighting skills and notoriety.

Up to the moment the Sixways Exhibition started, she had no one on her side. She needed to fight all on her own.

If he has already joined up with Rosclay, I'll need to change course to get rid of Jivlart before the match. I need to win the first match... Rosclay is the one I need to ensure loses, no matter what...

Even if it was merely an ostensible, forward-facing position, the Twenty-Nine Officials were originally only supporting one single hero candidate. The Second General, Rosclay the Absolute.

By crushing Rosclay first and foremost, she could bring the largest faction over to her side. That was Elea's goal.

There's too great of a difference in the total power we can devote to intrigue, and at best, I'll only be able to win one battle. But in the first round, if I defeat Rosclay at the start, I'll then be able to hijack *Rosclay's camp's plans for the second round and beyond. Who possesses the power most suited to become the hero. Who we should secure victory for. I just need to place Kia into that position, instead of Rosclay.*

Starting from the second round, when the sixteen candidates will be trimmed down to eight, the Queen will be spectating the matches in person. With but a word from the Queen, it would be easy to overrule which hero candidate Aureatia should be promoting.

It was for that purpose that she was also scheming to bring the Queen and Kia closer together.

Overwhelming power was already within Elea's grasp. All that was left was to obtain someone to support her.

I have the World Word on my side. A trump card that no one would even imagine exists.

She rubbed the bruise on the back of her neck again.

Kia had worried about this wound of hers and tried to take her out. A tiny child like her.

...It would be okay. Kia had plenty of faith in Elea and certainly wouldn't suspect a thing. She would never dream that she was being wrapped up in a conspiracy.

"I mean, you're lonely, right?"

It's fine.

Elea closed her eyes, as if to hide from the blinking lights in the starry night sky outside her window.

Elea had always been on her own. She didn't need to trust anyone.

Before her Sixways Exhibition match started, she would arrange all these schemes by herself.

First, Rosclay.

At the end of the darkness, there was sure to be light waiting.

A park at dusk. Rique the Misfortune was repeating the same explanation he had already gone over many, many times.

"Your enemy's not always going to stand pretty in front of you. You gotta pay attention to the edges of your field of view, too."

"Okay!"

Tu the Magic listened to his explanations. In her case, her replies were the only thing she got right.

"Until you get used to it, it's not the arms or their sights you have to really grasp but the whole silhouette entirely. Whenever someone moves, the shape of their outline is guaranteed to change, so with experience, you'll be able to pick up on what sort of movements they're looking to make next."

"Okay!"

"…You really getting this? Don't look at me, but look over toward that tree."

"Okaaay!"

A crack split through the air. Rique's arrow was faster than a bullet propelled with gunpowder.

Tu bent herself backward at the waist and dodged.

"I did it!"

"No, no, no! That's not it! I knew it; you didn't get it at all! You dodged that by looking first before you moved, didn't you?! That's not good enough!"

"What d'you mean they're different?! I'm dodging, aren't I?!"

"I'm telling you: Dodging by predicting the attack and dodging after *seeing* the attack are totally different. You gotta be able to evade attacks that can't be evaded. If you don't have extra time during your dodge, it'll be harder to shift to the next move. That's why it's important to dodge predictively for both offense and defense."

"But even if I get hit, I'll be totally fine."

Rique the Misfortune brought his hand down on his forehead and looked at the sky.

"Tu. I'm training you on how to dodge here, okay...?"

It was safe to say that the half day spent training had produced almost no results whatsoever.

Of course, Rique perfectly understood the source of her confidence. Tu the Magic was invincible. He doubted that there existed any method that was capable of bringing her down.

Nevertheless—Rosclay the Absolute. Alus the Star Runner. Lucnoca the Winter. Considering the numerous champions of the land, he couldn't say with absolute certainty that there was no way to defeat her.

...In which case, he thought, he needed to at least instill within her the skills of the average warrior.

If Tu was able to evade Rique's arrows with her physical abilities alone, the simple addition of some commonplace techniques would make her more than worthy enough to truly call herself invincible.

"...Tu. Do you want to win?"

"Yeah."

"Then, you gotta think. All the others are thinking with everything they've got. They're watching, moving, and fighting with all their strength. Because their lives are on the line. You're the only one not thinking things through."

"...I know. But do you think I can do that...? Does being born dumb mean you can't become a hero? I really don't think...I can ever become like you or Krafnir..."

"It's nothing but practice. Save the self-reflection for tomorrow. Day's already getting dark."

"...I can still keep going."

"Well, I can't."

Rique smiled dryly. Coaching someone with Tu's endless stamina was serving to coach Rique himself more than anything.

Tu the Magic was a perfectly flawless being, while simultaneously being an unpolished gem full of potential. In which case, just how much further was Tu's strength going to grow?

...Might not change at all.

Those had been his thoughts as of late. A keen emotion, in ways resigned, yet different, in some senses.

Her unchanging mental and physical state may have been a strength that only Tu possessed.

"Okay, then, see you tomorrow, Rique."

"Yeah. Tell Miss Flinsuda I said hi."

◆

Night. An ebony carriage slipped through an enormous metal gate. Amid the Aureatia hillside, where all the luxury residences were gathered, this estate stood out as particularly large.

The lady stepping down from the carriage, too, had the frame of a stage performer.

Her dress, neatly calculated down to each ring on her finger, if anything made her obese body seem even more graceful. Her name was Flinsuda the Portent, Aureatia's Seventh Minister.

She served as the head of Aureatia's medical welfare division, while also being one of Aureatia's prominent wealthy individuals, sparing no expense for herself or her surroundings.

"Oh my, oh my!"

Looking around the garden, Flinsuda let out a voice of surprise.

The flower bed that wrapped around the estate, filled with rows of every color of flowers, had been mercilessly destroyed. A hedge was cut down halfway, and there were the vestiges of a slash tearing through the hedge next to it as well.

Lying lonely on the ground below was a twisted and broken hatchet, clearly the deadly weapon responsible for the sight.

"Tu, dear!"

Flinsuda then discovered the young girl sitting in front of the entryway, hanging her head, her arms wrapped around her knees. She looked terribly depressed; her chestnut hair braid withered.

"Flinsuda... Sorry... I—I just...wanted to help...and when I heard that the gardener took the day off..."

"Well, now! You took care of the garden for me?"

"I watch the gardener every day...and I did the exact same thing...but..."

"Tu, dear... I don't know how many more times I can say it, but honestly..."

Her large body swept up Tu in her arms, and she roughly patted her head.

"I swear! You are *such* a wonderful child, dear! *Hoh-hoh-hoh-hoh-hoh!* There, there, now! Trying to help on your own like this, why, that's a fantastic attitude to have, dear! That alone is plenty! You don't need to worry yourself with cleaning all this; hurry up and hop into the bath, now. I'll have them prepare dinner, too. My sweet, sweet Tu!"

"O-okay...! Yeah!"

For the Sixways Exhibition, Flinsuda had planned to sponsor the greatest living Word Arts user, Krafnir the Hatch of Truth, as her hero candidate. Tu was an unconcerned party who happened to be given Krafnir's spot in the tournament—and nothing more.

However, the Seventh Minister loved her profitable hero candidate just as much as she loved her own riches.

Therefore, Tu was receiving the lavish support originally meant for Krafnir.

For instance, ever since Tu arrived at the estate, her exclusive apothecary stood in the kitchen. Her bath was also separate from the one the rest of the residents of the house used, the extension built onto the estate following her arrival. It was fair to say the young girl, her race still a mystery, was being treated just like anyone of minian race or better.

Flinsuda really is a nice person.

Following Flinsuda's directions, Tu was headed toward the bath.

Maybe it's because she has so much money.

Untying the knot on her clothes in the dressing room, she then took off her skirt and underwear, exposing her developed naked body. In the first few days, she had forgotten to even close the door behind her, but now she managed to take a bath by following the exact order she was taught to use.

Shutting the three-layered door like usual, Tu looked at the first bathtub.

"Today's tub is light blue..."

A temperature slightly colder than the outside night air caressed Tu's well-proportioned form. However, the feelings of hot and cold never tormented her and, in truth, would never injure her, either.

Her bare white feet descended the steps, and her legs left ripples behind as they sank into the water. Flinsuda was always telling her to make sure she soaked up to her shoulders.

After a short while, a voice came from outside the bathroom.

"Tu dear, have you already gotten in?"

"Yeah. What's in today's bath?"

"Hydrogen cyanide!"

The slightly blue-tinted liquid was a cyanide extracted from sinstralwort roots.

Soaked amid the deadly poison, the vapor compound alone was capable of easily killing beasts and insects, but Tu the Magic's skin was completely unharmed and maintained its youthful beauty, the liquid dripping right off her.

"Even hydrogen cyanide doesn't do a thing, why, Tu dear, you are incredible! Absolutely wonderful! Don't worry now, I'll be sure the whole assembly knows that you really are such a nice, strong girl!"

"*Hee-hee-hee*... You think...? I didn't really do anything; I was just born being fine with this stuff..."

Tu grew bashful and sank into the bath. She blew bubbles on the surface of the lethal liquid.

...The bath she had added to the estate was, to Flinsuda, nothing more than an experiment room to measure the limits of her new hero candidate's abilities. The chef and apothecary she hired for Tu both similarly experimented with the limits of Tu the Magic's durability day in and day out.

Boiling water. Liquid mercury. Various types of toxic substances. Flinsuda recorded her resistance to every possible type of attack, taking note of the mysterious hero candidate's objective strength and continuously updating the information.

Her goal was singular. She loved her profitable hero candidate just as much as she loved her own riches.

"Once you're finished, I have a new soup for you! I ordered it all the way from Caidehe!"

"Sure! But I'm gonna spend a bit more time here in the bath."

Tu the Magic nonchalantly got up from the deadly bathwater and headed to the second bathtub, separated by a door. This was a normal bath, for rinsing away all the toxic substances.

Even if she could feel the presence of extreme temperatures or stimuli, Tu wouldn't feel the intense pain that should accompany it. That sensation was blocked.

Nevertheless, she always liked the second bathtub over the first.

"*Hee-hee-hee...* It's so warm."

She sank her body into the pure bathwater. Resting her cheek on the edge of the tub, she closed her eyes in bliss.

Aureatia was a wonderful city. There wasn't any of the darkness or terror that ran rampant in the Land of the End. It was brimming with fun, warm, and delicious things. More than that, though, it was filled with lots of people. Flinsuda was here, along with Rique and Krafnir. She even made friends with the almshouse children.

...And finally, eventually, the girl she had met on that day, Queen Sephite.

"I love baths."

The mysterious and unknown Demon King's Bastard. She had the ability to receive good fortune.

Whatever circumstances she may have found herself in, she believed in a good world.

The fourth match, where Rosclay the Absolute would fight. The bracket of matchups for the Sixways Exhibition was, of course, something he had arranged himself.

Two small months before the bracket was finalized.

A meeting room in one of Aureatia's many civic assembly halls. While the facility was widely used among the citizens as well, there were few who would have imagined that there would be an important meeting that would sway government resolutions in one of its rooms.

That day, there were seven gathered in the meeting room. The primary attendant being Rosclay the Absolute.

He methodically cleared the interior of the room, placed a brand-new candle in the candlestick, and welcomed the attendants as they joined.

"Whoops. Looks like I'm the one holding things up."

The name of the mild and gentle older man was Nophtok the Crepuscule Bell, Aureatia's Eleventh Minister.

Tasked with oversight of the Order, he was also Kuze the Passing Disaster's sponsor in the Sixways Exhibition.

"Indeed, Eleventh Minister. We can get started immediately, but should we give you a short break first?"

"No, no... Don't mind me. I'm the one who's late. The excuse for my tardiness is that, hmm, I was giving bread to a child on the street, and well... No, never mind. Please, begin, Second General."

Nophtok scratched his head, looking uncomfortable, before sitting down in the empty seat.

"Well then, let me get straight to it."

An elderly man with a monocle spoke first.

A first-level instructor in the Craft Arts major, at Iznock Royal High School, Ownopellal the Bone Watcher.

In Rosclay's battles, he was in charge of Craft Arts support, generating straight swords for him.

"We're about at the point where we need to settle on a bracket. We can't postpone things much longer."

"The biggest problem is that bastard Dant sponsoring Zigita Zogi the Thousandth."

A snaggletoothed man with a wiry frame—Aureatia's Ninth General, Yaniegiz the Chisel.

The general who had been in charge of the northern front army during the Old Kingdoms' loyalists' suppression of Toghie City, along with Dant the Heath Furrow.

"He doesn't show any signs of going along with our scheme. Best to consider him completely part of the Free City of Okafu now. At the very least, he should be placed in a separate group, away from Rosclay... Either that or we could get rid of him before the match?"

"No dice. Dant's one of Her Majesty's favorites."

A tan-skinned man with dark-colored glasses. Aureatia's Twenty-Eighth Minister, Antel the Alignment.

In Rosclay's battles, he was tasked with providing Power Arts support that manipulated the trajectory of his sword.

"Looking at it a different way, Dant is keeping Okafu's forces in check. The moment he took them in, we lost our path to all-out war, as well. How then, will we dissolve Okafu under conditions that're beneficial for us and incorporate them into Aureatia? That'll be the direction going forward."

"…When all is said and done, we need to avoid the possibility of going up against any sponsors who'll give us trouble…"

A bald man, looking stern and grim—Ekirehjy the Blood Fountain, the royal family's governmental aide.

In Rosclay's battles, he was tasked with providing Life Arts support that enhanced the knight himself.

"For those with the most threatening sponsors like Mestelexil the Box of Desperate Knowledge or Mele the Horizon's Roar, let's place them away from Rosclay's side of the bracket. If we do that, then there won't be much interference in the first four matches of the bracket. We can let them have at all their schemes among each other, on their own side of the bracket."

"A different side of the bracket… If we're now talking about whether to distribute candidates into the final four matches…"

A man wearing thin glasses, with a sharp gleam in his eyes— Jel the Swift Ink.

A civil bureaucrat who first planned this Sixways Exhibition, wishing to reform Aureatia.

"Should the Order's recommended pick be placed on this side of the bracket or not. I'd like to decide on this today as it will affect the first round of the tournament."

"Hmmm, yes… Well, this is just my opinion, of course…"

Nophtok began. He was expected to fulfill his role in gathering information.

Therefore, he had already sent assassins against Kuze the Passing Disaster, working to verify the cleaner's fighting capabilities.

"I don't think the Second General should meet up against Kuze."

Much like Hidow the Clamp had done the same for Alus the Star Runner.

Nophtok the Crepuscle Bell, too, from the very start, was a sponsor *trying to defeat* his own candidate.

"My investigation of the past battles involving Kuze the Passing Disaster is, well…finished for the most part. If I was to sum it up in a word, then I'd say it was eerie. There's no cause behind the deaths that occur around him…"

"Wouldn't it be better to observe what he does in a fight rather than looking at past examples? Kuze isn't especially skilled himself, right?"

"Yes, yes. It's already been done."

Nophtok laid out several photos on the table.

All the photos showed the corpses of the assassins Nophtok had sent. The results of their autopsies, without exception, showed stab wounds from a short sword. One in the shoulder. One in the stomach. One in the leg.

"…As you can see. Well…save for the stomach wound, none of these are fatal spots on the body."

"And you're saying despite that…this single attack killed them all?"

"I'll say it again, if you'll allow me to offer up my own judgment… Kuze's power is exceedingly uncanny. I don't know if it's some causality beyond what the results here show, but…even without Kuze touching them himself, his foes die in a way I can only describe as spontaneous. He is likely the opponent the Second General should try the most to avoid in the first round… Therefore, I'm here to report that he isn't an opponent you can go up against for your first battle."

Kuze the Passing Disaster.

The Order's candidate had been regarded as the most suitable opponent for Rosclay to face in the first round.

Even as the reformation faction, including Rosclay, changed the status quo of Aureatia and showed the people the Second General conquering the Order's paladin, in the early stages, it would strongly impress on the citizens the need for a new social welfare apparatus and increase the likelihood that their systematic reforms went smoothly.

Nevertheless, at the same time, Rosclay could not afford to lose. On top of that, he was nothing but a normal minia, possessing no special abilities of his own. No matter how slim the chances may have been, as long as a match carried a possibility of an "accidental death," they would do everything in their power to avoid that danger.

Rosclay meditated, his noble visage never faltering, before thanking Nophtok.

"...I understand. Thank you, Minister Nophtok. Still, this is useful information. Let's use Kuze the Passing Disaster for a different purpose, then."

"I see... What purpose would that be?"

"We'll test Tu the Magic."

Rosclay signaled Jel with a look across the table, who in turn produced a thick bundle of documents.

This volume amounted to five days of records. It was clear that the person who recorded all this information had the luxury to employ a secretary with the knowledge necessary to leave behind such an enormous amount of written records.

"These are the experiment records that Minister Flinsuda has handed over as preliminary material. A very detailed record, including a study of the abilities Tu possesses, along with estimations regarding her actual combat abilities. A level of precision very much expected of Minister Flinsuda."

"So basically, she's using all of that to pitch Tu as fighting power for our cause, eh?"

Yaniegiz glanced at the documents. Though one of the Twenty-Nine Officials, he was unable to read.

"I mean, sure, why not. Easier to know how much you can trust someone if money's their only motivation."

"No... That may be a hasty conclusion, Yaniegiz."

Rosclay interrupted.

"I believe it is, in fact, because she always acts for the sake of profit that we need to take painstaking precaution and investigate her thoroughly, more than others who don't. Since there's a chance *she's already being bought off by someone else*. Although Minister Flinsuda can prove to be a powerful collaborator, I don't want to readily bring her over to our side. I see her as someone we wouldn't have to worry about if we make her exit in the early stages."

"Really now? But as far as I can see looking at the photographic records here, Tu the Magic is *actually* invincible. *Hee-hee*, I heard she didn't die even after getting showered in molten steel. Not someone who'll be easily killed..."

"That's right. That's precisely why we'll use Kuze the Passing Disaster."

Tu the Magic, believed to invulnerable to any and all forms of attack.

In which case, what about the Kuze the Passing Disaster's own ability, which could instantly kill the opposition with methods of unknown causality?

If they set up their match on the bracket, they could turn the two candidates killing each other into an inevitability.

Rosclay spoke.

"We'll send Tu and Kuze to the later bracket. A different group from mine, and we'll have these two fight each other in as early a match as possible. If Tu the Magic survives the match, then we'll be able to see that her fighting strength is indeed as advertised. In that scenario, then will be the time that we use whatever means necessary to thoroughly bribe Flinsuda or Tu the Magic herself to our side. If we have Tu the Magic acting outside the matches as a guerilla fighter, then we can control the entire Sixways Exhibition itself."

"In which case, what will happen if Kuze the Passing Disaster wins?" Antel asked.

Rosclay continued.

"As long as there's no urgency, we'll have him continue through the rounds naturally and deal with various risk factors for us. His status as a cleaner who brings instant death also means that he's guaranteed to eliminate his opponent, even when thrown against menaces like Kiyazuna the Axle and Lucnoca the Winter."

"There may be a situation where we'll need to urgently deal with Kuze. For example, in the event that it's evident Kuze stands against Aureatia."

"…Should that time come, then it'll be the Eleventh Minister's time to act."

"Yes, hmm."

Eleventh Minister Nophtok gave a flat, noncommittal response.

"*If it's just about dealing with him*, hmm. While Kuze may indeed be invincible, his weakness is clear as day…"

Rosclay nodded slightly. As long as they worked out a way to ultimately get Kuze the Passing Disaster out of the way, they could actually use him to proceed with the matches, depending on how they drew up the bracket. This was yet another special privilege afforded to the tournament organizers.

It was not only the one hiring them who could make use of an assassin.

"Based on that, we're faced with a different problem."

Securing victory in the first round—for Rosclay, it was the most significant problem of all.

He examined the possibilities of a second candidate he should face in his first fight.

This candidate was no exception to the others, posing some number of problems himself.

"What should we do about Jivlart the Ash Border?"

Jivlart the Ash Border—the head of the guild, Sun's Conifer, which rose up from its sham vigilante activities in Yataga Coal City. Amid the chaos of the True Demon King's era, they continued to add to their résumé without regard to the jobs they took. Then their power was recognized, and Jivlart finally achieved his debut in Aureatia as a hero candidate.

Although now their main functions were charity work and guarding the busiest sections of town, their behavior was that of a violent gang, intrinsically lacking the discipline of a proper mercenary guild.

In name recognition alone, within Aureatia, he compared favorably with any of the other Sixways Exhibition candidates. However, as for his actual abilities, he certainly didn't hold a candle to the strongest-ranked monstrosities like Alus the Star Runner, Lucnoca the Winter, and Mele the Horizon's Roar, and even when compared to those in the distinctly lower ranks of individual strength such as Rosclay the Absolute, Zeljirga the Abyss Web, and Zigita Zogi the Thousandth, he was lacking.

As Rosclay's opponent in his first round, he was the most favorable candidate of them all.

…Therefore, the apprehensions all those gathered in the meeting had about him weren't necessarily in regard to the man himself.

They were fears regarding the sponsor who stood behind him.

"…The Seventh Minister. Elea the Red Tag."

Antel muttered to himself, arms crossed.

"Problem's about whether she's worth trusting. She's a conspirator who'd give the Twenty-Third Minister or the Twenty-Seventh General a run for their money. I'd like to place her far away on the bracket, if possible. Our advantage lies in being able to bring sponsors to our side as direct allies. More than the fighting strength of a candidate, being able to place our trust in the sponsor themselves comes first and foremost.

"… If only Horizon's Roar didn't have Cayon with him, huh. If he didn't have that man as his sponsor, we could force the match to start at melee range and have a chance at winning…"

"Tsk, tsk, come now, Instructor Ekirehjy. Mele the Horizon's Roar is not as straightforward a champion as that, you know? Besides, even if we prohibited Horizon's Roar from using his characteristic fighting style, and Rosclay won, it wouldn't go over well if it was clear to the citizens what we did. I think it was a reasonable decision to avoid that."

"Rosclay. Have you considered a third possible option or further? The other remaining options are…Psianop the Inexhaustible Stagnation. Ozonezma the Capricious. Zeljirga the Abyss Web."

"Yes. First off, I think it best to avoid Zeljirga."

Rosclay immediately responded to Antel's question.

"Minister Enu isn't a man who's driven by ambition, but…he

has a wide network of connections, and his plans are even harder to read than Elea's. A troublesome opponent. One point is that we do not have a grace period to spare extra precautions on him... Also, regarding his candidate, Zeljirga the Abyss Web, whatever her circumstances may be, she was formerly with Obsidian Eyes. Even individually speaking, her spying and fighting abilities far and away outdo those of Jivlart's Sun's Conifer."

"Psianop, then."

"In Psianop's case, the difficulty lies in the rather high reliability of the report on Neft the Nirvana's demise. He should be disposed of in the same bracket, but I don't think there's a need to run the risk of fighting him in the first round. The remaining third option is Ozonezma... However, given that we know absolutely nothing about his true identity, in the event we're unable to get rid of him ahead of time, and we're forced into the ring, we won't be able to avoid it becoming a dangerous gamble. If we're concerned about the impression we're giving to the citizens, we want to avoid having me win by default in the first round, as well. Indeed, he would be the third-best option."

"Hmm... It seems like you've really delved into all his circumstances to make your decision. Did this for all of them, then?"

"Of course. Otherwise, someone like me wouldn't be able to advance through the tournament at all," Rosclay answered, a composed look on his face. In reality, however, everyone present knew just how much hardship the champion had struggled through— and how many considerations he made to keep up with these monstrous candidates.

However far ahead he looked, no matter how many elaborate plans he tried to weave together...any single misjudgment along the way would make it all collapse. Because Rosclay was but a normal minia.

How was he going to distort the providence of a fixed defeat and claim victory? If he exhausted whatever nastiness he had at his disposal, could he create a sliver of possibility? This stage, before the matches started, was the only battlefield that Rosclay the Absolute could completely control himself.

"Welp, with that said and done, it sounds like fighting against Jivlart'll be the safest option."

Yaniegiz spoke up in dissatisfaction, their conclusion having looped back to where they started.

Antel continued the discussion.

"We've also been investigating the Seventeenth Minister's motives on our end. There's no real indication that there's any stratagems in play around Jivlart. Presently, there haven't been any signs that another of the Twenty-Nine have won him over to their faction, either."

"In other words, she's on her own."

Rosclay thought for a moment. He, too, knew that Elea the Red Tag was a sharp and ambitious woman.

What then, if he was to think about things from her position? If she was preparing some sort of scheme to lead a mediocre man like Jivlart to victory in the face of the powerful opponents in front of him, it still meant that the hero candidate she chose to enact this plan was Jivlart himself.

Would she be able to navigate such a tightrope all the way until victorious?

At the very least, with him as her candidate, it wouldn't be possible.

"What about the idea she's prepared an alternative candidate for herself?"

If a participant drops out because of unforeseen circumstances before their match, the sponsor can select an alternative participant. Naturally however, it was not easy to find the kinds of powerful individuals who possessed the ability to fight through the Sixways Exhibition.

Antel answered. "There's no signs to suggest that possibility, either. Ever since her return from Eta Sylvan Province, the Seventeenth Minister has been spending all her time looking after Jivlart and Sun's Conifer. It's practically impossible that she could contact another powerful player while slipping through the watch of Sun's Conifer."

"Right. I have one other thing to add, regarding Miss Elea's movements. May I?"

"...Go ahead, Professor Ownopellal."

"She seems awfully devoted to the elf girl she brought back from Eta. She's worked on making her one of Queen Sephite's schoolmates and is trying to strengthen their relationship. This might serve as a helpful piece of info, wouldn't you say?"

"How old is she?"

"Fourteen."

"I see. Then that would mean..."

"...She's changed her approach to currying favor with the royal family by going through her student instead of herself...would be the long and short of it, I would say."

In which case, it was consistent with Elea's movements. She hadn't cast away her ambitions after all.

However, her methods weren't going to win the Sixways Exhibition, but ingratiate herself to the Queen and turn her into a puppet.

To the ambitious, the Sixways Exhibition was a perfect opportunity for a power struggle, but the risk was then very large. Elea was letting this opportunity pass her by because of that danger... and perhaps Rosclay needed to view this as her offering up a sure-to-be-eliminated candidate in Jivlart to Rosclay's camp—and seeking to preserve her own safety for the time being.

Rosclay brought his fingers together on top of the table.

"...If our series of conjectures prove true, it would mean Elea the Red Tag's designs are more long-term. In which case, I believe it would be correct here to enlist her as an ally. Professor Ownopellal. Have you been surveilling this elf girl's actions at school?"

"Of course, that is why I am here, after all. Incidentally, her name is Kia. She's a bit of an underperformer, academically. Though she's certainly a fun student to watch."

Elea the Red Tag hadn't joined forces with any of the other Twenty-Nine Officials.

Nor was she hiding some other powerful fighter in the shadows behind Jivlart.

So to achieve her own ambitions, she prepared herself another course to take.

Rosclay's reasoning judged that she wouldn't cause a problem. In battle, he was able to stifle his emotions and act with rationality. However, minia are not fundamentally creatures of reason. To wipe away their lingering anxieties, he would give a smaller push of assurance.

"Jel. Is Elea someone worth trusting? I want to hear your opinion."

"..."

A bespeckled man, looking sharp and shrewd. The Third Minister, Jel the Swift Ink. Among the Twenty-Nine Officials, he was openly hostile toward the Seventeenth Minister and continued to warn of the danger she posed more than anyone else. He was also the bureaucrat with the most outstanding executive abilities, leading the largest government faction, the reformation faction, with Second General Rosclay.

Ever since the meeting topic touched on Elea's person, Jel had kept silent. He knew that his own remarks would end up steering the direction their meeting took.

"...Just this once, I say we trust Elea the Red Tag."

"Really?"

Ekirehjy couldn't hold back his surprise. Jel continued dispassionately.

"I understand her excellence more than anyone else. Regardless of her lineage, I feel those with talent should be given an opportunity. Then, there's this Sixways Exhibition. If the day's come...where she's given a proper appraisal from us, as our ally, then the ambition propelling that woman forward may cool, as well. Beyond the simple logic, I want to gamble on that possibility."

"Understood."

Rosclay closed his eyes.

Even though he had asked the question himself, he never would have imagined Jel's answer.

Given that, however, he knew Jel was being sincere.

"Our first-round opponent will be Jivlart the Ash Border. We'll negotiate with the Seventeenth Minister and make preliminary designs on Jivlart himself, separate from Elea. Any objections to this policy?"

"No objections."

"Nooope."

"None."

After confirming everyone's consensus, Rosclay adjourned the meeting.

The commonplace minia had exhausted all the potential measures available to him. When it came to the tournament bracket, Rosclay's intentions were absolute.

Standing from his seat, Rosclay thought. Each one of the others was a peerlessly powerful fighter. Just how far would Rosclay's tactics, perfectly composed all the way to the final, hold true?

With the meeting over, the attendants began to depart one by one.

"Well, well, I gotta say, your yes vote was a real shocker."

Standing up from his seat, Yaniegiz looked at Jel, still reviewing the meeting material.

"Some slight sympathy for your blood relative, perhaps?"

"...She's nothing more than a base and illegitimate little sister. My personal feelings are closer to hatred than anything."

Jel's stiff expression didn't falter at all in the face of Yaniegiz's words.

He was always levelheaded and precise, like a machine.

"I will take responsibility for the resolution. No matter what."

Even when it came to the Seventeenth Minister and their shared father.

It was two small months before the beginning of the Sixways Exhibition.

The fourth match in the first round was, in some senses, the quickest to start, and in some sense, the first to have its outcome decided.

The pairings in the historically large tournament to decide the hero were certainly not chosen by chance.

However, the direction that his own fate would take was something even Rosclay the Absolute could not fathom.

◆

She had a memory from long in the past, carved deeply into her, that wouldn't disappear even now.

The window was open, and a white curtain waved in the wind.

In the bed, Elea's mother was fatally ill.

Beside her, there was a doctor to announce the time of death— and that was all.

There wasn't anyone else. No one besides the young Elea.

The dinner parties her father had hosted had so many people in attendance, and they were so lively and merry, and yet there was no one around the mother that her father must have, at some point in the past, loved.

...Even right then, as she drifted into death.

Since to her father, her mother was nothing but one of his mistresses, a prostitute from the slums chosen solely for her looks.

"...Listen, Mom."

Elea took her enfeebled mother's hand and gave her best smile.

Because she hoped her words would become the truth for her dying mother.

"Mom... Um... Y-you were happy, right?"

Her mother weakly returned Elea's grip.

Memories of strict disciplining were the only ones that remained. Her father, who almost never visited their house was much, much kinder than her mother.

Learn and get educated. So no one will look down on you.

Become elegant and refined. So no one will scorn you.

Every time she failed, Elea would get hit, and she would cry. Still, her mother had been lonely.

Elea knew that at night when her mother was alone in her room, she cried with far more intense grief than Elea.

The two of them had both suffered.

"E-even if Dad wasn't around the house...! We were totally fine without him, right?! Old friends came by, and you were all smiles, too, right, Mom?! And the food...the food, too. You said that those steamed eggs I made were tasty, didn't you…?! You even made that flower wreath when we went to Gimeena City! You read me books at night, too! Hey, we…we were both…we were both happy, right, Mom?!"

Wishing to keep her mother's soul from leaving her, she clenched down on her mother's hand with the strength of her wish.

She wanted to leave at least one little piece of happiness behind in her mother's head.

Elea wanted her mother to tell her that, despite her loneliness, despite being scorned by the world, the daughter she was so proud of had been her anchor.

"…Elea."

With a faint smile, her mother caressed Elea's hand.

Right now, her mother was alive. The thought was enough to make her tears spill. How could she be alive right now yet be unable to greet the next morning's dawn. And all without her father ever knowing about it.

It was too cruel.

"Mommy…can't ever be happy. Because Mommy's blood—"

Her smile cut into Elea's heart and never once left her.

"—is vulgar blood."

At the end of her words, the wind blew in from the window and carried her mother's last breath away with it.

Even after she heard the doctor give his short announcement, Elea remained frozen in desperate silence.

Elea spent the whole day lost in grief, but even more than that, she was terribly afraid.

Inside the dark manor, without anyone else there, she held her head in her hands and trembled.

I am, too.

She had her mother's blood in her veins. Blood Elea herself couldn't do anything about.

I'm the daughter of vulgar blood, too! I can't find happiness, either! No...! Dying all alone, dying while despised by everyone—I...I don't want any of it! I don't want to die like that!

Elea understood the reason why her mother had been so stubborn about educating her.

She learned the reason why her mother tried to keep that nice great-grandmother away from her.

As if propelled by an obsessive compulsion, she desperately persevered. To escape from the caste of the weak, destined to die in misfortune, disregarded by all. To reach the social echelons where she could change something through her own efforts, where she could earn recognition.

Learn and get educated. So no one will look down on you.

Become elegant and refined. So no one will scorn you.

I'm...I'm different from Great-grandma! I'm not like Mom! I'll become someone much, much greater, even all by myself...! I'll become a noble... An honest, and true, noble...!

Desperately sinking her teeth into it under candlelight, she studied script.

With the knowledge of written language she gained, she

rummaged through several reference books, to ensure her grades excelled more than anyone else in her class.

She had ruined her eyesight in the process, but she still continued. History. Geography. Physics. Word Arts. Finally, politics. She wasn't enough of a genius to always take the top spots in each subject. However, she ensured she wouldn't be looked down on by anyone. She also received humiliating support from the father who had abandoned his family. With it, she was able to continue attending the same type of school the nobles attended.

One day in the evening. That day, there were only three students remaining in the classroom, included Elea.

"Hey, Elea? I heard a rumor from my dad. So apparently, your mother was a prostitute from the canal town?"

"Whaat, i-is that...true? Elea..."

"......"

"*Pfft*, isn't that funny? I mean, such an adorable, model student, coming out of the belly of a whore. If you're a mistress's child, well, I just wonder, then, how you're making the money to attend school."

She thought she was lucky. Lucky that there were only three of them there.

Just before she returned home, Elea stuck a bottle in the bag of the girl who brought up the topic. It was a drug that generated heat with a relatively delayed chemical reaction. In the night, there was a fire at her estate, and her two young brothers and she burned alive with the rest of the family.

She felt very fortunate that she was able to save herself the trouble of having to kill the girl's father, too.

The remaining girl had been Elea's close friend, but the next day she was attacked by a thug and severely wounded.

She heard from the instructor that her face had been mercilessly crushed, and she'd likely be recuperating in a different city.

It's not enough.

Elea experienced nothing that could be called the joys of youth.

It's not just those girls, everyone's trying to kick me down! I need to be higher, high enough that no one can ever kick me back down... I don't want to experience these terrifying moments anymore! J-just how...how far do I have do strive...?!

The hearts of philanthropy or friendship were all superficial arrangements, and she considered her classmates and her instructors as enemies coming to steal her life, her pride, and anything else she had. Some sort of unidentified monster that delighted in such torment. In which case, her only choice was to eradicate them all from Elea's world.

However far she looked ahead, no matter how many elaborate plans she tried to weave together...any single misjudgment along the way would easily bring it collapsing down.

The True Demon King was still bringing ruin to the world. However, she was constantly forced to cope with an even more imminent terror.

Thus, until the day she graduated, she had been able to remain an excellent student. Using schemes, sometimes using her pretty features, she exhausted any and all ugly means to do so. Perfect, beautiful, and free of anyone's scorn—to become a true noble.

…Then she persevered endlessly.

She remembers the events of that day. The fireplace was illuminating the room. The previous Seventeenth Minister was sitting in an armchair. Elea was watching his back.

"Seventeenth Minister."

Elea had climbed up high to her position as the Seventeenth Minister's secretary.

Even then, it still wasn't enough. The Twenty-Nine Officials, all of them, knew Elea's lineage.

Her elder brother Jel was there. She was confident that everyone viewed her with hostility and was trying to kick her back down.

How far would she have to go to escape the stain of this blood of hers?

She needed to become even grander, even more important.

A beauty and light capable of concealing all the unsightliness and ugliness.

She was different from her mom. Different from her great-grandmother. Now they were nobility.

So no one would look down on her. So no one would scorn her.

"Would you relinquish your seat within the Twenty-Nine Officials to me?"

At the end of the darkness, surely there'd be light…

"*Ah-ha-ha-ha-ha*, come on, Kia. I'm long past the age where I can wear a hair accessory like this."

Elea was smiling. It wasn't the same as her usual smile, concealing her true feelings.

It was the carefree smile she had worn while she was working as a home tutor in Eta.

"Who says?! *Tee-hee-hee!* You look like a princess, Elea! It suits you."

"Oh, enough of the flattery!"

Colorful costumes were lined up on their left and right. The shop that had just opened up in Aureatia would take customers' pictures using the latest model of photographic camera. Anyone was able to pick out their preferred outfit for the picture.

Even an elven girl like Kia could freely dress up like a child of nobility, and Elea put on the type of clothes young little girls loved, and there wasn't anyone there to reproach her for it.

It was the day before the start of the fourth match.

The school Kia attended was closed for the day.

Because the match of Aureatia's greatest champion, Rosclay the Absolute, was just a day away.

The match to decide the fate of everything imminent. Kia took Elea out into town. Insisting that because such an important day was right at hand, it was all the better to completely clear her mind of any negativity.

Maybe she was supposed to have refused her. As far as Elea's plans were concerned, it was a totally meaningless outing.

"Hey, Elea."

Kia called to Elea through the curtain separating the adjoining dressing rooms.

"Lately, I've been thinking. Maybe my Word Arts aren't as almighty as I thought."

"...Why?"

There were no limits to the power of the World Word. If Kia wished for it, there wasn't anything she couldn't do. As far as Elea knew, this was a fact that left no room for doubt. Kia's Words Arts were capable of freely limiting an organism's growth, and back in the New Principality of Lithia, she had even been able to stop light itself.

"Well, I probably couldn't produce the same pictures that we took today of us dressed up all pretty, could I? I might be able to reproduce the photos once they were taken, but...if I tried making it just from my imagination, then it'd *definitely* turn out completely different from the picture we took today, right?"

"Right... You might have a point there."

She felt relieved. That level of restriction wouldn't pose a problem at all.

Though Kia was omnipotent, she wasn't omniscient. She couldn't cause any phenomena that was beyond her own imagination. Conversely, it was enough to make it clear that for simple effects like death or annihilation, she could bring them about without a second thought.

"Everyone in my village always said I shouldn't rely on Word Arts to get everything done. That's probably what you were trying to teach me, wasn't it?"

"...Yes. That's right. You could make a Lithia seafood dish appear right before our eyes, I'm sure. But as for what it should taste look or what it should look like... You wouldn't know without going there and having that dish for yourself. That goes for everything else out there in the world... That's why you need to know about all sorts of things. More... You need to learn about so much more."

Elea was saying things that made her sound like a teacher.

Forbidding Kia from using her Word Arts had been nothing but a means to hide the existence of the World Word and to prevent Elea from revealing her hand before tomorrow's match. At this point, there was almost no need to teach Kia any of this.

I wonder what it is.

From her time teaching in Eta Sylvan Province, she was a willful and brazen student who caused her more trouble than anyone else.

Elea would advance through this Sixways Exhibition and hold the top of Aureatia in her grip. If it hadn't been for the sake of her plans—she would've long since abandoned this home-tutor farce and sent Kia packing back to her forest.

Yet with her rebellious attitude, at the same time, Kia possessed a sort of carefree frankness.

She was kind, considerate to children younger than herself, and she spent time thinking over the things Elea had taught her, like she was now.

...Maybe it makes me happy?

She looked at the dressing room mirror. Elea was smiling.

This was her expression?

Even though tomorrow she would kill Rosclay and continue down a far more blood-drenched path than before?

I can't believe I'd feel happy to see a student's growth.

"Elea! Did you finish getting changed?"

"...I did. Are you ready, Kia?"

Elea's current appearance made her look like royalty. Though, the pretty jewels were faux gems to match the costume, and the golden hairpiece was a fake, mixed with other metals.

However, if Elea won, before long, even this sort of attire would become a reality.

So no one would look down on her. So no one would scorn her.

"My, how adorable, *Lady* Elea." Kia said teasingly, with a smirking grin.

"You too, *Miss* Kia," Elea shot back, looking at Kia attempting to appear mature by wearing an open-back dress.

"Elea! We still have two pictures left, so you have to come up with a different outfit. *I've* already got mine picked out. I've wanted to do this for so long."

"And to make sure I came with you?"

"Because it's a total waste! I mean, Elea, you're so—"

Kia abruptly cut herself off and dropped her eyes from Elea down to her feet.

"...Y-you're so...so lucky to see how cute I am, obviously!"

"Hee-hee."

An easily handled child. This young girl idolized Elea and showed her goodwill, exactly as she had planned. Though the girl wielded unrivaled power at her command, Elea was able to control her like this.

But.

"...Hey, Elea. That hairpiece, how much do you think it costs? My allowance might be enough to buy it, right?"

"You intend to buy it off this shop?"

"Well, really... I could make a hundred of these if I felt like it, of course."

Elea looked at Kia's face in profile. She was smiling blissfully.

Just like a normal young girl. As if her omnipotent World Word status was all a lie.

"...But. I want something real, not something I just made."

There wasn't a moment where Elea the Red Tag's mind was at peace.

She never once had a friend she could confide in.

If she won the Sixways Exhibition, it would be rewarded—the entirety of the life she had lived up until then.

◆

Kia had been patient through it all. Whether it was regarding her Eta homeland or Elea's current predicament, her concerns were only getting worse, but they weren't enough to make everything crumble down around her.

Putting on an air that nothing was much of a problem, she

brought Elea out to the photography studio and was able to laugh and chat with her for the first time in a while. Nevertheless.

"…Elea?"

Elea had collapsed on the floor in the middle of the living room.

Kia took a detour to watch a street performer, and Elea had returned ahead of her, which was why she hadn't been at Elea's side when…

"I'm okay. It's okay, Kia."

"That'll heal, right? With Life Arts…or a doctor…! C'mon, that wound will heal, right?!"

Blood was flowing from one of Elea's eyes. Kia was stunned.

"……"

"…W-well, say something, will you?!"

Pushing Elea aside, she stepped into the room.

Again, he hit her. Hit Elea. Hit her precious teacher.

Jivlart was lying slovenly on the sofa without a shirt. This man normally wouldn't be at Elea's house in the middle of the day on a holiday. Nothing of the sort had ever happened before.

Why?

Why? What reason did he have to do this? Was it something she'd understand when she became an adult herself?

She got angry.

It wasn't just Kia. The children in Eta all loved those sky-blue eyes of her. The eyes this man had hurt.

Though she knew that this hero candidate's victory was the only path to saving her homeland, she couldn't forgive what he had done.

"Jivlart!"

"What the…? Huh? Oh, it's you, Kia. Pipe down."

Even though he would be fighting against Rosclay the Absolute the very next day. He was supposed to have Kia's homeland on his shoulders… He was even harming his precious Elea, too.

"What…what are trying to do anyway?! Why do you torment Elea?! You're a hero candidate, aren't you?! Why the heck is someone like *you* in the fight to decide on a hero in the first place?!"

"*Pfft*…… Dumb kid."

Still sprawled out on the couch, Jivlart sneered at her.

"Because it's a good gig, obviously."

"What do you mean, 'gig'?"

"All right, I guess I'll fill you in, then. The match's tomorrow anyway, so there's no one to replace me, eh? See, me, from the very start, I made a promise to lose to Rosclay. You get it?"

"……!"

Watching Kia bite down on her lip in front of him, Jivlart continued, seemingly enjoying every minute it.

"I'm gonna lose and get paid for it. *Ha-ha-ha!* It's a helluva a story… Got neither kith nor kin, but me and the Sun's Conifer guys, all getting famous, getting recognition. Heck, even just a guy like me…a piddling, lowborn guy like me, being a damn hero candidate at all! Some well-to-do aristocrat gal ain't gonna be able to talk back to me!"

Lies—his hero candidacy, the talk of this man saving Eta for her—it had all been lies.

A lowlife like this had been crushing Elea under his heel this whole time.

"*Ha-ha*, ain't heard anything funnier, right?! Right, Kia?! You get it, right?! Growin' up out in the sticks with nothing…and now you're attending a school for nobles, so you know! We can rise up even higher from here on out, lemme tell ya! All those guys…who kept us underfoot, well, now we're gonna be the ones keeping *them* down!"

"…I'll kill you."

She realized it was the first time she had uttered those words at another person before.

How had it been when she was in Eta Sylvan Province? Had she ever said the words *die* or *kill* to another person?

At that moment, she understood clearly. It was people like this man here who were "enemies" worthy of such words.

"*Ha!*"

Jivlart mocked Kia with a laugh and went to leave her behind.

"Whoa, whoa, gimme a break. I'm real gentle with—"

"That's not it."

"……"

"You couldn't hit me, could you? It was always Elea. Always while I was still at school, in secret."

Kia took one step forward. Jivlart's sneering expression was tinged with the faintest shade of hatred.

Kia had never shown Jivlart her omnipotent Word Arts before. She always abided by Elea's instructions, never breaking them even once. In spite of that, Jivlart was avoiding Kia.

It could only be because, if he let Kia witness the decisive moment…it meant he would have to confront Kia. Nothing more than a child.

She closed the distance with another step.

"Jivlart. You. You're scared of children."

"…What the hell'd you say…?"

"You like children because they're honest, was it? Well, you're wrong. I'm not honest at all. You're always hitting Elea where I won't see you doing it, right?! What, don't tell me you want ignorant children to think you're a nice guy, or something?! You always run away from kids, giving the same excuse every single time!"

"Don't you screw with me, you little brat…!"

Contrary to his words, Jivlart was backing away from her.

Kia's presence made him get up, and she was chasing him toward the entryway.

Weak.

This man was weaker than a child. Ridiculous to even consider a warrior, he was just a puny minia.

"I was thinking the next time I saw you, I'd *make you cry*. Now I'll do something even worse."

For Kia, it was possible.

"Something you can't even imagine."

"You snotty… Sn-snotty brat. Watch me kill you dead. Try to screw with me, huh…?! Best not insult me. 'Specially if you don't know a damn thing about us. Dammit, I ain't running away! I ain't a kid! I—I used my own strength to— S-so don't screw with me!"

Jivlart brandished his sword. It was likely his usual attempt of plain intimidation.

His opening rush, his spirit, even his urge to kill itself, were all far, far too slow compared to a single word from Kia.

She thought that right now she could kill him. She had even decided on how he'd die. *Burst.*

"......*Burs—*"

"*Artpanon. Hamkest.*" (Deformed flower. Harden.)

"*Urk.*"

Jivlart stopped. Maintaining an expression of shame and anger, Jivlart collapsed and fell on his face in front of Kia.

Behind him, Elea had placed the palm of her hand up to Jivlart's back and was finished incanting her Word Arts. Far faster than Kia could try to kill him herself.

Jivlart had collapsed right at Kia's feet.

He didn't move.

"What?"

Kia looked down at the floor again. The tips of her shoes were wet. Jivlart's blood.

Blood spilling from Jivlart's mouth.

"Elea," Kia blankly mumbled.

"...It's okay. I changed the alcohol in his stomach...into poison."

"You did this, Elea?"

"......"

There was a liquor bottle lying on its side atop the living room table.

If the alcohol he had been drinking up until that point had been Elea's own, then as long as she aimed accurately at the position of his stomach, with Life Arts focused on the mastery of poison synthesis, such feats were possible. However.

"H-hey. Um. Elea..."

Then Kia understood.

She *had made Elea kill.*

Elea smiled awkwardly and gently embraced Kia.

"Kia......"

She was kind. She didn't get mad at Kia. Kia hated it. It had been that way ever since they had come to Aureatia.

A soft and warm body enveloped Kia.

"No, no, no. I—I don't want that, Elea."

Even in that instant, where everything had changed, one thing remained the same. What was Kia going to do? Elea's hero candidate had died. Eta was going to be destroyed. What did she need to do?

All her thoughts dissolved into a mess, and Kia stood, unable to make a decision.

"Elea, I...!"

When she tried to continue, the words caught in her throat. She realized she was crying.

A person had died. Right in front of Kia's eyes.

"I... I'm—I'm sorry..."

"Kia... Thank you for protecting me."

"I d-don't—I don't want any thanks."

"Hey, Kia? I'm the one who's sorry. Long before I worried about saving Eta... I should have thought about your feelings first. But with this, it's all over."

Elea's fingers gently stroked the hair on the back of Kia's head.

"I don't have any hero candidate anymore now."

"...Me!"

Kia returned Elea's hug with a strong embrace of her own. Though, with the girl's tiny body...she probably couldn't provide her with any serious sense of comfort.

Nevertheless, she could tell that Elea was trembling.

There was still one path left for Kia to save everything.

"Send me out there! I'll be your hero candidate!"

"...Kia."

Anything was possible for Kia. If she fought, she wouldn't lose to anybody.

"I'll go out there to replace Jivlart!"

With that, she had said the words herself.

Perfectly in line with the scenario Elea the Red Tag had engineered.

◆

"...Rosclay! Wait a minute, Rosclay!"

Yaniegiz the Chisel's call to Rosclay the Absolute to stop him came as he was stepping out into the castle garden theater arena, at the very last possible moment.

"Yaniegiz?"

Yaniegiz was out of breath. Rosclay could tell he was coming with truly urgent news.

"Y-you won't believe it...! Your opponent...Jivlart the Ash Border is dead! He died in an accident! Elea the Red Tag... There wasn't any time to search for a new candidate, but right before the match..."

"...What did you say?"

Rosclay was bewildered. How had something like this happened?

Elea's movements—particularly whether she had made contact with anyone powerful enough to possibly serve as a substitute candidate—had been under complete and constant surveillance up until the day of the match.

Given such a situation, could she have any possible reason to dispose of her own candidate? Did some unforeseen circumstances leave her no choice but to kill him? Could his death have been an honest and true accident?

"In which case...it doesn't sound like this match will end with a win by default, will it?"

"Yes, that's exactly right! She's already set up her replacement candidate...! The enemy isn't Jivlart the Ash Border... I-it's that girl! She doesn't have a second name! The Iznock Royal High School student, Kia!"

Kia. It was the name of the girl from Ownopellal's report.

A young elf girl who Elea the Red Tag had brought back with her from Eta Sylvan Province and who she was personally providing an education.

Her physical training scores were average. Her grades in classroom lectures were poor. Her grades in Word Arts studies were abysmal.

The plainly available information was enough, at the very least, to be certain that she was not a talent meant to be standing on the Sixways Exhibition stage as a fighter.

...What is her purpose here? Under these circumstances, it's too

late to cancel the match. *What is Elea the Red Tag aiming for by setting Kia up as her replacement? Is this girl supposed to be strong enough to advance through the tournament? Is Kia's student status not enough, and she needs to give her the title of participant in order to curry favor with the Queen? Or perhaps Jivlart truly did die in an accident, and she had no other person she could compel to take the stage?*

He looked at Yaniegiz. His breathing was ragged. Like Rosclay, he, too, was in turmoil.

The Ninth General, Yaniegiz, was one of Rosclay's compatriots, and they had fought together for a long, long time. He was waiting for a decision. A decision from the leader of their artificial champion, Rosclay.

Think. Think. Think. Given the already abnormal situation, I need to imagine the worst scenario. She's just a girl. Tu the Magic's just a girl, too, if only going off her outward appearance. What if Elea had been hiding a trump card, on Tu the Magic's level, for this very moment? Her Word Arts grades were abysmal. But that's just her classroom scores. Unlike any sort of physical abilities, she could feign those—a Word Arts user. Supposing she was one, what would be the focal point of her Word Arts in this battle? What will she do?

His thoughts whirled with tremendous speed. Even if he hypothesized that Kia was a Word Arts user, was there even a single plan he could come up with in this short time, the start of the match imminent, that could reliably seal off her means of attack and give them the initiative?

Defeat was death. At his back, death always loomed imminent.

Rosclay the Absolute's battles were a constantly repeating cycle of such extreme situations.

"Sprinkle water. Yaniegiz, can you sprinkle water as some special staging setup before the match?"

"Not an easy ask, no sir...! It'll be tight, for sure. We can rush a street performer over and mix in water as they sprinkle their confetti! Yeah, that'll work! What then?!"

"I'm presuming our enemy is a Word Arts user! With our arena already decided ahead of time, the focal point she'll use will either be earth or wind! We'll mix in water missing from the arena with those two properties and turn them to mud and fog! With the disparity in their characteristics, it'll delay the Word Arts invocation by a hair's breadth—and delay her move. In that delay, it'll be my only chance to close the distance and cut her down!"

"Rosclay! Your opponent... She's still a child, you know?!"

"That might be part of her calculations. That I...that Aureatia's hero would see his opponent's appearance and hesitate to attack! We'll try not to kill—no, *we'll make it look like we're not killing her*! Can you do it?!"

"At once...! Be careful, Rosclay!"

Rosclay advanced forward together with tensed resolve. Backing down wasn't an option.

The audience packed into the venue was at a loss.

An inconceivable and absurd presence was standing face-to-face with Aureatia's strongest knight. A pretty young elf girl, wholly inappropriate for this true duel arena.

Golden hair with streaks of white. Clear turquoise eyes, like a lake surface, perfectly positioned on her face.

Nevertheless, she was terrifying.

...*Kia. What is your second name? What are you going to come at me with?*

To Rosclay, this normal young girl, this unknown who should not be, suddenly showing up in the middle of his slowly and carefully built-up strategy, made him more terrified than anything else could.

"...So you're Rosclay?"

"......"

"...Aren't you cool."

The young girl simply looked up at Rosclay and muttered curtly to him.

Desperately hiding his fear of the unknown, Rosclay smiled.

"Thank you. Please don't be too hard on me."

Beyond her clothes, Kia didn't hold any vessel that would've served as a focal point for Word Arts. If she clearly had that sort of equipment with her, then Yaniegiz would've reported as much to him.

If this girl was going to attack with Word Arts, she would have to use either the wind or the earth, after all.

The adjudicator Meeka commanded they both space out from each other, and Rosclay measured the distance in the back of his head.

One step. Two steps. Two steps, and he was in sword range. Was that close? Or was that too far away?

Meeka proclaimed—

"At the sound of the band's gunshot…begin!"

Rosclay was listening to the beating of his own heart.

Time seemed to extend out for an eternity between Meeka's proclamation and the sound of the starting gun.

The band's gun was aimed into the sky. Nearby, a street performer scattered water all around.

Together with the pouring artificial rain, the ground of the garden theater grew damp…

…*No! That won't be enough moisture!*

The ground of the garden theater, also used as an athletic field, was blanketed with sand, which drained water well.

It was more precarious than he expected. Even with his intelligence and experience, he had been unable to perfectly predict everything down to the geological changes that would result from the sprinkled water.

The effect wouldn't be enough to delay any soil-based Word Arts. What if he used a technique to separate himself from the ground?

He revised his estimation of the distance between them to three paces. He needed to add one more to his opening steps, using the extra step to jump high into the air, and slash from midair, where Kia's height would make dealing with the attack difficult.

Using the hidden radzio he carried, he gave a new order to the personnel assisting him.

"Viga! I want your greatest Thermal Arts right as the match starts!"

<Yes, I know. We're delaying the band's gunshot on our end. We can do it right on your signal, Rosclay.>

There was no need to cut down Kia with his feet planted on the ground. With the sprinkled water, Kia had already been sprayed with enough moisture, while Rosclay defended himself with his insulated gauntlet. Viga, using long-range Word Arts through the radzio, would support him by using Rosclay's sword as the focal point for his electric Thermal Arts. He could place his trust in its accuracy more than any other, having used it to overcome many dilemmas before.

Hit with one attack. Focus everything on it.

A surprise attack from midair. The moment his sword connected, electricity would flow through it and knock out Kia—or immediately kill her—in one strike.

He didn't need to cut deep. If this attack felled Kia, then to the people, it would look as if he had knocked her unconscious with the back of his sword but without injuring her at all.

There wasn't anyone among the audience who would be able to verify the girl's fate when she'd be carried out of the arena.

...I'm sorry.

It was possible that all of this might have been nothing more than Rosclay's groundless fears.

She could simply be an innocent and misfortunate little girl. At the very least, she was still young, with a future ahead of her.

The fact that he was trying to cruelly end it all was both Rosclay's cowardice and the heavy responsibility of a hero.

If it wasn't for the eyes of the people around him, he could have saved her, just like when he had saved Iska.

He couldn't, though. He wasn't strong enough to win while showing his enemy such mercy.

Rosclay the Absolute was required to achieve an absolute victory.

Match four.

Rosclay the Absolute versus Kia the World Word.

I'm sorry, Kia.

Subtly rolling his wrists, he secretly gave the order to start the match. Rosclay could control the timing of the match's start. When the gunshot echoed, Rosclay was already moving his center gravity.

I'm sorry! I must…take you down!

Rosclay dashed with everything he had.

The opening steps of Aureatia's most just knight were as fast as bullets. Speed that was far too fast for the young girl to possibly react.

One step. He took his second ste—

"Bury him."

Suddenly.

Darkness enveloped Rosclay's sights. The earth ferociously bulged, as if opening up its maw, swallowing Rosclay and burying him completely.

Both his breath and his thoughts were cut off.

The audience's cheers disappeared suddenly, as if doused with water.

He had read the situation and correctly guessed his enemy was a Word Arts user. He had manipulated the arena environment and disturbed the focal point for her Word Arts. He had adapted to unforeseen circumstances and formulated a strategy. He had both an attack he expected to bring instant victory and the resolve to use it.

It was all meaningless.

Within the vast garden theater, the absolute hero Rosclay had already disappeared—on the ground where he should have been standing, there was only a silent mountain of dirt soaring up into the air.

The Word Arts of Kia the World Word were nearly omnipotent.

"Is that it?"

A delayed scream rose up from the surrounding seats.

Arrogantly looking past their cries, Kia turned her back on the champion's pitiful state.

An overwhelmingly unrivaled being, unknown to all, impossible to even theoretically hypothesize.

However far he looked ahead, no matter how many elaborate plans he tried to weave together...

"Guess I win, then."

...with just one single misjudgment...

The nameless citizens of Aureatia were always looking forward to Rosclay's victories.

The day before the match, in one of the commonplace shops lining the Aureatia streets, just such an exchange was underway.

"Hey, so for tomorrow's match. You're rooting for Rosclay, right, Deela?"

A boy leaned his body over the counter and spoke to the young man tending the store.

"...Yeah, I mean, it's Rosclay and all. Here, a screwdriver. That's all you need, right?"

"Hey, Deela! Is Rosclay really that amazing?"

"Yup. You'd get it if you had lived in Aureatia awhile like me."

While he treated the boy coldly, he didn't drive him out.

Speaking with his matter-of-fact tone, the store attendant continued.

"He isn't a champion for an unknown someone or other out there. He'll protect any citizen of Aureatia. Poor, orphans, it doesn't matter. Even out here, a district on the edge of the city like this."

"So then you have seen him before?"

"...Sure have."

Closing his eyes, the young man recalled his memories of the time.

The champion's flash, an honored memory left behind to all who witnessed it.

"He was up against a gigante revenant that apparently a self-proclaimed demon king created. Rosclay…kicked up the high wall, still in his armor. He ran up high enough to reach that monster's eye, and he threw himself into the air and cut the thing down… Can you believe that? That man… He's a minia, you know. Just the same as you and me."

"…*Ah-ha-ha*. Reaaally, though? After hearing everyone's stories, he definitely doesn't sound like one to me."

"He's a minia."

If he wasn't, he wouldn't have ever stood in front of such a calamity to protect the citizens all by himself.

All the people knew that he constantly kept training with his sword.

All the people knew that he would look out for all the citizens, regardless of their social standing.

"He doesn't seem that different from any of us, yet that guy's a champion."

"That's impressive. So then a guy like Jivlart doesn't stand a chance."

"…Everyone living in Aureatia is indebted to Rosclay. He's not any old champion… He makes you want to become just like him. If things go right, then someday—"

"Hey! Deelaaaa! Hurry up and close up shop!"

A voice came from farther inside the store. Already drunk. His impatient father.

The young man sighed and looked at his young customer.

"Sorry. Pops said we're closing up early today. Said it's a

preliminary celebration of Rosclay's victory tomorrow... Always something with him, seriously."

"Really sorry for bugging you."

"You're going to watch the match tomorrow, right?"

"......! Yeah!"

As he cleaned up after his final customer had left, the store attendant let his blank expression give way to a slight smile.

More than any champion spoken of in poems. More than the legend of Alus the Star Runner or whoever.

As if to confirm that which he believed in more than anything else.

"Rosclay's unbeatable."

◆

"Nooo, Rosclay...!"

"Rosclay!"

"It can't be... Rosclay!"

"Rosclay! Get up, Rosclay!"

Sorrow and bewilderment was filling the stands. Watching the progress from the half-underground entrance into the arena, Elea the Red Tag closed her eyes.

Kia had won. Finally, Elea could have peace of mind. A ray of hope, at last.

Kia is invincible. Faster than Rosclay, she bested him with a single word.

The fact was proven to her in the best way possible—that

Kia could go on and win the remaining three matches in just the same way.

The largest faction, ruined by their sponsored candidate, Rosclay, would need to incorporate Kia into their ranks, or the Sixways Exhibition couldn't continue on. Since they needed to defeat Lucnoca the Winter, who was bound to continue on advancing in the third match down the line.

The fearsome ancient dragon that easily butchered Alus the Star Runner and turned the Mari Plains into a frozen land of death. In front of now-evident disaster, there was none other than Kia the World Word who could accomplish such a feat.

Furthermore, if they were going to control Kia, it meant they absolutely couldn't eliminate Elea. It was for that reason she had spent such a long time building up a relationship of trust.

Her tutor, Elea, who Kia trusted more than anyone else.

The route to victory through the remaining part of the bracket had already been paved by Rosclay.

With this, the Sixways Exhibition was over.

"Silence!"

There was a clear and resonant voice amid the screams and uproar. The adjudicator tasked with observing all the matches of the Sixways Exhibition. A stout woman with a large frame, stern and solemn—Meeka the Whispered.

Her voice calmed the arena as it was descending into madness.

"As was agreed upon before the match! This true duel will be decided via one of two ways! A combatant is knocked down and doesn't get up. A combatant forfeits the match of their own volition."

Thus, with the match clearly decided to all present, she declared—

"However, Rosclay the Absolute has *not been knocked down yet!*"

Meeka's declaration.

It took a moment for Elea to understand what it really meant.

It can't be.

She felt like she was once again being dragged back into a terrifying dark abyss.

Meeka's expression was as firm as steel.

Her tone remained steady, as if she was narrating a clear and obvious truth.

"As long as this fact holds true, this match will continue!"

The crowd's cheers welled up once again.

The keeper of the judiciary. Aureatia's Twenty-Sixth Minister, Meeka the Whispered.

Neither Elea…nor even Haade had raised any objections to tasking her with observing all the matches. As the Twenty-Nine Officials all confronted and spied on each other, she was supposed to be the neutral adjudicator they had all agreed on.

She's been roped into the scheme, too… I can't believe they even got to Meeka. The adjudicator for the matches is our enemy—

She heard the cracking sound of something breaking. The mountain burying Rosclay's body was crumbling away, and it was slowly cut apart by a myriad of straight swords. Sword Craft Arts from his remote support.

No. She had a bigger problem than Meeka.

The fact that their fight was deemed to continue—the fact that the cheers were once again erupting through the arena.

From within the mass of earth, gaps appeared just big enough to breathe through, and a gauntleted hand appeared. Moving and grabbing a sword.

Elea gasped.

There was one more miscalculation. She looked toward Kia.

She didn't...kill him...!

◆

He wanted to gather his thoughts, but he was utterly drained.

His brain cells, cut off from oxygen, were reaching their limits just by maintaining consciousness, and various joints were dislocated or outright destroyed from being instantaneously squeezed under the earthen pressure.

Ignoring the intense pain, he fit his dislocated left shoulder back into place.

Gritting his teeth hard enough to draw blood, he nevertheless let out neither a scream nor a sob.

Because he was Rosclay the Absolute.

...Earthen Craft Arts. Irregularly fast activation speed...and scale...

Was his perception of them correct? This wasn't adequate contemplation but merely the work of confirming what he saw with his own eyes.

Laboring against the pain, Rosclay brandished his weapon.

Kia the World Word, already making to leave the arena, looked back at the knight dubiously.

She knit her eyebrows, as if she was looking at a true fool.

"...What?"

Fed up and disdainful—even then, to Rosclay, it didn't matter. Even in that brief instant, he needed time. The time from stirring the girl's emotions until she once again shifted to the attack. Time where, no matter how brief, he could study his enemy's true nature and pick out a route to victory.

Her incantation...was nonexistent. It wasn't a proper incantation. Her order to "bury me," was a signal to some other people. Using a radzio just like me...for support from someone outside the match... But no, given that I'm her opponent here, then the soldiers would've verified for me whether she possessed some communication devices or not... A cleverly disguised method... Is there some other method of making Word Arts work remotely...? No... That's not it...!

He couldn't get his thoughts together. It wasn't simply due to Rosclay's fatigue, either.

It was because, according to the known logic of this world, the phenomenon Kia manifested was far too abnormal.

Elea hadn't made contact with any other powerful players at all...! Even if there was someone here providing Kia support...! The only explanation is...with just simple Craft Arts alone, she managed to cast Word Arts...that possessed power and activation speed beyond even a self-proclaimed demon king's level!

And because he saw the conclusion he absolutely didn't want to reach.

If this phenomenon was being produced by some sort of mechanism, then he could prevent it from working. If he was able to perfectly see through the trick, Rosclay could conversely link it to a path to victory.

However, if there was *no sort of mechanism or trick at all*?

If the phenomenon he witnessed was the answer to it all—and that this young girl named Kia was a Word Arts user capable of using such tremendous Craft Arts?

Was it really okay for a monster of this level to appear out of nowhere without warning? A monster this ludicrous. This unparalleled.

...I need some path to victory—

Rosclay's body was once again covered in soil. It was instantaneous.

"Bury him... What's with you?"

It's impossible.

Once again, within his darkened, enclosed hell, this time he heard the sound of the armor on his right leg break apart. Kia's Craft Arts might easily be capable of strangling someone to death under the pressure of the soil. She was simply not doing so.

He had gained no new information. He was handled in the exact same way as before, and Rosclay was completely unable to avoid her attack.

"Ownopellal iokouto. Yurowastera. Vapmarsia wanwao. Sarp-morebonda. Utokma." (From Ownopellal to the soil of Kouto. Reflect in replica. Jeweled crevice. Standstill stream. Advance.)

A voice speaking Word Arts immediately resounded from a radzio and tried to bring Rosclay back into the fight.

It's impossible. Professor Ownopellal. It's impossible.

Due to the experience and judgment he had cultivated for himself, he unfortunately understood it more clearly than anything else.

Spitting up dirt, simply trying to walk forward sent an intense pain through him from the tips of his destroyed toes.

This is totally impossible for me... I wasn't able to devise any sort of measures for this situation. I wasn't able to estimate an enemy like this. I'm a mere minia. I can't win.

He wanted to collapse. He thought it was pointless.

What could he do up against an impossible-to-foresee and totally incomprehensible monster like this?

Stabbing his sword scabbard into the ground like a cane, Rosclay stood up.

"...Listen."

Kia let out an exasperated tone.

Rosclay readied his sword, just as his staggering amount of training had drilled into him.

Earnestly finishing this meaningless motion was enough to make a painful groan slip out from deep in his throat.

"I don't really want to be a bully here."

"...I— *Koff.* I'm a knight who knows nothing but the sword. I'd like to taste the honor of facing off against the pinnacle of Word Arts for as long as possible."

While he was spouting his cheap bravado, he hoped the next attack wouldn't come. Rosclay was floundering.

...Floundering for a way to kill this girl.

There was a by-product of the Craft Arts that dismantled the mountain of soil. Straight swords that were littered about the ground.

Due to their vast numbers, it should have, in fact, meant she couldn't keep aware of all of them.

"*Antel io Jadwedo. Laeus 4 motbode. Temo yamvista. Iusemno. Xaonyaji.*" (From Antel to the steel of Jawedo. The axis is the fourth left finger. Pierce sound. Descend from clouds. Circulate.)

The remote Power Arts support sent a sword flying. From a blind spot behind Kia, to sever her medulla oblongata.

The blade melted away and evaporated.

"?"

The girl's eyes widened, and she turned around to look at the sword's vestiges on the ground behind her.

It seemed she hadn't even noticed a surprise attack had come at her until it was all over.

"...Oh, I forgot to actually say it out loud, didn't I? *Protect me from all danger.*"

The Word Arts Kia had used during their match didn't end at the Craft Arts that sealed her enemies away in an earthen coffin. Keeping herself protected was a shield of Thermal Arts powerful enough to blast away steel.

Absolute defensive power that had fully warded her against the famous poison of Higuare the Pelagic, without her noticing a thing.

To Rosclay, from the start, this latest attack had been nothing more than useless resistance with little chance of success. However.

Is there even any chance...?

Swords physically wouldn't penetrate her. In other words, none of the methods of attack at Rosclay's disposable would have any effect on her at all.

The truth was enough to shatter his mind to pieces.

Falling to his knees in despair, he was on the verge of crumbling to the ground. He stepped forward to hold himself aloft.

Rosclay steadied his blade, the motions deeply ingrained within him, and stared hard straight at Kia.

Stop. It's impossible. I can't do anything.

Even though he wanted to drop his sword, even though he wanted to collapse, even if he wanted to scream that it was all impossible, he was unable to do so.

Rosclay the Absolute was forbidden from using the defeat condition known as "surrender."

"Huh... Excuse me...? This is weird, right...?"

It was Kia this time who puzzled over the true nature of her opponent.

Here she had thought that after showing off how overwhelmingly strong she was, there wouldn't be any need to fight anymore.

However, the adjudicator Meeka had declared the fighting

would continue, and Kia would still need to do something else in order to claim victory over the match.

"I mean… You get it, don't you? Any way you slice it…it's over. You're gonna lose."

"……"

Kia was far stronger than this Rosclay man in front of her. Stronger than any one of the other hero candidates entered into the Sixways Exhibition.

Be it Mele the Horizon's Roar or Lucnoca the Winter, with a single word, she could make them grovel before her. She had thought that that sort of fight would've been all it took to claim the glory of victory and the salvation of her homeland.

"What do you think you're going to do? From over there…and with those injuries."

"…Hrk, koff!"

Yet Rosclay the Absolute was abnormal.

With a body so covered in wounds, the young girl could plainly see it all with a glance, nevertheless, he stood true.

Kia remembered the words Meeka had said. The conditions for winning this fight.

"…Hey, so. I just need to make sure you can't get up, right?"

"I swear, I will—"

"Stop him."

Rosclay was crushed to the ground as if pounded by an invisible iron sledgehammer.

All the power was erased from his body, down to the tips of his fingers.

"...Look! He can't move at all now! Right?"

A flawless victory, indisputable to anyone there to witness it.

Kia smiled and looked toward Meeka. She looked to the spectators surrounding the area.

"Rosclay..."

"No, Rosclay...!"

"Get up! Rosclay!"

"Rosclay! Rosclay!"

Meeka was silent. She didn't declare the match decided.

Kia could keep these Word Arts active for an eternity. It should have been a clear and evident win.

Knocked down and doesn't get back up.

Everyone believed that Rosclay could still get back up from this situation.

Rosclay the Absolute was obligated to keep fighting until the bitter end.

"Roooosclaaay!"

"Don't give up, Rosclay!"

"Rosclay! Rosclay!"

"Rosclay!"

"Nooo, Rosclay, please...!"

For Kia, it was a terribly sickening spectacle.

"...What's with all this, seriously?!"

She looked at Rosclay, his movements halted. Naturally, there were no signs he would make a comeback.

...Far more than that, in fact. Kia realized the truth of the situation.

"Eek!"

With this, the Word Arts she could've kept up in perpetuity were expelled.

Rosclay grabbed the ground, coughing horribly, and stood up.

"Gahak...! Koff, hngh...gah...!"

No—he wasn't just having a coughing fit. It went far beyond that.

His coughs were equivalent to the panting gasps of a victim moments before they drowned to death.

Just then, Kia realized Rosclay's breathing had stopped.

Kia's awesome Word Arts had, faithful to her own will, stopped all of Rosclay's *movements*. Down to his involuntarily biological activity.

Kia backed off to avoid Rosclay. She didn't want to get close to him.

Rosclay couldn't even pursue her.

Standing squarely on the ground, he stared straight at Kia and properly readied his sword.

"Rosclay! Rosclay!"

"Rosclay!"

"Rosclay got up!"

"Rosclay!"

"Wh-why...? Why're you getting up?!"

The girl's appeal didn't reach the enthusiastically fervent crowd.

It was an awfully unfair and terrifying scene.

Why wasn't it all over? Why wouldn't anyone let it end?

"I—I… I'm clearly winning here, aren't I?! Right?!"

By this point, she was tearfully wailing.

Surrounded by the vast arena, everything was trying to make Kia out to be the enemy.

"Rosclay!"

"Rosclay!"

"Rosclay!"

"Rosclay!"

"Rosclay!"

Aureatia's strongest knight was standing. Dragging his feet along, he stepped firmly and drew closer.

Even when that state alone should have made it clear that he couldn't do anything.

The knight didn't withdraw. The minia didn't give up.

"After all that. After I had clearly had you totally beat!"

She wanted to win. She wanted to protect the homeland she held dearer than anything else.

What did she need to do? What did she have to do to win against this horrible foul play?

What were they trying to make her do? What did they expect Kia to do beyond what she already had?

"Kill him!"

Even though there was a voice screaming out to Kia, it mixed in with the cheers and didn't reach her.

Clinging desperately to the arena's entrance, Elea screamed.

It was clear by now. There remained only one way to decisively make this champion lose.

"Kill him! Killing that man…is the only way! Kia!"

◆

On that day Elea, secretary to the Seventeenth Minister, made her desires known.

"Would you relinquish your seat within the Twenty-Nine Officials to me?"

The elderly Seventeenth Minister laughed under his breath and seemed to brush off the conversation.

He must have taken his secretary's question as little more than a silly joke.

…Yet he then wore a distant, far-reaching look and gripped his pipe in his mouth.

The fireplace lit up his profile.

"…Well, now. I suppose when the time comes, it'll be passed on to you, then."

"You're toying with me."

"Not at all. You're young yet, but I think you're an exceptional young woman, worthy of a seat among the Twenty-Nine Officials. There'll be some who'll quibble about your heritage, but that isn't anything to get hung up on. From here on out, competent and capable people need to govern this country and be there to help the Queen."

Standing behind the easy chair he sat in, Elea was at a standstill, maintaining her smile. She didn't know what sort of expression she needed to twist her face into next.

The Seventeenth Minister was lying. The people who surrounded Elea were her enemies, scheming to deceive her and force her out of power. That was their sole objective.

"Everyone is drained and exhausted from the True Demon King's reign. Biases and prejudices regarding social status or lineage... At this point, the era where minia should be fighting against each other is long gone."

"……"

"I want to continue striving for such a world. Surely you understand, Elea."

"Seventeenth Minister. Did you know? The chef at the Porcelain Swallow was apparently arrested."

"...What are you talking about?"

The Seventeenth Minister turned to look questioningly at Elea.

She still wore the same gentle, beautiful smile. What sort of expression was she supposed to be making?

"That's the restaurant where I talked to the Eighth Minister this afternoon."

"I am aware. It's a wonderful establishment."

"Gahak, ungh!"

The Seventeenth Minister suddenly vomited, and an excruciating pain in his gut made him double over.

Once he had reached that point, he could only gasp out air, unable to breathe.

"...Even a wonderful restaurant like that isn't without its own base individuals, it seems."

"Gah, hngh, Ele—"

"In exchange for a trifling sum, they'll serve food exactly as they're told and ultimately sacrifice their own life in the process. Do you not think it's appropriate for them to face prejudice and bias? I'm sure that people of vulgar blood do that sort of thing, too."

"Hnah... Hngh, hah...haah, ah."

The toxicity in the seeds of the blue moon fruit was relatively low. Thus, should its poison lead to death, it was nothing more than an unlikely stroke of bad luck, only rarely befalling the elderly or sick, who were already in poor health.

As long as said toxicity wasn't strengthened with Life Arts.

Slipping Word Arts in between the gaps in a person's perception was an assassination skill. Before they had even begun their conversation...while the Seventeenth Minister was dozing off in his chair, Elea had finished the Word Arts incantation necessary to kill him.

"...Now, then. Please, say it one more time for me, Seventeenth Minister. Will you make me one of the Twenty-Nine Officials? Did you truly, deep down, wish to do so?"

"Hah! Hah! Anh, gahk..."

It had been a lie. Elea knew that from the beginning.

Everyone was an enemy. He knew Elea's lineage. As long as there was even one person who did, then one day, even this elderly man was assured to bring her to ruin.

"Is it absurd to divide and separate people based on their lineage or their social status?"

Elea pressed down hard on the Seventeenth Minister's shoulders, even denying him the ability to writhe in his agony.

Bubbles overflowed from the sides of the Seventeenth Minister's mouth, and even as the hemorrhaging of his stomach lining began to mingle with his spit, Elea continued to admonish him in his ear.

"...Now then, Seventeenth Minister. Were you kind enough to say the same things to my mother?"

"......! *Ugh, hnnnngh!* E-El...Ele...a..."

"My mother worked much, much harder than I did. To become a true member of the nobility. Striving so hard to be a woman worthy of you."

Cruelly holding his spasming shoulders, venting her pent-up years of spite, she still looked down at him with the same, perfect smile. Just as her mother taught her, with the beautiful smile she'd inherited.

Become elegant and refined. So no one will scorn you.

"Why are you so quiet?"

"......! ......*Hrngh!* ......!"

"Go on, now. Say it, won't you? That you lived a very happy life."

Watching the light in his eyes fade, Elea continued to address him up until the end. Just as she had before on that day.

With this, he would die. She had to confirm the truth for herself, or she couldn't find relief.

"That you were proud to have such a fine daughter."

"............"

The spasms stopped, and the strength drained from the shoulders she was pressing down on.

Looking at his face, frozen in his final moments of agony, Elea was finally able to wipe away her smile.

In the youth she had lived through, these moments were the only ones where she had peace of mind.

"Farewell, Father."

◆

"So this...is Rosclay's..."

Faced with the cheering blanketing the garden theater, Ninth General Yaniegiz couldn't help gasping.

They hadn't imagined it. The situation before that hadn't been included in their strategic estimations at all.

Even as Rosclay floundered so disgracefully, so clearly defeated, *the people wouldn't accept his defeat.*

The judges of it all wouldn't let Rosclay the Absolute lose. Even in this state, Rosclay was able to turn the spectators into allies.

"...Rosclay the Absolute won't lose!"

It was a sublime spectacle.

Both Elea...and Yaniegiz, as well, had failed to recognize the extent of Rosclay's influence.

Rosclay the Absolute. The pinnacle of valor. A true knight.

He was horribly wounded, without any hopes of victory, and remained unable to put up the slightest glimmer of a fight.

For the first time, he was laying bare a disgraceful sight that none of the citizens had ever seen before.

Rosclay strove nonstop to be perfect precisely because he believed that if he showed himself looking defeated to the people, it would all be over.

…He had been wrong. This wasn't the end of anything at all.

"Even if his preparations were meaningless…! I-if…it's plain to see he's been defeated! *That won't be enough* to finish Rosclay the Absolute!"

He had no way to victory. Nevertheless, maybe, just maybe.

It was the power to make even Yaniegiz, fully aware of the truth behind Rosclay's abilities, believe in such a possibility.

Meanwhile, underneath the audience seating.

Watching just as intently, Elea the Red Tag feared the same power.

I understood… Anyone who put themselves up against Rosclay would be stood up on the side of evil. The longer and longer this match is drawn out, Kia will continue to be at a disadvantage!

The match was dragging on. From the very start, the World Word shouldn't have needed to fear such a thing,

Whoever the opponent, with a single word, she could immediately bring the match to a close.

She should have been able to erase the champion without anyone in the audience understanding anything about how it happened—and make it clear that they needed a replacement in his stead.

"...Why?! Why, why, why...?!" Elea shouted aloud. Her voice reached no one.

"Don't you want to save Eta?! You're indebted to me, aren't you?! Your enemy's the very symbol of the nation that'll bring ruin to your homeland!"

At this point, Kia was hesitating to attack the hopeless Rosclay.

Rosclay would be eternally without a road to victory, but Kia wasn't able to kill him, either.

I would kill him if it were me. No matter what. I need to kill Rosclay, regardless of any malice or hatred toward him, or my happiness will never come. Kill him. I can't relax until I see him torn apart to shreds. If it were me... If I were the one...

Blood dripped from her right hand. She had been keeping a viselike grip on something in her palm, hard enough to draw blood.

...Aaah.

It was a hair ornament.

The hair ornament Kia had bought from the photography studio the day prior. An ornament made with the quality of a toy.

She had said it made her look like a princess, and it really suited Elea.

She's a child.

A normal child, who would pick out such a gift with her immature sensibilities.

She's...she's not like me...

Kia was just a child, merely gifted with the power of almighty Word Arts.

It was dark. Amid the underground darkness, the zealous cheers were the only thing that continued to echo around her.

In that place, neglected by everyone, Elea crouched down.

One after another, sinister black emotions welled up from inside her own heart. Anguish and regret, enough to make her entire life come to nothing.

"...Wh-why...? Why...? Such...such a simple thing!!"

Kia was a normal young girl.

A simple child who had lived in happiness without deceiving or killing anyone.

...In which case, what about Elea?

To Elea, presumption was obvious from a young age. Of course, she needed to kill.

Letting any of the enemies who threatened her remain alive was completely out of the question.

Elea didn't believe in a natural goodness in all beings that Kia took as a given.

"Why...?! Wh-what was...what was I supposed to do?! Why me...and me alone?!"

The green sunbeams filtering through the trees she saw in Eta. Days spent walking through the peaceful hills and fields. Changing into a costume and frolicking about.

She would sometimes behave like a child.

The teacher from the central metropolis would be ignorant of something the children in her care knew to be obvious, and when they'd ridicule her, she'd poke fun at herself.

She was constantly taught by her students about the youthful days she never had.

Because she'd never been a child.

Kia, totally unaware of anything, believed in Elea, got angry on her behalf, and was always trying to give something back to Elea.

Children given love *would end up like this.*

"...Kia!"

While Elea, to a...to a mere child, had...

◆

"E-enough already... End it..."

Rosclay the Absolute lingered in her sights.

This man would certainly not be a threat to Kia. Not only would piercing her all-powerful defenses be impossible, but even more fundamentally, at this point, he couldn't even take a step forward.

However, the presence in front of her was, without a doubt, a deeply obsessed specter, summoned by the curse of the masses.

Tormented with fear, Kia desperately tried to think of a way to defeat him.

She came to one terrible conclusion after the next. No. She didn't want to.

Even after she had brought all of Rosclay's movements to a complete halt, he still didn't give up.

"What am I supposed to do…?!"

What did she have to do to be able to defeat him?

Right now, it was Kia's side of the match that needed to come up with the answer.

"Surrender… Right, surrender! *Say that you surrender!*"

"Sur…"

Rosclay's trembling lips were forced open, and he spit up blood.

Physically controlling the movements of his mouth, she would make him say the words she wanted him to say. If that happened, then she wouldn't destroy his mind or end his life.

"Sur, rend…"

In that moment, Rosclay's right arm leaped up into the air. An instantaneous movement.

He cut his own throat with his sword.

"Eek…!"

He crushed his windpipe. Without a moment's hesitation or reservation.

Rosclay understood instantly that he couldn't let the people hear his words.

"Wh-what does that…what does it even accomplish?! Listen! You don't have any way to win, right?!"

"Gahak, koff!"

Rosclay gave no reply to Kia's words. He could no longer answer her.

His vocal cords and his windpipe were torn apart. There wasn't much time left before his breath would catch in his throat, and he would die.

The only choice was to make it clear to anyone's eyes that he couldn't stand up again—

"Tw-tw... *Twist!*"

"Augh, hngh!"

With a horrible splattering noise, both of Rosclay's legs were twisted backward at the knees.

She had to take both legs from him. If he was left with one, he'd stand back up again.

Blood oozed out from the flesh of his torn leg, and the champion's body was now unable to stand ever again.

"I-I'm—I'm sorry... Please, I'm so sorry..."

Nevertheless, the match wasn't declared to be over.

A wave of sorrow spread throughout the audience. Yet it wasn't one of a despair...

"Get up, Rosclay...! C'mon, stand up!"

"Use your sword, Rosclay! Cut off that demon's head!"

"Please... Please, Wordmaker, give Rosclay your divine protection..."

"Rosclay..."

"I believe in you, Rosclay!"

"Rosclay!"

"Rosclay!"

"Rosclay!"

They believed. Believed in the absolute champion's victory.

Such worthless prayers.

"This isn't right... A-all of you, something's wrong with you, all of you...! J-just let this person...just let him lose already! Can't you see?! Look at how beat-up he is! How do you expect him to stand up with his legs like that?!"

They weren't aware of it themselves. How could they fail to realize that they were the ones trying to kill Rosclay?

Kia could see. The champion she was fighting against was unmistakably alive, minian, and painfully tormented by each and every one of his wounds—Kia could see it all.

This was all plain fact to anyone who looked upon him, just as evident as Kia's victory.

Even with his legs twisted and broken, this champion still wasn't allowed to lose.

What did Kia need to do? What did they expect her to do?

Trust changes into faith, and excessive faith turns into unquestioning belief, and the extremes of unquestioning belief leads to fanaticism.

All the people in this vast arena believed in Rosclay. From deep in their heart.

"Foul play!" someone shouted from among the throng.

Even if she was a tender-aged girl...as long as she was Rosclay's enemy...

"N-no... It's not foul play... Truly... I really did this all on my own, so why...?"

She could hear a Word Arts incantation.

Right now, in this arena, if there was any clear foul play at hand—Kia looked at Rosclay.

"Egirwezi io rozsl. Meameaokea. Nomkloer. Ea kot aarmeal.

Wareaoir." (From Ekraezi to Rosclay. Trudging beast's path. Dwell in a single bough. Sword of all punishment. Expand.)

"Gaugh, hngh...mrrrn... Unnghh...!"

Rosclay had been forcibly holding in his screams, but he then let out a horrible, agonized groan.

The Life Arts coming in from afar were rapidly healing his throat and both of his legs.

Due to the exceedingly rapid healing, as a matter of course, his bones grew distorted and pierced through the skin on his knees.

The outer surface around the tip of his foot branched off, tearing away even more flesh.

While it was ridiculous to even call the resulting body part a leg, it made one single thing possible.

...He was able to stand back up.

"N-no... Aaah! Aaaaaaaaaaaah!!"

"Now, then—"

Drenched in copious amounts of sweat and stifling the intense pain, even then Rosclay smiled. While spitting out blood from his throat, freshly healed with Life Arts.

He was Rosclay the Absolute, after all.

"Let us give it our all."

The knight's body was sent flying. He collided at high speed into the edge of the garden theater and collapsed to the ground again.

Just then, Kia whispered her Word Arts, guided solely by denial.

"Fl-fl... *Hic, hnghh... Fly...*"

It was fear.

A tremendous fear that made an ordinary person forget their aversion toward murder.

Many people don't kill someone with a particular reason in mind. The kill simply out of fear.

Even Kia was capable of it.

"……"

Kia looked down at her own hands.

The sea of emotions billowing about inside her, in that single moment, seemed to quiet, as if she had never felt any of it in the first place.

"Ah."

She wiped her tears. With it, she snapped back to normal.

She moved just as she had before the match…as if she couldn't hear the voices of the crowd.

I…

A single fetter had fallen off her.

The tender-aged young girl, in that moment, for the first time, became cognizant of the truth in her own power.

……I can, do it…

She walked toward Rosclay, slammed into the wall.

Her father and mother. Her sister. Yawika and Thien. It was all to prevent her homeland from being annihilated.

She couldn't care less about Aureatia, criticizing her to their hearts' content, playing dirty and trying to pillage Eta for its resources. Even if, by chance, there were other faces mixed in among the masses that Kia recognized.

I have to do it.

If it was all to protect what she held dear… If it was while she had this resolve in her heart, she could definitely kill him.

This was an enormous change to the young girl Kia, but it was also the thought that her beloved teacher had continued to harbor every day.

I have to do it, I can do it.

Aureatia's strongest knight had collapsed facedown, almost as if he were sleeping.

…She didn't need to do anything special. If she gave the one-word command *Die*, she could bring his life to an end without any suffering, without witnessing any horrific spectacle.

"…The match's mine. I win."

"…Iska…"

The knight mumbled indistinctly as he lay on the ground.

"…Iska… I…… I…"

It was someone's name.

"Hngh, gauugh, bleeergh!!"

Kia vomited.

Thi-this person's… This knight's…

Kia covered her face with both her hands. She was trembling.

All the fear she had but temporarily left behind came surging back.

She realized she was a hair's breadth from dipping her fingers into a horrifying abyss.

Just moments beforehand—and over her own volition.

A person… He's a person…! A person, just like, just like me…!

He has someone dear, just like me... He's a-alive...just like me, and I...!

She had overwhelming power. Absolute power she had obtained out of nowhere.

Kia had a wish. She had something she wanted to protect. She needed to fight.

But did she need *to go that far*?

With her unfair powers, bestowed by the Wordmaker, she could make all her intentions come to pass.

She could crush someone who thought just as she did, who desperately tried to live in the world just as she did, under her foot.

Did she truly have to do *something like that* no matter what?

Without realizing it, she herself was transforming into a monster who harmed others without a moment of self-reflection.

What would everyone back home—what would Elea—think seeing Kia like that?

"Your power is a gift to bring happiness to others."

"I—I—"

It was at that same moment that someone's body hugged her close.

The body warmth, the soft feeling, enveloped her.

"This is the Seventeenth Minister! We surrender!" the intruder shouted.

"Elea..."

Elea was in tears.

"N-no more... Don't make her kill... Enough... Stop, please..."

◆

Kia could do anything.

While she may not have possessed a second name yet, with how freely she could do anything she wanted with her Word Arts, she could easily give herself a name someday that would astound everyone.

Five years earlier. The world beyond the forest was under the threat of the True Demon King's grave despair, and all the adults seemed to think that the Eta Sylvan Province where Kia and her friends lived was the only place left behind by the rest of the world.

The children like Kia and Thien were still young and hadn't been taught yet about the existence of the True Demon King, so they simply assumed that all the adults were discussing some sort of difficult topic.

Yawika was still very small, and while all the adults went to their gathering, Kia would often look after her. Yawika was an elf born with tanned skin, which was apparently somewhat rare.

Since Kia was the one looking after this rare child, the adults also showed her more respect, and she felt that they should've then been more willing to overlook her teasing and pranks.

"Kia, Kia."

"Yes, yes, what is it, Yawika? Sleepy?"

Kia had brought Yawika along to the lake as usual and was gathering mushrooms to use for cooking.

Frogs were croaking all around her, and Kia thought they sounded almost like musical instruments.

"Mrrrm, Kia, cheek!"

"Sheesh, what is it?"

Yawika's small hand slapped against Kia's cheek.

From an early age, Yawika had acted a bit spoiled, and while she wasn't great with words, she was a cheerful child who smiled often.

"If only you'd hurry up and establish your words so we could actually have a conversation together."

"Cheek! Cheek!"

Even in this world, where all sentient living beings could converse with Word Arts, it didn't mean that newly born children could eloquently use their words to communicate. As they began to grow, they needed to naturally shape their inner system of words. Along the course of learning their own unique words, they begin to realize that those same words addressed the people and things around them. These were the Word Arts that could bring about various phenomena.

As Kia dipped her toes into the cold lake, she addressed the ground right by her side.

"Grow."

With a speed that seemed to send pops into the air, mushrooms sprouted up from the gaps in the rock.

They were the mushrooms Kia was asked to gather for the

day's meal. She could make them grow right outside the house if she really wanted, without needing to come all the way out to the lake, but Grandma Micchi would get angry at her, so she thought it was better not to.

She claimed that mushrooms and fruits should each grow in their proper and befitting places, and if Kia kept using her Word Arts nonstop to make food, the forest might become sick.

I don't really think there's anything to worry about, honestly.

Kia could do anything. Whether it was creating, destroying, or even changing situations to be exactly how she wanted them to be.

With my power, I can reverse anything back to normal no matter what happens.

She used Word Arts once again on the mushroom.

"Disappear."

The mushrooms Kia made appear now disappeared. Just as things had originally been.

Before she had fully formed her own words, Kia was equipped with Word Arts that could make anything and everything obey her as she saw fit. Thanks to this, Eta was never lacking food, all the houses in the village had been renovated anew, and they were never troubled by terrible weather.

Kia thought she deserved even more special treatment if she was being honest, but nevertheless, just like the other children, she was forced to look after and care for Yawika like this.

Although, in Kia's case, she just needed to say, "Refresh the chimney," or "Make it rain until tomorrow," and her job would be over, so perhaps that was simply the way it was.

The adults were always hard at work tilling the fields, repairing the waterways, and trimming back the forest. If they asked for Kia's help, it was all work she could finish with a single word, but she understood that the adults all thought there was value behind things gained through this intense labor.

"*Ah*, now there's nothing to do, huh, Yawika...?"

That was why even Kia would bear with it sometimes. Even if the root vegetables she hated showed up in her dinner, she didn't change them into different ingredients like she did when she was younger. Nor did she interfere when someone was spending a lot of time and effort making a wooden chair, by using her Word Arts to finish the chair for them unasked.

As she continued to mature, Kia grew to understand she had a vague and undefined set of standards. She could use her Word Arts if it was to help create food. If she was going to create toys to play with, she could use them as long as she made sure to clean them up afterward. If it was for everyone's benefit, she could use them to change the weather. Manipulating the water level in the river wasn't okay unless it was truly and seriously for the sake of everyone, too, but if necessary, she would absolutely use them.

"*Grow. Disappear.*"

"Mrrrr, mrrrrn."

Yawika groaned. Perhaps she didn't like that Kia was playing with the mushrooms. It was truly very rare for Yawika's mood to sour when the two of them were together.

"What's wrong, Yawika? Are you all right? Did a bug bite you?"

"Mmrrrr!"

"Are you hungry?"

"Kia, bad!"

Yawika's nails caught a bit on Kia's cheek as she slapped her face.

"Ow! Sheesh, what's your problem?!"

She could do anything she dreamed of, and she was obediently looking after her, so why was she being treated like this?

"Why're you mad? Want me to sing you something?"

"Shoes! Shoes! *Mnnnh!*"

"*Sigh.* I still don't get it..."

Kia didn't understand children at all. As long as their Word Arts language was still undeveloped, they were halfway between a beast and a sentient person. Maybe Yawika's parents could understand what she was trying to say?

"Nooo! *Mnnnn!*"

Finding herself at a complete loss at what to do about Yawika's cries, Kia's eyes happened to fall on the mushrooms growing beside her.

Oh, right.

For some reason, up until that moment, the idea had never once occurred to Kia.

If her all-powerful Word Arts could bring forth anything and everything she wanted and even be capable of re-creating things entirely...

Perhaps she'd be able to make another person who understood Word Arts *do whatever she told them to*?

To Kia, it seemed like a truly genius idea. She had fixed up injuries for her parents and everyone in the village, but why then had she assumed she couldn't change their thoughts, too?

"Hey, Yawika."

Kia was truly just about to do exactly that.

There were no obstacles anywhere to stop her from putting it into practice, and a single instruction would have been all the incessantly crying Yawika would need.

"......"

Yet suddenly, her eyes stopped on the frog crying on the ground right next to Yawika. Truly, just a simple coincidence.

I mean, giving it a try on a frog first won't change anything, right?

Kia looked toward the frog and commanded it.

"Stop crying."

Instantly, the single frog in her sights stopped its croaking.

Up until that very moment, the frog had been desperately letting out a shrill cry without end.

"...Great. See, that went just fine. I'm a genius."

Absentmindedly patting Yawika as she wailed in her lap, Kia kept observing the frog for a few moments. The frog didn't cry.

As the collective choir of their croaks continued on loud enough to drown out the sound of the wind, the frog simply remained there, its eyeballs goggling about. Gradually, Kia began to find the sight unnerving.

This frog remained like this *because Kia had told it to do so.*

Even an overly serious boy like Thien would catch frogs and play with them, yet for some reason, the now absolute silence of the frog seemed a much more terrifying deed than dragging, spinning, and crushing one until it popped.

"G-go..."

It was okay. No matter what happened, she could do things over.

"Go back to normal."

The frog once again began to croak. Kia breathed a sigh of relief. Thank goodness.

"Yawika?"

The young girl Kia held in her arms was no longer crying.

"Huh? No way."

It was weird that she wasn't crying. After all, she had been in such a sour mood a few moments ago.

"Wait, but why?"

She was unsettled. She needed to ask an adult for help.

There was a voice—*gweh, gweh.* Kia's body trembled in surprise.

It was the frog's voice. It had gone back to normal—and was croaking again.

"...G-go—*go back to normal.*"

Kia once again used Word Arts on the creature.

She couldn't clearly say why. But she got the sense there was something off about this frog. Like the intervals and pitch of its cries weren't exactly how they had been before.

It wasn't croaking like it had been at first. It was as if it was croaking *in the way that Kia thought it had been croaking.*

"N-no, it can't be."

Kia hugged Yawika close.

"Kia, Kia!"

Yawika smiled, as if everything before had been a lie.

"C-cry. C'mon, cry."

She was scared. Even though it was only an insignificant frog she had changed with her Word Arts—and she hadn't actually used them on the tiny Yawika at all.

"Yawika. It's all just a joke, right? You're still you, right?"

"Cheek!"

She drilled her finger into Kia's cheek. Just like always. Like the Yawika Kia knew. Without scratching her with her nails at all...

There was no possible way to confirm it for herself. Yawika still hadn't fully developed her Word Arts. There wasn't any way to prove if she had been eternally changed forever or not, no matter what she did.

"Yawika!"

Kia roughly shook Yawika.

"Mww..."

No one had seen. Yawika might be *just as she was before*, and Kia wouldn't get yelled at—but it certainly wasn't okay to do such a thing without the world ever knowing about it.

"Mweh."

It was likely because her tiny body had been shaken so thoroughly—Yawika threw up the contents of her stomach.

"Weeeeeeh...!"

Then she started to cry. Just like normal.

"H-haaah..."

Kia lost her strength and sat down where she stood. It was a relief.

Thank goodness—she *never even thought* that Yawika would end up vomiting. Yawika hadn't been transformed into a version that bent to Kia's whims.

"Yawika..."

She stroked the young girl's back. What a handful, a truly troublesome child.

But that was the Yawika she loved.

"Kia."

Kia realized that, at some point, Yawika had taken off her right shoe. She had been so distressed that she didn't have the presence of mind to notice before.

"Aaah... Right. So that's what it was."

"Shoes! Look!"

A tiny frog had slipped inside her shoe.

She had been crying because it was uncomfortable. Once she was able to get it off, her mood improved.

There wasn't anything strange at all. That was the simple truth to it.

"I'm sorry... I'm sorry, Yawika..."

For a few seconds, she continued to embrace Yawika while she cried. The fact that, in that moment, she didn't go through with her intentions must have been the most fortunate period in Kia's life.

"I'm so, so glad I didn't use any Word Arts on you."

◆

In the middle of the garden theater, Elea kept her arms wrapped tight around Kia. Almost like a mother bird embracing her egg. As if to protect the girl from the noise and gazes of the audience.

"That's enough."

She wanted to cry more than anyone, and even now, Elea was truly the most unhappy of all, yet for some reason, before Kia, she spoke words of encouragement.

"All the scary stuff is gone now, okay?"

"...Elea. Elea."

Kia was crying. Never in her wildest dreams thinking that everything had all been staged by Elea.

"It's okay. I...," Elea said, stroking the child's golden hair. "I will always be right here with you, okay?"

She should have forced Kia to kill Jivlart.

If, back then, Kia had removed the shackles on her mind preventing her from murder, Elea surely would have won here.

More than anything, she should have understood that...and that was supposed to be her entire reason for summoning Jivlart to her house—why then, did she end him by her own hands instead? Why, in that one moment, had she made one mistake?

In any case, Elea had done it.

Before she could think things through, Elea had killed Jivlart with her own hands.

Why?

There had to be some reason. As she held Kia's tiny body and felt her quivering against her chest, Elea replayed the same regret over and over in her head.

Why? Why? Why?

"We've confirmed Kia's foul play!"

At the same time, the match adjudicator Meeka made an announcement.

"I will inform you all of the report I just received from our soldiers! We have several testimonies from our citizens! The Seventeenth Minister, Elea the Red Tag, made Kia stand on this dangerous battlefield...and provided her with Word Arts support from outside the arena! Therefore, for this fourth match! Kia is disqualified, and Rosclay the Absolute is declared the winner!"

There wasn't anyone in the audience who doubted these words.

The ear-rending cheers rained down on Rosclay as he remained collapsed on the ground and unable to stand.

The champion didn't get up, as if he was a godly idol with no mind of his own.

Supporting Kia in her severely exhausted state, Elea returned to the passageway.

Despite agreeing to make Jivlart fight against Rosclay, she had altered the agreement at the very last moment. To Aureatia, right now she was essentially a traitor.

"...Elea."

"It's okay. Breathe in, breathe out... Calm down, nice and slow, and it'll all be okay."

She rubbed Kia's back for her. A small back that made the World Word's power seem like a lie.

We'll get out of Aureatia...and flee somewhere.

A future of darkness. It seemed like there wasn't anywhere across the horizon for her to belong.

We'll conceal ourselves, get outside the city on the steam train... then, in a carriage together...

If she was with Kia, she just might be able to pull off such an escape.

A young girl with almighty power. Elea could control her. She knew she could make her fight against their pursuers from Aureatia and even make her kill their enemies. If they kept that up long enough, then escape was really in their grasp.

...I know. I'll be a teacher in Eta.

It seemed like a wonderful idea to her. In that tiny village, completely indifferent to combat or glory.

Playing together with the children, covered in flowers and mud.

Then, once more. She could look at the brilliant morning sun from the children's secret spot.

Just like that day...

Soldiers blocked her path.

"Seventeenth Minister. You must be tired. Allow me to accompany you."

"We'll guide you from here. Come. We shall bring Miss Kia along with us."

They were soldiers with Rosclay's faction.

Given that her almighty Word Arts had come to light, Aureatia would secure Kia for themselves. As for who was needed to control the World Word, Rosclay's camp now knew the answer.

The fight that Elea had gambled her life on had been a failure from the start, and the fourth match, not only before it even started…at the earliest possible point, had that outcome fixed.

Even then.

"I understand. Let us go together."

Elea smiled slightly.

She showered the soldiers' faces with the contents of the thin vial she kept hidden on her.

"*Guagh?!*"

"*Bwahk?!*"

"Huh, what's going on?!"

"Time to run, Kia!"

Even then, Kia must not degenerate into a weapon for the sake of Aureatia. That was how she felt.

Elea the Red Tag had been unable to obtain anything she had sought after.

She had blown it all herself.

In which case, if she could just get one thing right.

She pulled Kia's hand and fled. The Aureatia soldiers were trying to capture her.

The marketplace encircling the garden theater. Elea dashed across the midday market. The odd looks from the citizens pierced through her. Elea was a frantic mess, her clothes in disarray, covered in blood and tears.

Ah—Elea was supposed to always keep up appearances, to make sure no one scorned her, that no one looked down on her.

"Elea… Elea, listen to me! What're you doing?! Tell me what's going on!"

Kia was looking at her, too. The World Word Elea had discovered at the end of so much bloodshed was exactly as the preposterous legends spoke of…an invincible Word Arts user possessing absolute power.

However, they were a totally normal and innocent young girl who had never even experienced the death of someone close to them before.

I…

She had been jealous of Kia for being this way.

She ran.

Standing out in front of Kia.

To make sure she didn't see her face.

I'm so…so hideous…!

Outside the world that endlessly tormented Elea, there was a world like the Eta Sylvan Province, one of tranquility.

And living there had been a young girl who innocently believed in her.

A genuinely beautiful young girl, smeared by neither spite nor malice.

"Kia. I have something very important to tell you right now."

Elea stopped after they had reached the base of a long stone staircase.

There, she crouched down to Kia's eye level. Elea gave her a smile.

"Do me this favor, okay? Listen well to what your teacher's going to say, okay?"

"…Elea?"

Now.

Now was the time she needed to tell Kia the truth.

...The truth is: I've been fooling you.

Her turquoise eyes, like lakes filled with tears, reflected the world in its vivid, bright daylight.

The obvious and plain realization came to her, that the world reflected in a person's eyes was the one they saw.

I... In truth, I was just using you to gain power. All the suffering you experienced was all according to my designs. In truth... I'm a terribly vulgar woman who betrayed you through all of it. Even everything involving your homeland was entirely because of me.

Elea the Red Tag continuously used everything she could in order to survive.

She hadn't only deceived other people, but her own words and heart, as well.

Which was why this sort of deception was all-too-easy work for her.

...So. Everything here is my fault, so you alone need to escape.

With this, Elea gripped both of Kia's hands.

"I'm sorry for scaring you. Kia... You showed your unbelievable strong power out there, didn't you? That's why Aureatia's military is chasing after you. We needed to escape them."

"O-okay...right. You're right... I really did something terrible. Everyone's probably scared of me...and hates me..."

At this, Elea stroked her golden hair.

"Not at all. Ever since coming to Aureatia... You did a great job obeying my rule about your Word Arts."

"So um… Listen, Elea…! I—I…!"

Tears flowed from Kia's eyes.

"I just have to run away by myself! Th-that way, they'll just come chasing after me, right? I'm invincible, so I'll be toootally fine, okay…?"

Indeed. When it came to Kia, Elea knew everything about her.

Elea could even tell the lies that would lead Kia to this exact answer.

The Aureatia soldiers were after Elea. As long as Kia's weak point, Elea herself, wasn't there with her, Kia would be able to cleanly escape no matter how far it may take her.

"So um, Elea! No talk about any goodbyes or anything, right?!"

"Of course. Make sure you escape. I'll be here waiting for you the whole time. So please… Kia, be sure to use your Word Arts correctly."

It was a lie.

She had tried, more than anyone else, to make her use that power incorrectly.

"Because that…that power…is a gift, for bringing happiness to others."

A lie.

The World Word was a gift for bringing happiness to Elea.

Lies. Nothing but lies.

"Yeah… Okay…!"

"So for the time being…you've completed my lessons for you. I'll give you your second name now, Kia."

Elea brought her forehead to Kia's and announced the name.

It was a name that Kia herself had been completely oblivious to, yet it was more appropriate than any other.

"...World Word. Kia the World Word."

"My name..."

Elea acted as though she truly was a teacher.

Even as she resolved to tell her the truth, even if it was her final opportunity to do so.

Even if her ugliness ended up being exposed to everyone in the world, she wanted to remain this way in front of Kia alone.

Since Elea had always been the perfect teacher, beautiful and kind.

"...Thank you. Thank you, Elea."

Kia nestled in close and pressed her cheek up to Elea's own.

She took off the bandage over the eye Jivlart had injured and spoke.

"*Heal.*"

Then she smiled as she cried.

"I really do like those eyes. They're so pretty."

"Kia..."

"You know, Elea. The truth is, um, getting to spend all this time together with you...made me really happy."

"I was happy, too."

A lie. Not only these words, but everything else.

She had always been spouting nothing but lies in order to manipulate Kia.

"I love you, Kia... I do... I love you so much..."

Lies.

Another lie.

Elea the Red Tag was always telling lies.

Elea cried.

"I-it really is the truth..."

"...Elea. Miss Elea...was kind and pretty. Someone who everyone...was proud to call their teacher."

The young girl with the almighty Word Arts made one final wish to Elea.

"Find happiness!"

They were not Word Arts.

Yet more than any kind of Word Arts, such parting words were...

Kia. Elea's light, dearer to her than anything else, dashed off.

Her long golden hair fluttered, shining in the sunbeams and wind.

Elea turned her back and advanced toward the shade, diametrically opposite the young elf girl.

She wished happiness for Kia, more than anyone else. She wanted her to believe in the good.

Because Elea would carry all the darkness herself.

Kia, I—

One more time.

She found herself wanting to call out to the girl.

At that moment a soldier jumping out from the alleyway ran his sword through Elea's waist.

She collapsed. Her vision dyed dark crimson.

"...Ah!"

The Aureatia soldier who slashed her seemed more unsettled than Elea.

"...My apologies, Lord Jel!"

He reported to the man standing behind him.

"I only wanted to cut her legs to immobilize her, but because she suddenly turned around, my aim was thrown off...!"

"No matter."

A cold and levelheaded voice. She could hear the familiar tone of contempt.

Third Minister Jel was looking down over Elea.

"This latest incident has made it quite clear. Even if we spare this woman's life...she will persistently use others for her own self-interest. A she-devil who putrefies Aureatia from within. We shouldn't have ever given her a chance... I'll take responsibility for the decision."

...Ah.

There was something dirty right in front of Elea's eyes.

The viscera spilling out from her stomach was soiling the ground.

She always strove to be beautiful. She wanted everyone to view both her birth and her appearance as pristine and fair.

Aaah, my...my insides... Not this...

All of Elea the Red Tag was present in its hideous form and color.

Vulgar. Base. Vile. Crude.

"...I take responsibility for all of it. I was a fool, a fool for expecting anything of her."

...Stop. Don't...don't look at me... Brother...

As long as Kia could live on in happiness, that was enough. Yet. In truth, she...

She didn't want to die all alone.

She didn't want to die scorned by everyone.

"Die!" Jel shouted.

The levelheaded Third Minister made sure never to let his emotions show.

However, there was a distinct disappointment and rage contained in his shout.

"Cursed daughter of base blood! You betray your compatriots, manipulate a young girl, and kill...and even kill your own father! Don't you dare think someone like you will be given a chance to atone for this! Elea the Red Tag! A pitiful death is exactly what a wretch like you deserves!"

Amid the pool of blood, there was a golden glint.

The hair ornament. The one that really suited Elea, that made her look like a princess.

....

She desperately stretched her fingers out toward it.

There was sure to be light, at the end of the darkness.

But by that point, there was nothing. Her light had departed.

Before her fingers could reach the hair ornament, Elea's life came to an end.

◆

His optic nerves hurt. Even the glare from the lights was too bright.

Pain. Throughout Rosclay's entire body was nothing but intense pain. The pain that came from being remade with healing Life Arts.

Lying down on an infirmary bed, he spoke in delirium.

"...I lost."

Sitting at his side, Yaniegiz shook his head.

"That...is not so, Rosclay."

How many of Rosclay's wounds would recover? At the very least, he may have had more hope than Soujirou, who had completely severed his leg.

He was a champion who absolutely couldn't die. There were a total of four Life Arts specialists in charge of Rosclay's treatment. At least, they'd get him ready in time for the second round. Regardless of everything it would cost.

"...It was definitely your victory. If you hadn't been so well trained yourself, you wouldn't have been able to stay conscious in the face of those Word Arts. The Word Arts that demolished the mound of dirt and the Word Arts that healed your legs were all part of your preparations. Getting the Twenty-Sixth Minister to cooperate with us was also in thanks to your honest abilities."

Ninth General Yaniegiz concealed his personal history publicly, but Rosclay knew.

Yaniegiz was also born poor. An individual Rosclay had once saved in the past.

One of those who felt genuine pride at being saved by the champion.

"...That's just how many allies you've created for yourself. Far beyond what we imagined... Rosclay the Absolute has become a true champion..."

There was no room for any doubt. If it had been anyone else, they couldn't have brought down the almighty Kia.

"To all the people of Aureatia, you are a magnificent champion. Rosclay."

"...Still."

Rosclay mumbled as he stared at the ceiling.

"Elea the Red Tag had worked alone."

"......"

He had many more allies on his side than anyone else. The artificially constructed champion had won over the entire citizenry of Aureatia to his cause.

Nevertheless. If even a single element had gone awry, then there was no doubt...

"All by herself, she drove us all into a corner."

Match Four. Winner, Rosclay the Absolute.

Aureatia. At night, long after the sun had sunk below the clouds.

At this hour, the Order's chapel doors were locked, but it was also a time when regular believers normally didn't visit.

However, Kuze the Passing Disaster knew that there was someone who would offer prayers every day. When the bell sounded to let the faithful know the day was over, he would appear without fail.

"Hey, there. Haven't met before, have we?"

He was an ogre. A hero candidate by the name of Uhak the Silent.

Viewing him in prayer from behind, his back alone, wrapped in white vestments, was wider than the great shield Kuze wielded.

"See, my name's Kuze the Passing Disaster… Mind if I sit here?"

Uhak raised his head and stared hard into Kuze's eyes.

There was no reply. Thus, Kuze used the nonverbal reactions to carefully gauge Uhak's intentions. Just as he always did when speaking with Nastique.

"…Sorry. I'll try as much as I can not to disturb you, okay?"

The massacre at Alimo Row. According to the memoirs of the older woman and Order priest, Cunodey the Ring Seat, Uhak was an ogre who was born without receiving the blessing of inborn Word Arts. The investigative report produced by Hiroto the Paradox reached the same conclusion.

It wasn't that he hadn't composed his own words inside his mind, like with infants and babies.

Nor had he lost the ability to speak, or his hearing, from a permanent disability.

Despite having been proven that he didn't have any problem with either of these senses, the Word Arts for conversing, that even visitors were capable of utilizing, weren't present in Uhak the Silent—and Uhak the Silent alone.

One of the reasons for Kuze's visit to the chapel was to investigate Uhak the Silent, his presence the largest wild card for Hiroto's camp.

"It's my fault that I wasn't able to save Mother Cunodey."

However, Kuze had a far bigger reason than that to be there.

Cunodey the Ring Seat was dead. She was Uhak the Silent's and his sponsor, Sixteenth General Nofelt's, teacher and mentor— and Kuze's own as well.

That day the massacre occurred in Alimo Row. Kuze, visiting Alimo Row on his rounds, saw a burning red light in the direction of the church. He ran over, spurred by fear and impatience, but by the time he arrived, it was already too late.

The one who had slaughtered a majority of the rioting villagers was Uhak, now sitting beside him. But on that day, Kuze had killed many himself. Even if it meant killing and cutting his way through, he tried to reach Cunodey's side as fast as possible.

"...*Bweh-heh-heh*. Even now I still think about it sometimes, you know? Like, if my horse had been just a bit faster, or if I hadn't made any stops along the way... Stuff like that. You know, the day before that? I was with the Order in another town...and flying paper airplanes with the kids there. Ridiculous, right?"

He knew that Word Arts wouldn't reach Uhak the Silent. This was Kuze's one-sided confession.

It wasn't to earn the forgiveness from someone else, but a necessary act to try confirming with his own words where exactly the source of the sin lay.

"Hey. Uhak the Silent."

...As well as a crime that there was no longer any way to verify.

"When you killed people, was it painful?"

Uhak the Silent was an ogre.

Nevertheless, Kuze wanted him to adhere to the teachings of the Wordmaker.

As Cunodey's final disciple, different from Kuze and his deplorable state.

"Belka the Rending Quake...and everyone else in Alimo Row, they had all been alive. They had hearts, minds, and Word Arts. Even if, for example, the Demon King had broken their minds beyond saving... Honestly, no one should've died, and I shouldn't have made her kill anybody..."

That day, he had tried saving Cunodey, even if it meant killing the villagers. If he ended up surrounded by a group with murder on their mind, then Nastique would kill them. No matter how much Kuze tried to protect them, as long as everyone who he faced was an enemy, countless lives would always slip through his fingers.

It was a nightmarish crime.

"I wish it had been just me."

Silence was Uhak's only reply.

"...Sorry I didn't make it in time."

His mumble came out like a groan.

"Uhak. Listen... Truth is, even you *could've gotten through it all without killing anyone.* If you had adhered to the teachings, your heart would've been able to be saved. I should've been the only one to go through it. Just me..."

At the end of Cunodey's memoirs, she repented for accidently inviting so much death and chronicled the despair she felt at her inability to believe in the Wordmaker's teachings anymore.

Even if she was going to meet the same fate, he should have at least been able to give her a peaceful death.

Or perhaps to Cunodey, that had been the proper end for her.

To die after awakening to the truth that the hearts of beasts and the hearts of people were equally valuable.

"Thing is, Nastique... She can't get close to you. That power to nullify Word Arts has got to be the real deal."

They were the only two in the chapel.

The figure of the white angel, who was always supposed to be at Kuze's side, was nowhere to be seen, even by Kuze himself.

An unusual power to erase any and all supernatural phenomena. Kuze didn't know if such a thing truly existed, but that power was, in truth, driving away the invincible power of death that kept Kuze protected.

If there is actually a time when an angel, who's been alive since the creation, is supposed to die.

If Uhak the Silent simply had the will—would it be possible for him to erase the very existence of Nastique herself?

Nastique's presence, eternally lost. It was an absolutely terrifying thing for Kuze to imagine. However, if such an ending did exist for her, it also seemed, in some seasons, a type of salvation for him.

Nullifying Word Arts, huh.

Now, with this abnormality right before his eyes, Kuze was able to understand something very clearly.

Uhak *must not be allowed to appear* in the Sixways Exhibition.

The biggest priority for Hiroto's camp was being able to monopolize the information on Uhak the Silent ahead of time. To Hiroto's camp, Uhak wasn't a hero candidate they were meant to vanquish, but a trump card they needed to incorporate into their numbers immediately.

As such, Uhak's details were currently thoroughly kept hidden by Zigita Zogi's secret agent cells in various areas. On top of things, Uhak's sponsor, Twenty-Sixth General Nofelt, appeared to be covering up the incident in Alimo Row and would likely try to keep the true identity of his hero candidate hidden until the day of the match.

...Because simply revealing the truth behind Uhak was likely to change absolutely everything.

The fact that an ogre belonged to the Order. The fact that ogre had massacred a frontier town. As well as the fact that this ogre appeared in Aureatia as a hero candidate—and his existence itself negated the absoluteness of Word Arts, the very building blocks of their world.

What...? Just what are you thinking? What're you doing? Tell me, Nofelt.

Twenty-Sixth General Nofelt the Somber Wind. His relationship with Kuze stemmed from their shared childhood in an Order almshouse. Unlike the other children, he immediately started being promoted up the ranks in Aureatia, until reaching the top as the Twenty-Sixth General.

He was a companion who, unlike Kuze, had been able to go out into the light-touched world.

Everything will come to nothing. All the world will be unable to keep believing in the Wordmaker—and in the very world that the Wordmaker created for us all... It won't just be the Order that'll be finished, but the very world itself; I'm telling you... Shouldn't you understand that?

Nofelt was another man who had been too late.

Nofelt's unit had arrived in Alimo Row the day after Cunodey's death.

If even Nofelt, having won brilliant success for himself, if even the one among them who stood to become the happiest among them all, had given up hope in the entire world...

...Where are we supposed to find salvation?

If that wasn't a curse, but the cruel truth that filled the heroless world...

Then even Uhak the priest may not have been able to dispel that despair.

◆

Leisha was supposed to have been able to help this almshouse.

As she took bites of the crude wheat porridge, she couldn't stop the thought from crossing her mind.

The talk of her adoption by a wealthy frontier farmer had dissipated. She was terribly disappointed when she heard and wanted to cry, but she still remained with the Order, and when she considered she'd be able to see her beloved Kuze, that helped soothe her wounded heart ever so slightly.

"Hey, if I did actually get adopted…"

The meals had gotten a bit shabbier, but the building didn't change at all. It was just as filled with cracks as it had been before, the wallpaper design still outdated, still the same almshouse building that Leisha had long known and loved.

Even then, even if it didn't appear like anything was changing, they would not be able to keep things going as they had for long.

"I would've been able to give you all a bit more luxury, wouldn't I have? If they were getting a beautiful woman like me, why then, in return, I'm sure they would've donated a *hefty* sum for the honor. That's why, everyone, um…"

"…It's fine. This isn't your fault, Leisha."

Father Naijy, sitting across the dinner table from her, gave a fatigued smile.

He was a young priest in training who still couldn't read all the scripture. But he had always cared for the children's well-being, handling all the difficult things Leisha didn't really understand like money and their relationship with the assembly, so she thought he must have truly been very tired.

"Master Jivlart...the man who had long been lending money to this church, has died. It's my fault I wasn't able to create some means beyond his contributions to keep this church running."

"I've heard about this Master Jivlart person always providing for us, but...I never met him."

"That's right. For all of you, you're probably more familiar with that Tu girl who's been coming by lately to play with you all... But he had been here many times, starting way back. Apparently Master Jivlart didn't really want to show himself to children... He would immediately leave whenever you all came."

"Why?"

"He said he *didn't want small children to think of him as a bad guy. Ha-ha...* Strange, isn't it? I don't believe there'd be any child who would speak ill of him, myself."

"...I see."

A strange man.

However, Leisha felt a bit like she understood where he was coming from.

When Kuze the Passing Disaster would come visit, Leisha always strove to be as perfect as possible. If he saw her looking unsightly, her hair dirty, or her behavior violent, his heart's inclination to take Leisha for his wife might disappear.

Leisha had always been giving it her all. Since she was a beautiful girl who handled all of that.

"Maybe he was someone who other people couldn't look at charitably."

"......"

"Sinister-looking features, somewhat violent mannerisms, always acting childish—"

Had the family that was supposed to adopt Leisha heard some terrible rumors about her?

That her math grades were low, or that she got violent with the boys, or perhaps...it was the fault of some crucial lack of elegance that Leisha herself wasn't even aware of.

The *poor upbringing* that she had no way of subverting had eternally closed the door on the light she believed would lead her out from the shadows. The idea absolutely terrified her.

"...Even among people like that, there are good people like Master Jivlart, too, though. A person's outward appearance doesn't tell you everything, right?"

"You're a mature girl, Leisha."

"That's right. I am mature. After all, I have to be taken as a wife first. I've completely giving up on being adopted by any family. I'm going to stay with Father Kuze."

Father Naijy was awfully languid and listless. She could tell that, as he worried about the future of their orphanage, he was trying hard to bear with the death of their benefactor, Jivlart.

"When that time comes, I'll call everyone to the wedding...all the kids here—and you too, Father Naijy."

"*Ha-ha...* Thank you."

Naijy feebly chuckled.

After another big month or so, Leisha and the others were being taken in by another one of the Order's almshouses. There were some children who would be going to the opposite end of vast Aureatia. Others still would be going even farther, out to different cities entirely.

"So try to cheer up a bit, okay?"

"...You're right. I have to give it my all from here on out."

Three days later, Father Naijy passed away.

A carriage that happened by discovered his body floating in the nearby lake.

She also heard that, in a note he left behind in shakily disarrayed letters, he wrote out an apology to Leisha and the others.

She wished he had lived, even if he couldn't care for her and the others anymore.

It was two days before Father Kuze was set to fight in the Six-ways Exhibition.

Severely wounded in the third match, Ozonezma was resting inside one of the especially large buildings within Yuca the Halation Gaol's stable block, which had been turned into a medical treatment room.

Even after the match was over, he avoided revealing his aberrant appearance to the public. The hero candidate, gravely wounded in his honorable true duel, had his health ensured by the courteous care of Aureatia's doctors. Of course, to Ozonezma, possessing superb technical skill as a medic, performing the operations on him himself was a far more certain and reliable form of treatment.

"I brought her, Ozonezma."

Then, one day, Yuca appeared in his treatment room with a young girl in tow.

Long, firm limbs and a lovely chestnut-colored braid.

"YOU'VE COME, TU."

"*Whoooa*, what an incredible animal! So you're Ozonezma, right? I'm Tu the Magic! Nice to meet you."

Looking like nothing more than a healthy young girl at first glance, Tu the Magic was, as far as Ozonezma could perceive through his senses, more aberrant than Ozonezma, different not only from the minian races, but every other life-form under the sun.

"Your fur coat's all stiff... You have eight whole legs? So I guess you're not a wolf, then."

Tu the Magic wasn't intimidated at all, looking at Ozonezma's terrifying form, getting closer and patting him roughly. Although it wasn't exactly a pleasing sensation for Ozonezma's body, still not fully healed of all its wounds, he resignedly accepted the contact.

"I AM A CHIMERA. DID FLINSUDA GIVE YOU PERMISSION TO MEET WITH ME?"

"No worries there! She smiled and said it was okay, just like she usually does. She and Yuca seemed pretty friendly, too!"

"...I SEE. IT DOES SEEM, THEN, THE INTERPRETATION OF THE DISQUALIFICATION TERMS DICTATES NO ISSUE WITH CONTACTING A HERO CANDIDATE WHO HAS ALREADY WITHDRAWN FROM THE COMPETITION."

"?"

...Nevertheless, contact between a current candidate and a defeated one was still a risky proposition.

Amid the sixteen hero candidates, there existed those who were capable of achieving their goals by manipulating the defeated combatants, too. Zigita Zogi the Thousandth, who Ozonezma shared a cooperative relationship with, was one such individual.

"You don't look like me at all, huh. Yuca, are you really sure that Ozonezma's my big brother?"

"Don't ask me; really, I just repeated what Ozonezma here told me."

"...IT IS TRUE, TU THE MAGIC. YOU CONSTITUTE WHAT WOULD BE CONSIDERED MY SISTER MODEL."

He had felt it was a certain kind of destiny that Tu the Magic would appear at the same time as him at the Sixways Exhibition. The question was, though: How much did she understand about her own history and the purpose behind her creation?

Her opponent, Kuze the Passing Disaster, was an assassin who wielded a supernatural power of unequivocal instant death. At the same time, on top of that, she needed to take on the stratagems of Zigita Zogi the Thousandth and Hiroto the Paradox backing him.

IT IS HIGHLY POSSIBLE THAT SHE WILL DIE IN HER MATCH TWO DAYS FROM NOW.

This may very well have been his final opportunity to talk with her, too.

"THERE IS ONE THING I MUST KNOW, FIRST. HOW KNOWLEDGEABLE ARE YOU ABOUT YOUR OWN BODY?"

"Whaaaat? Um... I—I was taught about everything, sure, but...but of course I didn't remember any of that! I can't explain it that well."

"WHAT YOU DO REMEMBER WILL SUFFICE."

"...Ummm, well... Something about 'particles'? And al—uh, alignment... And the treatment? Of the heat generated... What was it again? Oh, cells...the next cells, uh... Hmmm..."

"...IN OTHER WORDS, YOU DO NOT REMEMBER THE THEORY BEHIND YOUR OWN CONSTRUCTION."

"But I know the important stuff, and that's all that matters. What's really important isn't how exactly you were born or whatever, but how you live."

A big smile spread across Tu's face, and she clenched both her fists.

It was clear from Ozonezma's eyes that she did this in an attempt to put an end to her explanation.

"DO YOU REMEMBER THE NAME OF THE PERSON WHO TAUGHT YOU THOSE WORDS?"

"...Yeah, sure."

Tu was honest. Her expression would rapidly fluctuate with her emotions in the moment.

Right now, her face showed she was trying to process some extremely complicated feelings.

As if she had recalled something she didn't want to remember, something she still couldn't fully get rid of.

"He's a super-awful guy, though."

"INDEED."

Seeing Tu's face, Ozonezma let out a weary chuckle. If a girl like Tu thought of him like that, then it meant the man really hadn't changed at all.

Even long after Ozonezma had left him behind.

"IZICK THE CHROMATIC IS A NASTY MAN."

".......! So you know him."

Izick the Chromatic. Ozonezma and Tu's creator—and one of the seven members of the First Party. The man referred to as the wickedest demon king of them all, before the appearance of the True Demon King.

Ozonezma raised himself up. Tu the Magic didn't fully understand her own body, after all. In which case, there might have been a significance behind calling her out to see him like this.

"I AM LIKELY ABLE...TO TEACH YOU ONCE MORE ABOUT YOUR BODY."

The Demon King's Bastard who, at some point or another, appeared in the Land of the End. Tu the Magic.

Ozonezma knew. She was stronger than anyone else in the land and, at the same time, more dangerous as well.

"TU THE MAGIC. YOUR TRUE IDENTITY IS..."

Late at night in Gimeena City. Kuze the Passing Disaster entered the city not in a carriage but on foot.

To ensure that no one could track him.

The night's temperature was on the chilly side, and Kuze's exhalations were misty white.

"…I've arrived in the city. I'm ready."

He used the radzio in his inside pocket to communicate with a distant ally.

In a position a little ways outside the city, his commander for the Sixways Exhibition—Zigita Zogi the Thousandth—was supposed to be on standby.

Goblins, a race thought to have been eradicated from the land. Among them, he was a champion, equipped with an exceptional genius for military strategy.

<Understood. Please leave the scene as soon as your job is finished. My soldiers can confirm the outcome for us. The most important point to keep in mind is that you cannot be caught in the act.>

Kuze had volunteered for this latest operation himself.

It was a job to grow Hiroto's camp's trust in him as an assassin.

More than that, however, it was a job, as the Order's cleaner, that would thwart a deed that threatened to shock the very world.

<I would like to give one warning—Nofelt has already sensed the possibility that he would be targeted and is acting accordingly. Should he be in hiding somewhere farther beyond Gimeena City, then I do not know if we will have a chance to trap him until the day of the match.>

"It's okay. Just gotta do it today."

The target was Aureatia's Twenty-Sixth General, Nofelt the Somber Wind.

They would dispose of Uhak the Silent's sponsor and lead Zigita Zogi the Thousandth to a win by default in his match.

With Uhak then becoming a masterless pawn, he would turn into an impossible-to-deal-with trump card in the Sixways Exhibition, with only Hiroto's camp knowing the absoluteness of his abilities. That was their plan.

<Master Kuze. Bloodshed is not entirely necessary to secure Uhak. The reason we sent you for the job, as you requested, was in part because you are the one with the highest chances of drawing Nofelt to our side. You both hail from the same almshouse, yes?>

"You've done your research, huh. That's right."

<Should information get out, and we can neither secure Uhak nor deal with Nofelt—that would be the most unfavorable outcome for you, yes? Our side can simply abandon you, pretend we're uninvolved, and that would be enough to settle things. An overstep on your end, however, will have ramifications for the entire Order itself.>

"...*Bweh-heh-heh*. Listen, you don't need to be so cautious, Zigita Zogi."

For Zigita Zogi, Kuze the Passing Disaster was the newest addition to their cause and an untrustworthy assassin.

Whether he could deal with Nofelt here would also serve as a test to see if Kuze could truly act under the strategic leadership of Hiroto's camp.

However, even excluding such circumstances, Kuze was resolved.

"...Nofelt is trying to expose that Uhak fellow right in front of the audience's eyes. The ogre priest who negates Word Arts. The criminal behind the Alimo Row massacre. I don't think for a moment that Uhak's mere existence is a crime, but...if the truth behind him is made known to the world, it'd be blasphemy against the Wordmaker... The Nofelt I know isn't the type of guy to do that."

Though he had long lost the qualifications to be a priest, Kuze was someone who shared an Order upbringing with Nofelt, and he was a paladin.

He needed to hear Nofelt's confession—what was he thinking?

"If you're going to make someone else do it anyway, I'd rather it'd be me."

<......*I trust in your abilities.*>

"Well then, there's just one more thing I want to know... Why did Uhak the Silent catch your attention? Truth is: There were other candidates you were looking to get your hands on and use as your trump card, weren't there?"

<You're absolutely right. Uhak the Silent is the highest priority in that regard.>

Hiroto's camp was gathering secret weapons they could mobilize themselves. Even under the condition that they couldn't be affiliated with Aureatia, there were many other figures who were worthy of being called invincible. Alus the Star Runner. Toroa the Awful. Tu the Magic. Mestelexil the Box of Desperate Knowledge.

<Among the sixteen hero candidates, there are individuals whose existences are maintained by the laws of Word Arts that exist beyond the laws of physics, including the construct races, dragonkin, and the gigante. Psianop the Inexhaustible Stagnation. Alus the Star Runner. Lucnoca the Winter. Ozonezma the Capricious. Tu the Magic. Mestelexil the Box of Desperate Knowledge. Shalk the Sound Slicer. Mele the Horizon's Roar.>

Zigita Zogi dispassionately read off a list of names.

<These eight among the sixteen participants would die instantly *should they be affected by Uhak the Silent's ability. Furthermore, he would suppress Toroa the Awful's enchanted swords and Rosclay the Absolute's Word Arts. Incidentally, your power would be included among them, too, Master Kuze. Also, this attack would not be limited to the arena and would be possible to use simply by having them observe Uhak among the audience, for example. A major factor regarding the information about this trump card is that only* we possess any of it. *Thus, the best option is to prevent any opportunity for Uhak the Silent to be exposed to public attention, just as*

you wished for, Master Kuze, and using him will keep his existence a secret.>

Should Zigita Zogi win the eighth match and advance, until the third match, Zeljirga the Abyss Web was the only candidate among those he could face who wouldn't be affected by Uhak's ability.

Indeed, if none of the other participants knew about the existence of such a being, then Uhak was the best possible piece to have under their control.

"...I got it. Sorry for making you explain all that for me. I guess I want to believe that this is really necessarily, is all."

<Master Kuze...>

Zigita Zogi's tone was always calm and composed.

A tactician who pushed aside his own emotions and always dispassionately conveyed the optimal strategy—and nothing more.

<You seem to have given up on letting Nofelt live right from the start.>

"...Guess so. I mean, am I wrong?"

The man who should have loved his comrades in the Order, just as Kuze did, was trying to curse not just the Order, but the entire world itself.

"...If I don't kill him, that might be it for all of us."

Nofelt had resolved to do as much. After Kuze failed to notice such anguish and abandoned Cunodey to her death, at this stage, what sort of words could he say to make Nofelt change his mind?

<Master Kuze. There are no absolutes in the world.>

"Fair enough. I feel the same way."

<I interpreted Uhak the Silent's abilities as simply a unique power that he was inherently born with, but...even making them out to be the Wordmaker's teachings may not be the real, absolute truth.>

"......"

If that was how everyone was going to face Uhak's existence, then perhaps Nofelt's deeds were, in fact, salvation to make the truth known to the world.

However... What about the things Kuze had protected up until now, piling up corpses as he went?

"Me, I don't want to think about that."

Both Uhak the Silent's and Cunodey's final moments. Kuze covered his face with one hand.

"I... I want to believe in the Wordmaker... There are plenty of people out there who have found salvation from his teachings alone."

<......>

"...Zigita Zogi. If I do let Nofelt go here, what will happen?"

He posed a new question, as if to shake himself free of his own mind.

Right now he needed to rationally paint over the sin that was going to occur that night.

<Nofelt departed Aureatia yesterday. His pretext was investigating the cause of the traffic generated by Ozonezma's match. He is scheduled to return home on the day of the eighth match. I doubt he will stay in town anymore. The transportation traffic Haade set up didn't just cover Gimeena City, but it extended in a wide area

*to the surrounding cities. In the meantime, any investigation would
appear natural, no matter where it occurred.>*

"Or putting it another way, no matter what happens to Nofelt,
no one will notice until the day of his match."

<You are absolutely right.>

Kuze thought.

…You really are an outstanding guy, after all, Nofelt.

He may have been very close to outwitting Zigita Zogi, the
most powerful tactician in the land. All with the simple yet bold
plan of leaving his hero candidate behind in Aureatia while he, the
sponsor, went into hiding.

He always had the smarts to react to situations like this, ever
since they were in the almshouse together.

Whenever he was about to be forced into handling an annoying job, he'd suddenly disappear right beforehand.

*<Of course, we'll need to identify Nofelt's hiding spot before the
night's over. I can send one of our units to sniff him out.>*

"Nah, that won't be necessary. If he's in the city, I have an idea
where he'd make his last stop for the night."

Kuze's footsteps advanced through the streets without any
hesitation.

He continued to speak briefly with Zigita Zogi before he cut
the radzio communication line.

Once he had lost his conversation partner, he realized it was a
terribly lonesome night.

Thanks to a wonderful miracle, we are all no longer in solitude.

Kuze arrived at a church.

He was confident that Nofelt was certain to be here.

All living things who possess minds of their own are all part of our family.

In his mind, Kuze recited the teachings he once learned.

He was unable to hope that doing so would bring some kind of salvation.

When he opened the door, he saw the figure of a man sitting down at the altar.

There was no one else. Nofelt the Somber Wind was here in this church.

"...Hey there, Nofelt. Haven't seen you in a spell."

"Ugh."

Even seated, Nofelt was very tall.

He had been ever since they were kids. Every year, he'd grow taller, as if to answer the expectations of those around him, like his body itself couldn't wait to broadcast Nofelt's prominent talents, even if the man himself remained silent.

Nofelt laughed foolishly.

"That obnoxious speaking style, gotta be Big Brother Kuze, huh?"

"That mouth of yours hasn't changed, either, has it?"

Kuze replied with a faint laugh of his own, and he started approaching Nofelt.

"Oh, mind if I take a seat?"

"And if I said no?"

"What? I'll still sit, of course. I mean, lemme tell you, at this age, it doesn't take much to make your back ache."

Kuze sat down next to Nofelt. Nor did Nofelt make any attempt to stop him.

Sitting side by side, Nofelt was indeed about two heads taller than Kuze. Just how old was Nofelt going to get before he stopped growing? Kuze wished he had the time to indulge in such earnest questions.

"Your back? At your age, seriously? Quit it with that. You're gonna make *me* look like an old man, too."

"...*Bweh-heh-heh*. Don't worry about that; we've both been old men for a while now. How many years do you think it's been since then?"

"Twenty-two...? Or it is twenty-three? *Heh*... I don't remember."

"C'mon, you gotta remember that much. As of two small months ago, uh, right, it was...twenty..."

"*You* don't even remember."

"...*Bweh-heh-heh*. Damn, it's that aging brain of mine."

Despite it being all so long ago, he could remember it even now.

The True Demon King was still a far-off incident in some place the kids didn't recognize, and even though they were poor, they were all able to help each other. The kids joined with the adults at work, they met many, many priests, and heard all sorts of words from them.

Then, even as each individual word vaguely blurred together, he remembered the many memories like a song he couldn't help humming to himself.

Nastique the Quiet Singer surely must have seen the world in a similar way.

Kuze believed so.

"…What d'ya say to a round of feather top, Nofelt?"

"For real?"

"I still have it. The one you left with me when you graduated. Here."

Taking a brass top out of his inner pocket, he tossed it to Nofelt.

Nofelt was by no means good at feather top, but the top was one he had always taken pride in. Seeing the dull gleam, unchanged from times past, he laughed.

"That's kid's stuff, c'mon."

"Hey, can't hurt every once and while. Here we go. Five. Four. Three."

"Whoa, whoa, whoa now. *Ha-ha*, wait, just hold up a sec, geez."

"Two. One, and—!"

Aiming at church floorboards, Kuze let the feather top fly. Nofelt's lagged slightly behind.

The two tops spun, letting out unique sounds as their spins cut through the air.

"We got yelled at whenever we did this on the church floor, huh."

"…Right. That didn't make any damn sense, for real."

"Especially since all the boards were level, and it had the most space. If I ever got to be a priest, that whole stupid rule'd be gone. But I guess kids these days don't play feather top as much?"

"Wait, Big Brother Kuze, you're still doing that Order stuff?"

—Indeed. Kuze couldn't leave the Order even while he betrayed the teachings more than any follower.

Would his mind be more at ease if he had lived without believing in the Wordmaker?

Could he have lived while pretending not to see the angel watching him?

"So was there some test to be a priest or something?"

"Nope. 'Paladin' is just a title, and I'm basically still rank-and-file."

"Huh..."

"I hate to admit it, but you know, Nofelt... You really are special. I'm glad you left. You've always been the smartest, even back then. With the huge body to back it up... I never thought you'd still be growing. Your parents must've really been outstanding, huh...to end up like you did."

"...Listen, Big Brother Kuze. That excuse's a bit unfair, right? I mean, none of us had any damn parents. Even if we did, they were assholes who abandoned their own kids, right?"

The feather tops continued to spin.

The brass surface reflected the warmly flickering candlelight.

"That's true. You...you worked hard, didn't you? You're part of the Twenty-Nine Officials, now."

"*Heh... Heh-heh-heh.* Shit."

The Twenty-Sixth General laughed. A dry, flippant laugh.

It slightly resembled Kuze's own somehow.

"I'm shit. Even after becoming so great and important, I'm still shit. A shithead just like my parents... Did you know, Big Brother Kuze? Granny Cunodey's dead. I... You know, I..."

Nofelt rested his forehead down on his hands, folded in his lap.

"...Really, I thought...if I became powerful and important, I'd be able to make things easier for everyone. Make sure that at every almshouse there'd be green strawberries after every meal...and use Kingdom money to have a cleaning lady at each one, too. Heck, I even thought for their scripts, they could use proper lambskin, you know... What else...? *Heh-heh*, ah right, there was another thing, too. I'd make it so the kids would be able to play feather top in church, right."

"I know. We all knew. Not one of us thought you abandoned us and left."

"...Stop, stop, it's super embarrassing! Hey, Big Brother Kuze. Everyone went and died. What am I supposed to do? I don't have anything I want to do anymore."

"......"

One of the feather tops' spinning wavered. Scraping against the ground with a clack, until it finally collapsed.

It was Nofelt's feather top.

"*Bweh-heh-heh...* I win."

"...*Pfft...* You just got lucky. This here's my Heron's Cry, you know."

"That's the thing. Sure, you learned fast, but your feather top was always weak, huh."

"No way... It's not weak at all. Rematch time."

The two synced up their breathing and dropped their feather tops.

The sounds of the spins reverberated on top of each other. From somewhere far off in the church, the wind howled.

"...Nofelt."

"What?"

"If I told you 'Don't give in to despair,' would you be able to stop?"

"......"

Nofelt looked at the high ceiling. After a long silence, he let out a sigh.

Only the clattering of the spinning feather tops echoed.

"Not happening."

"............"

"Hold up; my top looks like it's gonna fall again."

"*Heh-heh.* I win, again, General Pushover."

"Dammit... For real, this is so freaking... Ah, dammit! We're having another rematch, got it?"

"It'll just be more of the same, my friend. You trying to break your old record of eight straight losses from back when we were kids?"

"I'm telling you, if Granny Cunodey hadn't stopped us, I would've won the next nine straight."

One more time, their feather tops spun. The light of the candle continued to flicker unchanged.

Seeing the nostalgic scene in front of him, Kuze smiled. Laughing along as they did in their youth, and yet he knew they could never return to that time again.

"You came here to kill me, didn't you, Big Brother Kuze?"

"......"

"You know... I—I can't do it anymore. I can't. You see the look in Uhak's eyes...? See, I get it. Truth is, that guy... He hates all of it. The whole world and everything in it."

"That's all just in your head."

That day, Kuze saw Uhak. He was repenting.

They were eyes that wanted to atone for his sins against the world, but without having any means to do so.

"...Listen, Big Brother Kuze. If I said I was gonna use him, right...and turn this whole big farce upside down, what'd you say? Just destroy everything... *Heh-heh*, sounds like a blast, right? After he's made hero, he'll go up in front of everyone...and show them that Word Arts, the Wordmaker or whatever, is all a big load of crap...bald-faced lies..."

"It's okay, Nofelt. Enough, you don't need to blame yourself."

"I... The thing is—I... I'm just sick of this world. Seriously, it's hopeless, isn't it?"

"...You did everything you could. Look, it's not your fault, okay? Seriously."

One of the feather tops collapsed. Kuze hoped it wasn't the case, but he looked to see it was indeed Nofelt's top again.

All the many friends they had lived with, Cunodey and Rozelha, too—they were all gone.

Nofelt had left the Order. Kuze continued to remain in their ranks.

He had to protect the dying Order. Even if decay was the only path left, within it still remained the meaning to the life he had lived, the lives that the adults in the Order, and the children he wanted to protect, had lived.

"...I win."

"Dammit... Why can't I win, dammit...? Right up until the end..."

"We can keep going. I'll take you on as many times as you want…no matter how long."

"…Yeah, not happening."

As he flippantly laughed, Nofelt was crying.

Tears that he surely hadn't noticed for himself. When they were little, he made sure never to cry at all.

"This is hilarious, for real."

"…No one's abandoned you. No one. It's true."

He put a hand on Nofelt's shoulder.

Nastique was there. The angel was looking at the pair.

Then that same angel placed her blade in the back of Nofelt's neck.

Did he die?" That's right. I killed him.

Kuze mumbled. Was that the only salvation to be had?

Even if Nofelt had wished for it himself, there should have been another path available.

"…It's true… It's really true, Nofelt, believe me…"

The feather top was spinning.

There was now only one sheen of brass, illuminated in the candlelight.

◆

Ozonezma the Capricious's treatment room. Tu the Magic was squatting down next to the colossal chimera and listening to him explain the logic behind her own body's construction.

Her race and ancestry were checkered, more so than anyone else participating in the Sixways Exhibition.

At some point, even these truths are sure to be made clear.

Tu stared wide-eyed at Ozonezma, but eventually she began to speak.

"...I'm glad I didn't get paired up against you, Ozonezma. You knew more about me than I even do... If we fought each other, I probably woulda lost. That and you're my big brother, after all."

"INDEED."

Although the chimera Ozonezma was not a pure construct, from the moment he was spawned into this word, he had undergone painstaking adjustments at the hands of the self-proclaimed demon king of the First Party, Izick, and had existed as a living weapon. A solitary offspring essentially the same as a construct.

Connections for him had always been beyond any blood relationship, including his relationship with Izick.

Therefore, he wanted Tu to live, too.

"NOW, FOR THE MAIN POINT AT HAND. YOUR OPPONENT IN YOUR FIRST-ROUND MATCH MAY BE ABLE TO BREAK THROUGH YOUR INVINCIBILITY."

"You mean, Kuze the Passing Disaster?"

"...YUCA."

Ozonezma called out to Yuca, his own sponsor.

He had sunk his enormous frame into a corner chair inside the treatment room and was nodding off, half asleep.

"......Hmmm?"

"SORRY, BUT WOULD YOU MIND LEAVING US FOR A MOMENT?"

"Sure? Oh, but just don't start any fights, okay? This is my facility and all."

"WE WILL NOT CAUSE YOU TROUBLE."

Yuca excused himself from the room.

Ozonezma had made him leave because there was information he had obtained through Hiroto the Paradox included in what he was going to talk about next. Information that, having not entered Aureatia himself, he shouldn't have possibly known.

Even if Yuca or a subordinate of his were eavesdropping, Ozonezma was capable of sensing their presence. However, he knew full well that, when it came to Yuca, that was one thing he didn't need to worry about. He was an honest man.

"KUZE'S UNIQUE POWER IS INSTANT DEATH. AS LONG AS HIS OPPONENT IS A LIVING CREATURE, THIS HAS PROVEN TRUE FOR ALL HIS TARGETS. EVEN IF KUZE HIMSELF DOES NOT ACT, IF HE IS ATTACKED, HIS OPPONENT WILL BE HIT WITH AN AUTOMATIC AND UNSEEN ATTACK...AND SUBSEQUENTLY PERISH."

"...And I'll die, too?"

"I WOULD SAY...IT IS LIKELY SO. AS I JUST EXPLAINED NOW, YOU ARE, WITHOUT QUESTION, A LIVING ORGANISM."

Although Ozonezma was colluding with Hiroto's camp during his participation in the Sixways Exhibition, it was an equal partnership. He was not participating in the operation as intimately as Hiroto's adviser, Zigita Zogi.

Thus, he hadn't been informed by Hiroto's camp at all about the abilities and origins of any of the hero candidates from the fifth match onward, as they were outside of his part of the bracket. Considering there was a possibility Ozonezma could leak information, it was a valid judgment to maintain Hiroto's camp's advantage. Ozonezma understood this all as well.

However, for Kuze the Passing Disaster alone, he been informed about the man's powers.

Kuze was a collaborator who had been brought into Hiroto's camp after the start of the Sixways Exhibition. The information on him he had received by Zigita Zogi was, at this stage, proving to be effective.

IN OTHER WORDS, ZIGITA ZOGI. HE MUST BE TELLING ME TO USE KUZE'S INFORMATION LIKE THIS.

Ozonezma continued. "TU. DO YOU KNOW WHY KUZE IS COMPETING IN THIS FIGHT?"

"...Nope. He's from the Order, right?"

"FOR A LONG TIME, THE ORDER HAS SHOULDERED THE EDUCATION AND SOCIAL WELFARE FUNCTIONS OF THIS SOCIETY. ORPHANS WHO HAVE LOST PARENTS IN WAR. CHILDREN ABANDONED IN POVERTY. THE ORDER GAVE FOOD AND EDUCATION TO SUCH PEOPLE."

"...I'm visiting the church, too. I'm not doing it to pray to the Wordmaker really, but I made friends. So...I know that everyone's having a super-tough time right now."

Tu leaned forward and inquired. "Hey, so. Do you think Kuze's trying to become the hero in order to help everyone?"

"THAT IS LIKELY THE CASE. THEY ARE BEING DRIVEN INTO A CORNER. THE REASON IS BECAUSE THEY WERE FORCED TO BEAR RESPONSIBILITY FOR THE TRUE DEMON KING TRAGEDY."

"……"

The color in Tu's eyes changed at hearing the True Demon King's name.

The young girl was formerly called the Demon King's Bastard.

"THE WORDMAKER THEY PUT THEIR FAITH IN IS THE GOD WHO CREATED THIS WORLD. THAT GOD ALLOWED FOR THE EXISTENCE OF THE TRUE DEMON KING. THE TRAGEDY THAT THEY HAD NO HOPES OF FIGHTING AGAINST WAS SUCH THAT THE CITIZENS REQUIRED A TARGET TO POINT THEIR ANIMOSITY."

"That…that makes no sense. It wasn't anyone's fault. I mean, they could decide to blame someone and take them down, and that still wouldn't change anything…"

"TU. THIS SIXWAYS EXHIBITION… WHILE IT IS WHERE A HERO WILL BE DECIDED ON, IT IS ALSO A BATTLE OVER THE CONTROL OF POLITICAL AUTHORITY IN AUREATIA. IN ORDER TO REHABILITATE THE ORDER'S STATUS, KUZE THE PASSING DISASTER NEEDS TO PROVE THEIR POLITICAL WORTH. TO HIM, IT COULD BE SAID, THIS IS HIS SOLE OPPORTUNITY TO DO SO."

"But Kuze's attacks… They kill people, right?"

"YES. WITHOUT EXCEPTION."

"…Killing someone will save everyone in the Order?"

"I DO NOT FULLY UNDERSTAND KUZE'S INTENTIONS. HOWEVER, THAT WOULD BE THE CASE."

Tu looked hard at Ozonezma. Her green eyes were tinged with a faint light.

Tu combined an artless soul with an innocent sense of justice. There were times when that transformed into a cruelty that mercilessly eliminated one's opponents.

Ozonezma was only speaking directly with Tu for the first time, but he didn't want her to end up like that. If she learned about Kuze's circumstances and chose to withdraw from the fight without losing her life, that was enough for him.

"…TU THE MAGIC. WHAT IS YOUR REASON FOR PARTICIPATING IN THE SIXWAYS EXHIBITION? THROUGH MY FIGHT WITH SOUJIROU THE WILLOW-SWORD, I CAME TO UNDERSTAND SOMETHING… THIS SIXWAYS EXHIBITION IS A BATTLE OF SPIRIT AS WELL. IN ORDER TO TRULY STRIKE KUZE DOWN WITHOUT ANY HESITATION… YOU, TOO, WILL NEED SUITABLE CONVICTIONS OF YOUR OWN."

"I want to meet the Queen."

"……"

Queen Sephite. The young monarch who currently governed Aureatia, the last survivor of the United Western Kingdom.

Tu the Magic would have been present there, too, as the Queen's kingdom fell to ruin.

"I want to meet Sephite…and have her smile for me."

"...THAT IS ACHIEVABLE WITHOUT PARTICIPATING IN THE SIXWAYS EXHIBITION."

There were people who could effortlessly grant Tu's wish. However, even Ozonezma understood how difficult that would prove to be.

"Yeah. I know that. I... I just have to attend school. Rique told me that, too."

Tu smiled.

"But studying and stuff is still really hard."

Tu must have understood as well. That she was not of the minian races, but a being born with a deviate destiny thrust upon her, and that someone like her wouldn't be accepted by greater society.

The juggernaut, born into this world possessing nothing more than tremendous brute force, might have been unable to make her wish come true through any other means besides combat.

Kuze the Passing Disaster, and the Tu the Magic, would fight. If the end result had Kuze coming up short, then it would be a large loss for Hiroto's camp. Kuze had to win.

THE REST DEPENDS ON TU HERSELF. I... I HAVE, IN MY OWN WAY, FULFILLED MY OBLIGATIONS TO HIROTO.

Ozonezma closed his eyes.

...NEVERTHELESS, I DO NOT WANT HER TO FIGHT.

He hoped that the spear of absolute death and the shield of absolute arrest did not collide.

For even if Kuze won, and it was Tu who was found lacking... To Ozonezma, it would mean he would lose the little sister he had finally found.

◆

The day before the fifth match.

Despite the sun being high in the sky that morning, a thick, gloomy cloud cast a shadow over the almshouse.

Rique the Misfortune and Tu the Magic had visited this almshouse in Aureatia's Western Outer Ward, but along their path that day, Tu may have been deliberately more talkative with Rique than usual.

"Aigi's short but apparently really, really good at using a spear. They said that they've even beaten kids two years above them in practice matches before. Also... I thought Leisha maybe didn't like me very much at first, but you know, she's got a really, really good memory, and no matter what I say, she'll remember it all. Mie knows a whole lot about machines, and they showed me that they could dissemble a radzio and put it back together again..."

"Yeah."

Rique's reply was brief.

"......I wonder what'll happen to everyone."

"That's the one thing I just don't know."

As Rique and Tu approached the almshouse, three young men, lingering in front of the gate and idly looking up at the structure, came into view.

Tu thought that she felt like she had seen people like them before.

"...What're you guys doing?"

Rique let out a low voice. Today he had his bow with him. He had insisted that he needed to be by Tu's side and take precautions to absolutely ensure against a worst-case scenario befalling her the day before her match.

"Oh, great, Rique the Misfortune."

"Piece of shit."

"What're you doing here, asshole?"

The men all equally shared a boorish, rough air about them, and each hurled curses at Rique. It was there that Tu realized the truth behind her sense of déjà vu. The coats they sported were the same ones that Jivlart the Ash Border had worn when they came across him before.

However, Rique wasn't as angered or upset as he had been then.

"We came to visit the kids. The priest in training who was fostering and looking after them died yesterday."

"Erm, I'm uh, Tu the Magic."

The priest in training, Naijy, was dead. The young man who had come to greet Tu and Rique on their first visit.

He had seemed like an unreliable young man, but nevertheless, he would have been a dear figure to the children there. That was why, even as Tu had her match looming the next day, she had hastened with Rique to come visit.

"Seriously?"

"Naijy, too, huh..."

Rique opened his mouth to speak.

"......I heard Jivlart the Ash Border died."

"Huh? That ain't any of your damn business."

The various incidents that had accompanied the fourth match

days prior were still causing an uproar among the Aureatia citizens. The death of Jivlart the Ash Border, scheduled to fight in the match. It was announced that Elea the Red Tag, who had substituted her candidate and attempted to murder Second General Rosclay with foul play, had gone missing.

Jivlart's corpse was discovered inside Elea's residence. The cause of death hadn't been released to the public.

"…A little while back. The talk around a kid getting adopted from here got canceled. Naijy wasn't given a detailed reason why, but… He asked me for advice, wondering if maybe if the whole proposition had been involved with the slave trade."

"Quit yer yapping and kick rocks."

"*Heh.* What, are you interested in selling and buying kids, is that it?"

"Enough. I want answers."

Rique flatly cut them off.

"Jivlart the Ash Border was supporting this almshouse. Given his ample contributions, he should have had some voice in where the kids would be taken in. Was there some link with a slave organization behind the scenes? Assuming so, then the reason behind Naijy's apparent suicide…"

One of the young men grabbed Rique's collar.

"What the hell did you say?"

He scowled at Rique with bloodshot eyes. Theirs were eyes of hatred, of anger, and of bewilderment.

"G-go ahead. Say that one more time."

"…So you three… Why have you come here? Just what sort of

reason do outlaws like you have for getting involved with these kids? You understand? I'm looking for a convincing explanation here. If you can do that, then..."

Rique reached a hand out to his quiver, his collar still gripped in the young man's hands.

The experienced bow hand, more than capable of putting down the three simultaneously with his bow, even within range of their fists.

"Rique. Stop... Don't fight."

"...Sorry, Tu. But you can say that because you don't know."

The color of anger equally showed on Rique's face as well.

He fixed his eyes on the three members of Sun's Conifer and threatened them.

"Time for some serious self-awareness. You guys... What have you been doing up until now? How many clients have you betrayed; how much did you exploit the weak? After pretending to be heroes and getting into Aureatia, what were you trying to do next? I should've crushed Jivlart on the spot when I first saw him. I could've done it, and I even knew what to expect from Sun's Conifer, but despite it all, I... I was too soft, and now there's yet another victim!"

"Bullshit!"

The young man grabbing Rique's collar replied with a shrieking cry of anger.

"Piss off! Who the hell do you think you are, huh?! Jivlart... Jivlart selflessly provided for orphaned kids, and you have the gall to say that?! Always dredging up stories from the past and always treating us like garbage! You... You don't know what our home-land was like... What were we supposed to do?! You saying we *can't try to live an honest life*?! It was supposed to happen! The Six-ways Exhibition...was the hope that even guys like us could rise to the top! During the Sixways Exhibition... Aureatia'd recognize Jivlart, and then we'd all...all of us...all of Sun's Conifer—"

"Rique...!"

Tu cut in and forcefully tore them away from each other.

She didn't know what sort of suffering Rique the Misfortune had endured in the past, nor the type of life the Sun's Conifer members had lived up until now. She didn't understand either of their circumstances.

However, she thought that this hatred needed to be stopped by *somebody*.

"*Ha-ha-ha...* Honest? You guys? Honest?"

Rique spat as he covered his head once again with his hood.

"You really were just giving money to poor children without any sort of schemes up your sleeves? Don't tell me, did you want to be seen as the good guys or something? Just from doing the sort of superficial good deeds a child would think up...?! Were you seri-ously thinking that'd be able to write off all your crimes?"

"Rique!"

"Fine, so you *thought* of something, did ya?! You able to think up a way for idiots like Jivlart, idiots like us, to make it out there, huh?! What've any of ya done for us, huh?! What the hell do you know?!"

Sun's Conifer. Poor, uneducated young men who had climbed up from the frontier solely through violence.

Those who involved themselves with the guild would always get hurt. That was the *character* of their group.

"...Yeah, right."

This time, before Tu had any time to stop him, Rique instantly dragged the young man from Sun's Conifer to the ground.

"Enough crap! Don't think that sort of cheap...worthless talk about your rough life is enough to get the world to sympathize with you guys! You were just helping kids, huh...without anything in return? *Bastards like you, all of a sudden outta the goodness of your hearts?* How 'bout, if you got the time to play the hero, you go apologize to all those people you ruined to get here, huh?! People living honest lives to begin with, and you bastards crushed them underfoot! Give back everything you stole to rise up to where you are now!"

Rique shouted as he thrust with an arrowhead.

"Apologize to her...to that bride whom I wasn't able to protect! The Sun's Conifer!"

"Hic, mrrrm...bweeeh...!"

He was crying. The young man of Sun's Conifer, exuding an air of violence and brawn, was crying.

Unsightly—and unable to offer any rebuttal to Rique's sound logic.

Almost like a child, Tu thought.

Forsaken by this world, without any education or social status to their name...yet possessing only brute force as their way to resist that world. They had thought with such strength they would be able to obtain their wishes.

Violent and rough: children.

It's the same with me.

In that Land of the End, Tu the Magic had always been the Demon King's Bastard. She hadn't had any other means at her disposal to protect someone.

She thought that the men of Sun's Conifer were villains. They had, of their own free will, hurt those weaker than themselves solely for their own benefit. However, things were sure the same for Tu, too.

Exactly who would teach her the imagination to realize such sins?

For those who realized long after all the many crimes they had committed, how exactly were they supposed to make up for it?

◆

The almshouse courtyard. There was an ominous shadow lingering in a position to witness Rique the Misfortune's argument with Sun's Conifer in front of the gate.

The man was wearing long black clothes, similar to a priest's vestments though with a slightly different design.

...I can aim at Tu from here.

He was Kuze the Passing Disaster. The sole being capable of spurring the angel Nastique, bringer of absolute death, into action. An assassin's fight was not a face-to-face brawl with his enemy in an arena.

Naijy was dead. He died in despair at his, and the children's, future.

Learning of Naijy's death, Tu had come to check up on the children. He knew that she would be the type to do so.

I've heard all about you, Tu the Magic.

Kuze captured Tu in his sights from under the shade of a tree.

So they said your sprint's faster than a carriage. C'mon now, you can't be going all out like that when you're up against a kid.

Now, while she was bickering with Sun's Conifer, was his golden opportunity. He could lay the blame for Tu the Magic's sudden death on the hands of Sun's Conifer.

It was the reason Nastique the Quiet Singer was truly the strongest assassin of all. On top of the absoluteness of her lethality, the method was impossible to prove. Even supposing Kuze was amid a crowd at midday and faced off with another hero candidate and killed them, there wasn't anyone in the world who could produce evidence that Kuze was the cause of their sudden death.

Although everyone would understand it was inconceivable that a petty thug would be able to stab Tu the Magic to death, it was also possible to create a situation where there was no choice but to accept that explanation.

It's actually thanks to you that Leeno really started talking to everyone else, you know.

When an opponent went to kill Kuze, Nastique would kill that opponent.

However, there existed *one other condition* he had not told his collaborator, Hiroto the Paradox.

Heck, that even got Leisha to become attached to you. So that's why...

In order to make sure he didn't show that condition to anyone else, he had to stop the fifth match from happening.

Thus, Kuze would kill Tu.

He went to do so.

"This is…your first warning."

Voices, innumerable and inhuman, reverberated from the surrounding bushes.

The owner of the voice was nowhere to be found.

"Kuze the Passing Disaster. Leave until you are far enough away for Tu to be out of sight. At once."

No, that wasn't it. The voice's owner had long been visible. The gaps in the leaves of the trees. The spaces in the lawn at his feet.

Unnatural winged insects with a metallic luster were amassed in a swarm, enclosing around Kuze's feet.

"…*Bweh-heh-heh*. I've heard all about you… Didn't expect you to be such an overprotective guy."

The one who discovered the world's fifth system of Word Arts.

Now, with Izick the Chromatic's death, the person said to be this generation's greatest wielder of constructs.

"Krafnir the Hatch of Truth…!"

"I ALREADY HAVE A GRASP OF YOUR MYSTERIOUS ATTACKS. IF YOU IGNORE MY WARNING AND STUBBORNLY REMAIN HERE… I WILL INTERPRET THAT AS AN ACT OF AGGRESSION."

A former hero candidate who boasted a tremendous range of perception through his construct terminals.

Krafnir the Hatch of Truth. Even after he had relinquished

his hero candidate spot to Tu, her sponsor, Flinsuda the Portent, would never sever her relationship with a man as powerful as him.

Flinsuda had always let Tu the Magic move as she pleased in order to uncover anyone who went after her life and attacked her. From the very beginning, Rique the Misfortune hadn't been the only one guarding the girl.

Kuze raised both his arms. The stance of surrender.

"If I say I won't do anything, would you believe me?"

"Let's believe you. Though, let me make one thing clear. Until the beginning of the match tomorrow, we will not bring Tu out into public."

"......"

"You won't get any more opportunities to go through with your assassination."

"...And what if you disappear right now?"

"Want to try it?"

Turning aside his overcoat, he produced a small shield from inside. The bladelike insects didn't let the opening from his movement go by, and they rushed at him in untold numbers. Metallic revenant insects. Kuze smacked them down with his shield's breadth, but the swarm slipped through his defenses and tried to rend Kuze's eyeballs. All of them died and fell to the ground, without reaching their targets.

Are you okay—? Sure was.

"Naaah, let's go ahead and stop... This here's a church. Can't do this here, now can we?"

"As long as you are taking aggressive action, you can simultaneously deal with multiple targets at once. Not limited only to lethal wounds, you react to nonlethal attacks purposefully aimed at your eyes or arms."

Krafnir dispassionately analyzed Kuze's attacks. He was pressuring Kuze by showing him that as long as he continued to fight, Kuze would grow more and more disadvantaged.

"Dammit, since when can members of a candidate's entourage attack other hero candidates?! Krafnir...!"

"You have no right to say that right now... And I will warn you, Kuze the Passing Disaster. Complaining to the Aureatia Assembly about our infringement will be meaningless."

An ophidian revenant tangled around Kuze's right leg. Faster than it could sink its poisonous fangs into his shin, he slammed it, still wrapped around his leg, into a rat revenant. Using the edge of the shield, he severed the snake's head.

Krafnir was exactly right. The categories of participants in the Sixways Exhibition from the very start were not fair and balanced. There were those who would be criticized for foul play and those would be doing the criticizing.

Kuze the Passing Disaster was also a hero candidate *whose purpose was to lose.* To the point that his own sponsor was sending assassins against him.

There was buzzing to his rear. The winged insects were firing needles at him. Spinning around, he flashed his shield and blocked the needles. He had let some of them slip through, but they didn't hit him. He still had the leftover stamina to dodge.

"You're a surprisingly......swell guy, huh, Krafnir the Hatch of Truth."

"WHAT?"

"Forget it. Doesn't concern you."

The angel would kill those who tried to kill Kuze. There were no exceptions, even when up against a construct user whose true form was far away.

...Nastique's just killing constructs that're attacking me automatically. In other words, you yourself still aren't seriously trying to kill me.

There was the sound of wings above him. Kuze looked at the sky. A strange-looking flock melded into the clouds. Avian revenants.

Maybe he just doesn't have to.

The children couldn't see him, could they? Tu the Magic hadn't noticed him, had she? He took a defensive stance.

Curving in complex lines, the bird flock swooped down on him. He used the tree as a shield. It couldn't fully defend him. The thick tree trunk was instantly shredded and scattered everywhere. The birds circled back many times, and their slashing attacks kicked up a storm. One bird. Two. Three. Four. Five.

Five of the birds were killed by Nastique before he readjusted his stance and parried the next assault.

There were still three birds remaining. The insects encircled Kuze yet again. Rat revenants sprang forth, too.

Krafnir was purposefully only utilizing small-size revenants. He was trying to force Kuze to constantly deal with them and exhaust his stamina. It wasn't only Kuze's side who was trying to wrap up the fifth match without a fight.

"This isn't Word Arts or any type of magic item. Just what is this counterattacking ability of yours...?"

"WH-WHO'S TO SAY...? MAYBE I'VE GOT AN ANGEL WATCHING OVER ME?"

"Spare me the nonsense."

An arachnid revenant tried to slit Kuze's throat. It was intercepted and fell to the ground.

"......!"

Nastique wasn't the one who protected him. A chestnut-colored braid fluttered along behind her like a tail.

The young girl, her shoulder turned, looked at Kuze with one green eye and shouted.

"Kuze the Passing Disaster!"

He didn't want to kill. He didn't want to make Nastique kill. If the wish was enough, then it would have all been so simple.

Kuze the Passing Disaster's power wouldn't let him do such a thing.

Thus...

"*Bweh-heh-heh...* You found me, huh."

The spear of absolute death and the shield of absolute arrest.

In this Sixways Exhibition to determine the strongest in the land, there was no fifth match.

Their battle would ultimately be settled the day before their match.

Kuze the Passing Disaster versus Tu the Magic.

◆

Kuze the Passing Disaster was surrounded by an army. An army he could see—and one he couldn't.

It was small enough to lurk in the almshouse courtyard and avoid discovery at a glance, yet it easily wielded enough military might to bring death to an entire squad of the Aureatia army. Revenants made from the corpses of insects and small animals.

"Tu. Don't reveal yourself. The same goes for you, Rique."

Just how was it possible for a small flying insect's body structure to be capable of transmitting voice? Krafnir the Hatch of Truth was simply a construct master capable of such extremely delicate craftsmanship.

"Krafnir. Stop your attack. Kuze...hasn't done anything yet. Not a good move."

"...You're too soft, Rique. He was trying to kill Tu."

The bow-wielding dwarf was Tu the Magic's bodyguard, Rique the Misfortune.

Rique was already ready with an arrow nocked to his bow, but Nastique still hadn't reacted. The dwarf was simply readying himself to keep Kuze in check.

Then there was Kuze's opponent for the fifth match, Tu the Magic herself.

An invincible living weapon who possessed the physical and defensive abilities to completely nullify any and all attacks.

"Sorry... Kuze the Passing Disaster. I had no clue that Krafnir was out to get you. I actually want to fight you fair and square in our match... A win won the wrong way is totally meaningless."

Fair and square, huh. I'm not a splendid sorta guy like that.

Krafnir's hunch had been right on the mark. Kuze had indeed been trying to assassinate Tu before the match. The one attempting to avoid a fair and open fight was Kuze himself.

Am I...supposed to kill Tu now?

His target, Tu, was right before his eyes. If he used the other condition to send Nastique into action, he would be capable of disposing of Tu far more easily than in the situation moments prior.

However, the circumstances had changed. At the very least... he had been seen by the remaining two, Rique and Krafnir. In order to keep his trump card a secret, *he would need to kill these two as well.*

With that, he would add more unnecessary death, more murders running counter to his faith.

Keeping his aim fixed on Kuze, Rique addressed Krafnir.

"Krafnir. Did you attack Kuze under Flinsuda's orders? So she could sell the information on guys like this, aiming to attack Tu, to the other powers?"

"That's right."

"...I guess, then, I really don't gel with the way you guys do things. I'm saying this for your own good... Kuze the Passing Disaster. Leave. If you make contact with Tu, you'll draw false suspicions from Aureatia, too."

"*I* will? But not you all?"

He understood. From the very beginning, this was an unfair fight.

"Why's an Order guy like me...the one who's arousing suspicions for being at an almshouse?"

"He's right... We're the ones who should leave."

Tu cut in to defend Kuze.

"I've heard a bunch about you from the kids! They talked about how their beloved teacher's going to appear in the Sixways Exhibition! That if Father Kuze wins the fight, he might save the Order!"

"...*Bweh-heh-heh*. You shouldn't really be standing up for a villainous old dog like me."

Kuze sighed and tried to shut them out—the unclear and terribly dark emotions brewing inside of him.

Everyone said the Order was at fault. That the Wordmaker's teachings were wrong. The hero who killed the Demon King was just, the champions who displayed their honor on the battlefield were just, but the murderous paladin would remain unable to become a priest—and never again allowed to return back into the world's light.

"Kuze..."

"...THIS MAN HAS ALREADY SHOWN THAT HE IS WILLING TO ATTACK," Krafnir's bug ruthlessly announced.

"A HERO CANDIDATE TRIED TO KILL SOMEONE ASSOCIATED

WITH ANOTHER HERO CANDIDATE. YOU WON'T BE FIGHTING IN THE SIXWAYS EXHIBITION. YOU LOSE. KUZE THE PASSING DISASTER."

That had been the goal from the start. The construct user, never exposing his true form, had attacked Kuze, *left with no choice* but to automatically counterattack, from his disadvantaged political position.

It was not Tu the Magic but Krafnir the Hatch of Truth who was truly Nastique's natural enemy.

"Wait a sec, Krafnir."

Tu once again held him back.

"Kuze. There's something I've wanted to ask you ever since I first heard about you..."

"*Bweh-heh-heh...* You sure there's any fun to be had from hearing this old man's story?"

"Why do you kill?"

It was a terribly naive question. Cruel, like an inquiring child.

"That's a good question... I wonder why." Kuze mumbled.

The first time he had killed someone, he then thought about dying himself.

The despair from trampling, irrevocably, over the Word-maker's dogma.

However, the era of the True Demon King didn't even allow for such despair, either.

Amid the era of terror and murderous will, Kuze the Passing Disaster, spreading death simply from being wherever he stood, could truly only live on as a passing disaster.

Those who dared to kill needed to be killed themselves.

To Kuze, this was the righteousness he had taken up, even if it meant abandoning the Wordmaker's teachings.

He could only ever carry through on this righteousness, yearning for the faith he once held in his chest.

"...I don't care if I lose. Even if I can't win in the Sixways Exhibition...I think there's got to be some other way out there that'll let me see Sephite. That's why I'm participating."

"...Sephite. I see. So you want to see Her Majesty, huh, Tu."

There were mere children who could accomplish Tu's trifling goal without any obstacles in their way.

Conversely, however, there were some people who wouldn't even be allowed that much, unless they appeared in the Sixways Exhibition.

The world of light and the world of shadow.

"I want to help out the Order, too, you know. All I can do is fight, so if I'm able to help everyone by fighting, then I think that there'd be some meaning to the life I've lived! But even still. Everyone in the Land of the End, Rique, Krafnir...even the Sun's Conifer guys... Everyone has their own ideas and holds their own language. That's what the world outside was like... Kill it, and it's over... I don't want to kill you, either, Kuze!"

Tu's words were incoherent. Yet she had a genuine heart. Plain enough for Kuze to see.

"If you win, then maybe the Order might just be saved! But you really can't fight without killing anyone?"

"I can't."

Kuze shook his head.

"Tu. You've probably heard about my abilities from that Kraf-nir fella over there, right? No matter how much I may wish for it, that's one thing I cannot do. Anyone who fights against me is guaranteed to die. Regardless of my own wishes, I remain alive. And my enemy dies."

"In that case... If that's really the only option, I don't want to let you win after all, Kuze."

"......"

"...I mean, if you end up winning...then after that, you'll end up killing someone again, won't you?! You'll kill someone every time you win... Even the hero'd get killed! If that's the case...you'd be unable to be saved the most, wouldn't you...?"

"...Tu."

Kuze couldn't turn back.

In order to win, he killed Nofelt. He had been a close friend.

He didn't want to make Cunodey's self-sacrifice meaningless.

Maqure and the deceased Rozelha had entrusted their wishes to Kuze.

Then the children. There were children with futures, capable of protecting the faith, unlike Kuze.

However, for this girl.

Tu the Magic... So you're going look at me with those eyes, too.

Beautifully green pupils. Innocent, childlike pupils, capable of believing there was good in the world.

They were like the pupils of the white angel who continued to watch him.

"Tu the Magic. Please. If you let me win here... I'll withdraw in the second round. No more assassinations like this time, either. There is only one person...who I truly want to kill."

"...Until the next match?"

"That's right... Now, why did I go saying that? *Bweh-heh-heh...* I really hadn't intended on mentioning that at all..."

He hadn't even disclosed it to Hiroto. It was the greatest secret of the Order's plans.

"Why, then, I wonder..."

Why did he reveal it to this young girl...and not just any young girl, but Tu the Magic, his supposed opponent?

It was as if he was only going to kill one more person.

And he was begging her *to forgive him*, wasn't he?

"The second round...Kuze the Passing Disaster. Wait, you can't possibly mean..."

Tu wasn't the one to react.

It was Rique the Misfortune, his arrow still trained on Kuze.

Of those gathered there, he alone realized the meaning in Kuze's words.

...*Oh no!*

It all happened in an instant. Rique pulled back his bow. Then the arrow—

"Rique!"

"Get away from him! What this guy's trying to do? He's—"

That was the end.

Faster than the flight arrow could be fired, Nastique's blade brushed against Rique's arm.

The weight of the death, brought down in a split second, made Rique's arrow ever so slightly miss Kuze.

One of the reasons Rique the Misfortune had survived across numerous battles was because he would sense approaching death as a red flash of light—however, the angel of absolute mystery alone had been imperceptible.

"Rique! Rique!"

"I couldn't see it, ah…dammit…nothing at all…"

"Rique! Hey…c'mon, you're okay, right?! Nothing hit you at all or anything, right?!"

Tu screamed, even as the shallow cut running along his hand was plainly visible.

Feebly reaching a hand out to Tu's crying face, Rique groaned.

"…It's okay, Tu. It's all right…"

And then it was over.

He had tried to kill Kuze. Thus, he died.

In the midday almshouse courtyard, Kuze stood stock-still, aghast.

"You gotta be kidding me."

Both Kuze and Tu were trying to avoid a fight. Right up until that moment. Yet the death dispersed by Nastique had nothing to do with Kuze's own intentions.

A decisive failure.

He moaned in a voice too small for anyone else to hear.

"B-blast it… Damn, dammit all… Dammit…!"

He hadn't been able to avoid anything. It had been impossible for Kuze, possessed by an angel of death, to end things without a single sacrifice.

He had already killed. He couldn't stop it.

"*Weh, hic, Rique. Rique. Waaaaaah...!*

"Rique... Kuze the Passing Disaster, you bastard!"

Krafnir's myriad constructs were surrounding him. Tu's sights, emitting green light, were aimed toward him.

Nastique would make her move when intense murderous intentions were turned Kuze's way.

She'd end their lives faster than they could act on those intentions.

Everything. Anything and everything.

Murderous intentions focused on Kuze— Ah. It was all going to be for nothing.

"Can I kill this girl?" Please stop.

"Can I kill those who kill you?" No.

"Is it okay if I kill everyone?" Nothing in this world was okay to kill.

"Krafnir!"

Tu shouted, still crouched down beside Rique's corpse.

"Don't kill him!"

Her expression was hidden behind her bangs.

"Tu...! Because I'll get hit with his counterattack?! You think this is the time for soft naïveté?! Rique... Rique,

HE... HE'S BEEN KILLED! NO MATTER HOW MANY CONSTRUCTS DIE, THIS BASTARD'S GOING TO PAY!"

"E-even...even still! It's the same for Kuze! Even Kuze... doesn't want to kill anyone, either!"

It was like she was squeezing the words out of her chest.

As though she was shouting Kuze's own feelings in his place.

Still at a loss for words, Kuze shrunk one step back.

"......"

"Let's just end all of this. Enough of this, Kuze... People dying, getting killed... You're—you're fed up with it, right...? Right, Kuze?"

He couldn't believe it. Nastique wasn't killing Tu.

In other words.

I...

Tu the Magic wasn't showing any intention to kill him... Even after accidently killing Rique.

I don't want to kill. I truly didn't want to kill him.

There was no continued chain of murderous thoughts sent his way.

"...Hey, Krafnir. You think maybe I had things all wrong from the start...?"

"...Tu."

"I tried to make my wish come true...by becoming a hero candidate and winning my fights...but I never even realized that it might end up meaning I'd have to kill someone..."

"No, you... Tu. You're invincible. You have the power to win even without killing anyway."

"I… I'm not going to participate in the Sixways Exhibition anymore."

She personally rejected the chain of death and violence. That meant withdrawing from the Sixways Exhibition.

Thou shall not hate. Thou shall not harm. Thou shall not kill. Treat others as thou would treat thy own family.

"…TU. I… I'M GOING TO KILL. IF I WIN AND ADVANCE, THAT'LL MEAN MY OPPONENT DIES. I'M NOT GOING TO BACK DOWN NOW, THAT'S FOR SURE."

"I'm sure you can avoid killing them; I just know it."

Tu smiled, tears streaming down her face.

"…I settled things, without us killing each other."

Kuze the Passing Disaster bit his lip.

As if he were standing before a blinding light. For the sake of his faith, he had to betray someone he absolutely shouldn't, the person who believed in Kuze the Passing Disaster, even when he should have been her hated enemy.

"…This is farewell. Tu the Magic."

If the two of them had fought in the fifth match, would Kuze have been able to win against Tu?

He knew that answer ever since he heard about Tu from the children.

It was this very understanding that left him no choice but to assassinate her here instead of facing her in the arena.

Tu the Magic was kind. She had no intentions of killing Kuze the Passing Disaster from the very start. There was no way he would be able to kill an opponent who wasn't trying to kill him.

"…Hey. Kuze."

From far behind him, a voice called to Kuze.

The voice seemed to be in tears.

"I know."

He didn't have the courage to turn back.

"You…you can't kill people; you just can't…"

"…Of course not. I know that… I always have…"

Which was why he was the only one who should be burdened with the responsibility.

◆

The next day. One of the hero candidates, set to appear in the fifth match inside the castle garden theater, never appeared.

Checking the time, Twenty-Sixth Minister Meeka the Whispered declared—

"Silence!"

Her raised voice traveled well, even through the noisy spectators.

"…The significance behind consenting to the true duel in the Sixways Exhibition is to question the very resolve and courage of all those who would declare themselves heroes! Putting one's entire destiny, their entire lives on the line, and losing it all should they suffer defeat! Inevitable logic would dictate one should be fearful of such a thing, and no one unable to stand as a champion themselves should denounce anyone for this fear... However, I ask, just how terrifying must it be when compared to the True Demon King who our hero battled against!"

For these Sixways Exhibition matches, when one of the two combatants failed to appear...

"Thus, I, Meeka the Whispered, have decided that Tu the Magic does not have the qualifications to be the hero! The winner of the fifth match is Kuze the Passing Disaster."

Sparse applause, nowhere near the cheers of the fourth match, surrounded the black-dressed man.

"...Sorry." Kuze softly murmured with his face covered.

"I'm sorry, Tu."

She had left the spiral of conflict herself.

He had hoped she wouldn't show up there. That she wouldn't break her promise with Kuze.

Kuze was double-crossing Tu the Magic. The young girl who had been so willing to earnestly extend a helping hand.

Even if he hadn't told a lie, he was deceiving her. He was acting in opposition to the Wordmaker's teachings.

Tu the Magic. I... I...can't save you.

Neither Hiroto the Paradox's faction, who he was cooperating with, Nophtok the Crepuscule Bell, who had used assassins to probe into Kuze's abilities, nor Tu the Magic had a grasp on the other condition to triggering Nastique the Quiet Singer's attack.

By winning this very first round by default, he was able to keep that truth secret.

*　　*　　*

During the war with Lithia, he had killed Curte of the Fair Skies. He used his power to sever the life of a dying young girl.

In a church, he had killed Nofelt the Somber Wind. The general had accepted his own death without any resentment for Kuze.

Nastique the Quiet Singer's true power was not limited to automatic counterattacks bringing instant death.

The condition was line of sight. As long as they were within Kuze's sights, no matter who it may be…

He could kill them with just a thought.

That's why my assassinations are guaranteed to be successful.

He was targeting the life of a single person.

Tu the Magic. The sole person I'm trying to kill in my second-round match…

Rique the Misfortune had known Kuze's ability and still disregarded his own life to try to take Kuze's.

It was rightful rage and intent to kill.

The Sixways Exhibition held official royal games, and beginning with the second round, it was common knowledge that the royalty would come to watch the matches.

"I want to meet Sephite."

He had learned that this humble and simple wish was Tu's only desire.

I'm trying to kill…the Queen. That person is Sephite, Tu.

He would kill the hero. If the person who was finally left standing in the Sixways Exhibition was going to be treated as the hero, then in order to make sure that no hero was born, the only choice was to crush the Sixways Exhibition itself.

With the Queen's death, everything would be over.

Neither Hiroto the Paradox nor Nophtok the Crepuscule Bell knew the true reason behind the Order's participation in this fight.

Seizing on the Imperial Competition to assassinate the last member of the royal family. A wicked deed that would likely be passed down through generations.

Nevertheless, the group, only able to watch as they were carried away in the all-too-colossal current of the times...needed to make some sort of move right now. In order to make sure their compatriots were spared in the world coming on the horizon.

The Order was putting their final plan into motion.

◆

Rique the Misfortune died.

Kuze the Passing Disaster departed with his disappointment, and afterward, Rique's corpse and Tu were the only ones left behind.

Winged insects drifted in the air besides them.

"I... I TRIED TO MAKE YOU WIN, TU."

Even through his insect mouthpiece, Krafnir's chagrin came through clear.

"BUT I NEVER... I NEVER WANTED TO LEAD RIQUE TO HIS DEATH..."

"…I know that. Even Rique knew that, too."

Tu smiled. Ever since they had first met in the Land of the End, Tu knew.

"You're actually a good guy, Krafnir."

"…Are you really okay with this? Rique's death will be for nothing. There were almost no young men like him. I… I regret letting this happen…"

"Ah-ha-ha… Really, I guess…this whole Sixways Exhibition stuff might've been impossible for me from the start. I can't fight against Kuze."

"He's lying…! That 'condition' he laid out to you: It was an empty promise! He'll easily go back on his word!"

"I believe him."

Kuze the Passing Disaster. Sun's Conifer. And the Demon King's Bastard.

There were those in this world who were immediately distrusted. That may have been their own responsibility—and always correct, natural logic.

"I want to believe that Kuze's not going to kill anyone…that he'll be saved."

Even if reality differed, she wanted the world to be this way.

"Besides, I just need to go to school if I want to meet Sephite, right? Rique told me about it! I'll study from here on out…and pass whatever tough exam they throw at me, and then, and then… I'll see Sephite."

—and apologize.

"I... I MAY BE ONE THING, BUT YOU—YOU COULD'VE FOUGHT HIM...!"

The spear of absolute death and the shield of absolute arrest.

Within the Sixways Exhibition, the two individuals never truly exchange blows using these abilities.

"IF YOUR BODY TRULY IS INVINCIBLE...! IF YOU REALLY ARE IZICK THE CHROMATIC'S MASTERWORK! EVEN KUZE'S ATTACKS *MIGHT NOT HAVE EVEN LEFT A SCRATCH ON YOU!* IF YOU FOUGHT, THERE WAS A CHANCE YOU COULD WIN!"

Who was truly the strongest? Would a time come when the world would find out the answer?

"...Yeah. But...even if it all really was like that."

She wiped her tears. She faced Krafnir and gave him a smile.

No matter how cruel the reality she saw outside the fish tank was, even if it was different from the vivid colors she believed in...

"Even still, I wanted to save Kuze."

Match five. Winner, Kuze the Passing Disaster.

CHAPTER 16 ◆◈◆ Then the Twilight Bell Rings

That night, after the end of the fifth match and Kuze the Passing Disaster's win by default. The elderly Eleventh Minister, Nophtok the Crepuscule Bell, returned home to his residence, another man in tow.

The guest gazed out over the state of his home and spat out a single comment.

"What a dump."

The young man, cigarette in his mouth, left a crude and vulgar impression. The light fading from it, the cigarette itself almost gone entirely, yet he still kept it fast in his mouth.

"*Haah.* Is that so? If you compared it to the prosperity of everyone in Sun's Conifer... Well then, I suppose it may look a bit humble."

The young man's name was Giza the Wingsword. He was the second-in-command of the guild, Sun's Conifer.

Sun's Conifer—children who had engaged in the harsh labor of mining radzio ore on the frontier—started their own enterprise and climbed up from nothing amid an age of upheaval, unscrupulous about their means. However, their leader, Jivlart the Ash

Border, had suffered a shameful death right before his match against Aureatia's strongest champion, Rosclay, and the guild's path to rising further up in the world was severed.

Killed in a woman's house, there were those spreading slanderous rumors regarding Jivlart's abilities and conduct, and there were repeated incidents of their members hearing said rumors, and getting violent with the city's citizens.

Lacking a leader to set their course of action, Sun's Conifer was now losing their place within Aureatia. From the very beginning, they were uneducated young men who were unable to grow accustomed to the peaceful metropolis.

"However... Well, I think it's a perfectly adequate apartment to have a chat. At the very least, we won't have anyone listening in to what we say. There aren't any inhabitants on either side of me, you see. *Ha-ha...*"

"Spare me the stupid preamble. What happened to the person who killed Jivlart?"

"...Yes, yes. Let me begin things by saying Master Jivlart was killed by Elea the Red Tag, having rebelled against the Aureatia Assembly, and let's see... For example, whether it came from being seduced by her charms or that he was embarrassingly killed by a woman's slender arms—"

Giza's hands moved faster than his mouth.

He grabbed Nophtok by the collar, before then driving his fist into Nophtok's face. Blood spilled from the elder's nose.

"Gah, bwaugh."

"Go ahead, asshole, Hey. Say that again, why don't ya."

"I-it's not my... There are citizens repeating these sorts of rumors. *H-haah... Phew.* Pardon me. I—I need time...to get my breathing in order... What I'm saying is that...they're wrong. *It wasn't a woman* who killed Jivlart."

"......"

"You and your group believe as much, yes...? Hence why you're angry at the citizens' rumors. You have to find out the true culprit, the truth of the incident... I understand."

"Who is it? Tell me that first. Which asshole's the culprit? I-I'm going to kill them... I'll use Sun's Conifer's combined strength to turn 'em into mincemeat. Even if we pound them down straight to hell, it still won't be enough."

"...I require a bit of courage to disclose this fact...as it concerns my own reputation as well."

It was all a made-up story. He was relating a complete fabrication, the sort that Sun's Conifer would hope was indeed the truth.

Contrary to what he said, Nophtok held no value in his name or reputation.

Nophtok the Crepuscule Bell's official post was charged with controlling the Order. It was a position where he was simply denounced by the Order leadership for his supervisory responsibilities and criticized for the neglect.

Nophtok harbored, in some senses, a monstrous mental spirit that eclipsed all others, having worked unselfishly, going with the flow, and following the wills of others, and as a result, he arrived at the position most bereft of prestige, the seat of the Eleventh Minister.

Taking up residence in a housing complex in the slums while also being one of Aureatia's most authoritative individuals, the drab interior possessed neither furniture to indicate his tastes nor any articles that expressed his experiences in life.

It was a room where he simply ate, slept, and woke up. A life of this, day in and day out.

His disinterest was abnormal, completely different in nature from Yuca the Halation Gaol's own lack of unselfishness.

"I believe the Order I've been charged with...is involved somehow in Master Jivlart's death."

"...No way."

Giza answered incredulously, his face bright red.

"The Order... Those Order guys... Jivlart took really good care of 'em all... Said he loved the kids... That since the kids aren't prejudiced, they don't look at us like we're bad guys."

"Ah yes. I am aware."

It was because everyone looked at Jivlart so coldly that he had wanted children at least to think of him well.

A lowly, infantile thought.

Through an investigation, Nophtok already knew that even in Aureatia, their guild had continued their criminal activities. Unable to reform his fundamental evil nature, he instead tried to earn the approval of innocent children.

It was exploiting approval from the weak.

Nophtok felt that men like those in Sun's Conifer were the ones who truly needed to face punishment.

"There was a priest in training at the almshouse Jivlart

supported by the name of Naijy the Rhombus Knot. Were you aware of the fact that he died by suicide?"

"...He died right after Jivlart went. Like hell I'd forget. We... Right when we were talkin' about pooling money together and keeping that place going."

"I see. Did you consult with Naijy on the matter?"

"Of course we didn't. We wanted to get everything squared away and then go cheer 'im up."

"I see... In any event, one of the reasons for his suicide was an incident, see... Where he found one of the destinations he tried to send an orphan, in fact, turned out to be a slave trader."

"...What?"

"Indeed. An internal investigation proved that there is someone within the order who was tightly connected with such an organization. Master Jivlart must have realized that the almshouse he was donating to had this strange business going on. As a result, well..."

"Wait, wait, hold on."

Giza once again went to pull Nophtok in by his collar but realized what he was doing himself and stopped.

"Even if that was true... I can't believe Jivlart'd get knocked off by any regular bastard. The Order folks don't train for combat or anything. Who then. Who got 'im?"

"You appear to have realized the answer yourself, Master Giza."

Nophtok spread pictures out across the table. Pictures of assassins' corpses, the ones he had dispatched against Kuze.

"Dammit..."

Nophtok's job was always dirty work.

Thus now, with the winner of the fifth match decided, was when he truly needed to make a move. In order to dispose of his candidate.

"The order's paladin, Kuze the Passing Disaster. He is an assassin secretly working behind the scenes of the Sixways Exhibition. Conspiring together with Elea the Red Tag, he assassinated Master Jivlart."

Kuze had won. Not a simple victory, either, but a win by default.

There was a high likelihood that he and Tu the Magic, and thus her sponsor, Flinsuda, had made some sort of deal right before the match. The Order, as an organization, was on its last legs, but if they turned Flinsuda the Portent and her immense wealth into an ally, the power relationships in the Sixways Exhibition would shift dramatically.

It was possibly the Gray-Haired Child, instead. There was a chance he colluded with Aureatia's largest dissidents and used some scheme to dispose of Tu the Magic.

It would have been better if Kuze had simply won. A victory for Kuze means the death of his opponent... It means I wouldn't have to worry about there being any surviving pieces left in play.

However, given that he had taken moves to reject the match itself, he needed to fear the possibility that now Kuze the Passing Disaster and Tu the Magic were both rising in revolt against Aureatia, together. Once the strongest spear and the strongest shield had combined forces, there were very few players who could possibly topple their absoluteness, even among the other hero candidates.

At this point, I can still dispose of Kuze. Right now, while his vulnerability still remains in Aureatia... I can't let this opportunity slip by.

Nophtok the Crepuscule Bell mildly accepted being treated as an incompetent older man, never letting his artless and modest expression and tone falter.

However, he was a member of the Twenty-Nine Officials exactly because of his excellence and capability. On behalf of Rosclay, still critically wounded from the fourth match and unable to issue orders, he could move quickly to fulfill his own role.

"Kuze the Passing Disaster... Kuze, huh."

Giza the Wingsword's face twisted in anger, and he lit the cigarette in his mouth.

Nophtok heaved a fatigued sigh.

"I... I cannot stand that the Order has produced such a man. I needed to get your guild's cooperation in order to finally put him down for good."

"...Bring him on. Damn the bastard. I'll drop him down into the pits of hell."

The sole weakness of Kuze the Passing Disaster was clear. Even a powerless elderly man like Nophtok could dispose of him.

In order to enact his plan, he needed a myopic and ethically bankrupt group to work with.

"We'll take his *tools of the trade*, the children, hostage."

◆

A short walk away from the almshouse Kuze grew up in, there was a small pond.

A murky pond, dirtied by algae and mysterious plant life.

On the opposite shore, the old vestiges of a divine idol were buried in the roots, and while the children never paid it any mind, thinking about it now, it had been a spooky place.

The pond's waters barely came up to the children's knees, but since there was a cleaner and fish-filled river near the almshouse, none of the children played there. The only one who visited was Kuze.

Slipping out of the church complex late at night all alone, he'd often get yelled at by the priests.

To them, young Kuze must have been an awful handful of a child.

He was always alone as he traveled the somber path, stepping over the grass wet with night dew and hearing the chirping of insects resounding around him.

However, once night fell, there was someone there singing.

A tiny, faint, boyish voice.

It was a song no one knew.

Because the Word Arts weren't of this world.

He asked his friends, he asked the teachers, but there wasn't anyone who knew about the singer. It was a very quiet song, so Kuze thought that no one else could hear it except for him.

The nighttime memories remained because Kuze picked that time to go see her.

He thought it was a sacred spectacle, one that no one else should be there to witness.

Moonlight. The warble of the trees, waving in the wind.

A soft song, only audible in that moment when the world fell silent.

A beautiful terror and mystery, as if catching a glimpse of a far-off place beyond the reach of Word Arts.

It was an angel.

Pure-white hair. Pure-white clothes. Pure-white wings.

She had no weight. She was able to dance on top of a single flower petal.

A being who, during the time of creation, had been here with the original visitors to their world.

As though she had been left behind in the cogwheels of the world, her eyes couldn't see anything, and her ears couldn't hear. She was an afterimage of the creation, any meaning behind wielding the power she was given now gone, simply existing there until the day she should disappear.

Why was only Kuze able to see her?

Why did she choose Kuze?

Why did she bring death?

◆

The rain was pouring down in the Aureatia night.

Gas lamps were sparse in this town in the Western Outer Ward, and it didn't have the same activity seen in central Aureatia.

However, Kuze the Passing Disaster could hear the festival-like hustle and bustle echoing from afar.

"Light. Dammit, there's light. It's all up in flames! Zigita Zogi!"

He shouted to the man on the other side of the radzio. The first person he reported the situation to was Zigita Zogi the Thousandth, in a collaborative relationship with Kuze.

However, Kuze had once again been too late. He was sure of it.

<Please remain calm. That is just from their large numbers, the light from the lanterns and carriages of Sun's Conifer. There haven't been any reports of a fire from my surveillance unit watching the scene.>

"Still... Still, right now there are kids sleeping inside there! The guy who watched over the place, Naijy's gone, too, so there's no one protect them at night!"

That night, Sun's Conifer had mobilized in great numbers and occupied the almshouse.

Kuze had immediately learned about the trouble thanks to contact from Zigita Zogi, and rushed over immediately, but of course Ozonezma, still heavily wounded from the third match, nor Hiroto and Zigita Zogi, under surveillance by the Twenty-Nine Officials, could act directly in response to the situation.

<...Master Kuze. Should it be necessary, I can mobilize our goblin force and eliminate Sun's Conifer without issue. However, our opponent has this large number at their command. I believe

it's reasonable to think the news of a goblin unit closing in on them would instead fan the group's already excited emotional state. As for the excuse to give Aureatia's side of things, claiming we were independently cooperating with the city to maintain public safety...would be somewhat difficult. While suppressing the group itself may be possible, we might not be able to ensure the safety of the hostages.>

"...Zigita Zogi. You know, I... Bweh-heh-heh. I killed Nofelt. That's how far I went...to try to win the Sixways Exhibition. I wanted to help the Order. Truly."

<I understand. However, I am merely stating facts, while your contributions to the cause are a separate issue. Master Kuze, your objective here isn't eliminating this enemy, but the welfare of the hostages, correct? Please, remain calm.>

"No. You got it wrong. I'm not trying to fault you or anything."

Kuze smiled hollowly. It was self-deprecation about the irony currently attacking him.

"If it was Nofelt... I'm sure he would've mobilized the army for them immediately. See, he grew powerful and influential to help save the Order. If that's the case, then...just what did I do?"

<...In any event, Nofelt would not have returned to Aureatia until the eighth match, correct? Aureatia's handling of Order-related matters would have remained the same as it is now.>

"I... I had been his friend, too. He was even the one who taught me how to count. That guy even had that amazing talent of his. And yet..."

Kuze had several other Order comrades. Kind ones. Wise ones. Strong ones.

All of them were ground down together by the age of the True Demon King and would never return.

Kuze, alone, was now a shura.

<I will continue our surveillance. If some opening presents itself, we will immediately attempt a rescue. Report in if there are any negative developments... Finally, Master Kuze. I apologize.>

"...Bweh-heh-heh. For what, then?"

<It was a coldhearted operation. Everyone in this camp, myself included, are all pieces in play, but we are still living pieces. Even if it was by your own request, I shouldn't have made you kill your friend.>

"...Forget it."

Everyone living in this world had their own ideas and their own language.

They wanted there to be a wicked somebody who could bear the blame for their own suffering. It was a childish hope.

Perhaps it was because of such hopes that the True Demon King was born in the first place.

"I'll go."

Kuze had given up. Just like that day Cunodey had died. Like the day Rozelha had died.

<...Please don't give up, Master Kuze. If you fight, then—>

"Hey. Zigita Zogi. Don't you think maybe...maybe even I should be able to talk things out? Without any killing or being killed... Some kinda..."

If Kuze the Passing Disaster fought, there was guaranteed to be death.

That was why he carried a great shield. So that he wouldn't kill his enemies.

"...some sort of magical outcome like that."

A bell could be heard from the church. A bell announcing the end of the day.

The black-clad assassin flew into the middle of the light.

Even if there was nothing but darkness in the future beyond it.

◆

Seeing Kuze the Passing Disaster appear, Giza the Wingsword puffed his short cigarette.

"Well, now. Looks like you were in a real panic to get here, Mr. Assassin."

Giza was sitting down on the stairs in front of the chapel. Along with him, several members of Sun's Conifer were standing side by side nearby. He needed to get past these stairs and head inside to reach the almshouse. Passing right through the innumerable mob of Sun's Conifer members crowding around.

A gang clamoring under the bright lights and behind the chiming of the church bells. It almost looked like a festival.

"...Sorry. This old man'd really like to surrender right away."

Kuze raised both his hands while giving a flippant smile.

"Piss off."

His attitude seemed to have rubbed Giza the wrong way.

"Go on and die, right here, right now. You're the one who killed Jivlart, dammit. Can't complain if Sun's Conifer...if all of us gathered here kill you, yeah? Am I wrong? Making some mistake? After all the people you've killed up until now, why the hell are you the only one who gets to keep on living with that stupid grin on your face? Did you...did you really wanna win the Sixways Exhibition so bad that you used the dirtiest, sleaziest tricks to do it? Spit it out."

"Bweh-heh-heh... Well, let's see..."

He wasn't the one who killed Jivlart. Maybe he just should've said they had the wrong guy.

Tell them that he didn't care what happened to him, but he just wanted the children to be safe.

"I don't care what happens to me," huh?

It was terribly ironic. He truly felt that way deep in his heart, yet those were the only words he couldn't bring himself to say.

As long as he had Nastique's divine protection from death at his side, Kuze defenselessly exposing himself to the groups' murderous anger was essentially a decision to massacre all his enemies.

The intention to betray his faith and kill his enemies was all he needed for Nastique to slaughter everyone in his sights. However, Curte, who he had killed in Lithia, his former friend Nofelt, and Tu, who he had come very close to killing as well... Even after he descended into hell, Kuze didn't think he'd be able to forget about them.

"Bweh-heh-heh... Sorry. While I'm surrendering here, I'd like to talk a bit about Jivlart."

"Jivlart was..."

The church's bell was ringing.

Giza's voice trembled with anger as he spoke.

"...among all of us, the only one able to think about the road ahead. Said we'd do really amazing stuff once Aureatia recognized us... Told us that Sun's Conifer, that we'd become a guild beloved by anyone... He just needed to win in the Sixways Exhibition, and it was all gonna be smooth sailing from there, dammit! We'd be able to break off from all the crappy jobs we've been doing until now...with all of us living in houses, and with even bigger jobs, we were gonna get women, money, and hell, even families of our own, ya hear me?! That guy, that guy was the only one... The only one among all the rest of us worthless scum who could dream."

"...You don't say."

Jivlart the Ash Border's actual abilities were the most inferior among the hero candidates, and as such, he had been picked as Rosclay the Absolute's opponent in the first round match. He had heard the details from Zigita Zogi. That whether it came to prudence or character, he was no better than a frontier ruffian.

There was no way that was true.

"So he really was...a pretty important guy, huh?"

Jivlart the Ash Border should've made a far more outstanding hero than someone like Kuze.

Persecuted by everything in a dead-end world, he had been able to see a distinct hope.

He managed to give his dream to his comrades and guide them.

Both of these were impossible to Kuze. The salvation that he had discovered as he struggled in a sea of despair was nothing but even deeper darkness. In order to assassinate the Queen, to assassinate the hero, he was battling in the Sixways Exhibition.

"Don't you dare talk like you ain't got nothing to do with it, asshole."

Responding to Giza's anger, Sun's Conifer encircled Kuze.

They were clearly trying to kill Kuze. Anyone who tried to would die. They would die, and then someone else would be taken with revenge. Death would infinitely chain together and never stop.

As if it was the way the very world itself operated, they would die.

"You're the bastard who killed him, ain't you?! Leeching off the Order! Joining up with sleazy slave traders! Assholes like you are the ones tossing clueless damn children into the gutter, ain't you?! You... You're just like the bastards back in my hometown! When you heard we caught your 'goods,' you were the only one from the Order who came flying out here in a hurry, weren't you?! G-guys...guys like you being at the top's why even the damn Order itself...why the Order's ended up like this!"

"*Hah.*"

All the words Giza the Wingsword had spouted off were nothing more than misdirected suspicions, as far from the truth as they could possibly be.

The tragedy that had befallen the children was the result of the weakened Order being exploited by crime, and the reason the Order was weakened was because faith had been lost to the True Demon King, and they had been neglected in their state of decline.

Given that the story was consistent, despite being completely unfounded, someone must have planted it in his head. Kuze even knew what person would paint a picture like this, too.

"*...Ha-ha-ha...*"

However, Kuze laughed.

The all-too-ironic story made him unable to stop laughing.

Because it was also exactly as Giza said.

"*Ha-ha-ha... Ha-ha-ha-ha*, that's right. You're right..."

Kuze replied through his laughter.

"That's it. This old man... See, well... He's a wicked man. The Order...the upper echelons of the Order, they've been under the control of abject scum, see... Meanwhile, this old man's a killer— and selling kids into slavery...! Why not? That's rich. *Ha-ha, ah-ha-ha-ha-ha!*"

The church bell was ringing.

"Hey..."

Sun's Conifer were more perplexed than anything, seeing Kuze burst into laughter before them.

The wave of murderous rage that seemed ready to kick off at any second, for a very brief moment, stopped. However, the anger quickly swelled even larger and surged toward Kuze...

I really can't save them.

He was a paladin and a murderer. This sin of his was an immutable fact.

Tu the Magic wasn't there. From here, Kuze would likely kill a terrifying number of people. As a mass murderer, he'd lose his qualifications to be a hero candidate. Even lose the victory Tu entrusted him with.

Kuze laughed. He laughed so much that tears came to his eyes.

...I can't save anyone. Not as I am.

"I'm gonna hack you into mincemeat, you piece of shit."

Unsheathing a sword in each hand, Giza the Wingsword stood next to Kuze as he was crouched over laughing.

The swords were hanging over his head, he realized. Now was surely when an angel would come...

An angel will fly in, and...

Rain.

The light of the small moon through the clouds shone off the blade raised above his head.

It was headed toward Kuze's neck.

"Die."

There was a metallic clang. Kuze's gauntlet had reflexively blocked the blade.

For the first time, the defensive techniques Kuze had only even used to stop himself from killing his enemy had been used to defend himself.

"...Nastique."

It was Kuze's turn to look perplexed.

Instead of looking at Sun's Conifer as they surrounded him, raring to kill, he searched for the angel no one else but he could see.

"Where are you?! Nastique!"

"Sit still and die, dammit!"

"Gwaugh?!"

His stomach was punched hard. The blow was filled with an intense intent to kill.

The angel of death should've killed him in return for such an attack.

"Wh-what the hell's...going on here...? *Bweh-heh-heh...* Nastique..."

He was surrounded. Punched and kicked. As he took in the excruciating pain all over his body, and the even fiercer whirlwind of murderous rage, Kuze facetiously chuckled.

"...I... I killed Nofelt. He was a close friend."

Perhaps things had been the same for him and Nofelt, too.

"...If I had made it in time... You wouldn't have had to kill anyone at all... Despite all that...are you going to save me?"

His cheekbones broken and blood streaming from his eyes and nose, still Kuze's eyes weren't on the Sun's Conifer mob. Lingering beyond them was a large, silent white figure.

"Uhak."

In the Sixways Exhibition, there were two hero candidates from the Order.

Kuze the Passing Disaster knew that there was someone praying there every day. Right around when the bell would ring to tell the faithful of the day's close, he would appear there without fail.

The bell was ringing.

The gray ogre had a name. Uhak the Silent.

Thing is, Nastique... She can't get close to you.

"Quit yer laughing."

"We'll pull your guts out."

"Yer gonna pay."

"You're dead, Kuze the Passing Disaster."

Ahhh. They're trying to kill me.

So much murderous rage was being pointed at him.

I guess so. Only natural this'd happen to me, really. Always has been.

A club brandished by one of the gang went to shatter Kuze's ribs. He brought his gauntlet up against the strike and deflected the club from their hands.

A giant of a man sent kick after kick into Kuze's back, and he was rammed headfirst into the rain-muddled ground. Another one of the gang tried to get on top of Kuze.

"Die! Go to hell, bastard!"

"Nghaaaaaaaaaaaaaagh!"

With a stirring shout, he slammed his forehead into the top of his opponent's head. One of them tried to stab him with a short sword. Picking up his great shield off the ground, he slammed it into the ruffian's arm before the sword could find its mark.

He managed to do it all. He was able *to fight.*

"Uhak. Why—?"

Uhak simply stared at the scene. Even Sun's Conifer was unable to get close to the quietly lingering ogre. It was as if there truly was a holy priest standing there.

Struggling to stop himself from being swallowed by the wave of the mob, Kuze shouted.

"Uhak...! Uhak! Why—why did you kill others?! See, I really...I really wanted to know why!"

He punched. A punch came right back at him.

Adults fighting like a scuffle among children.

"I thought inside you...maybe you have your own beliefs... that are different from the Wordmaker's teachings...and let you kill other people. I...!" he shouted, drenched in blood.

Somewhere out in the world, there may have been a god who would forgive Kuze's sins.

Perhaps Uhak knew the truth, a truth beyond a faith composed from Word Arts. Nevertheless.

"I...!"

Even if he was able to learn mute Uhak's faith, Kuze would likely still pine for faith in the Wordmaker that was always out of his reach.

His heart, which felt such anguish towards the act of murder, was surely a form of salvation granted by the Wordmaker.

Knowing more than anyone it was sin, all he could do was fight and continue shouldering the burden.

"Die!"

"Evil bastard! We'll burn you alive!"

"Go to hell, coward!"

He could exchange blows. For the first time, Kuze *was managing to fight.*

It may have been a sin the angel wouldn't have forgiven him for, but for that sole moment, with Uhak the Silent lingering nearby—Nastique the Quiet Singer wasn't watching over Kuze the Passing Disaster.

He punched. He flung people away.

Kicks. Headbutts.

Alternating in turns, again and again, over and over.

"Haaah, haaah..."

"Why...why does this bastard...keep getting the hell back up?"

"Quit slacking off... Get to it! Hurry up and wring his damn neck!"

"This is... *Haah-haah*, for Jivlart!"

"...Bw-bwuh-bweh-heh-heh...heh-heh..."

Kuze laughed. He didn't even know what emotion was behind it, whether it was happy laughter, out of anger, or out of sadness. Before a group this size, he couldn't believe there was any hope of winning.

There clearly was, however, salvation.

A hope for even a man like Kuze, long shut away in the darkness of despair.

That's right. A guy like me. Even a sinner like me...

Might have been able to find his way to the children without killing anyone.

◆

The almshouse children had been rounded up and gathered inside the biggest dining room.

Leisha stretched up straight, raised her chin, and stared hard at the ruffians surrounding them.

Their gait and speech were terribly vulgar, and they seemed like villains. It was almost impossible for her to believe that these were the acquaintances of the same Mr. Jivlart she had heard Father Naijy praise.

"So like. What's gonna happen after we kidnap the brats?"

"What, you gonna look after 'em?"

"Oh, knock it off. *Koff!* I told ya: I don't got a thing for no little brats!"

"O-okay, in th-that case, can I—I take em? *Hya-hee, hee.*"

Leisha was disgusted.

The boys older than her hadn't been any help at all. Even after they spouted all that bravado when Father Naijy had died, about how they'd protect all the little ones until they found someone to take everyone in.

There were some boys taken down by two or three jabs to their head or shoulders, and others who started crying just from seeing it all happen. Even the boys who had continued to fight back were now limply lying around after having their hands and feet bound tight with rope.

Leisha was the oldest girl there, so this time, she needed to fight.

"Well, I'm not going to become the sort of adult you all are, that's for sure."

"What the hell's this one talking about?"

The ruffians seemed to have difficulty picking up the meaning of Leisha's words.

"*Ha.* Little runts just say weird stuff from time to time."

"Can't believe Jivlart supported these brats for so long. I couldn't even stand one of 'em."

"All right, little girl, then what *do* ya want to become, then?"

One of the men standing beside Leisha said this, out of either curiosity or derision. He looked older than the other ruffians, a man with thin hair and a smirk.

"I'm going to be Father Kuze's wife. We're going to live happily ever after."

"*Hee-hee-hee*, hey, this one's funny. Precocious little runt."

"...Were all of you raised without being taught the Word-maker's teachings?"

Even if they got violent with her, Leisha wasn't scared in the slightest. Though she was very scared of any wounds to her face, when she thought about then being forced to submit to them, she wouldn't be any different from the boys. They had been childish no matter how much bigger they looked, and thus she didn't fear them at all.

Besides, Leisha was a child raised by the Order.

She had learned through it all. What was right, what was wrong. These were things she knew she'd never disguise.

"I even feel bad for Mr. Jivlart. After all, he may have done all those nice things while he was alive, but here his own pals are doing something awful. You clomp around everywhere you walk, you throw spit wherever you want like it's nothing, and even your laughs are filthy. *Makes it clear what sort of upbringing you all've had.*"

Leisha was definitely not going to grow up to be an adult like them.

Someday, she was sure to be able to live a happier life. Holding on to hope, she could keep striving toward it.

Since, no matter what painful difficulties she faced, her spirit would be supported by the teachings of the Wordmaker.

Even without any family, even people in the absolute depths of misfortune, even children and the elderly—the teaching had saved the hearts of many people since they were brought into this world.

"Upbringing, is it?"

"What's with this girl? She the lone rich girl in here or what?"

"……"

The air among the ruffians changed. It wasn't the violent fervor they had shown from the beginning, but a sort of…cold murderous urge, mixed with fear, in response to some part of what Leisha had said.

I'm not scared whatsoever. Not at all.

Telling herself "whatsoever" might have been a lie. Her face was still the only part she didn't want injured, after all.

I'm sure things will get better from here on out. Even after my adoption fell through, even if Father Naijy's dead and the almshouse is going under. Father Kuze… After all, I'm going to be his bride someday.

His fatigued smile looked as if he was always lamenting misery and misfortune.

That was why Leisha felt she wanted to make him happy.

"Hey, this one's got a pretty face, doesn't she…?"

"Yeah. She's cute for a brat. I can make it work."

"She was getting' real cheeky with us and all."

"She was sayin' as much to Giza, too."

Even the ruffians were praising Leisha's features, too.

Of course. Leisha was the most beautiful there was. Normally, she would have felt pleased to hear their compliments, but there was something about the way they spoke that made her uneasy.

One of the men violently grabbed her hand.

"*Eek...!*"

"All right, you. Come with me into this room."

"Stop! Stop it, no matter what you do, I'm not going anywhere...!"

The adult man's grip was very strong, and Leisha was dragged off as if she was but a tiny bit of baggage. She had a terrifying premonition that everything was going to be ruined.

Something like this wasn't supposed to exist in the world Leisha believed in.

It was why she had never imagined it.

No.

Never imagined such a thing—that everything in her life would come to an end in wretchedness and misery.

"Come on!"

"No... Save me, Father Kuze!"

The door opened before the ruffian opened it himself.

A fist came flying in from the other side.

It connected with the ruffian's face and sent him flying.

A single man flew out from behind the door and protected Leisha.

With a bestial growl, he struck down all the ruffians in the room.

Frantically and slovenly, punching, pulling them down, hitting them with a broken piece of wood.

The man was wearing tattered black clothes, while his face was swollen beyond recognition and covered in blood. Nevertheless, Leisha immediately knew who it was.

"...Heyo."

"Father Kuze."

Father Kuze hugged Leisha in his big arms.

His usual ashy smell was overpowered by the stronger smell of blood, but his warmth was all the same.

"Father... Father Kuze!"

She knew from the very start.

Father Kuze was a paladin. He was always out fighting like this and protecting Leisha and the others.

No matter how battered he got, no matter how bloodied he became, he was fighting to protect someone.

"Thank you. Everyone's...everyone's safe. I stood up to them as everyone's big sister!"

"Ah-ha. Leisha, thank you...thank you for protecting everyone. Thank goodness. I'm really...really glad that no one ended up dead."

Looking up at Kuze's blood-covered face, Leisha smiled with the prettiest face she could muster.

She thought it was becoming of his future bride.

Kuze's face, scratched, bruised, and battered from fighting, was, to Leisha, the absolute most—

"Even when you're all scratched up... Father Kuze, you're still the coolest man in the world."

"Am I, now? That's right, huh. Normally...when you fight, you get all covered in cuts and scrapes like this, don't you...?"

However, Father Kuze gave an exhausted smile.

Despite being victorious in a fight he could pride himself on forever and then some.

As if it was the same smile he always wore.

"...*Bweh-heh-heh.*"

◆

Late at night. There was a knocking on Nophtok's apartment door.

If things went as scheduled, it was around when Giza the Wing-sword would be coming to report the results of the operation to him.

"Yes, yes. I'm coming."

With a pigeon's gait, he casually walked out to his door and opened it.

It was not Giza standing there on the other side.

"Oh?"

Looking at the blood-drenched man, enveloped in an even more lurid ominousness than usual, Nophtok spoke his name without any particular amount of surprise.

"Master Kuze the Passing Disaster."

"*Bweh-heh-heh...* Well, see, I was just nearby and dropped in. Do you mind?"

"I see. I do mind, in fact, but..."

Kuze was dragging the edge of his great shield. The wounds all over his body were deep, and he could no longer carry it on his arm. He had walked all the way there in such a condition.

"Looking at your current state, I don't think I can really afford to say that right now."

"I'm glad you're quick on the uptake... I don't need first aid or anything, and I won't ask you for any tea, so..."

With unsteady steps reminiscent of a departed spirit, Kuze stepped inside. In his wake, the floor was dirtied with splotches of dark-red blood, and Nophtok felt slightly disappointed.

"I see... So then, what is your business with me?"

"Ah yeah... Right. Let's get straight to the point. Sun's Conifer... You were the one who sent them to attack the almshouse, right?"

"Yes, that's right."

Kuze was an invincible assassin. From the very start, Nophtok had been prepared for any degree of retaliation from the man. If he had come to kill Nophtok in anger, then that would be the end of it anyway, and it was more productive to own up to it all.

"Hmm, given the state you're in now, it seems you killed quite a large number of them."

Were the children safe? Nophtok pondered.

The children of that almshouse, having lost their guardian just a few days ago, had been the easiest hostages to capture in order to threaten Kuze. There was no greater reason behind their selection than that. However, if possible, Nophtok wanted them to be safe.

"Didn't kill any of them."

A smile found its way to Kuze's blood-soaked face as he sat in his chair.

He looked extremely pleased.

"I... I didn't kill anyone. *Me*. I went all out and brawled my way through it all. Can you believe it?"

"No. I really can't."

Kuze the Passing Disaster could not have possibly resolved a situation without killing a single person.

In the following days, the almshouse massacre was sure to be treated as a major incident. The Sun's Conifer survivors would serve as witnesses, and Kuze the Passing Disaster would be stripped of the right to appear in the Sixways Exhibition. Even if he had failed to take the hostages, he had dealt with Kuze's presence, for sure. It was the scenario that Nophtok had sketched out for the operation.

"You can't force me out of the competition. I'm advancing to the second round."

"Hmm. I'm sure you understand, but I cannot allow you to do that..."

"...There's some fellas who do a real quick job out there. See, Yukiharu the Twilight Diver... I hear he's already writing up an article. In the end... After I rushed in and got the kids out of that, thing is, Zigita Zogi handled everything else for me... I barely made it through on my end, really."

"Twilight... Article? What are you talking about?"

Kuze continued, flashing a wide grin.

"An article on Sun's Conifer capturing and occupying the almshouse—and all the particulars around it... With photos of the scene printed next to it on the page... That'll get the information out there. With photos, it'll be certain and reliable evidence. It's called a newspaper article, apparently. I didn't know anything about it myself, though..."

Something was going on. That something was a presence backing Kuze, putting their schemes into action and using their influence far swifter and much earlier than Nophtok, including cleaning up the aftermath of the incident.

"You didn't kill anyone. Why was that?"

Nophtok repeated Kuze's previous words back to him.

"Ah well, I wonder why myself."

Kuze looked at the ceiling, leaning back in his chair.

"Must've been the Wordmaker's divine protection, wouldn't you say?"

"……"

"Did you know? It's always other people…who're the ones saving others."

Nophtok had no means of verifying the authenticity of Kuze's words. However—an information network was able to link everything back to Nophtok in such a short time. The name Zigita Zogi the Thousandth. Behind Kuze the Passing Disaster, there was a force threatening Aureatia, after all.

Though his entire operation may have failed, at that moment, Nophtok was able to finish things himself.

He took a deep break.

…*So it comes to this. Oh well.*

With this simple thought, Nophtok the Crepuscule Bell was able to choose his own death.

Kuze's sponsor was Nophtok. If his sponsor died, then he would lose his claim to fight in the Sixways Exhibition as a hero candidate.

Nophtok himself didn't possess the nerve to choose his own death, but even being the type of man he was, standing right in front of him was a means of certain and automatic suicide.

"Now then, Master Kuze. I will be killing you now."

The candidate murdering his sponsor—the most reliable reason for disqualification.

"What will you do then, Master Kuze?"

"...Nophtok." Kuze spoke with a gentle tone. "You yourself... were raised in the Order, too, weren't you? I knew for a long time what you were getting up to and all, but... Even still, I want to believe that there has to be some sort of salvation for you, right...? That maybe there was something that left you with no other choices."

"I... Well."

Had there been something like that? He got the feeling that, no, there hadn't been at all.

During Nophtok's childhood, the Order hadn't been in the same harsh situation it was now. Enjoying the favor and love of many people and perhaps in an attempt to pay it all back, he had ascended to his current position. As if someone had wanted him, too.

If there was a hungry young girl in front of him, he just had to offer her help.

Never propelled by his own resentment or anger, he simply had to live out his mild days and indifferently carry out the role requested of him. Even without the teachings of the Wordmaker, he thought that this unsophisticated, innate goodness in others was plenty by itself.

"Hmmm, I... I think I'm all set myself. Whether you believe in some salvation for me...or not, either way."

"Even still, I think, how great it would be, if there was."

He may have been right. If this salvation that he spoke of was *such a good thing*, then perhaps Nophtok would have sought it.

However, Nophtok was soon going to attempt to kill Kuze, then die to his instant-death ability, and that would be the end of it.

"Hey, Nophtok... What do you think when you see this?"

"......"

Nophtok could also read the Order's script. The script, by its very nature easily taught and widely studied by those involved in the Order, was capable of being disseminated to orphans, the poor, and other people in the lower class of society.

"This would be trade documentation. Yes... And one outlining technical medical treatment...and organ selling, at that."

"That's right. There were people using kids bought from the Order for that stuff. They were taking diseased organs that couldn't be regenerated with Life Arts and swapping them out with the children's fresh organs..."

"What an atrocity."

They were words from the heart. Nophtok didn't want children to meet such a grisly fate.

"There's stuff like this, too. Supplying materials for constructs. They were using minia as material to make revenants and skeletons. Using children from the Order. This, too. And this one over here, too. All of it."

Kuze produced document after document, stacking them one on top of the other.

The blood still dripping from his wounds stained Nophtok's study desk terribly.

"...Yes. Yes. It's truly heartrending. Within the Order's structure, it is impossible to prevent these sorts of crimes from happening... That is why there needs to be a new system in place to save everyone. You understand, don't you, Master Kuze?"

"Yeah. Of course I do. So you'll agree with me, then."

In the final document, there was a blank space.

"What in heaven's name?"

Still facing his study desk, Nophtok was at a loss for words.

"So all the stuff I've shown you just now, *let's have us be the ones who did it all.*"

The paper was a jointly signed certificate that showed the Order was involved in slave trafficking.

Why did he have such a thing? Why was it necessary?

"Wh-what is the meaning of—?"

"The Order's lining its own pockets. Using priests and innocent children for dirty business...they've distorted the tenets of the Wordmaker that are meant to teach people how to live decent lives and turned it into an organization that only brings people suffering. It's all...all because in the highest reaches of the Order, there are murderous scum, or scum only motivated by profit, doing what they please."

"...B-but that's not..."

The story that the people...had made the Order bear responsibility for the sorrow brought by the True Demon King. A negative reputation that Nophtok himself had let spread.

"*Things are fine that way.* We just have to make guys like us, the big shots in the Order, into the lowest scum in the world. All the people who've kept believing in the teachings...and the children, have done nothing wrong. It's not the Wordmaker's teachings that were at fault. All of it was entirely our fault."

"*Our...fault?*"

With trembling eyes, Nophtok looked over the list of signees. They were all signatures from the concerned individual themselves. Kuze the Passing Disaster. Maqure the Sky's Lake Surface. There were even signatures from the deceased like Rozelha the Contemplating.

Long before he died in that incident, they had gotten his signature on such a document. Still more. And more. And even more...

"*Eep.*"

Nophtok was scared.

The Order had a large amount of organizational power. While it wasn't fighting power, it was still enough for something like this.

And all of them, every one, voluntary.

They were trying to bear the unjustified sins, pushed on to them by the people, entirely by themselves.

"Ah right, I never told you, did I? See, appearing in the Sixways Exhibition? From the very start, it was to do this. In the second-round fight, I'm going to assassinate the Queen. It's the scum controlling the Order's plan to overthrow royal authority. That'll cancel the Sixways Exhibition...then all the wicked leaders in the Order, who'd make use of an assassin like me? Well..."

Why were they doing such a thing? Such a terrible thing?

The Order, supposedly the weakest organization of all, without any military power of their own, was in fact...

"Everyone'll be executed."

…enacting the most dreadful scheme in the Sixways Exhibition.

"Nophtok the Crepuscule Bell. My sponsor and the supervisor for the Order… You're the last one. There had to be someone who turned a blind eye to what the Order's upper ranks were doing, right?"

"I—I can't possibly sign off on something like this."

Just how terrible a crime would they commit just to save the Order? And while falsely charging so many people for it, too.

"I… I've never once had a hand in slave trafficking. A-assassinating Her Majesty, it's inconceivable. I don't have the courage for that. I didn't…I didn't do anything of the sort. Anything at all!"

"You're right. *You didn't do anything at all.* That's our crime."

A saboteur through negligence.

When it came to dishonorable slander, Nophtok the Crepuscule Bell had meekly taken it all in.

However, that was because said dishonor had been the truth of the matter.

He couldn't bear having such a crime be exposed for all eternity.

Why did the signatures continue to list so many names? What were they thinking? Were they really insisting that it was faith that drove this many believers into insanity?

Where was the salvation supposed to be in something this horrible?

"…See, look."

Before he could realize it, Kuze the Passing Disaster was lingering right next to Nophtok.

Like an angel. Like a god of death.

"Even you've got a heart that's terrified of sin. The heart that the Wordmaker gave you? You got it in here, for sure. *Bweh-heh-heh...* Good for you, Nophtok, being able to get scared like this."

Kuze was right. Nophtok didn't even fear his own death. He didn't place any value in his own existence. That was how it was supposed to be. There was a pen on Nophtok's study desk. He just needed to use the pen to try right now to kill Kuze.

His fingers trembled. He couldn't do it. He was scared.

"What's wrong? Go ahead and sign."

His spirit broken, Nophtok was unable to move under his own volition.

Despite profoundly wanting to run away immediately.

From where he was—and from the very world around him.

"Stop. Please. Stop this foolish plan. I beg you."

The Sixways Exhibition to Kuze the Passing Disaster was nothing more than a stepping stone leading them all to the gallows.

...And then. What was even more terrifying than that...

Even if all the names listed on the document were executed, *Kuze alone would survive on.*

There wasn't anyone who could execute a man capable of striking back against any murderous intentions against him.

He would shoulder all the crimes and continue on, alone. A living nightmare.

"You just gotta write your name. Hey? Do you want me to teach you how, Nophtok?"

They were supposed to have virtuous hearts. Both Kuze and Nophtok himself.

Nophtok had indeed helped the Order decline. Nevertheless, he didn't want a fate like this.

"Help. Save me."

Kuze's large hand made Nophtok grip the pen.

A bloodstained hand of death.

"You learned the script properly in the Order? How to write it, I mean. Right, Nofelt?"

"G-guaaaaagh...Augh..."

His head was pinned down, too. Fear had broken his spirit.

A heart that neither feared death nor sin. That was what he had thought.

Up until the terror from minutes prior, that's what it should have been like for Nophtok, and yet...

Everything Nophtok the Crepuscule Bell had constructed was all beginning to fall apart.

"Th-the state, this state the Order's in, i-it isn't only my fault."

"Sign it. Write your name, just like you learned how."

Thanks to a wonderful miracle, we are no long in solitude. All creatures with a heart and soul are our family.

"Save me. Please."

"That's exactly right. Make sure to pray to the Wordmaker first. Now sign it."

Be sure to talk things out. Since everyone was bestowed Word Arts by the Wordmaker to communicate with one another.

"Help me! Kuze! Save me!"

"Write."

Thou shall not hate. Thou shall not harm. Thou shall not kill. Just as thou would treat thy own family.

"Sign it, Nophtok."

◆

"Kill the Hero for us."

Even since he took on this earnest plea, before the start of the Sixways Exhibition, Kuze had been resigned to the sin he would bear.

The sky was clear, and the gentle sunlight bathed the world below.

It was these sorts of moments, for instance, when the angel would look at Kuze from the corridor window frame like she had something she wanted to say.

Her boyish short white hair and wings softly fluttered in a current separated from the wind of the real world.

Kuze left the confessional. Together with Maqure the Sky's Lake Surface, they discussed the hero who was arranged to be born from the Sixways Exhibition—and the Order's final plan. Their plan to shoulder all the crimes and ensure the survival of the Wordmaker's faith.

Kuze thought that Nastique must have known everything about what they had said inside the confessional, too.

"...Father Maqure's another really important person to me."

The angel lightly floating behind Kuze's back listened attentively to his voice with a curious look on her face.

At some point or another, Kuze had begun to think of her just like the children gathered in the church.

The sort of child who pays no attention to a boring conversation but waits for that moment to be engraved in their memories.

"That guy's like that even in front of regular followers, see? So the actual content of his sermons never gets across. He's always thinking about these sort of big-picture problems, you know, like about the world and society... His students have told him over and over, see, *heh-heh*... 'You should have become a philosopher or something.'"

When Kuze laughed, the angel would smile slightly, too.

"...Father Kuze!"

A voice brought Kuze to a halt.

It was one of the eldest orphans who had survived the tragedy that claimed Rozelha's life.

Even now, he'd recall the flickering memories of that day, when he killed Hyne the Swaying Indigolite.

The orphans and priest who just barely survived that incident were taken in by Maqure's almshouse.

"Whoa, whoa, none of that now. Can't call an old man like me Father—it's too rude to the other priest."

"But you were the one who saved us all, Father Kuze."

"......"

Kuze smiled ambiguously. *You're wrong. I'm weak. I can't protect anyone.*

During that incident, many believers died tragically.

Kuze had nowhere near enough courage to learn what this survivor had seen during the incident, what she had endured.

"I... I—I ended up surviving. Even though so many of the other kids died. Why were there some who died that day and some who didn't...?"

"Living on with those memories, that's just as painful. That's why really everyone's equal."

"But in that case...why are we the only ones who're forced to live with this pain?! What about all the other people in the world?! Do I... Do we have to suffer like this just because we're part of the Order?!"

Kuze tightly shut his eyes.

There were both children who died and those who got left behind.

There were those capable of living in the light and those who could only live in darkness.

Kuze, the only one under the divine protection of an angel— and everyone else, besides him.

As every living being in this world is equal, the Wordmaker bestowed them all the gift of language.

He laughed. He laughed facetiously.

Sorrow and salvation. Chosen ones. Destiny. He didn't hold any other answers.

"If it's not the sort of tragedy a person's strength can help save... then people can't save at all."

"*Bweh-heh-heh...* Sorry. This old fella doesn't have a clue. I'm not too smart, see..."

An angel that bestowed death. In this world, Nastique only bestowed her divine protection on Kuze—and no one else.

However, Kuze always hoped.

Listen. I'm begging you. You're an angel, right? Help. Please, Nastique—

He was always speaking into empty air.

She must be broken. Somewhere in his heart, he had realized it.

An angel of salvation, surely broken, who only protected Kuze.

Help everyone else, not me.

A young girl was dashing through the slums in a corner of Aureatia.

Cloaked in a dark-green robe, the hood pulled up hide her face, she ran from one dim alleyway to an even more darkly shadowed path, trying to avoid the eyes of others.

The slums road came to a dead end along the way, connecting to a canal. Standing close to the canal, the girl turned around and looked back multiple times to make sure no one was following after her.

Then she whispered quietly.

"Let me walk."

Like the magic out of a children's fairy tale, the young girl walked on the canal.

There was no one around to witness the remarkable Word Arts, an impossible feat even for the Word Arts users spoken of in legend.

The young girl was an elf named Kia. She now possessed a second name—Kia the World Word.

…I'm not going to run away with my tail between my legs.

The day of the fourth match, Kia had parted with Elea. In order to, one day, see her again.

Right now Kia, pursued by Aureatia, couldn't afford to make contact with Elea. But she just needed to clear the false charge of foul play against her...or if necessary, reveal to everyone that Rosclay was a false champion and make it possible to openly see Elea again...

If, however, I've already lost, there has to be something I can do.

Rosclay the Absolute's power had been far too tremendous. The power of numbers and faith, too great to be overthrown, even with Kia's almighty abilities. She knew she would need a different type of power.

For example, telling someone far, far grander than Rosclay...the truth of it all.

◆

The church in the Western Outer Ward had been attacked by Sun's Conifer.

Apparently most of them had been arrested for rioting, but Tu the Magic hadn't wanted to meet such an end.

Tu managed to walk the path to the church on her own without getting lost. Rique the Misfortune was no longer at her side.

"What am I supposed to do if I wanna meet the Queen?"

Thus, her words had now become a soliloquy.

Sephite. The last of the royal family, who she had met by happenstance on that day when the True Demon King brought ruin to the kingdom.

However, until she met Sephite again and spoke with her, Tu wouldn't be able to move herself forward beyond that day.

"Hey. Rique. Just once would be enough. Isn't there something I can do...?"

There wasn't anyone who knew Tu the Magic's true identity. Ozonezma's sister. An un-minian creation of Izick the Chromatic. A juggernaut of an unknown race. And finally, the Demon King's Bastard.

Tu was the only one who knew the truth of that day she met Sephite.

"I want to apologize to Sephite."

She casually crossed paths with a child, running from the far end of the alley.

Tu's memory told her that there shouldn't have been anything but a canal on the other end of the alley, but perhaps they had simply turned back after reaching the dead end?

"......"

When Tu turned back around, the child had also turned around to look at Tu. Maybe she had reacted to hearing Tu muttering Sephite's name.

A young girl. Blond hair. Turquoise eyes like a clear blue lake.

"Hello."

Underneath the morning sun, Tu smiled, her face blooming like a flower.

The young girl ran off without saying a word and disappeared into the shadows.

Light and shadow. There were those who won and advanced through the battle known as the Sixways Exhibition, and there were those who were beaten.

However, the story of the losers does not end with defeat.

To go and see Sephite.

The two girls, passing each other by in that fated crossway, held the same objective in their hearts.

Even if their paths there did not intersect right now, perhaps…

Afterword

Thank you for reading. I am Keiso. I don't believe there is anyone who would purposefully start buying this series at Volume 4, but if there happens to be anyone who has accidently done so, I absolutely recommend going back and reading from the beginning. The title is *Ishura I: The New Demon King War*. It's published on Dengeki Bunko's Shinbungei imprint.

As we're at Volume 4, at this point, I doubt there's many people who would like to hear an introduction to the work or how the author's been doing lately. For starters, I consider the afterword to have no value, thinking of it as nothing more than "some unwanted text tacked on to the back of the main story," ever since I was a kid, and I have never once read one from start to finish before. To the point that I think, if you're going to write one, it might as well have some sort of info that the reader'd find somewhat beneficial in their daily lives.

Thus, I will write about how to make a delicious Bolognese sauce.

Bolognese sauce is among one of the more advanced dishes within my living standards. As it requires you to cut several vegetables, control the temperature, and taste test, it is a bit of a labor-intensive recipe. However, on the other hand, if you make a stock of the sauce, you can freeze it even midway through the prep work, with its practicality being one of its strong points.

Now first, for the ingredients, you generally use three varieties of vegetables—onions, carrots, and celery—and finely chop them up into about the same size. It's fine if the amount of any of the vegetables is radically larger than the others, and those who aren't fond of carrots or celery can substitute them for other vegetables, however, I can't really imagine what sort of flavor a Bolognese sauce would have if it was made with any vegetables outside of these three. Please fill me in if you discover a tasty combination for yourself.

In the above process, I said to finely chop the vegetables, but for the past three years or so, I haven't finely chopped anything for myself. I do it all with a cooking device that, by pulling a cord, rotates internal blades to chop up everything inside its container. A truly excellent product, capable of being more finely tuned than a mixer, and producing uniform results much faster than I could with my knife skills. If you would like to purchase it yourself, at smaller capacities, it can be quite annoying and time-consuming to repeatedly take the contents in and out, so I recommend getting a larger size if possible.

Mix all the finely chopped vegetables together. With those, the Bolognese sauce is pretty much finished. All that's left is to cook the vegetables until they're heated through, mix in the meat, canned tomatoes, and seasonings, and that's enough. Thus, if you divide up this sauce base and freeze it, it will really come in handy the next time you go to cook.

There are some tricks when it comes time to cook the meat. Generally, it's fine to prepare a mixture of ground beef and pork of about ten ounces—about the same volume as the vegetables—but you do not directly add it in with the vegetables once they're finished cooking, and instead, I ask you to cook it in an empty frying pan after moving the vegetables temporarily into a separate container. Naturally, this isn't enough to warrant washing the frying pan first, and as for the separate container, you're going to be eating pasta later anyway, so just move them over to that plate for now.

The ground meat can be plopped in straight from the packaging and doesn't need to be broken up. Fry one side of the meat well in the oil left over from cooking the vegetables, and once it's browned, keep it collected into one piece and flip it over to fry the other side. If you mix it in with the vegetables, the process of frying the whole block of ground meat becomes difficult, which is why we removed the vegetables from the pan first. When you've fried both sides of the ground meat nice and solid, it should look just like a very lazily put together Hamburg steak. What's important is to fry it until it's nice and browned, without breaking it up, as if you break up the ground meat from the start, you'll lose both the nice browning along with the moisture in the meat, and it will become difficult to combine the fragrance of the char with the meat's natural flavor.

Next, you break up the meat. This is also an area where you can make adjustments for taste, but I detect more of the meat essence, so to speak, when it's broken up roughly and prefer that. When it comes to commercial, boil-in-the-bag Bolognese sauce, I get the impression there aren't many that contain any chunks of meat bigger than a mince. This is a point where this recipe excels, and since even with regular ground meat you brown it as one big solid mass, you can make the sauce with the perfect size meat chunks for you.

Next you reintroduce the vegetables you moved aside earlier, add a can of chopped tomatoes, and simmer the mixture. From here, as you simmer off the liquid to your preferred consistency, you can adjust the taste by adding salt and pepper, or any on-hand herbs, as you like, and once you finish it off with some pasta, it's complete.

One of the strong points of this recipe is its customizability.

I glossed over the seasoning step there, but the truth is, no matter what sort of seasonings you add in, you can usually end up with a delicious Bolognese sauce. Of course, it will taste great with just some extra salt, while for herbs, you can use pretty much whatever kinds you have available and have it come out delicious, and even if you throw in some red wine and cream, the tomatoes will bring all the flavors together on their own. Furthermore, you're free to choose the timing and amount when freezing it for later, whether it's after you've diced the vegetables, after you've cooked them, the actual complete Bolognese itself, or even those moments afterward where you stop and think *I may have made a bit too much…*, you can divide it up and throw it in the freezer—an advantage that lets you continue from wherever you left off in the preparation process next time. Naturally, finely chopped vegetables can be used just as easily in other recipes, and if you keep the prepped onions, carrots, and celery separated from each other, it gives you the possibility to use each one separately as well.

Finally, there's one big customization I'd like to introduce as an example. It's a technique that will let you completely change the dish if, as you're making the Bolognese sauce, you decide you want something else, you can add in curry powder flakes once you've combined the vegetables and meat in place of the tomatoes, and what was once meant to be Bolognese instantly transforms into *keema* curry. I think it's fair to say that this level of freedom to do everything at your discretion in the moment is a strength of Bolognese sauce.

Now then, I wrote at the beginning that afterwords are worthless, but they have an enormous amount of value to an author, and that is because I am able to use this space to thank all the people involved with the book. I would like to give my deeps thanks to Kureta-sensei for the many major jobs they handled, adding the illustrations to this volume, various promotional illustrations, and more, as well as to my editor, Nagahori, for all the wonderful advice they're constantly providing me, to the people involved in the publishing of *Ishura*, and finally, to all of you readers.

In the next volume, I think I will be able to finish writing everything up to the end of the first round in the Sixways Exhibition. Once the first round of the tournament is completed, that will mean that, numerically, half the total matches will be finished. I'll work hard to write it all the way to the end. Let us meet again. However, it must be added that, as I mentioned up top, I wouldn't be this far into the afterword as a reader myself, so I'm not exactly sure if this message of mine will reach you all or not...

HAVE YOU BEEN TURNED ON TO LIGHT NOVELS YET?

86—EIGHTY-SIX, VOL. 1–11

In truth, there is no such thing as a bloodless war. Beyond the fortified walls protecting the eighty-five Republic Sectors lies the "nonexistent" Eighty-Sixth Sector. The young men and women of this forsaken land are branded the Eighty-Six and, stripped of their humanity, pilot "unmanned" weapons into battle...

Manga adaptation available now!

WOLF & PARCHMENT, VOL. 1–6

The young man Col dreams of one day joining the holy clergy and departs on a journey from the bathhouse, Spice and Wolf. Winfiel Kingdom's prince has invited him to help correct the sins of the Church. But as his travels begin, Col discovers in his luggage a young girl with a wolf's ears and tail named Myuri, who stowed away for the ride!

Manga adaptation available now!

SOLO LEVELING, VOL. 1–8

E-rank hunter Jinwoo Sung has no money, no talent, and no prospects to speak of—and apparently, no luck, either! When he enters a hidden double dungeon one fateful day, he's abandoned by his party and left to die at the hands of some of the most horrific monsters he's ever encountered.

Comic adaptation available now!